PRAISE

"[A] moving novel . . . With beautiful prose and sustained suspense, Nunez's haunting story is a wonderful testimony to the strength and resiliency of the African diaspora, and will captivate readers with its well-drawn characters and first-rate storytelling."

—BEBE MOORE CAMPBELL

"This novel reads like a fable, with its legends, mythic creatures, and memorable characters. . . . And though it has become a cliché to call an author's writing 'beautiful,' this adjective accurately describes the writing in *Beyond the Limbo Silence*."

—ISHMAEL REED, author of *Mumbo Jumbo*

Discretion

"I recommend this novel ten-times over. I was due for a smart, well-written novel with depth of breadth and scope, and I got it in *Discretion*."

—TERRY MCMILLAN, author of *Waiting to Exhale*

"A mystical tale about love, passion, and the choices we make in life . . . A richly woven, multilayered work that is riveting from the opening paragraph."

—*Black Issues Book Review*

Bruised Hibiscus
Winner of the American Book Award

"An American masterpiece . . . Elizabeth Nunez, a superbly gifted writer has delivered a powerful and unsettling novel for all time and all people."

—SAPPHIRE, author of *Push*

"Hypnotic, searing . . . A story so explosive and disturbing, so brilliantly wrought, its images will haunt us in our dreams."

—KIANA DAVENPORT, author of *Song of the Exile*

Also by Elizabeth Nunez

Grace
Bruised Hibiscus
Discretion

BEYOND
THE
LIMBO
SILENCE

ELIZABETH NUNEZ

Ballantine Books • New York

For my son, Jason A. Harrell, who said to me in 1988 when he was eleven: "Mom, I'm going to grow an Angela Davis." That he and his generation may go beyond the limbo silence.

What in my view is remarkable about the West Indian in depth is a sense of subtle links, the series of subtle and nebulous links which are latent within him, the latent ground of old and new personalities.... The question is—how can one begin to reconcile the broken parts of such an enormous heritage, especially when those broken parts appear very often like a grotesque series of adventures, volcanic in its precipitate effects as well as human in its vulnerable settlements?

—Wilson Harris, *Tradition, the Writer and Society*

ACKNOWLEDGMENTS

Mostly, I thank Ivy Fischer Stone, my agent, for her faith in my work. I thank Seal Press for giving me voice; my editors, Faith Conlon and Deborah Kaufmann, who asked the right questions; Arthur Flowers, who demanded that I stretch myself; Francis Carling, a friend from my youthful days, who resurrected in time to challenge me again; my women friends who circled the wagons around me: my sister Mary, AnneMarie Stewart, Mary Taylor, Glenda Taylor, Lynne LaSala. Finally, I am grateful for residencies at Yaddo and The MacDowell Colony, where I wrote the first draft of this novel.

PART ONE

CHAPTER 1

My grandmother cried when I told her that a priest had given me a scholarship to go to a Catholic college in America. It was the first time I had ever seen her cry. I told her the news of my scholarship, more excited for her than for myself. For though this scholarship would give me the escape I craved, I knew that for my grandmother it would mean the fulfillment of the thwarted ambitions that for years she had nursed for her children. I expected praise, advice, reassurance, perhaps some words about how much she would miss me, but not tears. She had that reputation.

The women said she was mannish. At least my mother and my mother's sisters did. It was not a compliment. When I was a child, I thought this characterization of my father's mother had to do with her size and color and the fact that with six sons she was almost always surrounded by men. She dwarfed my grandfather by what then seemed to me to be at least two feet, but what I knew later, with the eyes of an adult, to be merely inches. Then, too, she had a body unlike that of any other woman I knew in Trinidad. Most were short like my mother and me,

3

though not as skinny. At twenty, I barely had a figure—slim hips, thin arms and legs, hardly any breasts. I thought I was unattractive. My grandmother, on the other hand, was tall and muscular—except for her enormous breasts.

I used to imagine they weren't really breasts at all, but rather two taut balloons that would burst the moment I touched them. My mother, like her sisters, had tiny breasts the size of loaves of hops bread, and when I rested my head on her chest, they flattened out easily against the pressure of my skull bones. I longed for breasts as large as my grandmother's and with the softness of my mother's. I got neither. My breasts turned out to be as small as my mother's and as firm as my grandmother's. But in the days when I wished that my grandmother would be like other grandmothers, that she would clasp me between her generous, plump arms and nestle my head against her warm cushiony breasts, I saw no beauty in hardness.

My grandmother's body was unyielding. Even the lines on her face and down her neck seemed held there by invisible wires. The parts of her legs I saw beneath her knee-length skirts were sinewy, too, and the short, laced boots she wore rainy season or dry gave the impression that she had just finished, or was about to do, man's work. Then there was also her hair, the most feminine part of her, my aunts said, though they disapproved of the way she wore it. The proper style for women in those days was to tuck their hair over a sausage-like roll that curled around the base of their heads. My grandmother wore her hair in a short bob. But it was curly, and in spite of the fact that it was gray, gave a youthful and frivolous cast to her face that was quite disconcerting against the firm lines of her body. Mannish indeed, but no one could ignore that she was a woman and had been a girl.

I think my darker-skinned aunts, my mother's sisters, envied my grandmother because of her pinky-white skin. (My mother, they believed, was the luckiest of them all. She was butterscotch brown, they would say, sighing as if they wished they could change their own blackberry complexion.) Of course, to them my grandmother's whiteness was additional proof that she was mannish. She was the color of the English, the colonizers who controlled our island. But they knew, and I did, also, that though her skin was white, my grandmother was not white.

Who could be pure white on an island that gave birth to calypso? my father used to ask. He told me that the English put wax in their children's ears and shipped them back to England to find husbands and wives before the sounds and sweet airs— the pinkety pang of calypso's sweet steel band music—could stir them to dream dreams of a world that needed no Prosperos. Still, some escaped. My grandmother's mother was one. Later, I discovered, nothing could shut out the music that filled her ears, not even a rope tied around her feet in a hospital in St. Ann's. My grandmother, grieving for her, built a wall of silence to seal in her secret when the people in town found out about the obeahman in Sans Souci sending signals with the sun. For love had trapped Bertha before her English parents could shield her from the Siren. So her daughter's eyes, my grandmother's, were washed by the rivers of Africa, wide and black and sparkling with the energy of rushing water. And her nose, scratched out in places where the air was weighted down with too much oxygen, pushed apart the thin nostrils that would have been the legacy left to her by her mother's people.

But in spite of the evidence of my grandmother's mannishness, the unkind gossip that sometimes peppered the talk among my aunts and my mother around the kitchen table, I was never convinced that my grandmother did not have the same feelings and yearnings as other women. I had cause to be certain, though, that she would not cry when I told her I was leaving Trinidad, for by then I had witnessed that she was, if nothing else, a master at controlling her emotions, a woman who had proven that nothing, not even the loss of a grandson whom she loved more than anyone or anything in the whole world, could bring her to tears.

I was ten years old at the time. My mother had sent me to my grandmother's to join the welcoming party for my eldest cousin, Alan, who was returning to Trinidad after spending ten years in England. Studying, my mother told me. Alan was my grandmother's first grandchild and old enough to be my father. My grandfather took me to meet him at the dock in Port-of-Spain. The ship that brought him was huge and white. At the tip of its hull, painted in big bold black letters, was the name of our recently crowned queen, *Queen Elizabeth II*. At the time I shared the awe my teachers had for her. *The sun never sets on British soil.* This young queen had the responsibility for us all, and the arrival of a ship named after her was an occasion for much pomp and circumstance.

Hundreds of people thronged the dock that day, pressing against the wooden barriers that separated them from the ship's passengers. The police brass band, comic to me then as it was now, played military marches in praise of our queen. The musicians looked like costumed players at Carnival: chocolate faces melting under stiff white cardboard helmets, white plumes fanning on top of brass spikes, brass-buttoned white jackets, heavy navy pants, black leather shoes crimping flat feet. But they were not players at Carnival; the uniforms they wore paid homage to the queen and to a system of government of which we were proud.

Down the steps streamed passengers sprinkled with confetti that fell like colorful rain from the hands of the ship's crew on the top deck. To the left of the ship's steps, I saw my cousin standing defiantly alone, his legs firmly planted apart, in one hand a spear and in the other an underwater spear gun. He reminded me of an African warrior, though the only ones I had seen at my age then were in my schoolbooks, and they wore grass skirts and carried no guns of any kind.

Long after my memories of the excitement on the dock that day dimmed, the image of the spear and gun remained with me as clear as the sparkling waters that cascaded over the rocks in Blue Basin. For my cousin—who had caused jaws to drop in disbelief when, with the accuracy of a seagull plunging its beak into a darting fish, he dove from the highest rock into that tiny pond we called Blue Basin—let that spear and gun distract him under the water in Maracas Bay. When he floated to the surface again, blood was pouring from his eyes and ears.

I learned about grief that night, the kind of bottomless, yawning grief that can find nothing upon which to anchor itself, that stretches itself out into a long howl ending in a hollow silence. I heard men cry that night: my father, his five brothers, my grandfather, my cousin's friend, his two brothers. The sounds they made were different from the muffled sniffles of the women. The men bellowed loudly in impotent rage, lashing out at a young man who so missed his warm tropical sea on that damp, cold island we called the mother country, that one night was all he could wait before he took his spear gun with him and dove deep, deep into the sky blue water. They found no water in his lungs, only blood streaming down his face from veins in his head that had ruptured under the pressure of the sea. Still, his fingers were locked around his spear gun, his knuckles turned grisly white.

"He must have thought he was a fish. The damn fool!" his father shouted through his tears. "Who the hell would dive down in the middle of the sea with no oxygen? Who the hell did he think he was? A damn fish? The Blue Basin champion? Blue Basin's no sea, dammit! The fool!"

My uncle railed against my cousin's folly, his pride, his

ignorance, his bullheadedness. He hurled blame at his dead son until he exhausted himself and only grief remained, releasing tears that poured without restraint down his cheeks.

My grandmother remained in stony silence. Not a word of consolation. Not a tear in sympathy.

Finally my youngest uncle, Melvyn, gathered up the courage to explain. He was with my cousin when he died. "We had a warning," he began cautiously. "I told him so. I told him—"

"What warning?" My grandmother's voice, soft but firm, stopped Melvyn in midsentence. "Go on, tell me. Talk."

"A big black fish like a giant dolphin. I saw it in the distance when our boat was out at sea. I saw it break through the water. It looked . . . " My Uncle Melvyn paused.

"Go on," my grandmother urged him gently.

"Like a woman."

Maybe it was his words alone that stoked his brother's fading anger, or the way he mumbled them under his breath as though ashamed for thinking them, begging some retribution that would have proven his thoughts wrong, but they revived my uncle and he flew into a rage again. "Stop it! Stop it! Not your goddamn stories and lies."

But my grandmother did not stop. "Like a woman," she repeated dreamily.

Melvyn's eyes darted nervously from her to his brother.

"With arms like a woman?" she asked. "Short? Stunted? But like a woman?"

My dead cousin's father stared at my grandmother in disbelief, his lower lip shaking, but he did not dare cross her. He unleashed his fury on Melvyn instead.

"Like a woman! You goddamn liar! You stupid fool! This is what you have to say when my son is dead."

"The Orehu," said my grandmother.

My dead cousin's father held his tongue and let her speak.

ELIZABETH NUNEZ 9

"The mermaid. The Orehu. She called your son home."

Later when he chose to forget that his brother had said he saw a fish like a woman in the sea and that his mother had named it Orehu and claimed it had called his son home, my uncle asked Melvyn to tell his story again. He would listen to his tale about a big fish like a dolphin.

Alan had laughed at him, Melvyn said, when he told him he had seen a big black fish with fins like arms rise vertically from the sea. "I laughed at myself, too. No fish has arms."

My uncle was satisfied. *Not like a woman.* He was reassured.

"Then what happened?" he asked.

"Then all of a sudden the boat heaved, as if a huge wave suddenly rolled under us. We both got scared. All along the sea was calm. Beautiful. The sun was in the middle of the sky. You could see sunbeams plunging to the bottom of the sea. They looked like tunnels of iridescent light. Tiny diamonds suspended in space." Melvyn's voice drifted. "You could see even the tiniest sea life. They were dancing in between the sea grass and the coral. It was—"

My uncle lost his calm. "What the hell does this have to do with my son?"

Melvyn shook the dreams from his head and tried to explain again. "He said he saw something in the water. He almost capsized the boat bending down to it. 'Did you see it? Did you see it?' He kept pulling my shirt. I thought I saw a cluster of sea grass shake as though something had hit it. I told him so. 'There. Look!' he shouted. The boat heaved again, and before I could stop him, he jumped into the water with his gun and his spear."

"Didn't you go after him?" Alan's father asked.

"I didn't see the fish," said my uncle Melvyn.

"Didn't you throw him the oxygen tank?"

"He disappeared before I could give it to him."

"Well, what did you do?"

"I waited."

"Why?"

Melvyn remained silent.

"There was nothing he could do," whispered my grand-mother.

"Nothing!" My dead cousin's father shouted to my uncle though he knew it was my grandmother who had spoken. "Nothing? For God's sake, he was your nephew. You could have gone after him."

"I thought he'd be back. He was a better diver than me."

"So you waited?"

My uncle Melvyn did not answer.

"When did you stop waiting? When? When?"

"The sun was so hot, I felt dizzy. I don't know how long I waited."

"The Orehu," said my grandmother.

"I didn't think I waited long, but I must have."

"Didn't you think that something had happened to him?"

"Just when I became afraid, I saw him floating on his back. Like he was sleeping. Except for the blood in his eyes. He was still holding the spear gun but the spear was gone."

"The Orehu," repeated my grandmother. She did not shed a tear.

When I returned home with my parents that night, my fa-ther told me about the Orehu. She is one of the gods of the Waraos, he said.

I remembered that long ago my grandfather had told me that when he was a boy, the Waraos came in their pirogues from off the coast of South America to sell their ground provisions in the markets in Trinidad. They once lived here, he told me. All the islands in the Caribbean were their home until the white man pushed them onto the mainland. The rain forests protected them there. The white man knew if he tried to follow them, the jungle would eat him alive.

On the night my cousin drowned, my father told me that the Warao god, Orehu, was probably a manatee, a sea cow. Sea cows are very rare, he said. Almost extinct. They rise up from the water to suckle their young. They have arms and palms without fingers except for thumbs. The Waraos love them and fear them. They have been known to carry the Waraos' pirogues on their backs safely through a storm, but then, at other times, they have pulled them down to the bottom of the sea.

I asked my father how did they do that: pull them down to the bottom of the sea?

"By some magnetic force, I suppose," he said. "Maybe ultrasound."

At ten years of age I was already a romantic. I invented the true story of my cousin's death. The fish he had seen was the tail fin of a mermaid. He had shot her with his spear gun before he saw her face, and when he did, he was so dazzled by her shimmering beauty that he fell hopelessly and completely in love with her. He was hers. He had no choice. He had to follow her wherever she took him. The rope between the spear that pierced her scaly thigh and the gun he held in his hand was his only lifeline to her. He held on to the gun until her jealous lover came to her rescue and severed the rope between them.

I did not share this true story with anyone, but it was a great comfort to me at my cousin's wake as I sat with the weeping women around his coffin. Only our grandmother and I did not cry. I wondered if she, too, knew the truth, but the next day when they lowered my cousin's body into the grave, my mermaid story could not stop my tears. At the sight of big men crying, even my grandfather and the priest, I wept uncontrollably for my cousin, who, after all, though he died for love, did not live to enjoy the island that he had waited for so long in that dark England place. Still, my grandmother's eyes were dry.

My mother was kind at first. She explained that my grandmother was in shock, but when for days and weeks after my cousin's death, my grandmother continued the unbroken rhythms of her life, acting as though nothing had changed, as though she had not planned and waited for years for the return of this grandson whom she had raised from babyhood after his mother died, my mother joined my aunts in pronouncing that my grandmother was a mannish, unnatural kind of woman, a woman who held back her feelings like a man.

They said some other things too, that I did not understand at the time. "It's mad Bertha in her blood. That Englishwoman tied to her bed in St. Ann's."

Those words would haunt me all my life. Mad Bertha. If she was in my grandmother's blood, she had to be in mine. When I learned about the music that trapped her to a rope tied to her bed, I feared that one day my ears would be filled with the music she had heard, and that I would slip into the same darkness that had imprisoned her.

But then, in those days, I thought my grandmother had the same strength of character and nobility as the queen of England, our young Queen Elizabeth who, though surely she must have cried herself to sleep when King George, her father, died, knew she had to be brave for us. There were people awake with the sun in all parts of the world, every second of the day, even when it was night in England, who were depending on her. She could not succumb to tears.

Now, at twenty, I no longer had such feelings about the queen. In fact, I had grown to resent her for her captivity of my island home, her continued policy of colonization. But I had not changed my opinion of my grandmother's courage and nobility, her selfless masking of her feelings. I knew that she felt pain and happiness like everyone else. I knew that although she did not cry, my cousin's death had wrung her heart. She saw herself as a partner with my grandfather, sharing responsibility for their family. She had to be strong; she had to set an example for us. So she wore her mask. How many times was I to wish I had that same strength, that stoic control over my emotions.

For a fleeting moment before I told her that I was leaving Trinidad, I thought my news might possibly sadden her. It occurred to me that the announcement of my departure would bring back memories of my dead cousin who had spent so many years away from home only to return to die. But I hadn't expected tears.

She was standing in front of the stove clutching a handful of seasoned raw chicken when I entered the kitchen. Hot oil bubbled in the black cast iron pot on the fire, filling the room with the familiar sweet scent of the burning sugar and garlic that women in Trinidad used to brown their meats for stew. I went to my grandmother with my news, giving her the facts the way I believed she would have liked to receive them.

"I have a scholarship to go to college in America," I said. "All my expenses will be paid. My books, my tuition, my food."

I saw the lines on her face grow rigid. She sucked in her breath with such force I thought something had happened to her. I rushed toward her but she put up her hand and blocked me. Then, as if nothing was wrong, she turned back to the stove and dropped the raw chicken in the boiling sugar. Hot oil shot out of the pot and rained on the countertop. The chicken hissed and sizzled like ice water on burning coals. Clouds of gray smoke climbed to the ceiling.

I stood near her until the sounds simmered down, waiting for her to speak. Only when she turned around did I see her tears. They rolled softly down her cheeks, caressing the rigid lines on her face, curling into the corners of her mouth. Her bottom lip shook. I wanted to hug her, to hold her, to do anything to stop those unnatural tears, but she walked past me to the kitchen table. I noticed her hands when she sat down. The spidery veins on their backs were blue and scraggly and her knuckles were pointed and white.

I tried to comfort her. "Don't cry," I said. "Don't cry."

The rivers of Africa rushed through her eyes. "Enough!"

She brushed the tears off her cheeks. The muscles on her temples twitched. She folded her lips into a tight knot and reached for the bowl of dasheen bush on the table.

"Are you sad to see me go? Is that it?" I dared to ask, thinking the improbable: I was the one to break her mask; I, who in the past year had spent so many hours locked in my room, was, after all, the one she loved most, the one whose absence would be too much for her to bear. But the lines in her face did not soften.

"There are things you don't know yet, Sara," she said. "Things you don't know."

I thought, perhaps, she had not understood me fully. I knew her ambitions for her children. Education was the only escape she saw for her sons from the future the colonizers had designed for them.

"College in America is like university," I said. "It's not what we call college here. I have a scholarship to go to a university."

All her sons had gone to St. Mary's College, the best education Trinidad offered, but it was not more than secondary school, two extra years for the more brilliant, the ones who hoped for a British scholarship to a university in England, or the sons of the plantation owners who could afford to pay. None of her sons went to university, though all finished the two extra years at St. Mary's. There was a rumor that my father had won one of the two university scholarships that the British offered once a year. Two for the entire population on the island. One chance in two hundred thousand. The British, or rather the agents of the British, of which there were more than a few on my island that was proud of its loyalty to Mother England, didn't give the scholarship to my father. His answers on the physics examination were too perfect, they said. Most unlikely. One chance in two hundred thousand. They discounted the fact that my father had a photographic memory and that he had gone weeks without sleeping, studying by the light of a candle, kept awake by the mugs of thick black coffee my grandmother had brewed for him.

Perhaps that was why my grandmother asked no questions when my cousin Alan left for England. Studying, his father said, though everyone knew he had no scholarship and his family had no money. No one asked where. Which university? There was an understanding in the family. I supposed my grandmother knew in her heart it was a lie.

"In America?" she asked. Her words formed more of a statement of condemnation than a question.

"Wisconsin. Oshkosh, Wisconsin. I have a full scholarship. Everything paid for."

"You'll be the second grandchild I'll lose to those big countries," she said flatly. "That's all."

I thought she was referring to the secret we kept about my dead cousin. By then I knew what everyone else had already known when I was a child. Alan was a link in a chain, on better days swinging buckets of coal from one man to the next, on others, descending deep into a black pit, lower than the depths of the sea that took his life.

"No, I have a scholarship. Really. I'm going to university."

"Dead people don't come back."

I thought I had not heard her clearly and asked her to repeat what she had said.

"Dead people don't come back," she said again.

I didn't know what she meant.

"Alan died in England way before he came back."

I held my breath. This was the first time I had heard her speak of him since his drowning.

"His spear and his gun couldn't help him. They were spoilt in England. The Orehu knew."

My eyes scanned the floor. I knew about her mystical and spiritual beliefs. They were part of the culture in which I was raised. My mother told me her stories, too—of the soucouyant and the diablesse. But I was twenty years old. A grown woman.

"The Orehu knows," she insisted, and reached for my hand, pinning it to the table.

I tried to move but she held me still.

"The Orehu knew what happened to him in England."

I fought with her. "Alan drowned right here in Trinidad in Maracas Bay. He dove too deep. He was too arrogant and foolish to take his oxygen tank."

I had already cast away my stories of mermaids and lovers. I had put them away with my other childish things.

"You may know too much for your own good."

I believed I was a grown woman, but she spoke to me as if I were not, and the truth was I did not have the courage to contradict her.

"You think I have nothing to teach you. You think only water can drown you."

I looked away. She gripped my chin and twisted my face toward her.

"Like America," she said. Her eyes pierced mine. Her voice seemed to come from the bottom of her throat, forced through her windpipe in a whisper. I became afraid.

She saw the fear in my eyes and slackened the pressure of her fingers on my chin.

"People think I say foolish things, Sara." She stroked my face. "But I know what I say. Listen to me. America is like the sea. You think it's good. You think you can swim in it and you'll be safe. Yes, you can find food in the sea. Plenty of fish in the sea. But when you're not looking, not thinking about it, America can drown you like the sea."

Her eyes turned glassy and her voice became more agitated and strained. "Your grandfather knows. Let him tell you about his brother, Thomas." She removed her fingers from my face. "Let him tell you about the big-shot dentist. 'America did this for him. America did that for him.' Told your grandfather we should move to America. Said your grandfather had a small is-land mind when he said his family was too black for America." She picked up the white kitchen towel hanging over the back of her chair and brushed the air. "America was good to him all right. Made him feel he didn't have to look over his shoulder. Then it got him."

She stopped waving the towel, pulled it taut and wrapped one end around her neck. The other, longer end, she stretched above her head. She looked like an animal about to be slaugh-tered. Her head dropped on her shoulder. She stayed like that for what seemed to me an eternity, her eyes continuing to stare at nothing, her lips moving as if she would speak and couldn't. I remained transfixed where I was, not knowing what to do, not understanding her. At last she loosened the towel and turned to me.

"Do you understand now, child?" she asked. Her voice seemed to carry the mysteries of the past. She was expecting me, blood of her blood, to understand, to know, but I did not know what she meant. "Do you understand me, big child?"

I said what I did not believe. "He was hanged?"

She laughed and brushed the towel back and forth across her shoulders. "And you want to go to America?"

"Then tell me." I was caught in her web, wriggling.

"The word is *lynched*," she said. "Lynched. Your great-uncle Thomas was lynched. Strung up on a tree, American style. No questions asked. No jury. Rope round his neck. His body like any old sack of black coals."

M y mother said that my grandmother was getting old and didn't know what she was saying. My grandfather's brother had been shot accidentally in a bar in Georgia. Not lynched. The police there said he resembled a colored man who had raped and strangled five white girls.

My father turned his back on me when I asked, but not before I saw anger narrow his eyes and set his jaw in stone.

My grandfather said that my grandmother had no right bringing up his brother's name from the dead. What happened in 1950 to his brother in Georgia would have absolutely no bearing on my going in 1963 to Wisconsin, which was way up north in America and as different as day from night.

"Too, besides," my mother reminded me, "the Americans saved our family. They are angels."

I knew what she meant.

CHAPTER 2

It was in 1956 that the Americans saved our family. Just a few weeks before our rescue I had hardly known they existed. Not that there weren't Americans in the world. I knew they lived in a place called the States. Wanna go to the States? Just came back from the States. Yeah, man, I have family in the States. I thought it was a stupid name to call a country. The States. I once looked for it on the map. We learned geography in elementary school but the only countries we studied, of course, were England and Western Europe, sometimes Australia or New Zealand, rarely the Windward and Leeward Islands or the Caribbean. I knew where the Americas were—North America, South America and Central America—but not the States. I concluded it must be New York because sometimes these words would be used interchangeably with the States. *Just came back from the States. Man, that New York ent playing it cold, man.*

I had seen some Americans in Trinidad. They had built a military naval base in Chaguaramus on the northwestern seacoast not far from Port-of-Spain. My uncles told me they remembered when they used to ride their bicycles from Diego Martin to Teteron Bay, but it was difficult for me to imagine any Trinidadian lying on the beaches in Chaguaramus, for that place was as foreign and distant to me as the States despite being just a few short miles from where I lived. Sometimes I saw the Americans when they came to Port-of-Spain to shop. Yankees, we called them as children and laughed at their clothes that no self-respecting Trinidadian would wear. Bright-colored pants, sometimes sun yellow or shocking pink. They had no shame. Pants cut off at the knees like overgrown schoolboys. We laughed at their hairy legs. No shame. Even the eleven-year-old boys in my class begged their mothers for long pants. They were a mark of maturity. And the shirts the Americans wore! They loved flowers. The bigger the better. Splashes of hibiscus or coconut fronds, bougainvillea or upside down flamboyant—whatever flower they thought we grew in the tropics. The English loved flowers on their clothes, too, but they were much more sensible. Tiny rosebuds, lilacs, a sprig of silver bells—subtle insinuations that nonetheless remained permanent on our consciousness: their master plan for owning the world.

Then there was always the inevitable camera swinging from the necks of the Americans. We posed for them, laughing, wondering why they got so upset when we refused their money. "What for?" we would ask. And even if we were tempted, how could we explain to mothers who knew everything that someone wanted to pay us merely for standing there, arms around each other, acting the fool. On Jouvay, the first morning of our two-day Carnival when people wore their silliest costumes, we dressed up like Americans. Grown men and women did the same. We put on the most outlandish colors we could find, clashing one against the other. Blinding lime green with sunset orange. Bleeding red with sea water blue. Cameras swinging. We laughed at ourselves talking Yankee talk with slurring *r*'s and vowels that whizzed down our nasal passages.

They had a fairy tale quality about them, Americans. Loads of money, big cars, huge mansions, hardly any children. I never saw an American child before I was twenty. Unreal people. The stuff of calypsos and the make-believe world of Carnival. Lord Invader teased us about them: *Drinking rum and Coca Cola/ Down in Point Cumana/ Both mother and daughter/ Working for the Yankee dollar.* Sparrow warned: *Jean, Dina, Rosita and Clementina, Round the corner posing/ Bet your life is something they selling/ If you catch them broken/ You can get it all for nothin/ Don't make a row/ The Yankees gone and Sparrow take over now.*

They came in black and white, the Yankees, but I thought them all the same: Americans, Yankees, as different from us as the English, distinguishable only by their accents and the penchant the English had for wearing cultivated flowers on their clothes, straw hats with ribbons or more flowers. White gloves in the middle of the day. But the Americans became real enough for me that June of 1956 when my schoolmates began to get sick.

June in Trinidad can be a month of contradictions. The two seasons meet then, the dry, swirling parched dust across burnt, brown grass, snapping twigs off half-dead trees; the wet, grumbling thunder around noontime, sending slivers of liquid silver rain gleaming in the sun. The devil and his wife fighting for a hambone, children chanted. Such it was that June. The sun and the rain. The dry and the wet. We were accustomed to getting colds then in that mixed-up weather. "It makes you stronger for August when the hurricanes come," my grandmother used to say. "Do battle with the germ in June and you'll master it in July." So at first it was not strange that the children in my town were sick in June—the burning fevers in the morning, the cold shivers by afternoon. The pains in the limbs were different. We couldn't explain them. A different type of cold this year, the older people said.

My grandmother told my mother to give me senna pod tea to drink every three days and to bathe me in shining bush tea water. Almost all liquid brews in Trinidad were called tea. Children drank cocoa tea in the morning, adults had coffee tea at night; we all drank black tea in between. We took orange peel tea for stomachaches and senna pod tea to cleanse our insides. I hated the taste of senna pod tea, not to mention the embarrassment of what it did to me, especially on a school day when everyone knew from my frequent trips to the lavatory that I had been forced to drink it. My mother added milk and sugar so it would taste like black tea but that never masked the bitter taste. When the sickness came that June, school children all over Port-of-Spain were going to the lavatory often and having many accidents.

For my shining bush tea baths, my grandmother sent a small bag of herbs that had been blessed, she said. We knew she did not mean blessed by the priest, and although my mother was a rigidly religious Roman Catholic, she dipped that bag once a day in my bath water. I asked her one night if the obeahman had blessed it. She slapped me. After my bath, she made me say the rosary with her. She said the first part of the Hail Mary, I said the second part: *holymarymotherofgodprayforussinnersnowand atthehourofourdeathamen.* I never heard the words. Just the music. The rise and fall of her voice. The cadence of the lines. Sometimes my mind drifted, but I always felt the beat and at her *blessedisthefruitofthywombjesus,* I would respond, *holymary motherofgod.*

Sometimes I thought of what we had done before the rosary. My mother would light a candle at the foot of the bathtub, dip the bag of herbs three times in the shining bush tea water and make the sign of the cross. I wondered if the obeahman and our parish priest met at the street corner.

One night my mother broke her silence during the ritual of
the bath water. "I don't really believe any of this you know, Sara,
but we can't take any chances. This sickness is so different."

But she believed. A few years later I caught her with her
obeahwoman. Three operations in England and still there was
only me. Then, desperate to give birth to another child, she had
the obeahwoman burn roots for her.

My friend Nancy was the first one in my school to die. She
leaned over to me one day in class and whispered that her legs
hurt her so badly she could hardly move them.

"Where?" I asked. "Which part?"

"The bones," she said. "Right in the very center."

They had hurt her before but not in the very center. I offered to tell the teacher but she shook her head vigorously. "It
will pass," she said.

It had passed before.

Her fever flared up after the noontime rain. We had found
shelter under sprawling, leafy branches of the tamarind tree that
shaded one corner of the schoolyard. It was still lunch recess
and while we had that freedom, nothing could send us back to
those hot, stuffy classrooms, not even rain. By accident I touched
Nancy's face. I wanted to point something out to her and my
hand brushed her cheeks. Her skin felt like burning coals. One
second later she slumped to the ground. She could not move.
The headmaster picked her up in his arms and took her home
in his car. She died the next day. We began to fear this June cold
that gave fevers in the afternoon and pained the legs.

The Sunday after Nancy's death my father took me to the
movies. This was an unusual treat. My father, who only seemed
to notice my existence peripherally when we sat together at
mealtimes, or when my mother complained about something
I'd done, or when I gave him those innumerable plastic ashtrays
for his birthdays, suddenly seemed to notice that I existed the

day that Nancy died. There were a lot of questions:

"Did you and Nancy share your juice at lunch?"

Yes, we always did, drinking from the same bottle. We were friends forever. For eternity, we had sworn.

"Did you share your sandwich with her?"

Yes, we did. She took a bite of mine. I took a bite of hers. That's how we ate our sandwiches. We were friends, sworn to eternity.

Yet I did not give my father any of these answers that traveled through my mind. "No," I answered to all his questions, not knowing why, but grieving so for Nancy that I wanted to be fiercely loyal to her. I wouldn't tell of the things we did together. They were her secrets and mine. My father was satisfied.

All that day I cried my heart out for Nancy, as much because I wouldn't see her the next day and we wouldn't be able to share our deep, dark secrets, the deepest and darkest of them about the silent, painful, mysterious transformations that were taking place under our nightgowns without our consent and against our wishes as because she was dead.

My father took me to the movies to console me in my grief. I was hardly consoled. I still thought of Nancy and her pain. The sudden and persistent aches in her legs. This, too, must be part of the transformation, we had thought when she first told me her legs hurt. A numb, dullish feeling, she had said. The soreness around the nipples, the flesh that was pushing upward, the funny sensations between the thighs. The bleeding. The legs had to be next. It was only natural. I was envious. She would be taller. Her bones were stretching before mine. We didn't think it would hurt as much as it hurt her. I didn't think she would die.

I thought of her for long hours at a stretch. Of our folly. Of my envy. If only I had told our teacher. Not that day—it was too late then—but on the days before when I wished that as had happened with her my pains would come. Her bleeding had started before mine and now her legs. If only I had told someone, I could have helped her.

In the movie theatre my guilt grew. I felt the numbness begin in my toes. A dull pain. It rose up my legs. My knees felt weak. The Von Trapp family had escaped Vienna and were now singing in America. My father leaned over to me and whispered, "Only in America. You could be a millionaire overnight."

The hills are alive with the sound of music.

He whispered again. "But not if they are Negroes."

I barely heard what he said, but in the flicker of light that crossed the screen I glimpsed his face. The anger there—raw and savage—sank deep into my memory. It was the same anger I saw years afterward when he did not answer my question about the lynching of his father's brother. Now I thought only of how much angrier he would become if I told him I wanted to go home.

My legs now felt like sandbags. They hung heavily from my knees. Then the pain began. In the very center of my bones. I tugged my father's sleeve.

"My legs," I whispered.

He looked down on me.

"They hurt."

He brushed his hand across my cheek. "No fever," he said.

"But they hurt. I can't move."

He touched my knees.

"I can't move them," I said.

"Let's go." He grabbed my hand.

"I can't move."

He stood up. The people behind us grumbled.

"Can you wait until the end of the movie?" he asked.

I shook my head. "I can't move," I repeated.

He picked me up in his arms.

That night the Americans came to help us. I can only guess how my father persuaded them to come to our house. My father was working then for the Ministry of Labor. His job was to settle wage disputes and to stipulate working conditions for Trinidadians employed by foreign companies. It was my father's responsibility to see that our people were treated fairly. Ironically, his orders from the government at about that time made the opposite appear to be true. He was the one assigned to inform the Americans that they could no longer pay wages to Trinidadians in U.S. dollars. Trinidadians were discovering that, with the rate of currency exchange, they could make a teacher's salary cleaning toilets on the American base. They began to pour into Chaguaramus in droves. The Americans found this amusing until my father stopped them. Workers could no longer be paid directly by the Americans. Wages had to be given to the Trinidadian government, which would in turn pay the workers based on the country's standards for fair wages.

The Americans were furious. An unheard-of demand, they said. Taking money away from people. It was the first step to socialism, communism to follow. Private enterprise, open competition, capitalism, monopolies, these had worked for them. How else would they get the best workers for the base? What did it matter if some mother was having difficulty explaining to her son that he needed to study math? The dollar was all that counted. And who needed math to clean a toilet bowl?

They blamed the British for their experiment in allowing a transitional government of local people. Independence was not guaranteed. The British were still the colonial rulers in Trinidad. What did they have to say? But the British were licking their wounds from the war, and the allure of days without nights—the sun never setting on lands they ruled—was beginning to wear thin. Let the Americans save the world.

The gifts from the Americans started arriving at our house that year: boxes of chocolates, cigarettes, chewing gum. My father returned them the next day, but the gifts kept coming, each

time more numerous, each time more expensive. Radios, cameras, watches, my father returned them all. The gifts became
more tempting: a washing machine that caused such arguments
between my parents when my father gave it back that my mother
did not speak to him for a week. Then a bicycle and a pair of
roller skates that sent me into a screaming frenzy when they
were all returned. But that night of my sickness I saw the captain of the naval base hand my father a small box of chocolates
and witnessed the humiliating smile of gratitude that crossed
my father's face as he accepted it. The shock of that moment
thawed my legs. The joints in my knees loosened. The resolute
chill that had taken hold of me in the cinema when I willed
myself to feel Nancy's pain dissipated. It seemed unfair. For a
box of chocolates. The wide grin on my father's face. The dull-
ness in his eyes. Captain McNeil slapping him hard on his
back, flicking the ashes of his cigar on my mother's polished
floor. I rushed to my father and grabbed the box of chocolates.
I tugged hard. He held firm. We struggled again. The tears
poured down my cheeks. He gathered me in his wide arms
and pressed my head against his chest. I heard the pounding of
his heart. It beat fast and furiously. He whispered in my ear:
"It's all right, Sara. All right. You'll be well now. You won't be
sick. We'll all be fine."

I wanted to say I was sorry—his broken voice shamed me
for my actions—but at that moment the American captain put
the needle in my arm and I screamed instead.

We were like thieves in the night, my family—Captain
McNeil with his parcel of syringes filled with Salk vaccine, my
father accepting the box of chocolates, all my cousins, the children of my father's brothers and sisters, lined up one by one,
accepting the American protection.

Polio raged through my town that year. June, July, August.
The lucky ones died, the less fortunate were fed into iron

machines, the courageous accepted their twisted limbs and kept on going. September. The English colonists brought the vaccine to our town, but by then it was almost too late for the children who lived on our block. By Christmas, about ten of them had disappeared.

Now the Americans had come to save our family again—me specifically. They sent a black Roman Catholic priest who spoke Yankee talk, but his was different from Captain McNeil's. His words drawled out slowly like hot tar. He said he was from Mississippi. 'Sippi, he called it. He said 'Sippi was just like Trinidad: "Same old hot sun, green grass, 'cepting there are no coconut trees and sugar cane. Only cott'n."

His mission, he explained to my mother, was to discover raw talent in the primitive world. My mother was certain he did not mean her world.

"So you're visiting our island on vacation, then?" she asked him.

The priest smiled. "I wish I could take a vacation now." He extended his arms. "All this here—this, too, is all part of my work."

"Your work?" My mother squinted her eyes.

"Your island is part of my territory. Jamaica, Barbados, Grenada."

"Your territory?"

"I explained it to you. I look for raw talent in primitive countries."

Ultimately my mother forgave him. She made peace with her conscience and with me. The American priest, she told my grandmother, who still insisted that the Americans had lynched her husband's brother, had chosen me because of my brains. There was some truth in that statement but also a lie, for by then, more than anything she desired, my mother wanted me out of her sight.

I had never made the top three in my class. Some years I came close. Yet if it was not true that I was brainy, it could be said I was studious. I had discovered the usefulness of that virtue quite accidentally—innocently at first, without any consciousness of its worth except for the pure pleasure I got from reading. Later, I deliberately set out to be studious, and, eventually, as my growing needs sought fulfillment in books, I developed a dependency on them that turned into an addiction.

Naively, at the early age of nine, I was drawn to books for the fantasies they allowed me: worlds in which Cinderellas became princesses, frogs turned into handsome princes and ugly ducklings, swans. Worlds where men, enchanted by the call of mermaids, followed them to their deaths. Later, after Nancy died and I entered puberty alone, my chaotic realization of my awakening sexuality drove me into a relentless curiosity about sex (*love* was the word I used then). I plundered *The Canterbury Tales*, bypassing imagery and metaphor—satire totally lost on me—and voraciously read and reread those passages that sent shivers of pleasure down through the lower part of my body. By the end of my first year in high school I could recite long passages of certain tales totally by heart.

It was Zeta who introduced me to romantic love. I met her when I was thirteen. Our island was an outpost in the British Empire and books took forever to get to our colonial library. The most modern we had were the novels of Jane Austen and Emily Brontë. Zeta had read *Pride and Prejudice,* and from her I discovered the first of the books that would thrill me with their stories of romantic love. The moody Darcy burning with desire for the unsuspecting Elizabeth: how many nights I dreamt of him.

We were secretive about our reading, Zeta and I, thinking

our parents would disapprove of our choice of books. We surmised from their adamant refusal to talk to us about our changing bodies, their furtive remarks about the visits of our "monthly friend" and the dangers of any contact with boys, that the books we read were sinful. But they were irresistible to us. Then, three years later, books and the studious posture became indispensable to me for reasons that had nothing to do with sex and romantic love. I discovered that if I could bury my head in them day and night, I could avoid the undeniable reality that my painstakingly slow and torturous metamorphosis from a girl into a woman, that had begun at the late age of twelve and a half, had resulted in tragedy. I had grown from an ugly duckling into an ugly duck. No swan for me. And my mother saw it.

At first she tried to reverse my misfortune, buying me the prettiest clothes, then straightening my coarse, thick hair. But my straightened hair hung limply at the sides of my face, exaggerating the huge roundness of my dark brown eyes and the dark shadows beneath them—vestiges of my Carib Amerindian ancestry. She persuaded my father to buy special fortified milk for me, and chocolates, and she fed me starches—rice, dasheen, cassava, yam—in the hope that my body would blossom out. But the bones in my knees and elbows still protruded, my chest stayed flat, and my hips, like a boy's, fell in a straight line from my waist. She tried shaming me: "If you keep your lower lip poked out like that, you'll grow up dragging your lip behind you. And for God's sake pinch your nose a couple times at night to get it growing right." Her threats did not help. By the time I was eighteen, I, too, had accepted the inevitable.

Books protected me from my mother's pitying eyes and my father's patronizing cheerfulness over my slightest achievement. My interest in reading was comforting to my mother, too. I was studious. At least I was not a total failure.

Was I smart? In Trinidad I never got to know. In my last year of high school, they said I suffered a nervous breakdown. I remember only the brightness of the light blinding me, relief coming only when I shut myself up in my room with my books. Four months before, I had fallen hopelessly in love with a boy, who, except for one brief afternoon, never again acknowledged my existence. My father, fearing the darkness I had withdrawn into, took me out of school. I was not permitted to take my final exams. There had been Bertha, his mother's mother, white as any Englishwoman, tied to a bed in the madhouse in St. Ann's.

The boy Eric and I had been friends since we were children. Our mothers had known each other for years. Then at Carnival time, in February of my last year in high school, he became transformed in my eyes, the dark and mysterious Heathcliff. He possessed no quality or characteristic that one would rationally and objectively compare to Heathcliff's, save perhaps one. He was not our neighbor's biological son. But it was not uncommon among women in Trinidad at that time to take another child into their families. Sometimes a relative or friend who lived in the country wanted to give her son or daughter an opportunity for a good education in the city; sometimes a friend or relative was too ill or too poor to take care of her child. But there were times when the woman who took the child, in some cases more than one child, did not know the parents. They were either dead or had passed the children on to a friend when they could not care for them, and the friend, in turn, had passed them on to another friend when she, too, could do no better. Such a boy was Eric. Our neighbor had gotten him from a friend who was emigrating to England. She had taken him when his mother died. My association of Eric with Heathcliff was based on that information alone. Later I was to see that I had instinctively made the right choice.

It was perhaps the more than usual merriment that takes over Trinidad at Carnival time that plunged me into a morose brooding about my plainness that year. My friend Zeta by then no longer needed books the way I did, though she, for reasons different from mine, also did not take her final exams. She had told me that she was having an affair with our history teacher's husband, who was an assistant editor of a local newspaper. Her plans were to leave school and work with him as an apprentice reporter. He had admired her writing, told her she had talent that should not be wasted on school books. This was the kind of romance we dreamed about.

She took me with her one evening to a Carnival fête at the home of one of her lover's friends. It was there, when I saw her lover hold her passionately in his arms, that the solid defensive wall of books I had built around me began to crumble. I wanted it too. I wanted to feel the passion Zeta now had, that I had read about in books. I wanted to experience love. Not the childish, teenage puppy love that collapsed our school girlfriends into endless giggles—Zeta and I sneered at that—I wanted serious, romantic passion. Yet no boy had shown the slightest interest in me and I had examined myself enough times before the mirror to know that I had not the vaguest trace of my mother's beauty in me. But one afternoon I felt the power my mother must have known all her life—the power she had in her ability to draw men to her, unwilling or not, like chips of metal to a magnet.

Eric had no intention of disturbing my world. A little too much rum without his parents' knowledge was all it had taken for him to see me as the object of his lust. In a darkened corner of my parents' living room, for that moment only, his hands groped my chest, searching for mounds of flesh that were not there. Frustrated, he slid his fingers up my thighs and reached for the space between my legs. The shock of ecstasy sent me reeling out of his arms, my body on fire. Eric did not try to hold me. He let me go and slumped to the floor in a drunken stupor. The next day when I sought him out for the passion I wanted again, he had already found another. I saw him pressing her against a mango tree in his back yard.

For weeks afterward I hid myself in my books behind my locked bedroom door. There were days when the depression that descended upon me wrapped me in a cloud so dark, so thick, I could barely breathe, barely turn a page. But there were other days when I wallowed in my misery, finding perverse pleasure in the pain I knew I was causing my mother. Someone had seen me burst into tears when I came upon Eric, his lips clamped to the lips of his new conquest, and had told my mother how the girl had laughed at me when I called out to Eric, and how he had chased me away. In a place as small as my island, secrets were not possible. How tragic, I thought, to be the most beautiful woman on the island—if I were to believe my father—and to have a daughter whom nobody desired.

"Come on out," my mother pleaded through the keyhole. "There will be other boys."

I flung threats at her with malicious glee. "If you mention boys again, I'll never come out."

Still, she did not stop trying to make me attractive to boys. Even when nothing came of her efforts, I would hear the disappointment in her voice and see the pity in her eyes. The disappointment was there in the most casual of her remarks: "Sara, why don't you go to the dance on Friday with your cousin?" Or: "Sara, did you know your friend Arlene is engaged? So young." The pity was there in the way she brushed the hair off my face and smoothed down my eyebrows. In the way she openly admired other girls in front of me. In the way she never told me I was pretty.

And, ultimately, I forgave her. She had tried to have other children, my aunt said. Three operations in England before I was four years old. She had no one to whom she could bequeath her flawless butterscotch brown skin, her soft curves, her lustrous, wavy hair. There was only me—a mockery of all she was.

Being studious was the least I could do to compensate for my betrayal of her. I could give her something to boast about. She could say to her neighbors: "That Sara, I don't know what to do with her. She spends all her time reading." It would be a complaint she could say with pride. I would be Sara, the intellectual; Sara, the bookworm. And when I would be in Wisconsin, out of her sight, my body no longer a reminder of her failure and mine, she could say more: "That Sara. All the boys who ask her to go out and yet it's the books, books. She'll marry books."

And there would be some truth in what she said—though I never believed boys would be waiting—for by the time I left Trinidad for America, I had read the best of the English writers our colonial library had to offer: Chaucer, Shakespeare, Spenser, Milton, Pope, Johnson, Byron, Shelley, Keats, Wordsworth, Fielding, Austen, Brontë, the Brownings and the few Caribbean writers who were available to me then—Mittleholzer, Selvon, Lamming, Naipaul. Yet I had never read a book by an American.

CHAPTER 3

September is the saddest time of the year to leave Trinidad. Like April of the country I would soon journey to, September ushered in new life from the destruction of the old. Out of the hurricane-whipped foliage rotted into the damp earth burst fresh-dressed greenery: new growths of delicate lime and dazzling emerald shimmering against the bold olive of trees that survived the hurricanes, coconut palms shaking hurricane waters from the spaces in their fronds, poui and immortelle disentangling themselves from the smothering grip of dead vines. Mango trees flowered: tiny white buds folded between new green leaves. The flamboyant spread out its thick brown arms and sprouted flames of fire, red and yellow, from its branches.

On the Sunday before I left Trinidad, already feeling nostalgia for the landscape that I would not see for years, my father drove me through the mountains north of Port-of-Spain to Maracas Bay, on the other side of the island. He wanted to say his good-byes to me, give me his last words of advice on the price of gifts.

Along the road he reminded me that this, too, the freshly

paved road on which we traveled, was a gift from the Americans to the Trinidad colonial government.

"They built it after the war," he said, spitting out the word *war* between clenched teeth, as he always did, as if merely voicing the word threatened to release an anger in him he had chosen to stifle. His older brother, George, obsessed by a sense of obligation to his mother country and deluding himself perhaps into believing that as a British subject he was a British person, had enlisted in that war.

Sometimes my father would boast about how his brother had learned to fly the British bomber planes in sixth months. "Just imagine," he would say in wonder, "one day before that, he'd never ever been in the insides of a regular plane."

At other times my father would grow morose and speak bitterly of the war that had taken his brother's life and the lives of the best of the young men in the colonies, and had given nothing back. But not so the Americans, he would tell me. They knew how to repay debts.

By then, I knew more about the Americans than I had as a child, and America had already begun to lose its fairy tale quality. A military air base at Waller Field stretched across central Trinidad; the farmers just rolled their belongings into bundles and left their lands when the British told them to move. And the naval base in Chaguaramus: the fishermen simply had to find new waters, and there would be no more family picnics on Sundays on the beach at Teteron Bay. All for fifty battered American destroyers when the mother country was afraid Germany would become their father country. And no one asked us anything, my father would shout.

Now I was barely listening to him, smelling the wind full of the sea, fishy and salty. Now my mind spun circles. Could I live without this in Wisconsin? Could I live on prairie lands whose borders touched only land and more land thousands of miles from the sea?

I pressed my face against the car window, greedy for the forests of fat-trunked trees, the clutter of leaves and vines on their tops, sifting the sun, the sudden surprise of precipices that plunged from dizzying heights at the edge of the road as we curled around the tight bends up the mountain to the sea. "For ninety-nine years," my father was saying to me. I shut off his words with the roar of the white surf crashing onto the huge rocks below us. I didn't want to feel his anger, not then, not when I was etching in my mind, for Wisconsin, white, frothy mists hugging mountain peaks, sparkling jewels reflected in the sun.

"Even the Americans knew that they had taken too much," my father said, and then mercifully, like me, he grew quiet, silenced by the beauty of the landscape.

I knew the rest of what he would have said. Even the Americans realized that the best seaports in Trinidad, Sunday picnic beaches, acres of cocoa fields and farmlands and anything else they wanted on the other islands, were too much to pay for fifty old destroyers when no one asked the people if they minded paying. And for ninety-nine years. It was too much. But when our car skated down the last stretch of road from the mountaintop and the bay appeared shimmering blue against the sunlit sky, its edges skirted with cotton white surf and then ivory brown sand, I was ready to forget. The road the Americans had built, giving Maracas Bay to us—though only to those of us in the middle class who had cars—eased the resentment of ninety-nine years. I was ready to filter out my father's words, his anger about discarded fuel and debris snaking down from the huge military ships in Chaguaramus, soiling our waters in Carenage Bay. Fishermen's sons, naked and brown like the earth, splashing in oil-drenched waters, wondering later about the eczemas that grew on their legs, pustulant and ugly.

On the beach my father made me peel my eyes off the sunlit sea. He wanted to warn me, as he had said before when we left Port-of-Spain, about the cost of gifts. I wanted to turn away from him, to keep my etching intact for Wisconsin, but he held my shoulders firmly and looked deeply into my eyes. He had something important to tell me, he said. Eric Williams had come back from America and he had learned a lot from him.

"When you get to that college in America," he said, "I want you to be careful. Don't let America fool you with its righteous words. Freedom, independence, the right to choose, justice—these are for them alone. Americans are sentimental. They cry and weep at the movies, at make-believe—but don't think real life moves them. Be careful, Sara. To them, you owe them every-thing. They owe you nothing. Your scholarship? They have paid for your silence and your friendship."

He spoke in generalities and I fought to understand him, abandoning the sea. "Not every smile is a smile," he said. "And you can lie with your face and keep your heart."

The sun blazed down on my back and burned the sand, and I remembered, and too late tried to erase the image of the other burning my father was pressing me to recall. "Not every smile is a smile." I knew what he wanted me to understand were his own smiles to Captain McNeil.

My back grew hotter and I placed my hand on the nape of my neck and felt my perspiration, hot and steamy as the water that rolled off the tool shed my father had burned, the tool shed full of Captain McNeil's gifts. He wanted me to remember the fire. To understand his smiles after he had accepted the Salk vaccine from Captain McNeil, to know why he accepted the other gifts that came after that, each one perversely less expen-sive than the other, each one larger and more cumbersome: a box of perfume for my mother, then a stack of towels, a carton of beans, bags of flour; cufflinks for my father, then a case of beer, cans of sodas, fertilizer for our lawn, chewing gum. Afterward my father would store the presents quietly in the tool shed, and his mood would darken and he would drift like a shadow through the house.

Each day I saw him grow more sullen and fall more deeply into a silence that even my mother could not break. Then another American, Paul Robeson, came to our island. Captain McNeil invited my father to a concert Robeson was giving at the base on Christmas Eve. It was the only gift my father ever truly accepted. Later, when he returned from the concert, my father set the tool shed on fire.

Our neighbors grieved for us: who would do such a heartless thing on Christmas Eve? My mother, uncanny, hiding our secret, fanned their sympathies. "All our Christmas gifts had been stored there," she said.

Her lie allowed for catharsis and permitted us to admit, while concealing the horrible truth, that my father had stored the gifts from the Americans there. It released the humiliation we had endured, the guilt we had not acknowledged, even to ourselves, when we accepted our vaccines in silence and watched helplessly as polio ravaged the children of our neighbors.

What price had my father paid for my life? The fire consumed the need to know, to give voice to the question. It eradicated from my memory, or so I thought at eleven years of age, my father's silent acceptance of the gifts from the Americans. Yet it left in its ashes suspicions that never died. Now, sitting in the sun on the beach at Maracas Bay, my father was to fuse forever the memory of that fire with the beauty of the landscape I did not want to forget.

"Just be careful what you accept from them, that's all. Just be careful what you take."

I would wonder later, why, in spite of what he knew, he let me go to America.

My mother also had her special good-byes to me. No more advice on how I could be transformed into a swan. No hair straighteners, food to make curves where I was all angles, clothes that would never make me look like her. I was leaving Trinidad, taking with me the embarrassment of her failure. Nor did she need to warn me of the price of gifts from the Americans. The fire had relieved her of guilt and she had chosen to forget. Now she could say, without betraying my father, that the Americans were angels. Yet something troubled her about the physical appearance of the American priest who brought the gift of my scholarship, and she wanted to protect me.

There should have been no reason for her to distrust Father Jones. He looked like us. Not that he resembled my family directly, but he could have been any one of the hundreds of Trinidadians who walked up and down Frederick Street in Port-of-Spain. He was about five feet seven, his skin the fresh, ruddy brown color of the rain-washed sides of a clay mountain, his hair, short and nappy, cut close to his head. He had a sturdy nose bridge with a matter-of-fact nose, open nostrils to draw in the air—attractive on a man of his complexion—high cheekbones and an expressive, generous mouth. He talked with his hands. Our instinct was to trust him. In one respect only did his physical features differ dramatically from ours. But this feature so dominated his face that, in spite of the similarity of the rest of his body to people's on my island, it filled us with an uneasiness that fought against our natural inclination to accept him as one of us. His eyes were the clearest blue, the color of the early morning sky.

Perhaps that was what troubled my mother most about Father Jones, though she never said so. Her final good-byes to me the night before I left were as enigmatic as my father's. She gave me a medal of St. Jude, the patron saint of impossible cases, and a bag of herbs. "Put it away and never use it," she said, pressing the bag of herbs into the palm of my hand and folding my fingers over it. "Never, unless you have to, and you'll know when that is." Father Jones, she said, was like us and not like us. More like Captain McNeil than like us. Yet, in the long run, she'd trust Father Jones first. But I should remember that, colored or white, all Americans were the same. When push came to shove, they would band together. Still, if she were me and she got into any trouble while she was in America, she'd ask the colored people for help first. She'd trust them first, but only after she'd prayed to St. Jude and put the bag of herbs in her bath water.

September in New York, six hours from Piarco Airport in Port-of-Spain, frightened me with its absence of greenery, its dead brown and gold leaves clutching desperately to dry branches, chilly winds plucking off withering stems, swirling brittle leaves into debris strewn by passersby, dirty yellow grass sprouting between broken concrete pavements, brown dirt hills in fields that would be richly green on the island I had just left. The woman who had come to meet me at the airport, a friend of my grandfather's murdered brother, was not unsympathetic. She kept her silence and let me stare gloomily through the car window at the dismal landscape on the drive from Idlewild Airport to her home in Jamaica, Queens. But when the taxi turned into her street of red-brick faced houses, she became impatient with my unhappiness.

"Look," she said, "some people would give their right eye to have the chance you have now."

My despair made me brazen. I didn't think the States would be so ugly. "My grandmother did not want me to come," I said. "She said America killed my great-uncle."

"Monkey chaser." The words hissed from her lips like venom from a cobra.

"What?" The muscles in my throat contracted.

"You. You, monkey chasers from the banana bush."

"Me? I?"

"Yes. You, monkey chasers from the banana bush think you know everything. Well, you don't know anything. Monkey chasers!"

The violence in her voice and the anger that flared from her eyes released the tears I had stoically dammed behind my wall of silence during that drive to Queens, and now they rushed down my cheeks uncontrollably. I had arrived in the country of the Americans, the fabled place of money, big cars and beautiful mansions, and all I saw around me was clutter—the clutter of brick houses leaning against each other, broken-down cars, twisted metal lining the pavement, people huddled at the corners of treeless streets. And now she had called me a monkey chaser, and my beautiful island home, the banana bush. Father Jones had made no mistake when he told my mother that he had come to Trinidad to find raw talent in the primitive world. That was how this woman saw my world, too. I was primitive, my island was primitive. She widened that gap between us— between her people, black and white, and me—to such a distance that I experienced an isolation for which even my self-imposed exile into a world of books had not prepared me. The strangeness of the place, the cool, detached weather, the lifeless trees, the squalor of concrete and brick and the brown and gold landscape triggered a longing in me for the radiant greenery I had left, and a sense of loss and regret for my folly, for my careless acceptance of the beauty that had once surrounded me, my easy willingness to give it all up.

Before I left Trinidad I had begun to miss the landscape. Now I knew that I would miss even more than that. Although I had accepted the priest's offer of a scholarship to a Catholic college in Wisconsin because I wanted to escape my mother's

pitying eyes and the guilt I felt for the unhappiness my existence caused her, now I knew I would miss her more than I had
dreamed possible. I would miss my father, my cousins, my aunts,
my uncles, all those who loved me. I would miss the people I
looked down my nose at, the ones who had seemed insignificant to me because I thought, from the books I read, that the
world of the big countries was filled with people more civi-
lized, more sophisticated—kinder. I never could have imagined
this utter feeling of isolation into which Mrs. Clancy's words,
spoken to me in the cavernous shadows of the back seat of a
taxi, now plunged me, a feeling of being completely severed
from the human race.

My mother had arranged for me to stay with Mrs. Clancy
for three days. She was to take me shopping to purchase winter
clothes. My mother thought that as I had never seen winter
clothes before, I should not try to buy them by myself. She had
prepared me to recognize Mrs. Clancy. Skin your color, she had
said. Her words were meant to comfort me, to make me feel
safe. But Mrs. Clancy was hard and jagged, sinewy muscles and
bones, blackness without luster. In her eyes was a pained expression that forced me to turn away or look down when she
faced me. She was my great-uncle's friend, my father said. His
last lover before he made his trip to Georgia.

She took me into her living room in silence and gave me a
box of tissues. I could see in that gesture, in the way she placed
the box gently in my hands, that she felt remorse for what she
had said, but her words continued to pain me, to keep the gulf
wide between us.

"Dry your eyes and sit down," she said. "Catch your breath.
I'll put your suitcase in the bedroom for you."

She came back offering me a glass of lemonade. "I shouldn't
have said those words to you," she said, her voice gentler than I
could ever have imagined it. "But it's best you learn now to be

tough. I hope these are the hardest words anyone says to you while you're here. Contrary to what I said back there in the taxi, this is no bed of roses you fell into, child."

The lilting way she pronounced the word *child* began to chip away at the isolation I had felt minutes ago. The familiar cadence of her speech comforted me and I smiled at her. We were seated facing each other on two enormous couches that crowded her living room. Thick red draperies embossed with white flowers fell from high white ceilings onto a dark red carpet and shrouded the room. It had already grown dark. The faint glimmer of the streetlights at the end of the block filtered through the white diaphanous curtains hanging limply between the parted drapes. Mrs. Clancy rose and turned on what seemed to be a showroom of lights. Still, the room felt close and I longed for the airy, light spaces of my mother's open living room with its many windows, wicker furniture and wood-beamed floors.

"You hear the accent, eh? Came here when I was a child, thirty years ago. Could fool some people though. Like your great-uncle Thomas." A vague softness crossed her face. "Thomas didn't know until it was too late that, like him, I came from the bush. He was so busy making it the American way. Didn't want to have anything to do with bush people."

She knew the words offended me. "I say bush people," she said, "but I don't mean anything bad by it, the way Thomas did. Sometimes the bush is better than all this concrete we have here."

I began to feel warmer toward her, the gap narrowing, the isolation less intense. She was my great-uncle's friend. Family almost. Curiosity finally broke down the remaining traces of my resentment.

"What happened to him?" I asked.

"Who?"

"My great-uncle Thomas."

"Didn't your grandmother tell you? He died."

"How?" I asked.

"How? How do people die?"

"My grandmother said he was murdered. Lynched."

"Lynched? Lynched? Where did she ever hear that?"

"Well, was he?"

She narrowed her eyes. The muscles on her face moved up and down as if she were chewing something hard. "Lynched?" She looked away. "I didn't think they heard that news in the bush." Her voice was barely above a whisper.

"What happened?" I asked.

"He forgot the rules."

"My mother said they shot him in a bar in Georgia, then they lynched him." I mixed my grandmother's version of the story with my mother's.

She laughed. "They don't lynch you when you dead, child. They lynch you so you can feel the lynching. So they can see the fear in your eyes telling them they have the power. Thomas was in the wrong place. He always thought he could go anywhere. I told him, a drop of black blood make you black, Thomas. He thought all you had to have was white skin. He came out different from your grandfather, you know. Same mother, same father. Portuguese and African, but Thomas took the white skin. He thought that made him white."

"And they lynched him for that?" I asked incredulously.

"Something like that. They're real hard on you here when you start thinking you're white. Thomas was a big-time New York dentist. He owned an apartment building in Harlem. He drove a Cadillac. He put his money in the bank on Madison Avenue. Big shot. But he didn't look where he was going. He didn't follow the rules."

I thought of my grandmother's words: *America is like the sea. You think it's good. You think you can swim in it and you'll be safe.*

"Did he rape those five girls?" I asked.

Mrs. Clancy threw back her head and laughed. "Rape five girls? Thomas? My Thomas? He was a gentleman, my Thomas." She stopped laughing. "I mean a gentle kind of man. A cultured man. That's what those rednecks hated the most. That's why they strung him up. My Thomas wouldn't hurt a fly. He opened doors for women and walked with them on the street side of the pavement. They probably knew he thought he was better than them. He probably called himself doctor. They wanted to put him in his place. All they saw was the bush. I don't mean Trinidad bush. Africa. All they saw was the jungle. To them we were animals. No, Thomas was in the wrong place at the wrong time. Here, if you're the wrong race, that can mean serious problems. Those are the rules."

I was to discover later, in June of the following year precisely, when three young men, two white and one black, passed through the town of Philadelphia, Mississippi, seeking answers for the senseless burning of a black church in Longdale, that being in the wrong place at the wrong time in the United States of America was a crime so heinous it was punishable by death. Even in a town named for brotherly love.

But Mrs. Clancy had her rules, too, her way of preparing me for America. I had to give her a dime for every call I made on her phone. The cash box was on the table next to the phone. Nothing is free in America, she wanted me to know, not even clean air. I also had to pay her the fifteen-dollar fare for the cab that brought me to her house, and five dollars for the one she called to take me shopping for winter clothes. She disregarded my downcast face and pocketed the money, reminding me that I was going to be all alone in Wisconsin—no mother, father, aunt, uncle or neighbor to help me out, to give me a dollar.

"How much money did you bring with you?" she asked me.

I lied, making it one hundred more than I had. "Three hundred dollars."

"And what do you expect to get with that?"

"My winter clothes," I said.

She laughed. "A warm coat, boots and a pair of gloves, the most. But that's not all the winter clothes you'll need. We'll spend two hundred here. You can take one hundred with you to Wisconsin. They plan to give you pocket money on that scholarship you have?"

I had not thought of pocket money.

"Well," she said, "you write your parents and tell them send you some, and soon as you get to that school of yours, you find a job. Hear me?"

On the last day I stayed with Mrs. Clancy I had five dollars left in my wallet. As far as Mrs. Clancy knew, I had one hundred and five. She came to help me pack clothes that were strange to me—a pair of long, gray knit underpants, two undershirts, a gray woolen scarf, a pair of black knit gloves, a black knit hat, thick gray socks and an ugly brown-and-black-tweed coat. She was pushing aside my thin, pastel-colored clothes from Trinidad to make room for the new drab winter garments she had told me to buy, when her fingers brushed against the bag of herbs my mother had placed between the folds of my nightgown. She pulled the bag out and brought it close to her nose.

"For protection?"

"Oh no," I said quickly. "My mother must have put it there by mistake."

"By mistake?" She peered into my eyes. "Don't lose yourself so fast, child."

I tried to explain again and she stopped me.

"When you get to Wisconsin, child, don't let them make you forget who you are. All a person has is who they know they are." She replaced the bag of herbs in my suitcase.

I wanted to tell her that the herbs had nothing to do with who I was or who my mother was, either. It was just a custom, a habit, a sort of extra protection, like the St. Jude medal I wore. We didn't really believe in it. At least, I didn't believe in it.

"Well, you're lucky, child. Many a day I wished I had my mojo bag."

The word made me cringe. "It's not a mojo bag," I said.

"You forgetting already?" Her eyes pierced mine. They were hard, condemning. "It's dangerous when you forget."

O n the airplane to Oshkosh I opened my wallet to count my money again. Five dollars. I did not know how I would survive. Then, opening the section that held the change, I found a fifty-dollar bill. Mrs. Clancy had put it there—her extra protection for me in Wisconsin. She, like my mannish grandmother who refused to cry, wore a mask of toughness.

And so I arrived at that tiny airport in Oshkosh, burdened with words of advice, warnings, dismal predictions, feelings of isolation and desolation and a yearning to return to the familiar—to the sounds, smells and warmth I had left behind in Trinidad three short days ago. When the tiny propeller plane I had boarded in Chicago touched down on that barren landing strip, my imagination was aflame with all that had been said to me about America. The warnings, disassociated in a new setting from the persons who had spoken them and the incidents that had given rise to them, stripped of almost any human, sympathetic context, became cold, objective realities that I was certain I would encounter. I began to fear that I, too, could end up like my great-uncle Thomas, that my face would be so unknown, my identity so unremarkable, that someone would come out of the dark, an authorized official of the law, and shoot me down, or lynch me, as they had lynched my great-uncle, because in

this great big place to which I'd willfully gone merely to hide
from my mother's pity, there would be no one who would know
me, who could say I went to school with her, or she was my
neighbor's daughter, or I knew her mother or her family, or I
was a good person, a young woman who would not hurt a fly.

My head also swirled with my father's warnings about the
price of gifts. Would the nuns make me pay for my scholarship
the way Captain McNeil made my father pay for the vaccine
that saved my life, in secretive little installments that would strip
me of my self-respect and pride? And could I withstand the
cold of winter?

Once, in the sweltering heat of the August hurricane season,
I tried to trick myself into believing the stories in the English
books I had read: winter was nicer than the sultry heat of the
tropics. I rubbed cold bottles of ice water up and down my
arms and legs and basked in the pleasant sensation of the soothing cold against my hot, sticky skin. But my mother broke the
spell I had woven.

"If you really want to know, put your arm in the freezer
and keep it there for ten minutes. Then you'll have an idea of
winter."

She would know. She'd been to England three times before
I was four years old.

At first there was only the tingling chill on my arm that
cooled the rest of my body, and then the prickly sensation that
comes with touching something hot. But finally I felt the pain—
brutal and burning. It seared through the bones in my fingers
and enclosed my wrists. I could not endure ten minutes. Three
was all I could withstand with my hand in the freezer. I had a
glimpse of a nightmare then: the unbearable pain in the joints
of my fingers multiplied when it spread to every bone in my
body.

No one came to meet me at the airport. I was somewhat

prepared for this because my plane was delayed three hours in Chicago. I was grateful, though, for the time to be alone. It gave me the chance to disguise my fear, to put on a smile, to reassure myself I had done the right thing. Wisconsin was not Georgia. The nuns would be kind to me.

I decided I would use the fifty dollars Mrs. Clancy had left in my wallet to take a taxi from the airport to the college. All along the ten-mile trip I could see the driver looking at me through his rear-view mirror.

"Going to work for the Sisters?" he asked me finally.

"I'm going to college," I said.

"Is that so?" The words blended into each other. *Izzatso*. The curiosity in his voice was edged with anger. He lapsed into silence.

I looked out the window less out of interest in the landscape than to avoid meeting his eyes in the mirror. Once we had passed a few concrete buildings, we entered vast open spaces of acres and acres of grain that flooded me with memories of the sugar cane fields that lined the road on the way to the airport in Trinidad. How familiar this now seemed. How beautiful. It was about four in the afternoon. It could have been morning. The sun was stretched out over the tops of the grain. Was it corn? It could have been maize or wheat. I would not have known the difference, but the sea of green it made, rippling right and left with the wind, shimmering against a backdrop of blue hills that merged with the sky so engaged me, so absorbed me that my fears about my isolation, my feelings of strangeness in this new country began to melt away with each mile on our approach to the college.

"Did you say you're going to college?" The driver spoke again and shattered my reverie. His emphasis on *college* was pronounced with such disbelief that it immediately triggered my defenses.

"I have a scholarship," I said, tearing my eyes away from the grain field. "The nuns are expecting me."

He looked at me through the rear-view mirror. Only his eyes were visible. Ice blue.

"How'd you get that?"

I didn't think blue could be so hard. Blue, I saw in the soft sky in Trinidad. Blue, in the warm turquoise sea. "The nuns gave it to me."

"What'd you do? Take some exam for it or something?"

"No, I just got it."

"Just so. Just got it. That's all."

I could hear the growing irritation in his voice and I clutched my handbag tightly. I didn't know what he meant, what it was that bothered him.

"They gave it to me," I said.

"What kind of English is that you're speaking?"

Ice blue again in the rear-view mirror.

"I don't understand," I said.

"Your English. Your accent. Where you from?"

I took a deep breath and forced myself to relax. "Trinidad."

"And where's that?"

"In the West Indies."

"And they went all the way out there and gave you a scholarship?" He took off his cap and whistled long and loudly. There was no music in the sound. "All the way down there?"

"I was lucky," I said, forcing a smile.

"For nothing? They gave it to you for nothing?"

"Father Jones," I began. "He said the nuns were looking for . . ." I couldn't finish my sentence. Primitive people with raw talent, Father Jones had said. "The nuns were looking for someone to help in my country." I tried again, groping for the right words.

"I have three sons myself," he said. He put his cap back on

his head. His voice was quiet now. Distant. "The oldest one goes to college in Milwaukee. Works thirty-five hours a week like me, driving a cab. Goes to school at night. Nobody came up to him or me to give him a scholarship. Not like we live far away like you. Just right down the road a few miles ahead. Wisconsin-bred and Wisconsin-born."

I felt a need to apologize. "I have to work, also," I said, the lie coming rapidly to my lips. "To pay for my scholarship."

His ice blue eyes caught and held mine. "Then that's no scholarship, lady."

I pulled away. "Well, it's part of a scholarship. I work and they let me go to college free."

"What kind of work?" His question came swiftly, challenging my answer.

I looked down at my hands. "Cook," I said. Miraculously, I had chosen the right word.

He grinned, brushed back strands of dirty blond hair that had fallen on his forehead and leaned back against his seat. "Thought so," he said. "Thought so." A satisfied smile crossed his lips. He didn't speak again until we arrived at the college.

All the nuns had come out to meet me on the front lawn. I saw them against the backdrop of a huge, dark building, their long white skirts and veils billowing out behind them in the sudden gusts of wind that accompanied my arrival. One of them broke off from the rest in a slight trot as the taxi pulled up against the curb. The Mother Superior, I correctly guessed, for she had been standing at the head of the open triangle they had formed. When the taxi came to a halt, she grasped the door handle and yanked open the door. In seconds I was folded into mounds of white cotton, my right cheek pressed painfully against the metal crucifix on her chest.

"We are all so sorry, so sorry." She tightened her embrace. "They told us you'd be here by six. Those commuter planes are always off schedule. We called. They told us the plane would be late. Just by chance Sister Agnes called again at four to make sure there wasn't another change, and there it was, you were already in and on your way here." She released me. "Come, come out. Welcome, welcome." She guided me out of the taxi. "Sister Agnes! Sister Maryann! Come, come."

The other nuns crowded around me. "Isn't she brave?" Mother Superior tightened her grasp around my shoulders. "Isn't she smart? How'd you know how to take a taxi? Of course it was the right thing to do. But all by yourself the first time in a new country? That was brave."

The smile I painted on my lips warmed them to me.

"What a face," one said.

"What hair."

"So thin." I heard another clucking her tongue and once again I was folded into mounds of white.

Mother Superior clapped her hands. "Sisters, sisters, don't crowd her." She pulled me away from the arms of the one who had called me thin. "My, my," she said. "My, my." Her eyes surveyed me.

The taxi driver came up behind us and tapped my shoulder. "Now, miss, who's going to pay the fare?"

Mother Superior turned to him. "Shame on you, Charlie. This is a special visitor from Trinidad. Miss Sara Edgehill. Miss Edgehill, this is Charlie. He does the regular runs from the airport into town."

Charlie shifted his eyes to the ground and mumbled, "Errands. I have a lot to do."

"So you have, Charlie. But the suitcases?" Mother Superior placed some folded dollar bills in the palm of his hand.

Charlie flashed me a look of pure hatred. It stung my eyes.

He went to the trunk of the taxi and pulled out my suitcases. "Here," he said. He dropped them at my feet.

"Aren't you going to bring them in?" Mother Superior looked at him, but something in the way he stepped backward toward the car, rubbing his hands against his thighs and shaking his head, warned her not to press him further. "That's okay, Charlie," she said. "Leave them here. We'll take them inside."

He drove off with such speed that the car wheels skidded against the concrete pavement.

What happened that evening is still blurred in my mind. I remember the shock of looking into a sea of white faces drowned in white cotton. I had never before seen so many white people, so white, all crowded in one room. I had been taught by nuns in the Catholic high school I attended in Trinidad, many of them from Ireland, some from southern European countries. All had been in the Caribbean so long that by the time I met them their faces were permanently tanned. Occasionally a new nun would arrive at the school and we would ogle at her whiteness, but she would be one, an oddity. Before we really got to make jokes about her—"It's a good thing Mother Angela has eyes or you'd think she has no face at all"—the nun would look like all the rest. There were some who couldn't tan but then their faces were covered in freckles. "It's a good thing Mother Perpetua has freckles or she'd have to hang a sign on her face." But I had never seen such whiteness gathered in one place. It frightened me.

At dinner my fear intensified. I began to feel this new, color-less world close in on me. Perhaps this feeling was triggered by the food which, coincidentally, was without color: white steam rising from mounds of fluffy white mashed potatoes topped with a pat of pale melting butter, white baked fish covered in a white sauce and slices of white bread served on white plates on top of a white linen tablecloth. Not even the tiny beads of green peas or the shredded lettuce broke the vast stretches of white-ness before me. Gradually the nuns merged one into the other, their faces lost in the voluminous folds of their habits, each growing increasingly indistinguishable from the other. I could feel them pressing me with more kindness, and then I was sucked down into a vortex of bottomless whiteness, my legs flailing limply from my body. White clouds, strangely ponderous and heavy, now converged upon me, enveloping me, smothering me. I gasped for breath and the clouds entered my lungs and expanded my chest further and further outward until I exploded and my body broke up into tiny fragments of white paper that gently floated up out of the vortex and hovered along the four corners of the ceiling. I saw the nuns raise their crucifixes upward and I felt myself grow lighter until tiny bits of me sprinkled down like the noonday drizzle. The nuns cupped their hands and caught me, and when they each had a little fragment of me, they clamped their palms together like the shells of an oyster and trapped me in the shelter of their goodness.

CHAPTER 4

The faces I saw in my room the next morning were brown. I thought I had died and gone to heaven. I shut my eyes tightly, counted to ten, and opened them again. They were still there.

"You're not going to faint again, are you?" The girl who put her hand on my forehead had a face like an exquisite mahogany African mask. Her almond-shaped eyes slanted mysteriously upward. Her long, elegant Nubian nose flared slightly at its end. Her lips were full and generous, the color of purple cocoa pods. A mass of tight black curls clustered around her face.

"You gave the Sisters a real fright last night." There was something familiar about the lilting way she spoke. A surge of happiness burst across my heart. She was a foreigner as I was; she was not an American.

The other girl in the room was lighter in color, her skin the shade of black tea drawn in hot milk. Her straight black hair was parted down the middle and fell along the sides of her face. Her eyes were smaller than the other girl's and sparkled with a kind of childish gaiety. She had a short, thin nose and a small mouth, but these, too, seemed animated.

The mahogany girl pointed to her. "This is Angela. My name is Courtney. We wanted to be here when you came, but we were invited out to dinner last night at the O'Brien's. You'll meet them."

Angela shook my hand. "The Sisters said you hadn't eaten a thing yesterday. You wouldn't touch dinner and then you fainted." She was also not an American. I couldn't place which country she was from, but I knew she was from the Caribbean.

"Fainted?" Then it came back to me, the blinding white. When I regained consciousness on the dining room floor, the nuns were hovering above me. Then there was an incredible softness beneath me, a gentle warmth over me and I drifted off to sleep.

Angela giggled. "That was so funny, fainting like that."

Courtney frowned at her. "This place can do that to you."

"There were so many of them."

She understood what I was talking about. "You might as well get ready. We're the only people in the whole college, in this whole town, who are not white. You can feel like a flea in a bowl of milk. Sometimes it's hard to stay afloat and not drown."

"Oh, Courtney." Angela shook her head.

"Angela loves them."

"The nuns are good to us."

"There were two Negro Americans living in Oshkosh when we came," said Courtney. "They left last week. Not by choice, mind you."

"That's not fair." Angela's tiny mouth shaped itself into a girlish pout but the defiance in her eyes cooled quickly under Courtney's steady, expressionless stare. She turned to me. "Don't let Courtney frighten you. People here are nice. Very nice."

"Maybe," said Courtney.

"The truth of the matter, Sara, is that Mrs. Smith said she

had left all her friends in Detroit and she was missing them."

"The truth of the matter," said Courtney, "is that Mrs. Smith couldn't find any friends here."

I wanted to return to the heaven I woke up to. "I'm starving. Where do you get breakfast?"

"Sister Agnes said you were to have breakfast in your room today."

"We are to eat with you," said Angela. "Here, it's all arranged."

"No. My God, that won't be necessary. I'm not sick."

"We want to." She uncovered a tray that lay on the desk next to my bed, which faced a large picture window. The sunlight, warm and brilliant, streamed through the glass. The leaves on the trees cast whimsical shadows across the room. I brushed aside Courtney's words. *Mrs. Smith could find no friends in Oshkosh?* Everything in that room suggested the opposite. The pink ribbed coverlet on the bed next to mine matched the one on my bed. There were happy posters on the walls, a white shaggy rug on the floor, and two tiny desks in the little alcove near the door.

Angela followed my eyes. "All the other rooms are decorated in the same way," she said. "Except, perhaps, the posters are different." I could not imagine that in such a place, in such pretty rooms, the people would not be as nice as Angela had said they were.

Suddenly I realized that I was to share this room with someone. Tacked on the edge of one of the bookshelves was a small sign. I squinted my eyes to read it. *Angela.* I breathed in deeply and then was ashamed for the relief I felt.

"You and Angela share this room," said Courtney, watching me. "Angela gave you the view."

I wanted to express my gratitude to Angela, but it was shame I felt under Courtney's sad eyes. Courtney knew I would have taken the bed near the door to have avoided rooming with her.

"I shared this room with Courtney last year," said Angela.

"In fact, you have her bed. It was her idea to give you the one near the window. Not mine. She thought you'd like to see the trees."

My shame deepened. "So where will you stay, Courtney?"

"She has a room all to herself," Angela answered for Courtney.

I thought I saw Courtney's face turn to wood, the African mask she resembled made real. But in an instant it was human again, the cool rigidity that had entered her eyes and had spread across her cheeks blinked away with a quick flicker of her eyelids. My head swirled. Was it she who blinked, or I?

She brought the tray to my desk and poured me a cup of tea. "With milk like the English, I bet." She handed me the tea with the milk in it already. "And no sugar. You don't like it sweet, do you, Sara?"

Her voice disturbed me. I was irritated by her insinuation that she knew me well. Yet she was right. I didn't like it sweet.

"Half a teaspoon," I said, quietly fighting a battle with her.

"You don't have to."

"Then none."

Angela giggled again. "Courtney's always doing things like that. She likes to pretend she's a fortune teller."

Courtney brought her face close to Angela's. She pressed her thumbs to her temples and stretched her skin back to her hairline. Her eyes disappeared in the folds of her skin, and the palms of her hands opened wide on the sides of her face fanned out her fingers like the fronds on a palm tree.

"Or vodoun priestess." The mask reappeared.

I could see the fear in Angela's eyes. They grew round and black. Her lips trembled. She backed away from Courtney and clutched her throat. Blood drained from her face and her complexion turned sallow. Courtney laughed and dropped her fingers from her temples.

Had I imagined the mask? Had the strangeness of the room

played tricks on me? It was easy to think so now with Courtney's laughter. Angela was smiling too. Color returned to her cheeks. She swiped her hand playfully at Courtney.

"You're always playing games with me."

Hadn't Angela seen it, too, the mask I had seen?

I tried to force her to remember. "Didn't Courtney frighten you?"

She laughed. "She's just silly. She comes from the bush."

I braced myself for Courtney's response, but she laughed also. Perhaps my mind had tricked me. Perhaps it was a game, a pretense, a private joke, yet I felt an undercurrent between them, cold and tense, in the absence of sparkle in their eyes.

"To Angela every place but here is the bush," said Courtney. There was no humor in her voice. "I'm from St. Lucia. Courtney Adams, a good English name for the daughter of a vodoun priest. And Angela's last name is Baboolalsingh—Angela, in honor of her mother country, England, and Baboolalsingh for her East Indian ancestors. She's your neighbor, you know. She's from British Guiana."

Angela passed me a slice of buttered toast and a sliver of ham and shook her head. "Courtney's always saying things in a special way. Her father is not a vodoun priest. African, I suppose. And both my parents are East Indians." I saw her glance quickly at Courtney, but Courtney kept her silence and did not contradict her. "I came in January," she continued breezily. "Courtney has been here since September last year."

"The nuns thought I needed a companion." Courtney's voice was dark and heavy with sarcasm.

"Anyway," said Angela, "the nuns gave both of us scholarships. I guess you are on the same program."

I nodded my head.

"I really like it here. It's terrific. The Sisters are wonderful. They're kind to us. They treat us really well. And the girls are very friendly. Most of them will be here tomorrow and you'll see. You'll love them. I know you're probably feeling lonesome now. I did when I first came but now I don't miss home one bit. You'll see. This is a really nice place and on holidays," she said between mouthfuls of bread, "Mrs. O'Brien usually has us to her home." She swallowed and added breathlessly, "Sometimes some of the girls invite us to their homes for the weekend." She paused and glanced slyly at Courtney, expecting, I thought, that Courtney would have something to say, but when it was plainly apparent that Courtney was absorbed with eating her cereal and was going to let her talk, Angela moved happily along.

"It's going to be like a real party next week," she said. "I'll introduce you to everyone. Molly, she's real pretty. Christina, or Tina as we call her, she's gorgeous. In fact all the girls are nice looking. Wouldn't you say so, Courtney? Courtney?"

"They're okay," Courtney said quietly.

"Just okay?

"Why don't you give Sara a chance to get to know them?"

"I just want Sara to know how nice they are."

"Nice and pretty. Nice and pretty and friendly and nice and pretty," Courtney chanted.

"Courtney's always funny. Don't mind her."

I didn't think Courtney was funny. There was a cold bitterness in the sing-song way in which she mimicked Angela's words. It was not only Angela she meant to mock but the girls, too. I found myself getting angry with her, with her unfairness in trying to spoil everything for me, to color my impressions of the other girls before I got to meet them.

"I'm really looking forward to meeting your friends, Angela," I said. "They sound great."

Courtney got up. "Look, if we are all finished eating, I'll take the tray back to the kitchen."

Her eyes met mine. They were profoundly sad.

"I'll see you at lunch time. Angela will show you around and take you to Sister Agnes."

I wanted to touch Courtney's hand, to stop her. I wanted to ask her to go with us but the dark mood that had begun to drape over her with Angela's increasingly bubbly descriptions of the girls now seemed to envelop her completely. She seemed to want to separate herself from us. Yet I felt she was offering me a choice, pleading with me to ask her to stay with me, to choose her. We are soulmates, her eyes said. She knew, without being there, what had happened to me the night before in the dining room when my body shattered into tiny fragments and fell like rain into the cupped hands of the smiling nuns. She knew how I liked my tea: milk, no sugar. She probably knew my isolation and loneliness. But I fought against my pull toward her. No, no more mournfulness for me. No more sadness. No more despair. I looked up into Angela's bright face. That's how I wanted to be. That's why I had left Trinidad. I wanted a new life. Hope. If Angela had found it here, why not me? If she had met friends here, why wouldn't I? If she found this college, this little town in America, so irresistible that it had faded her memories of her birthplace, why wouldn't I?

That was what I wanted: a new chance, a place to be myself, to start again. Somewhere I could become myself without hurting those whose expectations I could never fulfill, without cringing under the smothering pity of those I loved and those who loved me, knowing, both they and I, that I could never be what they needed me to be. I could not be for my mother the beautiful daughter she wanted, needed. I could not make up for the children she could not conceive. I could not mirror for my father the beauty he saw in his wife, nor be the son he did not and would not have.

I had escaped. I had chosen my escape here. I would make something of this, something of myself. I turned my back on

Courtney, swept away her moroseness in the dismal rubble of her unspoken words that presaged the realization of my worst fears about America and about the girls who would live with us in the dormitory. I threw them away along with the dark misgivings that Mrs. Clancy had triggered in me in New York. I chose the light. I chose Angela. I would let her be my guide through the College of the Sacred Heart for Women.

Through Angela's eyes I saw the freshly painted walls of the dormitory, each room neatly lined up in two rows, separated by a long narrow corridor with a white rubber-tiled floor. The building had three floors. I was on the first. All the rooms were decorated like mine: white-for-virgin floors, pink-for-girls bedspreads and white-for-innocence rugs.

Outside with Angela the landscape had not lost its familiarity. I gazed with longing at the miles of grain that grew in the fields across the road from the dormitory. But Angela shattered the fairy tale I was constructing. "That Courtney," she said, tossing her hair into the wind, "one day she told me that those fields reminded her of sugar cane estates in St. Lucia. She's so silly sometimes. Boy, did she learn fast." Long strands of black silken hair splayed across her shoulders like an open fan.

I wrapped my arms tightly against my chest. A gust of wind followed by another in rapid succession crawled down my back and chilled my bones. *Oh Courtney, you hoped as I did.*

I was fooled as you are going to be fooled, I could hear her answer.

I pulled my eyes away from the fields.

"And where's the college? Where do the nuns stay? Where did I have dinner last night?" I asked Angela, piling question upon question to bury my reemerging doubts. Angela, thank God, was blissfully unaware of how her casual remark about Courtney could have so easily been said about me. How I, too, saw sugar cane growing from those cold grain fields. She was eager to answer me, to fill me in with every detail of the College of the Sacred Heart for Women. She would take me to the college then and there, she said. And as I followed her up the mile-long stretch of solitary road that led to the cluster of buildings at the end of the fields, she lovingly recited to me the history of the college that she had so perfectly memorized.

The Sisters were originally a small group of twelve nuns who were members of a religious order dedicated to the care of the sick. The group had ministered to the farmers in northern Wisconsin for over a decade and when the wealthiest farmer in the state died, he did not, as Angela brightly said to me, "forget the hands that cared for him." He bequeathed to them his mansion and two hundred acres of farmland. The nuns moved into the mansion and sold half the acreage to build a small nursing home next door. They trained the daughters of displaced farmers, and, in fact, any girl who was willing to work, to be their assistants. As the years went by and their nursing home grew, the nuns expanded their training program to include girls from the neighboring towns. Some years later a few banking firms decided to establish their main offices in Oshkosh. The businessmen followed next, paying the nuns huge sums of money to rent their land. One thing led to another, Angela said, swelling with pride as if the nuns' success were her own personal triumph. The businessmen donated money to the Sisters to expand the nursing home into a hospital, and the training program became a school for nurses.

When the Wisconsin Department of Education required that nursing schools give their students liberal arts courses, the Sisters decided to go into the college business. The original twelve went to live in the hospital, and turned the mansion into a school building. Ten nuns were sent from the main order to establish the college. They became the principal faculty. They lived on the top floor of the mansion. Classes were held on the

first and second floors and the girls ate their meals in the basement. Angela told me that I probably had my fainting spell in
the nuns' banquet room on the parlor floor next to the admin-
istrative building, where she was now taking me to meet Sister
Agnes. She told me that the college was only five years old and
that there were a hundred and twenty students. Fifty were nursing students and lived in the hospital or at home. Of the other
seventy, fifty lived in the dormitory with us and twenty were
local residents.

Angela said that the school, not yet accredited, was like an
annex of the University of Wisconsin. It didn't bother her, she
said, whether the college got its accreditation or not, because
the nuns were nice and she knew that they would do their best
for her. Some of the girls, however, complained, or at least their
parents complained, that not having accreditation was tanta-
mount to having no college at all. It didn't make any difference
to her, but Angela was certain, anyhow, that the college would
get its accreditation that year. Once they were accredited, Angela continued, they would not need the University of Wisconsin and the spies that came around every month to poke
their noses into the classrooms.

I loved the story that Angela told me about the nuns. It con-
tained many of the fantasies I had sought out in books: selfless
saviors of the poor and dying, rich benefactors touched by their
kindness, rewarding them for their years of self-sacrifice. I loved
most the part about their turning clay into gold, taking an inheritance and increasing it tenfold, transforming a dream into a
reality that was larger than what they had first envisioned. Not
merely a nursing home for a few farmers, Angela bragged, but a
hospital *and* a nursing school *and* a college. It was the stuff of the
books in which I had immersed myself. Fiction made real.

I could make no sense, however, of Angela's chatter about
accreditation. I liked the way she said the word, the *d's* and the

t's bouncing against each other on the roof of her mouth. It seemed a genuine American word to me. I had never heard it before, nor seen it written in any book. It had a distinctive ring to me that conjured up images of the American spirit—the wholesome courage and gritty nerve of the pioneers I saw in the old cowboy movies that were exported to countries such as mine. There would always be a man with a heavy hammer raised above his head, driving a wood stake deep into the earth. His wife, in a pinafore, would be standing behind him, hugging a son and a daughter to her sides. One blow is all it would take for him to lay claim to the land in the Wild West where the deer, the antelope and the Indians roamed. In that one word that Angela repeated so many times as we approached the main entrance of the college, I sensed the thrill and excitement that must have scorched the blood of these owners of the New World. *Accreditation.* It meant validating your right to ownership, proving you belonged, you had the credentials. I knew the word had the same effect on Angela. I heard the nervous quivering in her voice when she said it.

"The nuns said we'll get our accreditation, but it doesn't matter if we don't get our accreditation right now, though it would be good to get the accreditation so the people from the University of Wisconsin will stop prying. In America you don't have to answer to anybody when you get your accreditation."

It was a new American word. I loved it.

I wanted to ask Angela the same question the taxi driver had posed to me: Why had the nuns given scholarships to three girls from the Caribbean? Why hadn't they chosen their own girls? But it didn't seem fair for me to interrupt the stream of Angela's pleasant prattle. She was taking such obvious pleasure in relating how the nuns had overcome every obstacle in their paths, as if their achievements were hers. Happiness bubbled out of her. I envied her. I wondered if I would be as fortunate to experience such joy in America, such happiness, such a sense of belonging.

By the time Angela had left me on the lawn in front of the college, explaining that Sister Agnes wished to see me alone, she had easily infected me with her gaiety. I saw now the elegance of the dark mansion which, when I first arrived, was merely a forbidding, shadowy background accentuating the blinding whiteness of the nuns' ballooning skirts. Now, because of Angela, I saw the mansion as a rich man's dream, perhaps an educated man who wanted to recreate on his own estate the sprawling manor house of a nineteenth-century English landlord. For though I had never before seen a building of this size or stateliness, I knew it through the Victorian novels I had read.

The building was set back on a wide, open lawn, shadowed by massive oak and maple trees, their leaves already burnished to a multitude of shades of red and gold. In New York these colors had reminded me of death, green having been the only color I had associated with life. Green on the leaves of trees at the height of the rainy season in Trinidad. Green drowned by the hurricanes. Green set on fire by the sun in the dry season, tarnished brown, sucked dry. Green made withered and lifeless until it curled upon itself, and fell off from trees like pages ripped from a book. Green floating to the ground with the red and yellow petals of flowers from giant poui and sprawling flamboyant. Green heroically rising again from the ground in September. Green basking in the brilliance of a sunlight made cool by the winds that followed the hurricanes. But now there were browns and golds and reds without the fiery heat of the dry season. Now there was brown floating gently off trees in cold, rainy-season winds, gilded leaves brushing against glinting flecks of light that sparkled off the metallic gray stone walls of the mansion.

Three turrets rose above the mansion's slated roof. A weather-vane poised atop the middle turret twisted with the wind. On each of three floors, a score of domed windows, divided by a center column of stone wall, protruded gently outward. I noticed the hospital, too, assertively attaching itself to the mansion, but it was a modern, concrete building of no particular distinction whatsoever and I chose to ignore it. Yet how soon was I to be reminded of it when I entered the mansion.

From the moment I opened the front door I saw the antiseptic whiteness. Any polished, dark wood paneling and ornate Victorian trimmings I had anticipated finding had been gutted out and replaced with plaster and Formica. Instead of deep, plush couches and oak armchairs, there were cheaply made wood benches. An array of brightly colored magazines were carefully placed on low Formica-topped tables. My disappointment must have shown naked on my face.

"It doesn't look the way you would expect, does it?" Sister Agnes came toward me. "We had to be pragmatic. Our students are young and energetic."

She shook my hand. "Come, follow me." She led me briskly down a narrow corridor to her office.

The beauty of her room caught me by surprise. This was how the rich landlord had furnished his dream manor. Beveled oak wainscots, four feet high, bordered each of the four walls. Above them, the walls and ceiling were white, made out of a rough-textured material, stucco perhaps. The floors were still the original wood parquet, partially covered with an Oriental antique orange-toned carpet on which stood an enormous mahogany desk with bright brass handles. Behind the desk were six oak-framed windows. Three dark green leather armchairs formed a semicircle around the desk. To the side of one was a low mahogany cocktail table with brass rings that matched the desk's. My eyes must have widened to round orbs. Sister Agnes was pleased.

"It's the only room like it in the building. The others were modernized to go with the times."

"It's beautiful," I blurted out.

"Yes, yes."

She was my height, no more than five feet two inches. When she stood next to me, I could see deep into her eyes. They were the color of the sea—blue tinged with green.

"So you are Sara, Sara Edgehill. I'm so pleased you're here. I'm Sister Agnes, the dean of students. We were so worried last night. We thought you were going to be sick again."

The word *again* snaked across my mind and made me uneasy. I lowered my eyes.

"Don't be afraid." She touched my hand and forced me to face her. "We want to know about all our girls and you are one of our special girls. We intend to take care of you while you're here. Sit. Sit." She motioned me to one of the armchairs. She waited for me to sit and then she walked around to the other side of her desk. "We understand you like to read."

She pressed her palms against the top of the desk and slowly forced her body into the large leather swivel chair. She was performing a sort of physical exercise, a habit she had probably grown into of putting the weight of her body on her arms and legs to strengthen the muscles.

"Father Jones said you like to read," she said again. She clasped her hands under her chin and rested her elbows on her desk.

"Yes, I enjoy reading."

"What kind of books?"

"All kinds."

"Your last book, for example?"

"*Wuthering Heights*," I replied.

She leaned back in her chair and swiveled from side to side. "The unhappy Heathcliff," she mused.

My early fear returned like slivers of ice beneath my breasts. *Heathcliff. Why did she say Heathcliff?*

"What else have you read? Shakespeare?"

"Yes."

"And your favorite play?"

"*Romeo and Juliet,*" I said, not stopping to think.

"Innocent love shattered."

I twisted uncomfortably in my chair.

"And what else?"

"What else have I read? Most of what was in our library."

"All those books?"

"It's a small library. There are no modern books. Chaucer. Only a few books past Dickens."

"Dickens?"

"I loved *Great Expectations.*"

"Father Jones said you were bright."

My face felt hot. "I just read," I said. "I like to read." Except, I thought, that one year when I hated the books I had read in class. My English teacher had turned Keats's odes into mathematical equations. She sent us scurrying for patterns of irreconcilable opposites and paradoxes. I began to dislike the poems I once loved. Wordsworth's poems no longer consoled me after I was made to beat out iambic pentameters and search for symbols and metaphors under every blade of grass.

"But you didn't take your finals?" She was looking as me intently, her sea green eyes darkening.

I bit my lips.

"Was it because of your problem?"

"Problem?"

"Your sickness. Like last night."

"I was just tired last night. I feel better now."

"Your nerves?" she asked, trying to hold my eyes. "You don't have to be ashamed. We have to know everything, you know, when we take you."

"My father didn't think . . . " I couldn't continue.

"You don't have to feel ashamed, Sara." Her eyes invited me to trust her.

"I planned to go to night school the following year and take the exams."

She opened a folder on her desk and hooked a pair of reading glasses over her ears. She read silently for a minute and then looked up at me over her glasses. "You were doing quite well in school up to that last year."

"I wasn't interested in school at that time."

"And now?" she asked.

"I think I'll do okay. I want to do well."

"And you think you're strong enough?"

"Strong?"

"Your nerves. Do you think you can take the pressure of studying?"

"Studying never bothered me."

"And last night?" She returned to her earlier question. "You can be honest with me. Your father wrote to us about your sensitivity. He said your nerves were bad. You were always tense. Even as a child."

"My father said that?"

"He was concerned. He knew we could help."

"My father wrote to you?" That had to be a lie, I was certain. He wouldn't tell our secrets to the Americans.

"Well, we asked questions."

"And my father told you?"

"Don't blame him. We needed to know why you hadn't taken your exams and he explained your sensitivity."

"My sensi—?"

"Your nerves, I mean. He said you are a bright girl and well-read, but that you were sheltered and not prepared for the world. He blamed himself. He said he didn't think reading was bad for you, but that you read too much. And when it happened, you weren't prepared for it."

"It?" I struggled to hold back my tears.

Sister Agnes left her desk and came around to where I sat. She put her arm around me. "Your father knows more about you than you realize. He was your first boyfriend, wasn't he?"

I did not answer her.

"It could happen to anyone." She rubbed my back, making tiny circles on my flesh with the tops of her fingers. "Unrequited love. The pain can be almost unbearable."

There was such sadness in her voice that I looked up and I saw reflected in her eyes the pain she had caused me to remember. She was staring far off into the distance. Sailboats drifted to sea in her eyes.

"Is that why I'm here? Why you gave me a scholarship?"

"No, and then yes. Father Jones picked you. He said you had potential. And then, we are a nursing order."

"But I'm not sick," I protested weakly.

"We could help you."

"I just didn't want to take my exams and my father said it was okay."

"What happened to you last night was almost the same thing," she said. "Your feelings are too strong. You must learn to control them or they'll control you."

"I have controlled them," I murmured. She had to bend her head to catch my answer.

"You have. So you have, Sara. Feelings are good. It's good to feel sadness and happiness and anger and love." She paused, her voice suspended on the last word. "Even love, Sara," she repeated. "But you must control that with your will, too. Yes, love, love, Sara but not only with your heart but your mind." She came closer to me. "Know when to let go."

I thought of the story I had invented when my cousin drowned. He had held on to that rope and the mermaid took him down. He did not want to let her go. Love had given him no choice. He held on to her until he drowned.

"You are a lovely young woman. One day a wonderful man will fall in love with you."

"Lovely?" Only when she answered me did I know I had asked the question aloud.

"Yes, lovely and young. You must strengthen your nerves while you're here and love will happen to you again."

"Lovely?" I repeated.

"Your eyes are like bottomless wells. Someone will fall in love with your eyes when you return to your homeland."

I flung my arms around her neck. She hugged me, too. When finally she released my grasp, she said with a voice that didn't fool me with its sternness, "You've got a lot of work to make up, Sara. You have a lot of studying to do. You need to strengthen your nerves. Don't go fainting again. You can't go through life being overly sensitive. Pull yourself together. Study and make us proud. Okay?" she said. "Okay? Now go on, Sara. I'll see you tomorrow when the other girls get here."

In the stark stillness of the dormitory bathroom, gleaming white against sterile metal, I studied my face in the mirror. Lovely, she called me. Eyes like bottomless wells. Bottomless wells that no one had seen before. Not Eric. Not my mother. Not my father. I stared long and hard, examining my eyes, widening them, narrowing them, turning them from side to side. They were lovely. I was lovely. *Lovely,* I said, and my tongue and lips shaped the sound. *Lovely.* I shaped the other sounds. *Like bottomless wells.* My eyes grew moist. *Like bottomless wells.* I gave voice to the words and my eyes filled with water. They were my father's eyes I saw reflected in the mirror, my father who had betrayed me, betrayed himself.

There was madness in his family, some people had said. He knew I had heard it too. It came from my grandmother, that mannish woman who couldn't cry. Wouldn't cry. They said her mother had abandoned her and had gone mad.

I had to pass the rum shop on the way to my grandmother's house. One day I heard them talking, their anger at withering limbs and dying passions breeding malice, fermenting with the alcohol they used to douse memories and the futility of their desires.

"She white, yes, but she Creole white. She nigger white. She whitey cockroach white."

I was only fourteen.

"Such a lady. Such a little brown lady." They mimicked my stylish walk. I was practicing to be my mother, head held high, hips swaying right and left, back held straight, disclosing no movement.

"Little lady with the white cockroach granny. Little lady, do you know, little lady, your granny's mammy was mad? Do you know, little lady? We saw her, little lady."

One of them, the oldest of them all, a bone dry woman, her wizened face sprouting curls of gray wire, her bent body reeking of urine and raw cane rum, held me fast.

"I saw the whitey cockroach, the white nigger. I saw her in the madhouse in St. Ann's Hospital. She sitting in a corner rocking a baby." She made a cradle of her arms. "No baby, but she rocking. Then she lift up she dress for her teats."

The old woman pulled up her tattered shirt and the people in the rum shop howled with laughter.

"Yes, just like these teats. Dried up like these teats. She took out she teats and give them to the baby, but there was no baby."

My father and I talked about this encounter once. Only once. He was at home when I fled to our house from the rum shop, not stopping to visit my grandmother. My trembling frightened him.

"They remember another time when people like my mother

were their enemy," he told me. "They remember when their parents were slaves on sugar estates owned by people who looked like your grandmother. They can't forget or forgive. They say evil things to make you feel their pain."

But he hid the real truth from me. I had read *Jane Eyre*. I knew about the mad Berthas, the white Creole women in the West Indies who had gone mad with their guilt. Neither fish nor fowl, neither European nor African, but now born and bred West Indians, they were left to face the relics of slavery, the scuttle that was left behind when the Europeans left. And the guilt, mostly the guilt. Our mad Bertha, my grandmother's mother, was made even more insane when she tried to cross over. When she thought, *Wasn't I now West Indian? Shouldn't I now choose one of them? One of us?*

But Bertha's parents were born in England, and when she chose a black man, became impregnated by a black man, they set her adrift on that wide Sargasso Sea. The English did not want her, the black people laughed at her, so she took her place, drifting, drifting, and set her baby free.

I witnessed the stone wall of silence that my grandmother built around herself when someone dared to question her about the past. And I kept her secret and my father's secret. I saw him looking for the seeds of my madness that day when, in sympathy for my dead friend Nancy, I developed the symptoms of polio. I saw my father looking, but I kept his secret. When Eric rejected me and I shut myself up in my room with my books, I saw him looking, but I kept his secret. Now he had betrayed me. He wrote to the nuns about my sensitivity, my problem, my nerves. But I was not the one who was mad. It was she. That was why he allowed me to accept Father Jones's gift, though he would try to warn me it would have a price. No, like my mother, my father needed me to be out of his sight. I reminded him of the one thing he wanted to deny.

I could not sleep that night. But when morning came and Angela pulled off my covers, gushing like a schoolgirl, "They're coming. They're coming. Wake up, Sara. They will be here in no time," I made myself begin the process of forgetting. No tears, I promised myself. I would become my mannish grandmother.

CHAPTER 5

They were not, as Angela said, all beautiful, but never had I seen all in one place such a range of color in eyes and hair. Some had hair like the sunset and eyes green as the marbles I played with as a child; others had hair like straw and eyes blue as the ocean. Some had black hair like Angela's, long and straight, and eyes brown as mine, some lighter, some darker. So many colors. Their skin tones ranged from pink to ivory to the palest of beige—the color of tea with milk. And some had freckles—tiny dark dots scattered across their cheeks. I saw full lips, thin lips, no lips. Thin noses, long noses, short noses. But these girls weren't all beautiful. Not to me. Different, strange, but not beautiful. Beautiful, still, to me, my mother: curly black hair, brown eyes, butterscotch skin, high cheekbones, generous hips and a backside that swayed to the rhythm of her stride.

But the girls weren't ugly either. Strange, odd. I had not thought there could be so many colors at the end of the spectrum of the rainbow, light fading into so many shades of pale. Yet there was a sameness to them all: the absence of brown in their skin, lips and noses that never stretched as far or as wide as ours, backsides that never reached the same height, but more than that. Happiness was spread out unabashedly on their faces as if they knew the world was theirs, as if they had never known deprivation or loss. I saw them jump out of cars, sprawling and spacious, I heard them shrieking and laughing, arms thrown around each other, dancing to music I did not hear, parents, sometimes grandparents, in tow, burdened with loads of luggage, spanking new.

In Trinidad we were more guarded with our joy. We knew happiness was never permanent. It could be snatched from us without warning: a disease we could not control, a vaccine that arrived too late, a deceptive sea that could lift a pirogue in one swell and claim the one we loved most—a son, a grandson, a cousin.

Angela, kneeling on my bed, her nose and hands pressed against the windowpane, also watched their arrival. Unburdened by the reserve I had learned, she hopped up and down as each girl arrived, sometimes rushing to the door, squealing, "I hear them! I hear them! They are coming!" But the footsteps would pass our door. Still, she was not deterred. She would grow sad for a moment, but within seconds would regain her optimism, tossing her head as if to chase away doubts that vexed her, she would return to the window hoping, believing, but not so much that she dared open the door, even a crack, when footsteps approached us.

Courtney was nowhere to be found. Since we last had parted on the first morning of my arrival, I had not seen her. She did not join us at lunch as she had promised and she did not come to dinner. I asked Angela if she knew why.

"She's working," she said. "Courtney needs the money."

"What about you?" I asked. Sister Agnes had explained to me at dinner that my scholarship covered the cost of my tuition, books, food and board. I was beginning to worry about where I would get the money for clothes and necessities such as toothpaste and soap. I still had the fifty dollars Mrs. Clancy had given me and the five from the original two hundred I had brought to America. I thought about the coming winter and the clothes I would need. Perhaps the coat, gloves, hat and scarf I had bought in New York would be enough.

"I work, too," Angela was saying, "but not like Courtney."

"You work? What do you do?"

"I sing."

"For money?"

She laughed at the surprise in my voice. "I sing for local people at private parties. If they're having a dinner party or a luncheon. Sometimes Mrs. O'Brien—Mrs. O'Brien first arranged it for me—sometimes Mrs. O'Brien hears about a convention going on in the one hotel in town, or the Lion's Club meeting or the Rotary Club or the Knights of Columbus."

"I didn't know you could sing."

"How could you? You just met me." She giggled. "There's more to me than meets the eye." In a flash her eyes moved away from mine, leaving behind the imprint of an unspoken challenge: Can you see below the surface?

Something—instinct, I supposed, the cultural ties that bonded us, our common Caribbean roots, our difference from the rest, intuition—stopped me short of asking her why she did not go out to meet the girls. Why stay here with me behind closed doors? But I no more wanted to expose her than to face the answer myself. It was easier to pretend with her that this was the way it should be: the girls getting their last chance to say goodbye to their families and we having the good sense, the manners, the compassion, sensitivity and thoughtfulness, to stay out of their way.

"To tell the truth," said Angela, "even I didn't know I could sing. Yes, some tra la la in the bathroom. Once I sang in the school choir, but people back home would laugh if I told them I sing for money. What really happened, though, is that Mrs. O'Brien had some people over for dinner and she invited me to meet them. They asked me all sorts of questions about British Guiana—how hot it gets, do we have snakes, what kind of houses we live in. Questions like that. Then one of them said she liked West Indian calypso and she began to sing, 'Come Mister Tally-man, Tally me Bananas.' Before I knew it they asked me to sing it and I did. I sang 'Jamaica Farewell,' 'Yellow Bird' and 'Kingston Market.' They loved it."

"But those are not calypsos," I protested.

"To you and me, but not to them. Anyhow, they ask me to sing at their homes and they pay me. I sing about once a week and I make ten dollars, sometimes fifteen on a good night. It's enough for me. I asked Courtney to join me. I was willing to split the money with her, but she's real shy. I bet you can do it with me. Can you sing?"

I laughed and shook my head.

"Well it doesn't matter. Do you know the words to 'Jamaica Farewell' and 'Day-O?'"

"Yes, sure."

"Then that's all you need. I'll tell Mrs. O'Brien. We could do a duet. Maybe they'll pay us more. Will you do it?"

"What about Courtney?" I asked, my thoughts flipping back to that proud mahogany girl I had just briefly met.

"She has a job."

"Where?"

"In the cafeteria kitchen. She makes more money, she says, and she needs it. She sends half back home to her mother. She works whenever she's not in school. Day and night. I don't know how she does it. She never sits around and talks with the girls or anything. If she's not studying, she's working or she's in school.

Work, study, work, study. That's all Courtney does."

Her resentment was thick. "Is that why you're not room-mates this year?"

We were both facing the window when I asked her that question. There were just a few girls left on the sidewalk. Most of them were already inside the dorm. We could hear their voices, loud and gay, up and down the corridors, shutting us out. I knew Angela wanted to be with them. I wondered if her resent-ment toward Courtney had to do with having been trapped into living with her. If her anger now was sparked by her real-ization that none of the girls whose voices she could recognize had knocked on our door or had introduced their parents to her. But when I asked my question again, she jerked her head suddenly in the direction of the door and I had the distinct impression she was afraid. There was panic in her rapid movement. It was as if she thought someone, Courtney, I sud-denly realized, were waiting outside the door, listening for her response.

"Look, Sara," she said, "Courtney's strange. You know that joke she made about being a vodoun priestess? Well, that's no joke."

Angela's face was dark and drawn. How easily her girlish giggle had fooled me. Now I saw that it was quite possible that she was a year, maybe two years, older than I.

"She was just joking with you," I said.

"She keeps dolls. I saw them. Little black dolls in the bottom of her drawer."

"So what?" I would not let her infect me with her childish imagination.

"Do you know what the little dolls are for?"

"For goodness sake, Angela."

"She has pins in them."

"Pincushions. She uses the dolls for pincushions."

"Five pincushions? That's how many dolls she has."

Soucouyant, diablesse. The Orehu. I carried to Wisconsin a bag of herbs that had been blessed by an obeahman. I fingered the St. Jude medal that hung from the silver chain around my neck. "It's none of our business," I said.

"Well, it was my business. I got out of there."

"Did she know you found them? The dolls? The pincushions, I mean?" I had unpacked my bag of herbs and placed it beneath my clothes in the middle drawer.

"God, no. I wouldn't tell her that. But I asked Sister Agnes if you and I could be roommates. I said something about making you feel at home the way they tried to for me with Courtney. Nobody knows why I don't share a room with Courtney. Except you. Nobody."

She was lying. I could tell from the way her eyes grew wild when she said *nobody* that she had not told me all. She still hid her secret from everybody. Yet I resisted her attempt to draw me into complicity with her as if we shared a common pact that excluded everyone. Excluded Courtney.

"It's the African in her," she said. "All that mumbo jumbo. She's pure African, you know. Not colored like you. I can see you have white blood. You and I are more like them," she said.

Now I closed ranks completely with Courtney. I, through whose veins ran the blood of slave masters, closed ranks with her with my African blood. I was in a foreign land; the girls outside my door did not look like me or speak like me. It was natural I would form a bond not only with Angela, but also with Courtney. We three were foreigners, but we came from the same region; we had the same histories. Yet in that similarity was our difference. My African ancestors and Courtney's were brought to the Caribbean as slaves, chattel, commodities to be used and then traded or put out to pasture. Angela's ancestors came as indentured laborers. No slight difference in countries where the people had learned to mimic the intricacies of the British class structure. Angela's people had been treated as human beings—men and women looking for work, for a way to feed their families. They had been given land, five acres if they worked on the sugar estates for five years. Each time they raised a scythe, each time their machetes fell on the thick rounded stalks of sugar cane, each time the thin, razor-sharp leaves cut vicious welts into their legs, each time they blacked out under the burning sun, they knew, they understood the difference.

I used to see them in St. James, dancing with a half moon on their shoulders in the early dawn of their Hosay Festival: small men, almost still boys, with thin legs and pubescent muscles straining against the firm flesh of narrow torsos, shoulders struggling to stay steady, then loosening under the weight of a hundred silvery stars scattered on sky blue paper glued to the wooden frames of two half moons they had made the night before and had nailed to the front and back of a piece of wood that protruded from the center like a stick on a fan.

These were Muslims, the descendants of the prophet Mohammed, their rightful place as caliphs stolen by murderers hundreds of years ago. And still, in Trinidad, their people remembered. Muslims and Hindus, it made no difference. On that day in Trinidad they were one. East Indians: Hindus joining Muslims and separating from us.

They danced in pairs in memory of Husain and his brother, Hasan, eyes black and glazed, their thick, straight black hair gleaming with coconut oil slicked back against faces contorted with pain. The strongest would raise the half moon high above his shoulders and dance in wide circles to the pulsating rhythms of the Hosay drums behind him, but few had that kind of endurance, that kind of grace. Most jerked their bodies in a half dance, their palms sweaty and raw with bruises from frantically clutching the center stick, knees weakening under the strain of a deceptive half moon, weighing more than these boys, not yet men, had bargained for.

These dancers were the heralds. They came before the sun reached the center of the sky, dancing in the day with the thousand silver stars and half moons of many nights of sitting around fires, stretching goat skins for drums. Later came the tadjah, the tomb of Husain, rolled on wheels and pulled by half-naked men in white dhotis. Ten tadjahs down Western Main Road one year, another year more. Families—Hindu and Muslim—vied to outdo each other. They sculpted magnificent temples with meticulous detail out of papier-mâché and wood. There were arched windows and entranceways, their edges shiny and glittery, domed tops with silver moons balanced on their peaks and encircled with stars. Many rooms in Husain's tadjah. On the sides of the tadjahs they glued strips of colored metallic paper—white, silver, gold, orange—and tiny bits of mirror. Then when the sun went down, they threw all the tadjahs, every one of them, into the sea, a sacrifice to their gods.

Angela's people celebrated their rituals and left the rest of us in awe of the waste, unable to comprehend how they could withstand the knowledge of the futility of the hours they had spent carving and painting; how they could watch with such dispassion as the temples sunk beneath the muddy waters of Carenage Bay.

One early Hosay morning, as I stood with my mother and our neighbors at the edge of the pavement, an incredible thing happened. One of the dancers fell. I had seen him tottering seconds before under the half moon, sweat pouring down his temples, hands clutching desperately to the center stick, slipping, then clutching again, fatigue wearing him down. But I did not think he would fall. The local rumor was that none of these boys, almost men, ever fell. But I saw this one's knees buckle and his eyes roll in their sockets, and then he crumpled to the ground at my feet. I thrust my body forward to help him but my mother pulled me back before I could touch him. Then I saw the whip.

The half-moon dancer was about my age, just two or three years older. His body writhed on the cool morning asphalt with each stroke of the whip. The Indian women on the other side of the street drew their saris across their faces, and stayed still. The drumming intensified. The other male dancers, boys themselves, braced sagging shoulders. Half moons danced in the sky. Bodies moved in a wild and strangely thrilling dance. The Indian fathers applauded. A curtain was drawn between them and us.

I asked my mother why she had stopped me from helping the dancer.

"None of our business."

"But how could they be so cruel?"

"It's not for us to understand. It's their culture."

Their culture. The East Indians with their difference from us. Later my father would tell me that I would have brought dishonor to the half-moon dancer had I helped him.

The English colonists had long ago banned the beatings but still they persisted. My mother's neighbor, a very black woman with hard eyes, explained: "Is their pride. They want to flaunt it in front of us. All that Hindi they speak. A real Hindu from India can't even understand a word they say. They just want to make sure the white people know they different from us. You think they like that beating? They want to say they have culture. So the white people know they not like us. So they treat them better."

I had no basis for believing her, except that otherwise she had seemed a kind woman. She had a julie mango tree in her backyard that bore fruit long after the season had ended. Every week she would give me a mango despite knowing that at that time of the year she could get a good price for them and she needed the money. Her husband, she told me, couldn't find a job.

"It's all those Indians leaving their cow patch. They make the white people think they better than us, so my Egbert have no work. White people giving Indians all the work."

Now I was to understand her resentment and feel a self-righteous anger toward Angela for her attitude of superiority toward Courtney that, I thought, ultimately, Angela would soon have toward me.

"Our countries are closer to each other than yours is to Courtney's," Angela said, finally noticing my silence after her remark that she and I were more similar to each other than Courtney and I. "I knew *we* would be friends right away."

I felt a fierce loyalty toward Courtney. "We should all be friends. There are only three of us against all of them," I said.

"Against?"

I had not realized that I'd used that word.

"You mean *among*," she said, looking at me closely.

"Among," I corrected myself.

"Because they are not against us," said Angela. "That's how Courtney thinks. They want to be our friends. They do everything to make us feel at home. It's just Courtney."

And I wondered, looking out the window with her at the last of the girls tripping merrily into the dormitory, pressing my nose and hands like hers against the windowpane, I wondered: Was it just Courtney?

I met Molly, the girl Angela called her very best friend, that first day. She came bounding into the room almost at the moment when Angela, having observed to me that the last car of parents had left, flung open the door.

"Oh, Angela, I missed you." Molly hugged and kissed her. I did not think she noticed my presence. She was brimming with news about the past summer. I could barely make out what she said, she spoke so rapidly, and my ear, not yet accustomed to the nasal rhythms with which to me all Americans spoke, strained to understand her. There was Yellowstone Park and Los Angeles, California. A boy she met on a trip to Mexico. A University of Wisconsin boy. "Gee, wasn't that the best luck?" And then there was bad luck. She was forced to go with her parents to Italy on their annual trip to visit her grandparents. She couldn't stand leaving the boy behind. They called each other every day. Sometimes twice. "Gee, didn't my parents get mad. Serves them right, though."

Through all her happy recounting, Angela mirrored the emotions on her friend's face. She smiled when Molly smiled, pouted when she pouted, frowned when she frowned. I remained the silent observer. Then Molly, spent, having told her story for the second time, asked, "And what about you, Angela? What did you do this summer?"

For the first time since Molly had entered the room, Angela looked across at me. Her eyes pleaded with me to save her, but I did not know how. I did not know what she wanted me to say. Molly, who still took no notice of me, pressed her. "Tell me, Angela, tell me what you did."

"I stayed here in Oshkosh." Angela's words betrayed no feeling, neither disappointment nor joy. They were said as a matter of fact, not meant to elicit response and certainly not the pity that gushed from Molly.

"All alone here?"

"Well, not alone. There was Courtney and the Sisters. And the O'Briens took me out a lot."

"But you didn't go anywhere?"

"Well, yes, of course. To the movies. Sometimes for dinner at the O'Brien's. "

"Why didn't you tell me, Angela?"

"It was okay. I didn't mind."

"You could have stayed with me."

I saw Angela blink. Blood rushed to her face. I knew immediately that Molly was lying, but Angela's words revealed nothing. No hurt feelings, no anger.

"I prefer being here," she said. "I told you that in the spring." She reached for my hand. "Look, I want you to meet my friend, Sara. Sara Edgehill." She pulled me from where I sat on the bed in the corner.

Molly's face lit up and she hugged me, too. "So you are Angela's friend. She told me you were coming. I'm Molly, Molly Lorenzo."

Pretty Molly, I thought, *pretty as Angela said you were.*

Molly had soft, doelike brown eyes, a perfect oval shaped face, a straight nose and a full mouth. Her straight brown hair was streaked with gold and cascaded over her shoulders. She was Angela's height, a little pudgy, but the firm fleshiness of her arms and hips added to her attractiveness. Pretty Molly. Rich Molly, who traveled to places about which I had only dreamed. Going to Italy for her was bad luck.

"You took Angela from me," she said.

"Took her?"

"She told me you were coming. I wanted to room with her this year."

I glanced at Angela. She was still smiling; her eyes revealed nothing. Had she planned for me so long? Didn't she say Molly was her best friend?

"She said you had already arranged to room together."

"She said we had arranged . . . ?"

"Well, didn't you, Angela?"

But Angela was saved from answering Molly's question. The girls who had kept her waiting with her nose pressed against the windowpane, now rushed into our room, but I wondered as I watched her collapsing into giggles, returning the hugs and kisses, what lie would she have told just then? Why was it that after all she had said about these girls, mimicked by Courtney—nice and pretty and friendly and nice—she would choose me, whom she had not yet met, instead of Molly? But it was difficult to believe that these girls could be to blame for I saw them fussing over her, their voices laden with regret: "You stayed here alone? Only the O'Briens? Just to the movies and dinner? Oh, Angela, why didn't you tell us? You could have stayed with us." Watching their faces, hearing their words, I could not doubt that Angela was loved.

Finally Angela introduced me. "This is Sara Edgehill. A friend from Trinidad. Trinidad?" she answered a question. "It's about seven miles off the coast of South America. Well, not so close to British Guiana that we can see each other's countries, but close.

"Yes, we speak with almost the same accent. Our countries are close to each other. I mean, her island is close to my country.

"No, our accents are not really British. Well, I suppose because the schools in both our countries were run by the British. Well, and then, there are a lot of English people in British Guiana and Trinidad."

She fielded off questions with an alacrity that amazed me. Nothing wiped off the smile she had planted on her face.

"Slavery? Oh no. We are a protectorate of England. It's the same arrangement you have with the Virgin Islands. A colony? Yes, but we have our own government."

I watched her duck and glide, a boxer, fending off the responses they sought like a pro, letting nothing unsettle her. But, finally, one of the girls, a little redhead with thin arms and acne scars across her face who had been quietly staring at me while the others probed, asked: "How is it she doesn't look like you, Angela? How is it her hair's not straight as yours?" And Angela, my giggly, girlish roommate, suddenly became serious.

"We are the same, Sara and I. We are West Indians."

But two weeks later the girls forced her to choose between

them and me. It started as a joke. Or so I thought. Six of us were in the laundry room in the basement of the dormitory—Angela, Molly, three girls whose names I hadn't memorized as yet and me. We had just returned from our half-mile walk from the mansion where we had dinner every night. A school bus would take us back to the dorm if we met it immediately after dinner, but we were always late. I, deliberately so. I was still uneasy in a crowd of these girls who chattered mindlessly and cheerfully as if their youth would never end. Most of them were about eighteen, younger than Angela, Courtney and me, but by no more than two or three years. Yet that difference seemed to entitle them to a youth we had long lost. They frightened me with their childish happiness; they behaved as though they never had cause to cry, as though they knew they would never know sorrow. Their world was a paradise in which nothing was serious. Even my accent was cause for joy. It tickled them pink.

Tickled pink. It was one of those metaphors we used in Trinidad, hardly conceiving that in the countries of its source it was meant to be taken quite literally. Tickled pink. I saw their faces turn rosy with laughter. "'Con't'? 'Con't'? You mean 'kain't'? 'Kain't.'" They turned pink. Tickled pink.

In groups of ten or more of these girls I felt an alien, an outsider, a person apart. I was shut out from their laughter, their happiness. They were Rousseau's happy natives. Fresh children of a New World that they had already won for themselves. I came with my self-consciousness, my memory burdened with histories of slavery, exploitation, colonialism, deprivation—minor triumphs, also, to be sure, but always achieved through struggle and effort. They would bombard me with their innocence, asking questions that I would not dare ask for fear I would reveal my ignorance.

"Where is Trinidad?" they would ask.

"In the West Indies," I would answer.

"Where is that? Near India somewhere?"

"No. That's what Columbus thought. He thought he was going to India when he sighted our islands. Because he was traveling west, he called our islands the West Indies."

"Oh, Columbus discovered your island?"

"Well, no. The Amerindians were there already. There were the Caribs, the Arawaks, the Waraos—part of the chain of the great empires in Central and South America, the great Inca, Aztec and Maya nations."

"But Columbus discovered your islands for our world. Right?"

"Right."

"So where's the West Indies?"

"Let me see . . . South of the Tropic of Cancer but still very north of the equator. East of Central America . . . "

"The Tropic of Cancer? Where's that?"

"Twenty-three degrees north of the equator."

"Oh."

"Well, in relation to your country, just off the tip of Florida."

"And Trinidad? Where is it exactly?"

"It's much farther south, off the northern tip of South America."

"My parents went to Brazil there one year. Is it near there?"

"No, much farther north. Near Venezuela. Yes, about seven miles off the coast of Venezuela."

"Near Angela's island?"

"No, Angela doesn't come from an island. She comes from British Guiana, which is on the continent of South America. Actually it is next to Venezuela."

"I thought they only spoke Spanish there or some other foreign language. Angela doesn't speak Spanish at all. Only English, like us."

"Well, the British colonized us, too."

"Too?"

"The same way they colonized America. We were all part of the British Empire, so we speak English. Now we're like you. Independent. We got our independence from England last year."

"But you speak a different English," one of them would insist. And so the questions would continue, and so my answers, as I floundered my way through a geography and history that was foreign to them.

Ah, but how well I knew their history, or thought I did. In 1962, that last year before I left Trinidad, my father took me with him to Woodford Square to hear Eric Williams, the man who would become our first prime minister. Williams had recently returned from years in America. He told us stories about the fighting spirit of the Americans to set us on fire on the eve of our independence from British rule. The Americans, he said, had defied the British. They had refused to follow the British religion or to pay them taxes. Later they fought a bloody war against the British for their freedom. "Live free or die" was their slogan. This history was the real source of the joy that seemed to bubble so freely and naturally from these girls. They had won the right to be themselves. They had severed themselves from the weight of an ugly past. They were not Europeans with a suitcase of memories. They were Americans, a new people in a new world. I envied their absence of baggage. How was I also to know about their shame? Their enslavement of black people?

Eric Williams spoke about the enslavement of Africans, but on other days, days when my mother no longer allowed me to go to Woodford Square.

"The dregs of society are now coming out there," she said. I knew she meant the poorest and the blackest of us.

Perhaps had I gone I would have made sense of my grandmother's tears. I would have seen in her act of tying the kitchen towel around her neck like a hangman's noose that there was another history about America I had not yet discovered. But it would be much later before I would witness the legacy of American shame. After Eric Williams, I went back to my English books, my English education, and learned other things about America through British eyes.

I learned that while in fact America was no longer a colony of England, it was, as it were, a stepchild of England. Fearing the consequences of this, my mother had taken me to the Ministry of Education of the spanking new independent country of Trinidad and Tobago. She wanted to know whether the government would recognize my education in America as legitimate or equal to a college education in England. She wanted to make certain that when I returned to Trinidad I would get a good teaching job—one with status. She had heard the horror stories under the British government. Great-Uncle Thomas's story was one of those. He was not, as I was originally led to believe, a willing immigrant to America. He, too, had dreams of returning to his green grass island. But the British colonial rulers told him when he came with his dentistry degree from the University of Chicago that dentistry in America was not dentistry in England. It was not a matter of license; it was a matter of education—American versus English. My mother thought the situation would be different under an independent Trinidad unfettered by British regulations, but she wanted to be sure. The black man at the ministry who took her question looked surprised.

"Of course, there's a difference in the education," he said. He, like so many of the officials who replaced the colonists, was still in love with England. "The British were at it centuries before the Americans, so of course it can't be the same. But Wisconsin? Yes, we've heard of Wisconsin. The University of Wisconsin? Well, yes, if she gets an honors degree. Yes. We would consider that from the University of Wisconsin."

How was he to know, my mother and I as well, that the College of the Sacred Heart was *in* Wisconsin, that it was not a college *of* the University of Wisconsin?

Yes, I knew about the history of these girls in my bookish way but they knew nothing of mine. And when they pried me with their well-meaning questions, I felt even more distant from them, more and more conscious of my Trinidad self. So I avoided the crowds in the bus. I chose Angela's little group, which, already having included Angela, hardly ever noticed I was there. On that particular evening, however, two weeks after Angela had so staunchly aligned herself with me—*Sara and I are West Indians*—they chose to discover me. Innocently, believing that they were the world, they were the children, they were the people, they had defined Angela and now they wished to define me.

Molly started first. "Hey, Sara," she said, opening the faucet in the laundry sink. "Bet you don't have water like this in Trinidad."

Angela laughed and winked at me. A joke. I played along.

"No, we don't," I said, straight-faced. "Not like this water."

Molly paused and studied the water flowing on her hands from the faucet. "Bet you use rainwater where you come from."

"Sure," I said.

"This must feel different to you."

"Yes. Very different."

"What's it feel like?" another girl asked, I thought without humor. "I mean, rainwater on your body?"

"Soft," I said. "Real soft." My mind drifted away to another place, to other times when I stood outside on the grass, turned my face to the sky and let the rain soak me, splash through the strands of my hair and run in tiny rivulets under my dress. "Soft and smooth. And sometimes hard," I said, still dreaming.

"Which is it? Soft or hard?"

"Soft and hard," I said. "Hard when it falls on you. Soft when you hold it in your hand. Sometimes we'd catch it in a large tub. We'd put a wire netting over it so no leaves or branches would fall into it. We'd collect the rainwater there, and later, when the tub was full, we'd dunk our buckets in and take what we need."

"Balancing your bucket on your heads. I knew it! I saw it on a post card!" one girl shouted triumphantly. "Show us, Sara. Show us how you do it on your island."

My mind refocused. "What?" I asked.

"Show us. Show us how you do it."

"Do what?"

"Balance the bucket on your head."

"I don't know how."

"Come on, Sara. Show us."

"We had faucets in our house," I said lamely.

"You know you didn't, Sara. Show us."

"Really. Truly! Ask Angela."

"Put the bucket on your head, Sara. Don't be silly. It's only us. Show us how you walk with it in Trinidad. Show us."

One of the girls stretched out her arms and began to walk the length of the laundry room, holding her head stiffly, balancing an imaginary bucket on her head. "You have to be careful so that not a drop will fall. Side to side, moving the hips only with the legs so the bucket stays straight. Like this. Now show us, Sara."

"We have faucets, too, just like these, in our homes. Water is piped from our reservoirs into our homes exactly as it is here. I thought you were joking. We collect rainwater, but only for fun and to wash our hair."

"And you wear grass skirts, too. I saw it on a poster."

"That's in Hawaii. That's their native costume." I looked help-lessly at Angela. She shifted her eyes from mine. She was laugh-ing. *With them.* She had joined them in their joke on me.

"Put the bucket on Sara's head," said one of the girls. "She's too shy."

"Wait." It was Angela who spoke. "In Trinidad they wrap a towel like this." She rolled a towel and wound it around her head. "Then they put it on like this. Here." She flattened the wound towel and placed it on my head. "And then they put the bucket—"

She reached for the bucket, but I had ducked my head. I pulled off the towel and dashed it to the floor, and feeling a humiliation deeper than any I had experienced before, I ran blindly up the stairs to the room I shared with Angela and flung myself across my bed dissolving into tears. I heard them laughing outside my room. Angela's laughter was the loudest.

Why was I crying? Because of Angela's conspiracy with them, her betrayal of me? She said we were the same. We are West Indians, she said. Or was I crying because these girls had managed to make me ashamed of myself, of my people? How much different was I from my mother, who cringed when Father Jones declared that he had come to Trinidad to look for raw talent in our primitive country? I had never thought of my country as poor. We were not rich as the Americans, but we were not poor. We had food to eat, places to live—not mansions, but homes, comfortable homes. But perhaps we were primitive. I had not thrown away the bag of herbs my mother had pressed into my hand. It still lay hidden under my clothes in my dresser.

Winter came fast for me my first year in America, only four short weeks after I had arrived. By late September the gilded leaves of oak trees were trembling with the cold and clutching desperately to stems grown too weak to save them. A soft wind fluttered through the oak, and the leaves shivered and fell like rain showers in the middle of the dry season. I buttoned up my sweater and put on my scarf. By October hardly any leaves were left on the trees. These giants that had taken decades to grow tall, now stood naked, their trunks exposed, their branches outstretched like powerless arms. October was easier for the grain fields. No slow death as leaves turned new colors, then grew thin and fluttered away. Someone came with a machine and razed down the sheaves while they were still green. Their thin stalks collapsed on the still warm earth.

I tried not to let these thoughts of dying, death, destruction and decay penetrate my consciousness. I did not want my problem, if I had one, to surface here in America—my great-grandmother Bertha stirring in her grave. Madness was not something I allowed myself to think of. Even though I knew my father thought his grandmother had entered my veins, I blocked out that possibility from my mind. Yet Bertha tried to pursue me with her guilt about her abandoned baby and a whole tribe of Africans she had reduced to chattel. I fought to disown her. She had let guilt and her love for a black man plummet her into darkness.

If crying was what I should not do, allowing myself to feel too much, as Sister Agnes said, then to protect myself from Bertha I would not cry. I would not feel. Angela's little betrayal then meant nothing to me. That was the way the world was, the natural course of things that the weak submit to the strong as the oak trees did to the rhythms of the seasons. What should Angela have done? Cut herself off from the girls to go sulk in her room like Courtney? Angela was one of the survivors, one of the sane ones who knew how to play the game. She chose the winning side. Angela would be the way the girls wanted her to be. They had made the world, and if in hot countries the natives wore grass skirts and balanced buckets of water on their heads, so be it.

"Don't take it so hard," Angela had consoled me when she

returned to the room we shared, later that night, giving me time to imagine her and her friends laughing themselves to tears over my humiliating exit. "You don't always have to explain yourself to them. You know who you are. They aren't interested in knowing that. They just want you to tell them that they are right about who they think you are. What's so wrong about that? Give them their fairy tales. When I first came I used to try. I heard you tell them that Columbus story. Well, I tried, too. Columbus, I said, had made a mistake. He thought he was going to India but he landed in the Caribbean. But he called the islands the West Indies, anyhow. They said that was an understandable mistake. Look at you, they said, 'you're Indian and you're from the Caribbean. Columbus must have seen people like you.' Do you think I tried to explain to them how the East Indians were transported to the Caribbean? No, Sara, you're wasting your time. Look at Courtney. She has no friends. I let them have their way. It's easier. If I could give you advice on how to get along with them, it would be this: Give them their fairy tales. I give them what they think are calypsos."

"But what about your self-respect?" I persisted. "How can you let them think of you as some primitive savage?"

"I take care of my self-respect," said Angela. "You don't have to bleed over everybody. People don't always have to know how you feel."

And there it was again. Feelings. Bubbly Angela had achieved what I had yet to learn to do, what my father had warned me I must learn to do: *Don't let them see in your heart, Sara.* But, I wondered, if and when the time comes, will they know how to act? Will their silence so have killed feeling that they will have no passion left to make a choice?

The cold fall winds threatened to strip me of my resolve to steel myself against tears. When the winds thundered across the barren plains, knocking down branches, sending leaves scuttling across the grass to huddle in trembling mounds on fences and curbs, I felt such a longing for my warm place, my green grass home, that I stayed in my room and cried in my pillow at night. But the day came, finally, when I decided I would be strong. I put on the tweed coat that I had bought with Mrs. Clancy, and the gloves, hat and scarf, determined that as long as I was going to be here for the winter, I would make myself ready for it. The clothes felt strange on my body, heavy and cumbersome, but outside when the wind began to circle my legs, I felt warm and comfortable.

On that day, I had my longest conversation with Courtney since we first met. I had seen her off and on in the dorm, or on the road to the college or in the dining room. We would speak briefly. She was always in a hurry to go someplace else. Once she said to me, "I see you're adjusting to Oshkosh. You seem to get along perfectly with the girls." She was smiling but I felt her words were meant to chastise me, to insult me. After that, she seemed to be deliberately trying to avoid me. I would see her between classes, but somehow before I could speak to her, she would slip down a corridor, race up a staircase or turn in another direction. I asked Angela. She responded with a shrug. "That's Courtney. She prefers to be by herself." That day, however, we almost collided. A sudden blast of wind had gusted across the open field toward me. Using my head as a battering ram to defend myself from its icy onslaught, I was hunched over my books, unable to see in front of me.

"Hey, watch it. Wait a minute." I immediately recognized Courtney's voice as she held out her hand to stop me. I looked up. She was smiling. "Where have you been? I hardly see you around."

"You mean you," I said. "I hardly see *you* around."

She widened her almond-shaped eyes. "I see you at dinner."

"Yes, but you hardly speak to me."

"Should I? You and Angela seem to be such good friends. You seem to be doing all right with the girls too."

It occurred to me she was angry, jealous, perhaps, but when I looked at her face, she was still smiling.

"You could come and sit with us," I said.

"Is that an invitation?"

"Do you need one?"

"I don't see you coming to sit with me," she said.

I began to feel guilty and resented her for it. Many times I had come into the cafeteria and taken a seat at an empty table. Sometimes Angela sat down with me, sometimes she did not. Courtney never did.

"Well, we don't always have to sit together," she said, that smile still on her face. "They may think it's a conspiracy. And who knows?" She winked.

I shivered against the wind. Her eyes gave me no reason to think her words were meant to be taken seriously. Still, I felt the need to be certain. "You're funny, Courtney. Really you are."

"Sometimes," she said. Her voice was grave.

I looked away from her. She was making me uneasy. *What conspiracy?*

"So where are you going all dressed up like that?" she asked and snapped me out of a dark mood.

"To class, obviously," I said.

"You look as if you're ready to brave the Arctic snows. Don't let Angela catch you in that getup. You'll embarrass her."

"What getup?" I looked down at my tweed coat and then at her. She was actually quite fashionably dressed. She wore a short cranberry-and-blue tartan plaid skirt, a white buttoned-down blouse, a cranberry cardigan, white socks and oxblood oxfords. I wondered how she had learned to dress so well. In the distance I saw the girls spilling out in little clusters on the front lawn of the college. They did not have on coats, either. When the wind

tossed their short skirts up their backs, they laughed. They un-
raveled long strands of hair that twirled around their faces like a
spider's cobweb and shook their heads free. I thought, *what kind
of people are these who would play with a cold wind?*

Courtney followed my eyes. "It's a beautiful day," she said.

"I'm freezing." I pulled my hat over my ears.

"Don't be silly. It's still fall. What will you do when it gets
cold?"

"Die," I said, and made a brring sound with my lips. "I feel
warmer dressed like this."

"Because it's not cold. Girl, you better get yourself ready for
winter. This is just the start-up. Don't you have sweaters?"

"One."

"And wool skirts?"

I shook my head.

"Are those all the winter clothes you have?" she asked, pok-
ing her finger at my coat. "What are you going to do, child?"

I clutched my books to my chest and looked away from her.

"Do you have money?" she asked.

"Fifty-five dollars." She could hardly be a year older than I,
but she made me feel like a child. I could withhold nothing
from her.

"I'm not prying for prying's sake, you know," she said softly
and touched my shoulder. "I want to help. I know how you
feel."

She had taken hold of me again, the way she had when I first
met her. I felt a strange connection to her, a bond. Her eyes
spoke to me: *Hold on to me, lean on me. I can take care of you.* I
shook my head, half comforted by her caring and half fearful of
the strange power she seemed to possess, feeling as Angela must
have when Courtney changed her face into a vodoun mask and
frightened her.

I brushed away the fear. "I think I have enough money," I

said. "I think I'll be okay."

"You'll be okay. I know it," she said.

I wished she wouldn't sound so mysterious, so all-knowing. I forced myself to laugh. "You say that like you really know," I said.

"Oh, I really know," she said, and smiled again.

I wanted to get away from her. "I have to go to class." I took a step forward to the college.

"Wait." Courtney looked steadily in my eyes. "Don't believe all the things Angela said to you about me."

I thought of the little dolls. Five of them under her clothes in her drawer.

"Angela's different from both of us," she said. "You know that."

In my drawer I had a bag of herbs blessed by an obeahman.

"I have to go," I said.

"No. Wait. What are you doing Saturday?"

I felt my body grow hot under my heavy clothing. I took off my scarf and unbuttoned my coat. The wind that curled down my neck felt surprisingly refreshing, not cold and deathly as it was when I started my walk. Courtney watched me loosen my clothes.

"You better take that coat off," she said. "And that hat, scarf and gloves. I warn you, they'll laugh at you." She narrowed her eyes. "Angela the most."

For a long second she kept her eyes fastened to mine. *She knew. She must have seen me run out of the laundry room. She must have heard the laughter.*

She walked around me, stretched her hand to my shoulders and took off my coat. I let her take it. There seemed nothing else I could do.

"Give me your other things, also," she said. I gave them to her. "Here. Take my cardigan." She pushed my arms through the woolen sleeves. The sweater felt good. Warm. Just right.

"Look, I know you have to go to class now, but would you like to go with me to the O'Brien's next Saturday? Around seven."

"And what about Angela?" I felt a perverse sense of satisfaction in asking her that question. There had to be times when Angela had laughed at her, when the girls had snickered and Angela snickered, too. Courtney exposed me; I would expose her. We were both vulnerable to the kind of humiliation that made us ashamed of our past. But if this were true, Courtney never admitted it. She looked straight at me and never flickered an eyelash.

"She's going to be busy," she said. She spoke without emotion.

I pressed her. "How do you know?"

"Ask her," she said, and shrugged her shoulders as if it did not matter to her whether Angela came with us or not.

"I will," I said.

"Fine."

"Okay."

She looked over at the girls, still playing with the wind. When she turned back to me I thought there was something she wanted tell me about them, but instead she asked, "So?"

"So what?"

"So will you come?"

"Yes," I answered quickly. "Yes, I'd love to."

"Good. I'll meet you in front of the dorm at seven."

"What about my clothes?"

"I'll leave them for you in your room."

"But I'll be cold on the walk back."

"No." Courtney looked at me sternly as if she had given me a command, as if her one word had the power to change the way I felt, to change the effect of the cold on my skin. Then she grinned, touched my arm briefly, and walked away.

CHAPTER 6

The girls never questioned me again after that evening in the laundry room, nor did they apologize. Perhaps, they had decided that ultimately I was more like Courtney than like Angela, and as their days were to be filled with laughter, they needed no thin-skinned girls crumbling into tears over one silly mistake they had made. How were they to know that in Trinidad people wore the same clothes as Americans and that water was piped into homes from reservoirs? They had seen the pictures the missionaries had brought back from Africa. And what was the money for that the nuns collected from them every month, the hundreds of dollars their parents donated to the missions?

"Did the nuns find you the way they found Angela?" Molly asked me the morning after I had tricked Courtney into including Angela in her invitation to the O'Brien's. I had decided to wait until we were on the morning bus to the college before I asked Angela if she wanted to go to the O'Brien's with Courtney and me. I wanted to be in a safe place to hear her lame excuses, to see her meaningless smiles. I did not want to be tempted to ask her questions about Courtney that I did not want answered. I had planned to sit next to her before anyone else did, but Molly squeezed past me and pulled Angela next to her. Now they both sat behind me.

"How did they find you, Sara?"

"What do you mean?" I was cautious, remembering how she had trapped me before.

"How did you find out about this place? For God's sake, Oshkosh of all places?"

The Catholic missionaries were looking for primitive people, savages to civilize. A blue-eyed black priest from Mississippi came to Trinidad bearing gifts. My mother feared his eyes, my father, his gifts. I shook off the memory.

"An American missionary came to my town," I said.

The girl next to me beamed. "My father gives thousands every year to the missions. Literally thousands." Her voice sang the words, the notes high and strident.

"How did you feel?" Molly's breath was warm against my neck. "What was going through your mind at that exact moment when you knew you had a scholarship? Exactly when you knew? Weren't you the happiest? Weren't you the luckiest? What did your friends say? Bet they were green, absolutely green with envy."

A flash: Zeta telling me I ought to think about it a little longer. "You don't just pack your stuff and move millions of miles away on a moment's notice, Sara. What do you know about this Father priest? I don't like his eyes, Sara. What do you know about these American people or about that college? I don't like it, Sara. Why don't you stay here, Sara? Why do you want to go and leave? Why do you want to leave me?"

But then Zeta also knew everything: the closed bedroom door, the stories we read that didn't come true for me. "You think too little of yourself, Sara. You think running away will help that? You will go from the pot into the fire. Run, but you can't run from yourself."

No, my friend did not turn green with envy, Molly. Anger, yes. Weeping with grief when I insisted.

"So what did your friends say?" Molly's breath brushed my skin again. The pores on my neck opened.

"Happy," I said. "They were happy for me."

"It makes it all worthwhile." The girl sitting next to me chirped like a bird. "That's what my mother tells my father every month when he has to stuff those envelopes. It's the least we can do. All that poverty."

"Money can't always make you happy."

"What did you say, Sara?"

"We are not beggars and I'm sure you don't do it for nothing."

"What?"

"You get something back." The girls around us grew quiet. "The satisfaction," I said. "Helping the underdog." The words flew from my lips as sarcastically as I had intended them.

Angela caught up with me when we got off the bus. "You are always so serious, Sara. Smile a little."

"You smile." I struck out at her and shattered any chance that she would say yes to me now.

"If that's the way you want it, but you could be grateful, you know. Show a little appreciation. It won't kill you."

I ran to my class.

For some time now it had become obvious to me that Angela was finding me a liability. She wanted peace with the Americans. She wanted them to like her, to be her friends, and she was beginning to believe that I was more like Courtney than like her. The silence grew between us, not the silence of spoken words, but the silence of the ones left unsaid. For Angela was too in love with cheerfulness to sit stone-faced with me in the same room. She continued to be friendly toward me, to be bubbly and cheerful as always, but when we talked, she touched on nothing personal, nothing intimate, nothing below the surface.

There was not the least indication on her face—not a darkening of her eyes, a frown on her forehead nor coldness in her voice—to warn me that she had ceased to see me as the long-awaited compatriot, the fellow West Indian for whom she had given up a chance to room with her best friend, Molly. She spoke no words that betrayed the truth that she was separating herself from me as she had already done with Courtney, but almost every night she would disappear from our room after dinner. When she returned, she acted as though nothing had happened, as though she had not left me alone for hours. She would chatter merrily about the events of the day as if she thought I cared, though she had to know I did not care. She would insist on giving me this and that tidbit of news: Did you know . . . ? Did you hear . . . ? Guess what Molly told me? There would be no emotion on her face, except childish excitement, none expected on mine even when it was apparent that we were, for all purposes, ceasing to be roommates—that all we did was share a room.

At first I welcomed the silence, especially in the mornings when I awoke before everyone else to listen to the deep-throated hawking sounds of the big-feathered birds that raced across the sky, their calls so different, so new to me—nothing like the sweet trills and melodic whistles of the birds that sang in the orange tree near my bedroom window in Trinidad, their blues, reds and yellows dotting the green leaves. But I loved the energy and muscle of these strange big birds. The huge V they made in the sky seemed to puncture the clouds like the steel tip of an arrow. They had a sense of purpose and direction. They were going south to warmer lands, leaving behind the frigid weather I had so foolishly and so willingly chosen. I had read about the winter migration of birds in my geography books in school. And now to see it!

I loved other mornings sounds as well: the hushed whisper of quilted booties against tiled floors. I had only known the loud slap, slapping of hard leather slippers on polished wood. Now this. Even the muted rustling of the wool blanket as I shifted my body in the bed was different and pleasing to me. In Trinidad, we used only one sheet on our beds. Now I slipped into a pocket like a kangaroo's pouch and curled my legs into my chest like a fetus, safe and warm in its mother's womb.

I loved the quiet swing of the well-oiled bathroom door, too. No ubiquitous sea-water salt in the air to cause hinges to creak and squeak with rust so that everyone knew where you were going, where you had been. I woke up early for the privacy and still emptiness of rows of sinks and shower stalls, the absence of the sounds I disliked in Trinidad. When I returned to my room after my shower, Angela's mindless chatter was bearable. It did not intrude on the pleasures I still savored: the intimacies of the morning. I did not need more from that girlish young woman who only got serious enough to tell me one day: "You don't have to bleed all over them. You don't have to let them know how you feel."

Later, on the bus to breakfast at the college, the sounds around me were harder to endure. Angela was always at the center of most of the conversations. I felt myself envying her ability to forget, the ease with which she had freed herself of the baggage I still carried. Yet I knew when she waited with me, her face pressed to the windowpane, as the girls, her friends, streamed in the dormitory from their summer vacation, that she must have felt some anger, some resentment. She had to have known that something was wrong about not feeling free to rush out to them while their parents were there.

And if it was gratitude she felt—as she thought I should

feel—or appreciation for the money their parents had donated, the scholarship they had made possible for the three of us, that certainly was not enough to compensate for their humiliation of her. Surely she knew what I knew: her people had written language thousands of years before the forefathers of any of these girls had lost their way into the Caribbean, and awed by the art they saw there, brought in guns to steal gold, and left behind diseases that decimated empires.

And if Angela had forgotten all that, she must have seen the Hosay temples in Guiana—the intricacies of the tadjah, Husain's tomb, the half moons decked with a thousand silver stars. Even if her family were now Catholics, they must have helped her understand what my mind could not comprehend: the control, the discipline, the sacrifice, the mystery. Centuries of civilization had imbedded this ritual in the memory of her people. Centuries, so that they could repeat it with flawless detail in spite of the brutal middle passage, the years of indenture, the backbreaking work under the scorching heat of a relentless sun in interminable cane fields. But if Angela had these thoughts— these girls with their guileless ignorance, their assumption of superiority, their patronizing generosity, had troubled her—she concealed them well. She never seemed unhappy; she never seemed angry. She always seemed anxious to be with the girls.

Then came the Saturday nights I dreaded, nights Courtney, too, must have known in the College of the Sacred Heart, nights that made her have such pity for me that she invited me to go with her to the O'Brien's. Perhaps she had caught a glimpse of me the Saturday before, sitting in the TV den, the light extinguished from my eyes. Though I hardly ever saw her on the weekends, she must have experienced those Saturdays when she first came to the college, when she felt a loneliness so complete and terrifying that she was moved to save me from it, if only once.

It should not have mattered to me when the girls left. In Trinidad I had known no nights like theirs. No cars screeched up to my front door. Here, bright-faced young men from Oshkosh, Green Bay, Kenosha, Racine and Fond du Lac slammed doors, banged fenders and blew horns, impatient to be with young women they found beautiful. Inside, young women bustled up and down corridors, burst into each other's rooms, flung dresses on bed rails, scattered makeup on dressers, chattering and laughing endlessly. No young man had ever come to take me out in Trinidad. I had no hair to fix for some boy, no lipstick to put on, no dresses to iron, no dates to talk about. But still I felt an emptiness when they left, which reinforced my feelings of exclusion already cemented during the days before, when I heard them planning and making arrangements—even those girls who had no dates.

At the beginning, Angela too was left behind when the girls went out on Saturdays. But if their absence mattered to me, it did not seem to matter to her. After the last girlish squeal died down, when the stampede down the front steps ended and the cars screeched out of the driveway, she pulled us from our rooms—the shy ones, the ones too fat, too skinny or not considered attractive enough to fit into the happy world of the other girls—and transformed our dismal group into a raucous pajama party. She had discovered an old popcorn machine in a pile of discarded junk in the basement and set up chairs around the TV. Within minutes after the girls had left, we would be doubled over with laughter at the antics of *The Beverly Hillbillies*, our mouths full of popcorn chased with soda.

Finally the girls asked Angela out. One of the young men, it seemed, wanted to date her. I did not know whether this was true or not. That was what the girls in the TV den said when one night there was no Angela to brighten our dour faces, no cheerful splattering of popcorn to delude us with fantasies that on Saturday nights we had fun, too. But Angela did not tell me she had a boyfriend, and gave me no hint of where she had been when she returned to our room that Saturday nor the Saturdays after that.

I did not doubt that Courtney, who had the uncanny ability to surprise me with information it seemed impossible for her to have, knew this, also. But I resented the fact that she acted as if Angela had rejected only me and not her as well. Wanting her to admit this, I foolishly trapped myself into a confrontation with Angela.

It was already Friday and I could put it off no longer. I decided to ask Angela in the privacy of our room that morning, the moment she woke up, if she would go with us to the O'Briens', but it was she who caught me off my guard.

"Were you watching me sleep, Sara?"

I jumped back, guilty, and too late tried to compose myself. She had caught me looking at her, searching for the places on her face that I thought might expose her true self. Her eyes had been closed, but her lips, free from conscious control, were clamped together tightly, the muscles in her lower and upper jaws pressed against each other, clenching her mouth shut as if to silence any sounds that might escape unwittingly from her throat. I thought of the senna pod tea my mother gave me at the end of every week with the same regularity with which, on Saturday mornings, she dusted and polished and cleaned every corner of the house. She held my nose and mouth shut until, struggling for air, I was forced to swallow. What sounds were pushing against Angela's lips? What words might she say if I could unclench them? I half expected her to wake up gasping as I did when finally my mother removed her fingers from my mouth, but her lips slackened to an easy smile and her breathing came even and calm.

"Well, were you?"

Embarrassed, I tried to find the right words to explain. "I was waiting for you to wake up."

"Do you do that every morning?" The smile disappeared. The eyes, fully open now, were challenging me.

"Of course not."

"Then why now?"

"Oh, don't be so serious, Angela." The words echoed in my mind and mocked the many times she had said exactly the same to me. I searched again to find a way to start, a way to ask my question before she could probe further. "I wanted to ask you something. That's all."

"What?"

"I wanted to know if you'd like to go with Courtney and me on Saturday to dinner at the O'Briens'." Saying it finally, I felt a weight lifted from my chest.

"Saturday? Which Saturday?"

"This Saturday."

"You mean tomorrow?"

"Yes, tomorrow."

"But today is Friday."

"Yes, I know."

"Why didn't you ask me before?"

Was she that clever? I couldn't figure out where she was heading—whether she was about to say yes and was chiding me for having taken so long to ask her, or whether she was looking for an excuse to turn me down.

"I didn't think you'd be interested," I said.

"Who didn't think I'd be interested, you or Courtney? Because that Courtney thinks the worst. She's paranoid."

The word surprised me, not that it was in her vocabulary, but that she used it so intentionally. I had not thought she troubled herself to form studied opinions of people, least of all of Courtney.

"I don't think so," I said. "She thought . . . we both thought you would be busy."

She twisted a lock of her hair around her finger.

"If you'd asked yesterday—I promised Molly." She looked away from me.

"Well, if you can't . . . "

She sat up in her bed and faced me again. "I hope you know what you're doing, Sara. I wouldn't get too close to Courtney if I were you."

My throat tightened. Once again she had squeezed me into a corner and asked me to choose. But why her? She had offered me nothing. Was it anger or jealousy that set my head on fire? Yet when my words came out they sounded like a whine from a spoilt child, pouting because she couldn't have her way.

"I don't see you asking me to go out with you wherever it is you go."

She got out of bed and put on her robe. With her back toward me she said, "Don't ever say I didn't warn you about Courtney."

I could hear the slap, slap, slap of her slippers down the corridor to the bathroom door. The sounds they made were distinct, familiar, and filtered through the cacophony of voices with their nasal twangs and alien accents. Long after I had switched to quilted booties, trembling from the cold that curled up my feet and ankles from the tiled floor, she still wore those slippers from British Guiana. Hers were dark brown. They were decorated with ornate swirls, curlicues and flowers that were pressed into the polished leather. Those slippers were the only evidence I had up to that moment that she remembered the past.

I had agreed to meet Courtney on the front steps, but instead I waited for her in the TV den. The dorm had a peculiar shape. Both ends of the building curved inward like the speaker and receiver of the old black telephones we used in Trinidad. Along the spine were the bedrooms, while on one end was the entranceway and on the other, the den. The nuns must have had the building specially designed this way, for there was a clear view of the den and the lobby from either end. Behind the lobby was a bedroom where an old nun stayed. I rarely saw her. Sometimes her shadow would drift down the corridor at night and I could hear her hushed whisper, "Lights. Lights." But most of the time I was already asleep when she came by.

Our curfew on weekdays was eleven. We had to study in our rooms from seven to nine. Absolutely no visitors were allowed in our rooms during this time or after eleven o'clock. We had to keep our doors open during study period so the old nun could inspect our rooms. It was not uncommon for her to knock on our door after lights out to make certain we had no visitors. It was not always so, the girls told me with a snicker. Just two years before, the rules were different. Then someone questioned the two girls who never came out of their room. "Never," one of the girls told me knowingly. "Never. You know what I mean. *Never. Ever.*" It took me weeks before I understood her meaning. Me and my Victorian novels.

But though our door was open, I knew Angela felt closed in, penned like a caged animal during the study period. Our desks were on opposite ends of the room so I could not see her face, but I could hear her chair sliding back and forth restlessly. She would stack books upon books on the floor, then pick them up, open them, flutter the pages and shut them noisily. She would do anything to stop the stillness, the quiet. She seemed to be afraid of silence, to fear that in those moments suspended between the bells that announced the beginning and end of study time, some terrible thought would escape past her defenses and enter her consciousness. That she might be forced to confront the question: What was there in the College of the Sacred

Heart that gave her such cause to bubble over with happiness?

She was like the moths my cousins and I used to imprison when we were little. We pinned back their wings and squeezed them down the long necks of rum bottles, and then, with the kind of cruelty only children have at a certain age—pure and guilt-free—we watched them beat their wings with such speed and desperation that bits of their thin covering floated down to the bottom like specks of dust. If only they knew how to retreat, close their wings and ease their bodies through the opening in the bottles. When the bell sounded the end of the study period, Angela bounded off her chair and raced through the door to her girls. She hardly took notice of my presence.

On Saturdays there was no study period and the curfew was extended to midnight. From the den it was possible to see the girls in the lobby rushing to their dates and so be forced to face the reality that we were the ones who were not wanted. But Angela saved us from that vertiginous descent into self-pity. She arranged for us to meet in the basement at seven to make the popcorn for our TV parties. I knew she had chosen that time deliberately. By the time we got back upstairs, all the girls were gone. That was Angela. She would not let them or us see her bleed.

I thought it was safe then for me to wait for Courtney in the den at seven. From there I could see her when she came to the lobby to meet me. Even after Angela started going out on Saturday nights, the girls still stayed in the basement until after seven. But when twenty minutes passed and Courtney was still not there, I panicked. Suppose she had come and I had not seen her? Suppose the popcorn-making girls returned and found me sitting there, dressed in my best skirt and Courtney's cardigan? What lie could I invent to conceal my date with Courtney? Mysterious Courtney. Paranoid Courtney. Courtney who hardly ever talked to them, who thought they were against her. I ran to her room. She heard me before I could knock on the door.

"It's open. Come in, Sara."

The door was resting lightly on the latch and opened easily upon my touch. Before I saw Courtney, I saw the photograph. She must have arranged it that way. She must have placed the photo so that anyone entering her room (rare as Angela said that was) would see it first, and then, like me, would lose vision of everything else, would see nothing but that photograph pinned to the center of her bulletin board like a picture in an oversized frame. Four black women in mourning clothes stood in a semi-circle around four tiny coffins, their stony faces barely visible under thin black veils that fell over their foreheads. *Children! Babies!* I sucked in my breath and my eyes found her.

"Yes," she said, as if she had heard the whisper in my mind. "Yes, children."

And then I smelled the burning herbs, the sweet sickly scent that unhinged a memory I had locked deep within my subconscious, broke it free and sent it spinning before my eyes.

A canal running red with blood. Me, barely eight, racing home in a starched blouse and Scottish plaid skirt, new books hugged tightly to my chest. It was September. The thick carpet of green slime at the bottom of the concrete canals that ran along the sides of the houses had been washed clean by the August rains. Water gushed from houses, bouncing bubbles of soapsuds and the peelings of raw yams and cassavas. But the water from my house was pink where it emptied into the wide gutter along the street, red where it poured from the pipe on the ground in the back of my house. Blood red.

I clutched the bib of my uniform and rushed to my mother's room. It was there I saw her: the midwife, the obeahwoman. That was what my father called her when he came home later that night weeping and cursing, hugging and kissing my mother, then weeping and cursing again. "That damn obeahwoman and her evil roots. Eleanor, Eleanor, how could you let her come here? To our home? To our bedroom? How could you?"

My mother. Three operations in England before I was four and no babies but me, not looking a speck like her.

For weeks I had known something was wrong. The sounds had filtered through my dreams in the early morning until they woke me up and I bolted upright in my bed, cold, damp sweat on my forehead. I pressed my hands against my mouth to force my silence and swallowed hard to push back the tears.

Every morning the sounds were the same: deep groans and gagging from the bathroom, a sudden gush like water from a faucet splashing into the toilet bowl, my father murmuring helplessly, "Eleanor, Eleanor."

At night I heard my father trying to comfort her. "Eleanor, Eleanor."

My mother sobbed. "Not this one, too. I can't lose this one, too."

They said nothing to me. They pretended I couldn't hear. Like all children from Trinidad I was to ask no questions. *The violet by a mossy stone / Half hidden from the eye!* Wordsworth praising his Lucy, the English girl; my father imitating him for his dark-skinned daughter.

My aunts came to our house every day that August into early September. "No, no, Eleanor. Why do you punish yourself so? Is nothing you did bad in your life. This one will make it. You'll see."

The priest came to pray for my mother. My father held my hand tightly while the priest circled her, swinging his incense censer. My mother sat on a cane-backed chair in the center of the drawing room. Smoke curled around her head and choked her.

Dominus vobiscum.

The prickly rash that encircled the priest's neck grew redder and mounted his face. It was still late August. Most of the priests were at their retreat houses at the beach. My father must have paid good money for this one to leave the cool shade of the coconut trees along the sandy beaches near his seaside home.

Dominus vobiscum.

My mother rushed across the room, vomit spewing through her fingers.

Three operations in England to have babies. My mother knew she was cursed.

I heard her talking about the obeahwoman in hushed arguments with my father at night. I crept to their room and pressed my ear against the thin wood door. *A baby. Another pregnancy.* My father kept saying, "We'll go to England. Things have changed. More advances." My mother wept. Words such as the obeahwoman, the priest, slid through the spaces in her tears.

I thought my mother was dead that day when I saw the canal run red, but when I came into her room, she was lying on the bed, her back propped up against a stack of pillows, her nightgown drawn above her knees, her legs spread apart. I saw blood trickle down onto the newspaper beneath her and I gasped. A fat old woman dressed in white snapped her heavy hand over my wrists and stopped me from rushing to my mother.

"Cover it! Cover it now!" The woman dragged me to the table near the window.

My hands shook as I put the brass cover she had handed me over the burning herbs. My head spun with the sickly sweet scent of the smoldering fire.

"You see too much. Cover it!"

I saw my mother, her arms outstretched, reaching for me. She reached and reached but I collapsed backward before she could hold me.

Now Courtney was smiling at me. "You know this, what I do?" The girl from St. Lucia, her accent thicker than I had ever heard it before,

I did not answer her.

"Yes, you know it from La Trinite. Trinidad. *Oui? Oui, ma soeur?*"

The daughter of a vodoun priest. That's what Angela said. I had laughed at Angela.

I found my voice. "Why, Courtney?"

"Is nothing. I burn a little incense for the dead, that's all. I say a prayer before we go. Some people I knew. Like family, but not blood relatives."

She coughed and the accent I knew returned—middle class, educated. "Sorry. I did not mean to keep you waiting."

Sorry. As if nothing had happened. She combed her hair and put on her sweater. "Let's go. Come." As if nothing had happened.

Along the way she tried to calm my fears.

"That's how we pray for our dead. You remember, Sara. Didn't you do that in Trinidad? Back home the priest threw so much incense on the coffin, you didn't know who was crying from grief or who simply got smoke in their eyes."

I forced myself to smile. I wanted to forget the red blood in the canal, the red blood on the newspaper under my mother's legs, the smell of burning incense in her room.

"And you remember how hot it was? All that concrete. Like they were building churches for cold weather in Wisconsin!"

My smile deepened.

"I remember once, at the funeral for my aunt, my uncle fell right across the coffin. In the church! In front of everybody! Well, they all said how he wanted to go in the grave with his wife. How he was overwrought with grief. How he couldn't take living without her. And of course, his mistress was sitting right there in the back of the church. You know a funeral back home is an event. Nobody missing it. Not even girlfriends. Well, his mistress almost died with shame. Everybody tut-tutting around my uncle and saying that Edmund must really have loved his wife. See? Who knows what goes on behind closed doors? Never meddle in husband and wife business, they say. And all the time it was just incense suffocating the man."

She was erasing the memory. Still, I persisted. "Were you close to those children?"

"Which children?"

"The ones in the photograph."

"It's a long story. I was just praying for them. You also used incense in your church, didn't you, Sara?" She diverted me in the direction she wanted. "Didn't you?"

But I was not fooled. I would know that sweet sickly odor anywhere. It was roots she was burning. Like the roots the obeahwoman had burned at my mother's bedside. Roots for my mother who could have no more babies. Roots for the baby's blood running red down the canal along the side of my house.

At the O'Briens' house I would learn who the children were. My visit there would open a window to America for me, an America hinted at by my grandmother, with a towel around her neck like a noose, and my father, with his guilt and prophetic words on the price of gifts. Then, after that evening, I would never again be able to return to a childish innocence in which evil existed only in books or in places far remote from where I was. But my journey to that realization would be long one. It would begin with my resistance, my longing to see the world as I wanted it to be, my reluctance to accept that I could not separate myself from what was taking place in America in 1963. That I could not be an outsider. It would be a journey that would end in my beginning, that would return me to the purity and source of a racial past I had not yet acknowledged, and would link me irreversibly to black America.

PART TWO

CHAPTER 7

I had drawn a picture of the O'Briens in my mind. She was blond, long-legged, slim-waisted, beautiful; he, dark-haired, tanned, square-jawed, handsome. I had formed them from the images I had seen on the television shows that were aired in Trinidad: *The Donna Reed Show, Make Room for Daddy, Dr. Kildare, The Fugitive*. America's beautiful people. No Negroes other than Amos and Andy. In the absence of black people in the town and on the television screen in the den at the dorm, these images threatened to erode the pictures I had etched on my mind for Wisconsin: Trinidad's beautiful people—café au lait, butterscotch brown, dark chocolate, midnight black—lips full, cheekbones high under dark eyes, buttocks round and generous. Television was working its magic on me, entering my consciousness so cunningly, that before I was aware of it, it was beginning to redefine my sense of beauty. Sometimes when I looked at Courtney I found it hard to remember I had thought her face exquisite; I had thought an African mask exquisite. Then, afraid I had lost myself, I would rush to photographs I had brought with me of my aunts—dark skinned, brown eyed, curly haired—

and of my mother, whose beauty I prayed to inherit all through my miserable adolescence, to remind me. To set me straight again.

But television fixed my expectations of Americans. Though in church on Sundays and in the streets I saw plump ones and ones so thin they could be blown away by the wind; ones with noses too long or too big, lips hardly evident, hair like dry grass; some so pale I thought them ill, these seemed anomalies to me. For television had fed me nightly with its own vision of Americans. They were coppery bronze, slim, stunning. Perfect.

But the O'Briens were not perfect. They were, in fact, quite ordinary, like the people who lived on my street in St. James. He was of average height and size, less than six feet, neither fat nor slim. There was nothing remarkable about his face except his nose, which was long and pointed and reminded me of Pinocchio. But when he smiled, his brown eyes sparkled with genuine pleasure and he seemed an honest man, a good man. Average. One no more or less likely than another to tell a lie.

But Mrs. O'Brien was all warmth and kindness. Her eyes were soft brown and her curly auburn hair was streaked with gray. Her hips were wide and her breasts, big and billowy. When she saw me, she pulled me to her bosom. My face sunk into a pillow stuffed with goose feathers. Soft. Warm. Cuddly. Safe.

A sweet, sweet longing—a hunger with which I had learned to live—in an instant remembered and satisfied: the taut balloon breasts of my grandmother; the hard-crusted bread loaves on my mother's chest. But after the eternity of a second, the feeling evaporated, and embarrassed, I wriggled in her arms to free myself.

"Sara, at last."

Courtney smiled.

Jim O'Brien clasped both his hands over mine and shook them warmly, and then led me inside, to home, for the first time since I had left Trinidad. Home, though of the magazines that were scattered in the lounge at the college: a brass fireplace, enormous thick-tufted pink sofas, high-backed armchairs covered in a tapestry of pinks, blues and greens, thick beige carpeting, wall to wall, lace curtains at arched windows, a chandelier, Tiffany lamps on low tables. Home. Not my mother's home or the homes of her friends, but home. A home.

Courtney watched me like a satisfied cat, pleased with the smile she believed she had orchestrated on my face.

"Are you glad you came, Sara?" She came close to me and murmured in my ear.

From the corner of my eye I saw another man. He had come through a door in the dining room while Courtney was bending her head toward mine, whispering, "I have a surprise for you."

I looked up and saw him and an ice cube dropped to the bottom of my stomach.

"Sam. Sam Maxwell," Courtney said and pulled me toward him. "A friend from Milwaukee."

His skin was mocha brown and shone like fine polished leather, soft as satin. His hair, jet black, was cut close to his head. He wore loose tan pants and a soft ivory knit shirt that hugged his perfect shoulders.

"Not boyfriend," she winked at me. A Cheshire cat.

His mouth was generous, his lower lip fuller than mine. It broke into a broad grin and his eyes crinkled. He kissed her, and with his arm around her shoulder, turned to me. "So you're the Sara Courtney has told me so much about."

The ice cube melted into a pool of cold liquid. *Eric!* My voice disappeared in the back of my throat.

"Sara from Trinidad."

I coughed and sound returned. "She didn't tell me about you."

He laughed. "Just like Courtney."

But the eyes were not as hard as Eric's. They were warm and sensitive.

"Well, what do you think?" Courtney was still orchestrating. She addressed the question to Sam.

"Oh, go away." He pushed her gently.

"Well?" she insisted.

"Sam's a good friend," said Jim O'Brien. "We like him."

"You're embarrassing Sara." Mrs. O'Brien's breasts rose and fell. The flowers on her dress spread out, then folded again. She tugged Mr. O'Brien's sleeve. "Come, help me in the kitchen."

"Well, what do you think?" Courtney pressed Sam again.

"She's beautiful." Sam shook my hand.

My face burned. I put my other hand to my cheek. It felt hot.

"Don't flatter her. It will go to her head." Courtney grinned at me and then walked out of the room behind Mr. O'Brien.

In a hazy swirl of emotions, I saw her leave with the O'Briens. A big-breasted woman and a room full of light and color reminding me of home had thrust me into nostalgia, and a handsome man was awakening in me feelings dead since Eric.

"Sara." He repeated my name. "So you are from the land of the hummingbird and the steel band pans. I heard your steel band in New York."

I looked up at him. Nothing about him was like Eric.

"In Radio City Music Hall, of all places."

"Oh," I murmured.

"They played Chopin, Beethoven, Tchaikovsky, Mozart. All in one evening. It was incredible."

He smiled, and when his face settled again, a disturbing sadness entered his eyes and in the creases around the corners of his mouth. Tamarind. The brown fruit I loved as a child, its flesh sweet, yet sour, curling around a hard, black stone; its outer shell tough, ridged, yet brittle. Easy to crack.

"I couldn't believe they couldn't read music. That's what my friend from the West Indies told me. Is that true?"

I had calmed myself now. My fingers were loose. The memory of Eric had faded. "Yes," I said.

"That's unbelievable!" His admiration was honest and direct.

"More than that. Some of them can't even read or write." Pride calmed me completely.

"Impossible!"

I grinned.

"Like magic," he said.

Calypso beat her steel band pans and made music out of old oil drums. I laughed out loud.

"No, really. I mean it. It was magical to me. I kept looking for the violins, pianos, flutes, clarinets."

I shook my head. *Calypso in the pan yards in Laventille, behind the East Dry River and in the La Basse. Black corbeaux perched on long legs on top of garbage, their wrinkled heads bobbing. The English were not the only ones who put wax in their daughters' ears. Middle-class black mothers did, too: my mother and the mothers of my friends, frightened by the slip backward, the slide downward. The pull of the Pinkety Ping Pang of Calypso's steel band pan.*

Magical? It was hard to keep from laughing again.

"It seemed impossible. I knew there had to be a piano hidden somewhere. A violin."

"Well, did you find any?" I was beginning to like this man, forgetting my nervousness.

"Nope," he said. "Just the steel band pans."

"Nobody ever noticed that before."

"I don't believe you. They made those pans sound like a symphony. Like any instruments they wanted. I was impressed."

"They play calypso best, you know," I said, "but when they used to play years ago, the middle class ignored them. Then the English people asked them to play their music. Now they can play anywhere, even in New York City."

He shifted his eyes and scratched his chin.

"There is always a tendency to do that," he said. "To see things through their eyes. I'm sorry, Sara."

Television and its magic. I was guilty also, struggling to keep my pictures intact.

Courtney returned with the O'Briens, bringing out platters and bowls of steaming food, and seeing her, I seized the opportunity to escape from Sam, from the seesaw of emotions that he caused in me. He was not like Eric. He was a world nicer.

At dinner, the O'Briens talked about the nuns and the college and the farms that were there before the farmers had been forced to move. They recited tales I had already heard from Angela: about a philanthropic landowner who had left his inheritance to the nuns. About the Sisters' struggles and sacrifices. Their successes.

I listened politely, noticing that Courtney remained silent throughout the entire recitation except when Jim O'Brien commented on how lucky we two were to have a scholarship from the nuns. Then she exchanged glances with Sam and her eyes turned hard and cold and her lips narrowed.

Soon the conversation would change dramatically. By the end of the evening I would know the names of the four children who lay in the coffins in the photograph in the center of Courtney's bulletin board, and I would see another side of Sam that would both frighten me and endear him to me.

"Whatever happened to the Smiths, Jim?" Sam asked, moments after Mr. O'Brien had commented that the nuns had good hearts. Every year they had managed to find space in their budget for one more. First for Courtney, then for Angela, now for me. I tried to smile, hoping that would be sufficient indication of my gratitude. That he would not notice the thin line of Courtney's mouth. Then Sam asked his question.

"I guess they just missed their friends back in Detroit," Mr. O'Brien replied, not noticing Sam's eyes.

"Come on. You know the real deal. The truth." Sam's voice had a hard edge to it. Acid. Tamarinds, sweet and sour, burning at the image I had of his gentleness minutes before. Courtney sat up in her chair. Mrs. O'Brien's hand flew to her bosom.

Mr. O'Brien did not seem to notice any change in Sam. "What truth?" he asked, cutting into his steak. "They moved back to Detroit, Sam. It was better for them."

"Better for them or for you?"

"Better for them, of course."

"I think you preferred it that way."

Now Mr. O'Brien heard the acid. It hissed through Sam's clenched teeth. He put down his knife and fork.

"What's up, Sam? What's wrong?" His nose receded. Retreated under a forced grin.

"You know what I'm talking about."

"The Smiths. June and Charles."

"I was asking you what happened to them."

"But I told you." The grin faded.

"Here, man. Here. What happened to them here."

Mr. O'Brien turned to his wife. "Why is he so angry?"

Sam answered before Mrs. O'Brien could speak. "I'm not angry, man. I just don't want you pretending."

"Pretending what?"

"Now, Jim, you know what Sam's talking about." Mrs. O'Brien patted her husband's upper arm.

"No. What's Sam talking about?" Mr. O'Brien's long nose turned from his wife to Sam and back again like a weather vane. Deep furrows gathered in his brows.

"They shut them out of your little town," Sam shouted. "They! You!"

"For God's sake. Martha!"

Mrs. O'Brien turned her head and avoided her husband's pleading eyes. I glanced over at Courtney. She was looking at Sam, her face animated. A cheerleader. Her eyes sparkled.

"Okay, who's going to enlighten me?" Jim O'Brien faced Sam again. "What's this all about, Sam? Tell me."

"He's talking about when the Smiths left, dear." Mrs. O'Brien spoke quietly.

"Why," Sam said. "I'm talking about *why*."

"I don't understand any of this. The Smiths came to say good-bye. They had dinner with us that last night. Didn't they, Martha? Didn't they?"

Mrs. O'Brien clutched her blouse and nodded.

Mr. O'Brien turned to Sam again. "They were looking forward to going to Detroit. They were excited about seeing their friends. Believe me, Sam. There was nothing else."

I felt sorry for him. His cheeks had turned red with his earnestness, but Sam would not let him go. He leaned over the table and brought his face close to Mr. O'Brien's.

"I'm talking about the rock throwing," he said.

Mr. O'Brien looked down on his plate. "That happened six, seven months ago," he said. "Way before they left. And they caught the boy who did it. His parents paid for the window he broke."

"Didn't they tell you that everyone had stopped speaking to them?" Sam pressed forward again.

"They said they were lonely. That's why they were going back home to Detroit."

"For God's sake, man, wake up. Why don't you face it? *Everybody* stopped talking to them. Everybody in this all-white town of yours. They gave them the cold shoulder. Sure, that boy's mother paid for the window. She sent an apology. Then everyone shut them out. Remember?"

"How could you say so? How do you know that?"

"They told me, man. If you were listening, you'd have heard them too. What'd you expect them to tell you? That you ran them out of your little town? I was right here sitting next to you at this dinner table. And they were right here. Opposite to your wife. There." Sam's eyes were blazing. He pointed his finger at me. "Right there where Sara is now. They told you."

"They said they wanted to go home. They were homesick."

"They said they felt like aliens from outer space."

"Yes. Then Martha and I told them they were welcome here. In our home."

"In your home, yes, but not in your little town." Sam leaned back in his chair. He looked exhausted. Beads of perspiration had formed on his brow. The fire had left his eyes. "You'll never understand," he said. "Even when it's in your back yard, you won't face it. Everything is roses for you."

"Nothing's happening in my back yard." Mr. O'Brien dug his fork into a piece of meat.

"Four little girls in Birmingham. That's in your back yard, man. Why don't you wake up?"

"That's in Alabama. Not Wisconsin." This time Mr. O'Brien's eyes were the ones that burned. His voice shook when he spoke.

"In your back yard." Sam leaned forward again.

There was something in Sam's face that frightened Mr. O'Brien. He flinched and dropped the fork that seconds ago he had been waving in the air in front of Sam.

"In your back yard," Sam was repeating. "And we don't even know their names."

Mrs. O'Brien removed her hand from her husband's arm. Her eyes were misty. She got up and went into the kitchen.

"Their names, man?" Sam was whispering now. "Their names."

Courtney reached over and held Sam's hand. "I have their photograph." Her eyes met mine. "It's on my wall."

I looked away.

Sam smiled at her. His voice was quiet now. "It's important not to forget." He spoke directly to Mr. O'Brien. "They just bombed the church and four little girls were gone. Don't you know, man? Can't you remember? In your back yard and mine. Remember, man?"

Courtney found my eyes again. *Remember, Sara? The photograph on my wall. Remember?*

"Yes. Yes."

It was Mr. O'Brien who spoke, echoing my silent words and at last the tension was broken and the words flowed freely without fear, without restraint. Alabama. Birmingham. Bombs. Explosions. Guns. Four girls crushed. Two little boys shot. Riots. The police. Mr. O'Brien allowed Sam to say it all while he nodded his head and looked sad. Courtney drank in every word.

I examined the wallpaper on the dining room wall. Pretty pink flowers, blues and pale yellows, some still in buds, bunched into bouquets, stems twisting like veins, leaves pressed out flat, edges scalloped. They matched the flowers on the high-backed armchairs in the living room. I shifted the leftover food on my plate and saw flowers there, too, on the bottom, the same shade of pink as on the dining room chairs.

Mrs. O'Brien returned from the kitchen with dessert. She offered me coffee from a pot on a tray, next to a sugar bowl and a creamer, all made of shiny silver.

I shook my head. "I prefer tea," I said.

Sam smiled at me for the first time since dinner.

"With milk, like the English," he said. "And they probably got the habit from India."

"I don't know," I said. "The tea, yes. But I'm not sure about the milk."

He laughed. "Well, they had to lighten it."

More laughter. We had tea and coffee, cake with pineapple in the center and whipped cream and strawberries on top, and ice cream and apple pie, also, if we wanted while sitting on plump sofas near Tiffany lamps.

Home.

I had another passion besides books when I was a girl: the movies. I went to see one—sometimes a double feature—every Saturday afternoon as religiously as I went to Mass on Sunday mornings. At first I went merely imitating my mother, feeling grown up and responsible with my girl cousins when we took the bus up Western Main Road in St. James, past the Roman Catholic Church, its front yard dotted with gravestones; past the clutches of colored flags atop bamboo poles in the front yards of the Hindus; past the green and white mosque, its tiny square openings like eyelets puncturing its domed top; past the stores teeming with shoppers, children tugging on the skirts of mothers, mangy dogs sniffing at food baskets. Between the shops were houses with huge balls of black-speckled green ferns dangling on chains from the ceilings of open verandahs. There was also the new Ju-C soft drink factory where grown men still pressed their faces against the glass window, trying to unravel the mystery of empty bottles clanking down a conveyor belt before being swooped up by mechanical arms, filled and then capped. Past the factory were more houses and stores and a police station fenced in by white pickets, brick barracks farther on to the left, near the open fields where light-skinned girls in short skirts played lawn hockey, next to the oval stadium where my father practically lived during the cricket season. Finally, the Roxy on the right standing majestically apart from them all.

I was the oldest cousin. At eleven, my aunt let me babysit for her two daughters for a shilling and a free movie. Later in the afternoon my mother would go with my aunt to the four-thirty show. I should be in the country with her, my grandmother would say when we visited her after church on Sundays. The theatre was not a place for a decent young lady.

But for my mother the theatre was an obsession. She and my aunt didn't go to the same movies we did. Ours were for children: *The Mark of Zorro, The Three Musketeers, Tarzan and the Apes, Shane.* Westerns about cowboys killing Indians. Their movies were romances. I saw the posters pasted on billboards of cinemas whose names mimicked British theatres: Roxy, Rialto, Empire, Strand, Globe. Passionate men clutched willowy women in their strong arms; lovers raced toward each other across a green meadow; women gazed starry-eyed at a far horizon.

My mother started going to the movies not long after that day I came home from school and saw the canal running red. Later, after my father chased away the obeahwoman, he called the doctor who came with his black bag and silver stethoscope, which he pressed against my mother's chest. Then he pulled my father aside and spoke to him in hushed tones. *Can't. Too late. If that woman wasn't here . . . Don't know what she did with those roots.* My father wrapped my mother in a blanket, lifted her in his arms and put her in the back seat of the doctor's car. I saw blood seep through her clothing and spread down her legs. When she returned from the hospital, she told me it was all over.

"You're all I have, Sara," she said.

She was sitting up on her bed, her back to me, and I was doing what I loved best to do in the world—brushing her curly brown hair, loving the way it bounced back with each stroke of my brush. Soft. Light. My hair, at that time, was always plaited in two thick ropes crossed over each other on the top of my head like a crown of thorns. I was barely listening to her, brushing, brushing.

"You won't have any brothers and sisters," she said.

I brushed.

"Did you hear me, Sara? No brothers or sisters."

The fat obeahwoman clamping my hand down over the cover of the incense censer. I saw too much, she said. I saw the canal running red. I smelled the sickly sweet odor of her obeah roots. I knew it then. No brothers and sisters. And when they took my mother to the hospital, I saw blood leak through her blankets. I knew then there would be no babies.

"Not ever," she was saying. "Not ever. No more children. Ever."

My brush flew through her hair. Tiny wisps of hair broke loose and fluttered down to the bed.

"They took everything. The womb. Ovaries."

I brushed. The bristles scraped her scalp. Brown curls dotted the sheets.

"All of it."

She was crying now. She reached for a handkerchief beneath her pillow and blew her nose. Still I brushed until she spun around, the red in her eyes, tiny tributaries of blood crisscrossing the whites.

"What are you trying to do, Sara? Take the hair out of my head?" She snatched the brush from my hand and shook my shoulders.

My lower lip began to tremble. My eyes filled with tears. I leaned against her and she hugged me.

My mother could never conceive again, she told me, no matter who prays for her: the priest, the woman I saw in her room—no one. The doctor couldn't help her. Roots, saints, burning candles—nothing could help her now. The utter despair in her voice left me limp. Three operations in England before I was four years old, my aunts had said. I wept with her.

Two weeks later she began going to the movies. I, copying her, offered to take care of my cousins if she would let me go to the two o'clock show. Then I met Zeta and realized the power of books to transform the realities I did not wish to face. And the movies—my mother's movies—became a passion for me too.

The theatres then were divided into three parts—pit, house, balcony. Pit was the nearest to the screen and the cheapest. All we had money for. It was separated from house by a low, black cardboard partition. Ten minutes after the movie started the people in pit would jump over the partition to house. Zeta and I stayed where we were. After the loudest and the rowdiest had left, it was quiet around us and the screen loomed larger than life, pressing its images on top of us. We would lean our heads on the back of our seats and allow ourselves to be transported to other worlds: worlds where women were beautiful, men were handsome and lovers were faithful; worlds where evil forces intervened—unsuccessfully—to pull lovers apart; worlds where no matter what, in the end the lovers would be in each other's arms, swearing eternity.

There were other movies, also: England celebrating its victory over Germany. Bombs zoomed down from a swarm of tiny planes. Loud explosions blasted tall buildings apart. Tongues of fire licked the skies. People huddled together in bomb shelters. Afterward children pulled twisted toys from the rubble of brick and smoldering debris. And on the high seas ships were swallowed into holes dug by torpedoes. But in the end, always, the red, white and blue of the British flag. "God Save the King." The screen went black. The doors were opened. Sunlight streamed in, bright and reassuring. There were no wars in Trinidad. No bombs, no torn buildings. No broken bottles to slash limbs. No blood. No dead bodies.

I had this same feeling of disbelief when I sat in the dining room at the O'Briens' and heard Sam speak of bombs in a church in Birmingham, Alabama, hurtling bricks and slabs of concrete on four little girls. Four little girls crushed to death. Bombs turning pews into stacks of splintered wood. Bombs burying ankles and legs, splitting open jaws and shoulders, spraying blood. Bombs scattering people, triggering riots, bringing police on horses and cars with sirens. Bombs setting fire to a policeman's brains, unleashing such hatred that guns exploded and two little black boys lay bleeding, dying on the street.

After Sam had told us all, after he had drained us dry with the horrors of Birmingham, we sat there silent, in a daze, until Mrs. O'Brien reminded us of dessert. Then the screen in my mind went black again. The sunlight streamed in. *Ice cream and apple pie? Pineapple cake and whipped cream? Strawberries?* The movie had ended. It was not real. Nothing Sam had said was real. There was nothing in that room to remind me of a black family stoned out of Oshkosh, four little girls crushed in a church in Birmingham, two little boys bleeding to death on an asphalt street. Light glittered through the crystals on the chandelier and cast the colors of the rainbow on the thick carpet below. A brass fireplace shone and overstuffed sofas comforted us.

Mr. O'Brien wanted to give us a ride to the dorm but Courtney insisted. "We prefer to walk," she said. "We need the exercise."

I resented her presumption of my needs, but I said nothing. The O'Briens too did not protest. The streets were safe in Oshkosh, Mrs. O'Brien said. Danger came only through the television tubes and to a doctor running from the law in search of a one-armed man who had murdered his wife.

And if we needed help, Courtney reminded me when we were a good distance from the O'Brien's, she had her roots.

"You know what I mean, Sara? Voodoo. Obeah."

I looked away from her. *And the five voodoo dolls I called pin-cushions?*

"What's the matter, Sara? You don't believe in it?"

"Not educated people," I said. "We should know better."

Roots burning at my mother's bedside, burning, also, under the photograph of four coffins holding four little black girls. Roots in a bag under my clothes in a drawer in my room.

"Yes, you should know better. You should know where you came from."

I turned away from her.

"I wanted to leave early because of Sam," she said. It was an apology of sorts. "That's why I said we would walk. You don't mind, do you, Sara?"

"Because of Sam?" My head was still swirling.

"He and Mr. O'Brien needed the time alone to sort things out. They usually get along pretty well. It's just that Sam is hurting from what happened to the Smiths. You know it was the Smiths who introduced Sam to the O'Briens. They thought that because Sam was a law student at the university in Milwaukee and Jim O'Brien was a lawyer, they would have a lot in common. They never argue. Tonight was unusual. But I think Sam is finding it hard to forget what happened to the Smiths. They came to Oshkosh when Mr. Smith got a contract with the Wisconsin State Highway Department. He is an engineer. He said he liked the peace and quiet in Oshkosh. Detroit was getting too busy for him. When his contract ended, he wanted to stay. Then that boy threw a stone through their window."

I listened, burying broken windows, bombs, four little girls, bones scattered in a church in Birmingham, Alabama—repressing pictures that might remind me of the noose around my grandmother's neck. This was Wisconsin, I reminded myself. Oshkosh. A town of quiet, tree-lined streets. Electric lanterns on tall, black poles spread a blanket of golden light on freshly swept pavements, scaled up trees and painted a flurry of shadows on the whites and pale blues of pretty fairy tale houses. Wood burning in fireplaces sent blue smoke up red brick chimneys. Little china figurines peeked out of windows blocked colonial style in perfect squares by white strips of solid wood. Behind them shaded brass lamps cast a soft light on polished furniture (not necessary to put curtains on living room windows in Oshkosh, except for lace, thin and transparent to catch the light), and on a row of brass-knobbed doors were straw wreaths decked with flowers and ribbons.

On green lawns in front of the houses in Oshkosh, I saw male servants. Always freshly painted. Always ready. Always black. Hands outstretched to take coat and hat. Two black girls could walk through streets like these at night and be safe. White people would nod their heads and smile. Say hi.

"So how did you meet the O'Briens?" I asked Courtney.

"I didn't meet them. They met me."

"What do you mean?"

"What I said. They met me. Or Mrs. O'Brien did. She needed some black people to save and there I was. Of course, the Smiths were here before me, but you know what happened to them."

I did not like the tone of her voice.

"I thought you liked the O'Briens," I said.

"I do. I just don't trust them, at least not Mrs. O'Brien. Her grandfather was an abolitionist during slavery times."

"Then you have all the more reason to trust her."

"I would, if she would stop looking for Negroes to save. She grew up in Boston. That's where she met Mr. O'Brien. He was from Wisconsin and when they got married, he brought her to Oshkosh. God knows, looking for Negroes in Oshkosh is an impossible mission. A hand is more than you need to count us."

"I thought she was pretty nice to us."

"She always is, and I really like her. I wish she'd stop her crusade, that's all, and see us as human beings. I get tired of being a Negro that some white person feels he has to save."

Was that what my mother resented when Father Jones said he was looking for raw talent in primitive countries? Did she suspect that Father Jones did not see her as a human being the way he saw himself?

"Sometimes it's easier to be with Mr. O'Brien," Courtney was saying. "Did you hear what he said about the Smiths?"

"Sam didn't seem to like what he said."

"But at least he saw them as human beings first. As regular people who were missing their friends the way regular people do. Sometimes I wish Mrs. O'Brien would see us as normal people who get sad, not because we are black, but because we are just like them. We miss our families and our friends, too."

A car full of screaming girls whizzed past us. Someone shouted my name. I saw Angela's brown face in the rear window. She was not smiling. I knew Courtney saw her too, but she said nothing. I waved and Angela waved back. A tiny movement of her hand, palm opening and shutting. A baby's wave in the midst of wild gestures, arms flung out of windows, bouncing back and forth.

When the car was out of sight, and had turned the bend to the fields leading to the college, Courtney told me again that I would lose myself if I forgot Trinidad. This time I thought she meant Angela as well. And I wondered if she had noticed the leather thongs Angela wore. Did she see that they were made in India, that curlicues and the imprint of frangipani were pressed into the leather?

CHAPTER 8

S am called me the next morning. I wasn't surprised. I accepted his invitation to dinner as if I were accustomed to being asked out to dinner by a young man. I assumed the posture of someone who was self-assured, confident. I gave him no clue that his was the first genuine invitation I had ever had from a man. Perhaps this was not difficult to do because I had sensed that he liked me and his call now confirmed that.

"Sara, this is Sam. I wonder if you'd like to have dinner with me?"

I accepted immediately. "Yes. When?"

"This evening."

"When?"

"About six. I could meet you at the college."

"No. I'd rather I meet you."

"Where?"

"Don't you know a restaurant here?" I asked.

"I'm not from Oshkosh."

"Neither am I."

He laughed.

"There's a diner," I said. "At the corner of Fountain and Main. I passed it last night. We could go there."

"Good, we could meet outside and take it from there."

"Okay."

"At six then?"

"Six," I said.

I surprised myself with my boldness. But away from my mother's pitying eyes, the guilt I felt for disappointing her, protected by the anonymity I now had, the girls so preoccupied with their own personal appearance that they had little time to observe mine, I was beginning to see reflected in the mirror another me, a me not as distasteful or as unattractive as I had been led to believe.

"Lovely," Sister Agnes had called me. Eyes like bottomless wells. Yes, Sam must have noticed them, too.

I was thin, but not skeletal. In fact, in some clothes, attractively slender. Small bosom, narrow waist, but well-defined hips, thighs and legs. My complexion was not bad. Almond color, though with the absence of sun my skin had lost most of its reddish undertone. My cheekbones were high, and my eyes, my bottomless wells, sparkled when I laughed. My mouth, I now saw, was my mother's. Sensitive. Expressive. My top lip curled up at its corners when I laughed, and my bottom lip, the one my mother predicted would trail on the floor behind me, drooped a little when I was sad. My nose that I had never pinched, not once in spite of threats, had grown smaller with my widening cheekbones. Perhaps I was not lovely, as Sister Agnes had said, but I was not ugly.

Courtney caught me looking at myself in the mirror in the foyer where I had just hung up the phone. She had probably heard one of the girls calling me to the phone, singing my name down the corridor. But when I saw her face, suddenly, out of nowhere, my heart jumped and I spun around wildly.

She held me firmly by my shoulders. "What? What's the matter?"

"You came so suddenly. You frightened me."

She laughed. "Oh, Sara," she said.

"Why did you do that?" I asked, my fear subsiding.

"Do what?"

"Come upon me so suddenly."

"I saw you looking at yourself in the mirror," she said.

I shook myself free of her hands.

"Don't worry. He likes the way you look."

Now I was angry. "Were you listening to my conversation?"

She ignored my question. "I have some clothes that would look good on you," she said.

I turned away from her.

S am was waiting for me in front of the diner when I arrived, dressed in Courtney's clothes. She had left them for me outside my room. She was right. I looked good in them.

Sam seemed more handsome than he did the day before. He wore a light beige crewneck and darker wool pants. A burgundy scarf hung loosely around his neck.

He walked quickly toward me the minute he saw me. "I came early," he said. "I didn't want you waiting for me."

My face burned.

He took my elbow and led me through the main entrance of the diner. People turned in their seats and looked at us. Not shamelessly. Some, when they caught our eyes, spun around quickly again; some pretended that they were looking at something else; others smiled weakly. I had seen those looks before. Countless times at the college. Even from the nuns. A fish in a glass bowl. I had grown to expect the stares when I walked into a room full of white people. Courtney had warned me, but I had never been able to stop myself from feeling like an exhibit when they looked brazenly at me, an ant drowning in a sea of milk for their pleasure.

It wasn't easy for the people in the diner to stare at us. They were stuck in rows of booths along the sides of both walls. When we came through the front door only those facing us could see us—though Sam told me afterward that the ones near the windows had seen us long before we crossed the street and had sent the message through the room. "Like the beat of African drums or your steel band pans," he said, grinning.

Forks froze in midair before mouths opened wide. A flutter of whispers. The backs of heads revolved slyly. Smiles. Blushes. Something suddenly remembered to tell the person behind them so they would all look natural.

"They think we may be the new Smiths moving in," Sam murmured in my ear.

There was bitterness in his voice but he was smiling, and I let the upward curve of his lips and the warmth of his breath on my neck banish the traces of anger that lingered beneath his words.

A thin middle-aged woman in a frilly white apron, red rouge smeared over her pale skin, brown roots stubbornly visible under bleached blond hair, showed us to our seats. We sat down and the exhibit ended, forks returned to mouths, dishes clattered. A low, pleasant hum filled the room. A regular diner on a regular Sunday evening.

"They see we won't bite," Sam whispered.

The waitress smiled. "Menus?"

Sam took them from her without a word.

When she left, he leaned over to me and closed in our world. "Were you surprised I called you?" He smelled of wet grass after the rain in Trinidad. Fresh. Clean. The earth remade.

I shook my head.

"Did you expect me to?"

"Yes."

The glowing inside my body burned through my clothes and I ran my fingers around the collar of my blouse to let in air.

"Warm?" Sam asked and he took off his scarf. The collar of a pale yellow shirt barely visible above the neck of his sweater lent a boyish cast to his face.

I nodded yes. I wanted to take off Courtney's sweater but I worried I would mess up my hair which I was wearing short now. In Trinidad my hair would have curled tightly with the humidity. In Oshkosh it bounced with the cool, crisp air. Almost like my mother's.

"Pretty sweater," Sam said.

I changed my mind and quickly smoothed the crewneck down over my hips.

"Cranberry is your color."

"I never wore this color before. It's not a color we have in Trinidad."

"Yes, all those bright, tropical, sunshiny colors."

"Dark ones too, but cranberry is not one of them."

"Suits you."

Courtney was so sure the sweater would look good on me; that he would like it. I shook the thought from my head.

"Sorry about last night," Sam was saying. "Jim got me upset. I usually don't get that angry. As a matter of fact, I usually keep my feelings to myself. I don't want you to think I go around hollering."

"I don't think you do that."

He leaned back in his seat and rubbed his chin. The smell of wet grass drifted back with him, and in its place, suddenly overpowering, were the pungent odors of sauerkraut and bratwurst, reminding me: Wisconsin.

"The Smiths were my friends."

"So Courtney said."

"I didn't like Jim pretending that the Smiths had a choice about leaving. Choice? Who has a choice here? I wanted to explain. To tell you."

Like a schoolgirl, I had allowed myself to be fooled again. He wanted a chance to explain. That was why he had asked me to dinner. This was not a date.

I twisted in my seat, angry with myself for my foolish vanity. Yet what else would I have done on a Sunday evening? Closeted myself in the library with a book? Sat at my desk pretending to study while listening so, so carefully for the squeal of Angela's voice above the din of girlish giggles? I was adjusting and readjusting my mind when Sam spoke again and sent me, once more, to the top of a seesaw.

"Hell, who am I fooling," he said, throwing his arms in the air. "I couldn't get you out of my mind last night. It was unfinished business. Heck, I had just met you and there, boom! I was blowing up about stuff and I didn't have time to finish."

"Finish what?" I asked, my heart beating rapidly.

"Finish meeting you."

Silence fell between us. Had I heard him correctly? I shifted my eyes across the table in front of me. Mercifully, the waitress returned. I ordered pot roast, baked potatoes, string beans and salad. Sam said he would have the same.

Green eyes flashed. Dry blond hair, the ends bleached white, brushed frilly shoulders. "Good choice, honey," she said. She smiled, and the red lipstick she had deliberately applied over the edges of her lips spread grotesquely out to her cheeks. A clown's face. I felt sorry for her.

"New in town?" She batted false eyelashes.

Sam answered her gruffly. "Hungry."

She turned away without another word.

"She was just being friendly," I said.

"Like the way they were to the Smiths." The acid returned.

I looked away from him.

"You've got to watch this Wisconsin friendliness," he said. "It can trap you."

It didn't seem to trap Angela. "A lot of it is well meaning," I said, still pitying the clown face. How could she think that lipstick would make her prettier?

"Sometimes. So tell me about you." His eyes lit up. Tamarinds. The sweet side. "How do you like it here?"

"Okay," I said.

"Okay? Don't you miss Trinidad?"

"I have to get a college degree," I said. "That's all I think about."

"All? Don't you do anything else? Go out?"

"Sometimes," I lied. I didn't need him feeling sorry for me. "When I have the time."

"You don't only have to study, you know." His face grew serious. "Don't let the nuns make you feel too grateful."

Courtney, wincing under Jim O'Brien's praise for the nuns, but there was Angela too, telling me I should show a little appreciation. And my mother. She called the Americans angels. They had saved us from polio. They would save me now. They would give me an education that would make me attractive to suitors, if not beautiful. We both pretended there would be no price.

"You're giving them something, too," Sam said.

What? I couldn't imagine. But it was the *what* that woke me up sometimes with dreams of a burning tool shed and the sun blistering my back on the beach at Maracas Bay. The *what*, I wanted to know, yet not know, preferring to think that four years was not much to ask. I could wait till then. Then I would have my degree. I would go back to Trinidad, free, independent, needing neither mother nor father to take care of me.

I turned the conversation to the safety of our talk the night before—before dinner, before the talk of the Smiths, Birmingham and children murdered by bombs and bullets.

"What was the name of the steel band you heard at Radio City Music Hall?" I asked.

"The Pan Am North Stars."

"Oh, they come from my town, St. James. The best of the best."

"Have you heard my music? Jazz? The blues?" He turned the cards of the small jukebox against the wall at the end of the table. "The Beatles, Elvis, Pat Boone, Frank Sinatra, Andy Williams," he murmured, flipping the pages. Then he stopped and looked up, frustrated. "Naw, they won't have our music here. Have you heard the blues? 'God bless the child who has his own,'" he sang.

The waitress returned. A strange look between a smile and a frown crossed her face when she heard the tail end of Sam's song. I thought she wanted to say something to him, something friendly, but within seconds her lips closed. She put his plate down hard on the table and eased mine over to me.

"Billie Holiday," Sam was saying. "Have you heard her?" His eyes, cold, followed the back of the waitress.

"My uncle brought some blues records from America years ago. I don't remember Billie Holiday."

"I'll send you a record."

"I don't have a record player."

"Play it in that den you have in your dorm. There must be a record player there."

I nodded.

He leaned toward me again. "Better still," he said, "I'll give you the record when I see you again."

Again? My heart flip-flopped. Then he touched my hair and said he loved the way the curls bounced. "It's so pretty."

A small piece of my mother, a sliver of her beauty, at last. I smiled.

He said he liked the way I wore my hair—short and natural, without any chemicals. I didn't say anything about how the weather had changed it; how I was afraid that when summer returned, warm and humid, my hair would turn kinky and I would not be able to find a hairdresser who'd know how to open the curls again.

He loved my eyes, too, as Sister Agnes had told me a young man would. One day.

"What did you want to tell me about the Smiths?" I asked him, forcing myself to reality, afraid that the spell he had woven around me would not last, that when it ended, I would not be able to withstand the heartbreak.

He leaned back and told me more, this time without the bitterness and hostility he had hurled at Jim O'Brien. He told me of the good times he and the Smiths had shared: baseball in Milwaukee, swimming in a lake near Fond du Lac. "The Smiths had been thinking about buying a summer home in Fond du Lac," he said, "before they were stoned out of Oshkosh."

I lowered my eyes.

"Well, not stoned. Actually, it could have been an innocent accident. They may not have done it intentionally, but when they stopped speaking to Charles, I knew there was more to it. Charles and June left a month before they bombed that church in Birmingham."

He said *they* as if the they who threw the stone accidentally, the they who stopped talking to the Smiths, the they who threw the bomb in the church in Birmingham during Sunday School while the children were still in their seats were all one and the same.

Suddenly I felt afraid. "Do you think they will do that here? That the bombing will happen here?"

Sam shook his head and laughed. "No," he said, and reached for my hand.

The warmth of his skin on mine melted my fear. *What happened to my brother will have absolutely no bearing on your going to Wisconsin, my grandfather had said. Wisconsin is way up north in America and is as different from Georgia as day from night.*

"Don't worry, Sara. You're safe in Oshkosh. There aren't enough of you to threaten them."

I missed the irony of his words, but it did not matter. His smile reassured me. The north was not the south. I was not in the wrong place at the wrong time. Birmingham was a scene in a movie.

The screen went black. The lights went on. I was in Oshkosh again. One day I would ask Sam to tell me more, but not now. Now I wanted to be on a date. Now I wanted to be pretty. Now I wanted to be the daughter my mother had hoped for but felt she did not have. There was a handsome young man sitting opposite to me. He loved my eyes. He loved the way the curls bounced on my head.

Sam ordered dessert and talked again about returning to Oshkosh to bring me a blues record.

"I used to come here quite often when the Smiths were here," he said, "but I stopped coming. Now I have a reason to return. So?" He looked directly at me. "Will I see you again?"

"If you come back," I was cautious.

"I will."

He bent over and kissed my cheek. "You are a beautiful girl, Sara."

Insecurities vanished in a second. The past of fearing this would never happen to me was gone.

CHAPTER 9

What I said to the taxi driver would come to be after all. I was to be a cook at the College of the Sacred Heart. Even less. I was to be the cook's assistant. The taxi driver's world would be in sync once again. There would be no need for ice blue eyes to stare me down. The social hierarchy that he believed had been thrown into chaos when I—a black woman, a college student and passenger—sat in the back of his cab with him as chauffeur, would be restored.

In the weeks that followed after Sam left, the weather grew colder and colder. Trinidad was becoming a distant memory— a dream. When the first snowflakes fell in early November, I wondered whether there was, indeed, such a place where the sun shone all year. Such a place, I thought, if I could find it, if it did exist, would be where I would want to live. I could hardly bear to remember I had just left such a place. I borrowed more clothes from Courtney, piling layers of thermal underwear on my body. Now I wore two sweaters instead of one and two pairs of pants, and under them, leggings. I was growing thick with clothing but still my body refused to adjust. Still my blood flowed thin, remembering.

I looked through the windows at the girls outside and marveled at them, their seeming ease with the weather. The girls wore miniskirts over thin tights, below light, waist-length jackets. When the first snows fell, they ran out on the lawns, shouting with excitement. Snow got trapped in the strands of their hair and in the necks of their shirts. They loved it. They cupped their hands to catch the flakes; they opened their mouths and let them fall on their tongues.

When the first rains fell after the dry season, I did as these girls. I rushed outside to feel the new rain splash across my head and trickle down my face. I licked it with my tongue. I swallowed it. But this was snow, bitterly cold, like the inside of a freezer, only worse. Where the snow stuck to my skin, it pained me to the bone. How different these girls were from me. How different the climate was from what I had known.

Angela, too, seemed unable to adjust. I saw her fighting the wind behind trees, pretending, laughing with the girls, but I knew that her bones shook exactly like mine. She made happy comments to me about the weather. "It's thirty-five degrees. Oh boy, I can't wait for the winter." Or, "It's going to snow tomorrow. Wouldn't it be great to have a white Thanksgiving?" But she didn't fool me. I saw her put on her layers of thermal underwear. In early November she dressed like me, her body imprisoned under thick pants, multiple sweaters, a heavy coat and a scarf wrapped around her neck. She never asked where I got my clothes, but I knew she noticed that the ones I wore belonged to Courtney. Sometimes she'd say, "That's familiar." Or, "Haven't I seen that?" But Angela didn't raise questions leading to answers she didn't want to pursue. How I got my clothes was my own business. Whether I was cold or not was my concern.

She was happy. Life was not for worrying.

Courtney worried, though.

"I think you need a job," she said. I had recently borrowed her sweater for the fourth time. "I'll talk to my supervisor and see if she can do anything for you."

Meanwhile, I heard from Sam. His calls and letters kept my mind from dwelling on the horrible possibility that it could get colder than it already was. I told myself I wasn't falling in love with Sam, but with his ideas. My classes at the college had turned out to be a disappointment. I was learning nothing new. All the work I was being given I had already done in my last two years of high school in Trinidad. I was growing bored with my classes, with two exceptions: I was being introduced to American history and to T.S. Eliot, the latter only accidentally when some lines from "The Hollow Men" appeared in an essay we read in a composition class. *This is the way the world ends/This is the way the world ends/Not with a bang but a whimper.*

By some strange coincidence these were the words Sam quoted to me the second time he called; the first time he merely wanted to tell me that he had arrived home safely and had enjoyed meeting me.

"I wonder what Jim O'Brien thinks about what's going on now in his own backyard in Alabama? Have you seen the O'Briens lately?"

I'd seen them again. They had invited Courtney, Angela and me for dinner the Sunday after our meal at the diner. There was no talk of Alabama or the Smiths, bombings, riots or stone throwing.

"What's happening in Alabama?" I asked, reluctantly pulling out the images I had pushed far back in my mind. *I was in the right place at the right time. Here there was new snow and girls with miniskirts chasing the wind.*

"The world is ending with a whimper," he said.

I held my breath.

"In Alabama and Mississippi," he added.

The Eliot poem. I tried not to think of what he might mean. I thought this instead: how similar we were. Soul mates. He loved the very lines I had memorized.

"Didn't those nuns tell you?" he asked, forcing me to focus again.

"No."

"It's gotten worse. People are being beaten to death."

"Who? Where?" I felt my fear rising. The image of my grandmother, a kitchen towel twisted around her neck, shimmered before me.

"In the streets of Birmingham," he said. "Haven't you been reading about it in the newspaper? Haven't you seen the *Oshkosh News?*"

I didn't answer. I couldn't tell him that since I had been in Oshkosh I had not read a single newspaper. There were none on the tables littered with magazines in the dormitory lounge.

"I can't believe you don't know about this," he said. "Where are you all out there? In another world? I thought you understood what I was talking about when I was in Oshkosh. Don't you know this country's falling apart at the seams?"

I didn't know. I had no reason to know. He had said I was safe in Wisconsin.

"They're clubbing us to death in Alabama, Sara."

"I thought there was only one incident. I thought it was finished."

"Didn't you understand me?"

"You told me about the bombing. I didn't think there was more."

"The world is ending with a whimper there, Sara. George Wallace is killing us and the country does not care."

I tried to make sense of his words. "Why?" was all I could say.

"We want the Highlands, too, and the Massas say no. It's for them only."

I didn't understand him.

"I'm talking about integration, Sara."

"Integration of whom?"

"Blacks and whites."

I thought of my half-white grandmother and my mother of many bloods, many races. I thought about me.

"Look around you in your college and in your town. Haven't you noticed? White people don't want black people living with them or going to school with them. The governor of Alabama, George Wallace, has ordered his police force to stop black children from going to public schools that white children attend. Didn't your holy nuns tell you about this? Weren't they outraged?"

Sam seemed consumed by a rage greater than I had witnessed at the O'Brien's. I did not understand its source. Here in Oshkosh happy girls bounded merrily through clean, white snow. There were no traces of the whimper he had heard. I could see nothing to fill me with his passionate rage.

What he told me afterward seemed like stories, events I jumbled with what I had read in books. They belonged in remote places, to remote people. I could view them dispassionately and say, with sympathy, "They shouldn't do that to people. That's not right to do that to people." But I could not feel as Sam felt. The people he spoke about were unreal to me, as foreign as the girls in Oshkosh. The images he gave me blurred with the movies I had seen on Saturday afternoons in Trinidad, with their images of passion, romance, the horror of war, cruelty and injustice. But when the lights went up, everything disappeared into the celluloid. The events I saw then were pieces of fiction, dreams in the mind of an imaginative writer.

What Sam said to me on the phone and wrote to me on the

days that followed about the brutality in Alabama, the bloody beatings of children in Birmingham, had that cinematic quality of make-believe. Nothing around me in Oshkosh gave validity to the painful pictures he was painting, the feelings he was trying to convey. For all I knew, talking to the girls and to my teachers at the college, the world that Sam filled my ears with did not exist, for here was snow and laughter and young women who played with the wind. Here, nothing gave truth to the stories Sam wanted me to believe.

Sam didn't always call me with his anger. There were other calls.

"I really miss your eyes."

"You hardly know me."

"They are haunting me. You have mesmerized me, Sara. I can't get you out of my mind. When will I see you again?"

"I don't know."

"What about Thanksgiving? Can you come to Milwaukee?"

"I don't think so."

"You could stay with some friends of mine."

I didn't answer him.

"I'll arrange it. I want to see you again."

So money became a necessity, not only for warm clothes, but for Sam, to travel to Sam. I wanted to see him again. Yet, even then, I wasn't sure how I felt about him. Perhaps I didn't want to be fully aware of my feelings. But this much I admitted to myself when finally I asked Courtney if she had heard from her supervisor about a job for me: I was not only interested in Sam's ideas but in Sam as a person. As a man.

Courtney found a job for me in the middle of November. She warned me I wouldn't like the work, but it paid well. I was to be the assistant to the cook in the hospital kitchen. I would earn one dollar and fifty cents an hour for fifteen hours of work a week. It seemed like all the money I would need. Then

I remembered the taxi driver's prophetic words. *Thought so. Thought so.* I had come to the College of the Sacred Heart to be a cook.

The day I started to work in the kitchen, Sister Agnes called me to her office. I had received the results of my midsemester examinations some days before and knew I had all A's. I felt confident then that she would not prevent me from working, but there was no smile on her face when I entered her office. She barely looked up, and kept drumming on a sheaf of papers with her pencil. The lines on her face were rigid.

I had seen her several times since our first meeting. She had always smiled at me encouragingly. Sometimes she asked about my classes. Once we had lunch together. She laughed at the way I dressed. She warned me it would get colder and advised me to let my body acclimatize itself to the weather. She persuaded me to take off one of my sweaters. We never spoke again about my illness, the problem she had identified after I fainted in the nuns' dining hall on my first night. On the contrary, she remarked on how well I seemed to be adjusting. The O'Briens had given her an account of my visits to their home. They had found me an extremely well-mannered young person, she said. The report pleased her, but I worried that they might also have mentioned Sam, and that she would feel the need to warn me again about my problem. It was the latter fear that came to mind when I saw the serious look on her face.

She asked me to sit. There were some things about me that were bothering her, she said. I swallowed hard, tried to steady myself. No, it would not be good for me to have my problem again right there in front of her. But Sam was not what she had on her mind.

She got up and circled me. "The Sisters are wondering," she began slowly, "about your grades, Sara."

My fear left me. "I did my best."

"Yes. They were wondering how . . . I mean, do you think you're pushing yourself too hard?"

"Too hard?" It was about my problem after all.

"Your grades. All A's."

"Is something wrong?"

"No. Not at all. We were just wondering."

"I did most of my courses already, in my school in Trinidad. I'm not pushing myself. Really, I'm not."

"Most of them?"

"Yes."

"I thought you didn't finish your last year."

I knew where she wanted to lead me. She wanted to remind me of that last year, of my problem. "I don't study all the time," I said.

"Then your grades?"

I had discovered that according to the American system, I had actually finished high school when I was sixteen, and had taken the Cambridge School Certificate examination. The extra two years I spent in high school were actually the equivalent of one year in college. Yet the nuns had not given me credit for them.

"I'm learning many new things," I said, "but a lot of it is repetition."

"I see." She stopped circling me. "And you don't think that job in the cafeteria will be too much?"

"No."

Suddenly she smiled. Sea green eyes became alive and warm again. "No, neither do I, Sara. Neither do I."

Later, as tears streamed from my eyes while I was chopping an onion by the kitchen sink in the cafeteria, Courtney came by to visit.

"Hey," she said. "It's not worth crying over. They think you cheated on your exams but you know better. Don't let them get to you. They simply don't believe that black people have brains. They can't handle your intelligence."

I thought, after Courtney left, how my teachers in Trinidad would have laughed at her. *Intelligent* was not a word they would have used to describe me. They would have said I was a plodder—studious, perhaps, but not intelligent. But in my last two years in high school, I was in the class of the brightest girls on my island, the class for those who aspired to go to university, which seemed only possible then for a handful: those who won the few seats available at the University of the West Indies, and those who were smart enough to get one of the five scholarships to British universities that the colonial government offered. Out of my class of twenty, only two were white. I thought them exceptions. White women on my island never needed to trouble themselves with books. Bank teller jobs or positions as assistants to managers on the family's estate helped them pass the time before rich husbands came along. If rich husbands did not surface, there was always England.

A ll through the first weeks of November I waited for Thanksgiving without the slightest idea of the meaning of the holiday, viewing the day simply as a marker for when I would see Sam again. My days followed a simple pattern of classes, work, study, read and sleep that left no time for brooding or nostalgia, until a letter came from home, always written by my mother, but always signed, also, by my father, always containing messages he had sent to me.

Wisconsin would have been unbearable if I had allowed myself to believe those letters. My mother wrote that she and my father missed me. She said that since I left, there was no one to brush her hair. That she loved the times we were alone. No one understood her as I did. "You are flesh of my flesh," she wrote.

My father asked her to tell me that he was proud of me. The nuns had sent my grades to him. "Smart like a true Edgehill," he told her to write. *Bertha was an Edgehill.*

I read my mother's letters once. Once was all I dared. I folded them neatly and put them in a box in my dresser drawer. I did not take them out again. I knew the truth. I would not let myself be trapped by lies that would make it impossible for me to survive here, in this bitingly cold place, with strangers who never stopped staring at me. I had agreed to come because I wanted to please her; I wanted her to be pleased with me. I wanted to give her something she could be proud of, that she could boast about to her friends. She had given birth to a daughter who looked nothing like her. Her beauty had been squandered in her womb. If I were to believe her now, if I were to believe she loved and missed me, if I were to believe my father was not afraid that mad Bertha lurked in my veins, I would have to confront a waste so enormous that I would find it impossible to live with myself, to forgive myself. I would have to accept a burden too great for me to bear: I had exchanged green grass, blue skies, white sands, the sun in my face for nothing.

Sam wrote to me, too. His letters were full of the truth, terrible and terrifying. He wrote about the bloody beatings on the streets of Selma and Birmingham. He told me about the blinding torture of tear gas that burned the insides of eyes like lye poured on a fresh wound. About the snarling dogs whipped into vicious frenzy by officers of the law, who chafed at their own bits with their hatred for black people. "But why?" I would ask, and he could give no reason that made sense to me.

I thought of a country so rich that it could bring its bulldozers to Trinidad and cut through our mountains of stone merely to get to the beach on the other side. But I didn't tell him that. I thought of the tourists, our flowers in their hair, running to catch us in the sun, lining up our children against the trees and snapping with their cameras as if memory would not be enough, as if the beauty they saw in the little black boys and girls they had chased had blinded them completely from the horror they should have known: they had stolen these black boys and girls from Africa; they had brought them in chains to the New World. The ancestors of so many Europeans had obliterated the Amerindians here: slaughtered them with guns, devastated them with disease, forced them into the Amazon. But I did not tell Sam that.

Once Sam called me, holding back his tears. Only I could understand, he said, that he felt each rip into human flesh: the hard, razor-sharp fangs of dogs tearing into the new flesh of innocent children, the long, jagged trails of blood pouring down the sides of slashed faces, the yawning wounds, the bones exposed. And what are you doing there in Oshkosh, Wisconsin? What are they doing there?

Nothing, I might have answered him. Nothing. But I did not. We might have been on another planet. In another time. Had Sam not filled my ears with the terror in Mississippi, Georgia, Arkansas and Alabama, I would not have known.

"And all for the rights of black children to go to school," he said. "All because white parents do not want their children to sit next to black children."

It made no sense to me.

I knew that the same scenes he saw on the television in Milwaukee were aired by the stations in Oshkosh. But why hadn't I seen them? he wanted to know. In the TV dens of the College of the Sacred Heart, there was no room for Selma and Birmingham, nor for suffering and grief. There was only *The Beverly Hillbillies, The Fugitive* and *The Ed Sullivan Show.* And Sullivan did not expose Alabama. Elvis Presley and Pat Boone were singing and dancing all over America. The Beatles were becoming the new rage.

"That's because it's not white flesh being ripped apart," said Sam when I told him of my failed attempts to turn the channel to the news. Yet, still I suspected that what he saw in Milwaukee would not be what the newscasters in Oshkosh would choose to air on their prime-time news.

I asked Courtney. She knew about the riots. In her own way, she echoed Sam. "Things fall apart," she said, surprising me with Yeats. Then I remembered she read Achebe.

"But aren't you worried?"

She dismissed me. "A time will come when we can do something," she said.

I had the strangest feeling she did not mean *we* in the general sense. She meant us both: She and I.

Soon, I convinced myself that Sam was exaggerating the truth. It was not difficult for me to think that way. My history classes sang praises to America's romance with liberty: the pilgrim fathers; the Boston tea party; no taxes without representation; a constitution that guaranteed freedom of speech and the right to pursue happiness. I could not imagine that the atrocities Sam was describing to me would be permissible, even possible, in a country with such a history. I was beginning to believe that Sam had fallen prey to an overly sensitive imagination. When next he called me, I was cautious.

"Sam, you're taking this too much to heart."

I had underestimated his anger.

"You, of all people!" he shouted.

I searched for the right words to cool his rage. "It will pass, Sam. It will pass."

"How can you say that?"

"Sam, I know how you feel."

"I thought you did, but now I'm not sure."

"Sam, I know it hurts you to see your people suffering . . . "

"They are your people, too, you know. Your people."

I stayed silent.

"That's why I liked you, Sara. I thought you understood. You'd know what I meant."

I did not want to lose him. "Yes, Sam," I said. "I understand. Yes, I understand." But I did not. Not fully.

My words calmed him. "Will you come to Milwaukee at Thanksgiving?" His voice was tender. "I want to see you again. I've asked my friends. You can stay with them."

"I'll try," I said.

"Good. Stay as lovely as you are till I see you."

Lovely. The word banished all my fears. *Lovely,* as in love.

I longed to see Sam again, but late that November, seven days before Thanksgiving, America went into mourning, and personal longings and hopes gave way to a collective anguish that smothered the country well into December. It was Christmas before I saw him.

I would not have believed those childish girls capable of grief. It was Friday, November 22. I had read late into the afternoon in one of the tiny lounges on the third floor of the college mansion, vaguely aware that the room was gradually emptying. I thought I heard sobbing, but when I looked up no one was around. By five o'clock, I shut my book and began the half-mile walk on the road that wound through the razed wheat fields to the dorm. The road was deserted, no girls anywhere. No short skirts blowing in the numbing cold. No merry greetings like the cheerful tinkle of pebbles thrown into shallow pools. Not even the occasional car or tractor that usually whizzed by, causing me to huddle deeper over my books. The biting wind rolled against the barren fields and pitched dead wheat stalks onto the asphalt road. They crunched underneath my feet and made sounds that echoed in the stillness.

I opened the front door to the dormitory and the stillness

followed me inside. Then I heard the crying, the terrible yawning sobs.

President John Fitzgerald Kennedy had been shot, mowed down by the accurate bullets of a skillful marksman. I did not even know who he was. He had been president, the girls told me, for more than three years. In Trinidad, with our eyes on England, few of us had ever heard of him.

"That was what they were waiting for," Sam told me through his grief that night. "Now they'll understand suffering and pain."

Another man who would become a thousand times more important than Sam in the history of this country, another black man filled with rage a hundred times more intense than Sam had ever known, a man who saw the dogs with their bloody fangs, not in the sheltered quarters of his room, but on the wide, open avenues of Selma, Alabama, a man who had been there during those days, said something bitter and unwise the day after Kennedy was shot. Said Malcolm X, burning with revenge for his slaughtered brothers, the assassination of John Fitzgerald Kennedy was a simple matter, a case of "chickens coming home to roost."

The snow fell heavily on Oshkosh at Thanksgiving. Not the little delicate flakes of early November, bouncing against shafts of sunlight that beamed down from the blue sky. This snow fell in heavy blankets, in dismal shrouds of white, blotting out the sky and closing off the sun. This snow draped itself over leafless branches and weighed down pine trees, hiding their greenery. The wind did not disturb the grief, but stayed out on the edges of Oshkosh, mourning with the town.

I had heard that Thanksgiving meant turkey, dressing, gravy, mashed potatoes, candied yams, string beans, cranberry sauce, apple pie, ice cream, family and good friends. I could not tell if it was so that Thanksgiving. Sam did not stay in Milwaukee. He went to New York. He told me something urgent had come up.

A meeting he could not miss. Courtney, Angela and I ate with the nuns in their white dining room, outsiders in the midst of their grief. If we ate turkey, I do not remember.

A change came over the girls when they returned to the college after that Thanksgiving. I did not know whether it was caused by the sudden presence of death in their lives, the shattering of the fairy-tale world they seemed to occupy, or by another, deeper feeling of loss—the kind that unlocks unselfish actions and makes a person sensitive to the feelings of others. The kind that comes from the unexpected absence of something taken for granted, before, not treasured. Perhaps in September the newness of being without parents, the illusion of independence and freedom, had made these girls forgetful. Perhaps the brevity of the vacation at Thanksgiving, the memory of home and family suddenly realized, present and in the flesh, and then in an instant evaporated—returned to thoughts and the conjurings of the imagination—had given them occasion to pause, and, thinking of home and missing it, they noticed me again.

At night, at the end of study time, they came looking not only for Angela, but also for me. They offered me candy, cake, treats brought from home. They showed me their photographs.

And what about your home? they asked me. Do you miss your family? Will you see your parents at Christmas?

I answered them the way I thought they wanted me to answer, for they asked me these questions in rapid succession and I sensed their anxiety, their need for reassurance: they wanted the world to be right again. Yes, I said, I missed my family. Yes, I missed my home. Yes, I hoped to see my parents at Christmas. But I knew the last answer was a lie and I suspected they did, too. Neither Courtney nor Angela had gone home last Christmas. None of us would go this Christmas. We were scholarship students. Scholarship students did not have money to travel to the Caribbean in winter, even if we lived there. It was understood that if we could afford the airfare, we could afford tuition.

Molly was the first to invite me to meet her parents. They had come to Oshkosh to attend a convention of the Knights of Columbus. She invited me after she had asked Angela, and after they had both decided that they needed me. At first I thought the invitation was genuine, and thinking that Thanksgiving, or perhaps the assassination of her president had matured her, opened her eyes to worlds other than her own, I accepted. Too late I realized her purpose.

She came with Angela. They sat next to me at lunch in the cafeteria. Angela spoke first.

"Molly's parents are in town," she said. "They'd like to meet us."

"For dinner." Molly smiled. Her eyes shone and lit her perfect oval face.

Things had changed. Sam had said so himself when I had spoken to him the week before. It was a new time in America, with a new president in the White House, one who had fought for integration, Sam said. Twice the girls had invited me to go with them to the movies. Now Molly. I said I would go.

"Angela says you might sing with her."

"Where? When?" I felt my old guard rise.

"In the hotel. At dinner, silly. Angela said you can do a duet. She said you know all the words."

"The words?"

"We can rehearse tomorrow night." Angela, looking steadily at me, spoke as if this were something we had done before.

"Rehearse?"

"Right after study period."

"I can't."

"Then this evening."

"No. I mean . . . you know I can't sing. I told you."

"You don't have to. I'll carry the main tune."

"I can't."

"One song."

"No."

"Come on. Stop being a party pooper." Angela tossed her hair. Molly giggled. I began to feel foolish, the party pooper Angela said I was.

"My father said the Knights of Columbus will pay you."

"Come with me just this once, Sara. I know you can use the money."

Clever Angela. She had watched me in Courtney's clothes, missed me at dinner and still asked no questions. When finally I told her I was working in the hospital kitchen and eating dinner there, she just shrugged her shoulders and said, "Seems as if you and Courtney have your secrets."

She had said something similar when I came back with Courtney from the O'Brien's. "You and Courtney are becoming a twosome." Now she was pulling in her rein, making me feel guilty for my friendship with Courtney, as if I were the one who had excluded Angela. As if it were not she who had disappeared from the TV den, without a word, on Saturdays.

"You never go out with me, Sara. This is only one night. Just one song. I'll do the rest. Only *Yellow Bird*. You know that one. Please, Sara. I need another voice." She pleaded with me.

"My parents are dying to meet you," said Molly. "Angela said she and you would sing. It's my father's convention. He'd be really pleased. I've told them so much about you."

"Please," said Angela.

"In front of all those people?"

"I'll be singing with you."

"My parents really want to meet you, Sara." Molly's voice was as sweet as sugar.

I let them persuade me. I pushed aside suspicions that I had been invited only because Angela needed me for a duet. Perhaps this was the way the world was now. I preferred it to the photograph of coffins and the suffocating smell of burning roots in Courtney's world. To the horror stories Sam had told me.

"We'll have fun."

Angela wore a sari. I should have known the moment I saw her that this was to be no ordinary outing. No ordinary evening of fun with Molly's parents. What I did not know then was that I would envy her, and in the end, discover I was not much different from her.

The tight-fitting bodice of the sari exposed her flesh—smooth, firm, coffee brown—from below her breasts to her waist. Around her hips she had wrapped a matching thin orange fabric embroidered with silver. It fell over an ankle-length half-slip and left a trail of more fabric which she draped across her right shoulder like a shawl. It made a transparent veil for her naked torso, at once sensuous and demure. She wore heavy silver bangles on her wrists and silver high heels on her feet. She had lined the insides of her eyelids, top and bottom, with the black paste I had seen Indian women in Trinidad use, and in the center of her forehead, just below the part in her hair, she had filled a circle, a little smaller than a dime, with red lipstick.

An East Indian princess. A bride. The wife of a Hindu priest. She brushed away the shock on my face when I returned from the bathroom and found her dressed.

"It's my best outfit," she said.

"I didn't think you wore saris."

"Sometimes," she murmured, her eyes scanning the floor.

I put on a skirt and sweater.

"Don't you have a flower for your hair?" she asked.

I looked at her and frowned.

"Here." She pulled out a red silk hibiscus from her drawer. I moved away from her.

In the lobby, I waited, in my coat, for Molly's parents. Angela wore hers over her arm. Her sari was the first thing Mrs. Weaver noticed when she came to meet us with her husband. She went directly to Angela.

"How stunning. How beautiful. You *must* be Angela."

The black lining under Angela's eyelids had widened her eyes. Now they were rounder and darker, shining beneath the red dot on her forehead. She adjusted the shawl of her sari and wrapped the ends over her arm, close to her wrist.

"Isn't she beautiful, Philip?"

Mrs. Weaver was a television-beautiful woman. Her blond straight hair was cut in a page-boy style just below her ears. Makeup covered every line on her face. Blues and beiges darkened her eyelids, pink swept across her cheeks, ruby red outlined her lips. I saw Molly's resemblance to her when she turned her cheek for Molly to kiss. They had the same straight nose and oval face, the same firm fleshiness to their bosoms and hips.

Mr. Weaver pulled Molly to him and wrapped her in his arms. He was a tall man with a slightly bulging stomach and receding hairline. Mrs. Weaver glanced at them briefly and then turned again to Angela.

"Those silver bracelets are gorgeous."

"They belonged to my grandmother," said Angela. The bangles on her arm clanged against each other.

Mrs. Weaver smiled at me, a weak smile that formed a thin line and quickly faded in the corners of her mouth. " I'm glad you will sing with Angela tonight." She did not wait for my response.

"You call it a sari, right?" She fingered the silver embroidery on the edge of the sari that fell across Angela's arm.

"They are real silver threads," said Angela. "My grandfather brought it from India."

Girlish Angela. Coy Angela. She batted blackened eyelashes and lied without shame about grandparents almost dead from starvation in India before the British came with their offer of indentured labor on sugar cane fields in exchange for five acres of land. It was so in Trinidad. It had to be so in Guiana. Silver threads for saris would be the last thing they would put in their bundle of rags.

But the British had taught us well. They had poisoned us with their system of class stratification. In countries such as ours where the majority was dark skinned, it was essential to identify a marker, a way to tell the difference; to determine who was better than who. Race was not as important as class. This was what Angela wanted the Weavers to know, for which she had planned. She wanted them to know she was no ordinary Indian, that before Guiana, her people had not been indentured laborers; they were important in India. Even through my eyes she looked important, sophisticated. This was why she wanted me to wear the hibiscus in my hair. She wanted the Weavers to know I was different, too.

Within minutes I would fall prey to the same need to be a person not a race. Sam had said his people were my people, also, but I wanted the Weavers to know we were as complex and as diverse as they were. My parents were not ordinary people, either. They were middle class; they were literate; they were well-read. And when, in the car, Mrs. Weaver noticed my accent, I emphasized it and became proud of ancestors who were never mine, who had tortured mine.

"Just like the British," Molly's mother said. "You speak so perfectly, dear."

I beamed. "Well, Trinidad was a colony of England until just one year ago."

"You pronounce your words beautifully. Not like many of the people here."

I smiled. *Not like many of the people here.* The sudden rush of pride, its source not considered then, not analyzed. I did not stop to think who she meant.

"I could listen to you speak all day. Couldn't you, Philip?"

"I've always admired the British accent," Mr. Weaver said. "So cultured."

"Don't ever lose it," said Molly's mother.

The feeling of being special. In the hotel lobby I ignored the smiles that turned sour the moment we entered, the voices that suddenly descended to a low murmur, the heads that turned, the stares, bold and brazen. When the hotel manager rushed toward us and Molly's father stopped him—"They are with us. Foreign students"—I pretended that the smiles that returned were warm and genuine from the ladies with their high-pitched greetings and nervous laughter, and the men, pumping our hands. We were different, Angela and I, she with her sari and silver bangles, she and I with our accents. And I wondered how much more special I would have been to them—exotic, even—had I worn the silk hibiscus in my hair.

Angela sang first, a Hindi song she said she had learned from her parents. Her voice wailed with the high notes, her head and eyes moved from side to side, like a snake. Her shoulders straight, her elbows bent, the palms of her hand outstretched on either side of her cheeks. I almost did not recognize her.

The Knights of Columbus, seated with their wives around tables covered with pink linen and laden with pretty china and glasses stuffed with flowered napkins, dropped wads of ashes from cigars into glass ashtrays, put down beer bottles and stared in amazement. When Angela ended her song, they applauded.

Exotic Angela. She announced that she and I would sing calypsos, and she pulled me from my seat. Embarrassment waned under the unswerving attention of the Knights and their wives, the interest they seemed to have in us. Their admiration. I, enjoying the false superiority specialness brings, not seeing then that I was a bug on a microscope, did not deny that the songs we sang were calypsos—"Jamaica Farewell," "Yellow Bird," "Haiti Cheri," "Island in the Sun." When I didn't know the words, I hummed. Angela sang them for me. I discovered a voice I did not know I had. I basked in their appreciation.

At dinner one of the Knights asked me how we got our independence from England.

"I heard, without bloodshed," he said.

And Eric Williams popped into my mind before I could suppress his image. I saw him that day in Woodford Square when I let Zeta persuade me to cut school after lunch. He was standing on a raised platform under a samaan tree, hands punching the air, the cord from his hearing aid trembling with his passion, the crowd black and sweaty below him, clenched fists raised above their heads.

I suffered detention for a week when I returned to school the next day. My mother cried: her daughter with a bunch of hooligans. Then, during my last year in school, just a few months before our bloodless independence, my history teacher, a French Creole, infected me with her nightmares, and that crowd in Woodford Square mushroomed into the unruly rabble my mother had claimed it was.

"They are organizing to take what we have worked for," the teacher told my class.

We, the black middle class, sitting primly in starched blue and white uniforms, pleats pressed into place, turned our faces dutifully toward her.

"Let them find jobs. They won't have the time to be loitering around Woodford Square in the middle of the day. The next thing you know they'll be in our schools sitting next to you.

How'd you like to have the daughter of your mother's maid sitting next to you in class?"

She frightened me. They said she had relatives who lived on the other side of the East Dry River. My parents had a maid who lived on the other side of the East Dry River. I loved her. But when I turned twelve and started secondary school, my father pulled me away from her.

The school I attended was Catholic. When the British settled in the Caribbean, they invited the clergy to set up secondary schools for their daughters and sons. There were four such schools on my island: a boy school and a girl school run by the Anglicans, and a boy school and a girl school run by the Roman Catholics. You were admitted into these schools in one of three ways: either your father was a European colonist, or he had money, or you won a scholarship. Zeta's father had money; I won a scholarship.

On the first day of school, my father began my real education.

I was sitting in the back seat of the car nervously biting my fingers. "Ena say dat dis school harder dan de odder school I was in."

I was hoping that my father would comfort me and ease my fears, tell me I had nothing to worry about; that I was just as good as the girls who went to that school. But his hand flew across the back seat. The car swerved. He grabbed the collar of my uniform. The car swerved again. He slowed down and pulled over to the curb.

"Ena said *that this* school is harder *than the other* school I *went to*. Repeat it." His eyes blazed. "Repeat what I said, Sara. Now."

I repeated his words, my words sounding so different when he said them. I erased the *d*'s and replaced them with *th*'s, I changed the tense, my lips and tongue imitating the English accent he had used.

When he calmed down, he told me that I was not a little girl anymore. He recited a bible verse about putting aside childish things.

"People know who you are by the way you speak," he said. "You are not like Ena. You are different. You are middle class. If you speak like Ena in that school, they'll think you come from the other side of the East Dry River."

"Yup, the people down South could take a page from your book." One of the Knights puffed his cigar smoke in my direction.

"Yeah," said another. "I don't see what the Negroes have to gain from all that burning and looting."

"Jesus," said another. "Give them an inch . . ."

Molly's mother rescued me. "You know this doesn't have anything to do with Sara." She waved them away and when she spoke again of how intelligent I was, how cultured, and when the ladies remarked again about my accent—*very British*—I, too, allowed them to separate me from those burning and looting Negroes as I had allowed my history teacher with her fears of being recognized to carve a space between me and Woodford Square, so that when independence came I did not know how. Bloodless, perhaps. But I couldn't tell for sure.

At work the next day, standing side by side with Courtney in the kitchen, scraping the remains of that evening's dinner into the garbage disposal, I flinched when she asked me about my evening with Molly's parents.

"Did they like you as much as they liked Angela?"

My face burned.

"Or more than they like the Negroes in Alabama?"

I buried my chin in my collarbone.

I sang once again with Angela, pretending, exaggerating all that Sam now told me about Johnson, about his refusal to sign the Southern Manifesto in 1956 protesting the Supreme Court's decision to outlaw segregation. Twisting it to suit the optimism I wanted, the guilt I needed assuaged. Everything was all right again. It had been a bloodless revolution. One so quiet I did not know when it came.

Christmas brought its own bittersweet pleasures. My mother sent me a fruitcake, which she had put in a round biscuit tin taped shut with black electrician's tape, packed in a box stuffed with newspaper, wrapped in four sheets of heavy brown paper and sealed with another piece of electrician's tape and tied in a fisherman's knot with brown string. And still it leaked. When I picked up the cake in the post office it reeked of rum and molasses and glazed fruit, a sweet and heady aroma that filled every corner of the room.

Courtney was with me. I was glad she was there. When I handed my claims ticket to the mailman, I knew he had been waiting for me. His head bobbed up and down like the slats of a window shutter: up to me—opening; down to the ticket—closing; back to me again. A nasty look. His lips turned downward in a sneer; then he turned his back on me and left the room. I could hear scornful laughter from behind the partition where he had disappeared.

"Jesus, it stinks."

"Joe, you gotta hold it. It's your job, Joe."

"You're the one that got her. Your luck, Joe."

"I'm not carrying this. Naw. Not me."

"*Rum and Coca Cola/Working for the Yankee dollar.*" The calypso. Lord Invader sung derisively.

"Jesus Christ, man."

Pale skin lost its summer tan. Almost white as dough. Green, gray, blue eyes. Unyielding. I felt them on me cold, scornful. The mailman brought out the box my mother had so carefully prepared and wrapped. Months ago she had soaked the fruit in rum; the baking was done in late November. And now the mailman was holding it out to me as if it were garbage. Dark stains of molasses and rum had spread out along its four corners.

How I had craved the taste of black cake when the girls put up the Christmas tree in the dorm. For pigtail swimming in vinegar, limes, onions and green hot pepper. For pastelles made with cornmeal and wrapped in smoked banana leaves. In her last letter to me my mother had promised to send me this cake. How I had dreamed of it. Now I felt such shame.

"I'll take it," said Courtney. "It's mine." She reached for the box, her face an African mask, serene and mysterious, her almond eyes narrowed almost to slits piercing the mailman's heart. He backed away.

"I have ginger beer and sorrel," said Courtney when we were back at the dorm. "Bring your cake."

And she made it right again in her room. Black fruitcake soaked in rum. My mother's best. Or, missing Trinidad, I thought it was. Afterward, there was ginger beer burning my throat and opening my sinuses, and red sorrel, sweet and spicy, with black cloves floating to the bottom.

Courtney and I celebrated Christmas in her room the day the girls left for home. Molly had taken Angela with her. I did not mind, though Angela felt the need to explain: "Only one of us can go at a time." But I did not want to have to face the Weavers again. I wanted to forget that evening when I took praise for my accent and kept my silence. When I allowed Mrs. Weaver to separate me from the burning and looting Negroes. I was glad Molly had chosen Angela. My guilt lessened. Now Courtney was making it feel like Christmas at home. And she had no incense censer. No burning roots. Yet the photograph was still there on her bulletin board—four black coffins, four mourning mothers. But I did not pay attention to the image and neither did Courtney.

Later that evening Sam called. He would spend Christmas in Oshkosh. With Johnson in the White House, a Southerner but a good one, Sam saw hope for his country. He came to Oshkosh with fresh optimism. He was lighthearted, full of life and I fell in love.

Sam stayed for ten days, from Christmas Eve to the day after New Year's Day. Jim O'Brien invited him, Courtney said, because he wanted to make up for the quarrel they had had the last time Sam was in Oshkosh. Otherwise Sam would have had to remain in Milwaukee. His home, South Carolina, was a long way from Wisconsin and Sam had no family there, either. Both his parents were dead. He had spent last Christmas with the Smiths.

I listened to Courtney but I was not convinced. I didn't think Sam had come to Oshkosh to see the O'Briens. I knew he had come to see me. Our letters and phone calls had brought us closer. I was beginning to feel more at ease with him. I was opening myself to him. He seemed to have no expectations of me. No questions about the size of my nose or my protruding lower lip. No need to make me fit any dreams he may have had of beautiful women. He seemed to accept me the way I was, and for the first time in my life I felt liked.

I spoke easily to Sam about my days in Oshkosh, my classes, my work in the hospital kitchen, my friendship with Courtney. Only about Angela was I guarded. I didn't tell him about the two times I had sung with her at the Hotel Dixon. Nor that Oshkosh had its own version of the stories he had told me. Nor that the Knights of Columbus thought there was much my people could teach his about getting their share of the pie. Nor of my silence, as if I had agreed. As if those Knights were right. I didn't tell him that I felt ashamed of myself afterward and that I wanted to forget. Now, while waiting for him at the train station, I thought only about the last time we parted. About how he kissed me on my cheek.

This time his kiss was different. As soon as he saw me, he ran to me, wrapped me in his arms, pressed his lips on mine and there was passion. Not the savage greed I had known from Eric, but the desire of a man who loved me, who missed me, who longed to be with me. His arms held me safe in a cocoon and pushed the world away. I felt loved and wanted. I could not have dreamt such pure joy, imagined such happiness from all the books I'd read, from all the novels of romance. When at last our lips parted, he murmured, "You don't know how long I've wanted to do this." And I, who had been warned to hold in my feelings and had been learning to control them, whispered back, "I think I love you."

The words left my lips before I was conscious of knowing I loved him. Sam held onto them and made them right. "I know I love you, too," he said.

I remembered little about what we did at Christmas, where we went, who we saw. Courtney was with us sometimes, clicking her tongue and saying in mock disgust, "You two act like silly children." Jim O'Brien teased Sam: "I thought you came to see me. You never seem to have time to talk." On Christmas Day, Mr. O'Brien made a toast to brotherhood between blacks and whites. Sam, pressing his fingers into the back of my hand, was smiling. "Things will be better." Later the two men talked about their dreams for the country. They did not mention Alabama. No more about bombings, about little children murdered. Sam talked about his meeting in New York. About a group of students, black and white, who were going to Mississippi. About a new era in America in which the children would correct the mistakes of the parents. Busloads, he said, were on their way to Mississippi. Black people will have the power of the vote. The world would be made right again.

On New Year's Eve Sam told me all about himself. Winter, I was discovering, had its pleasures: a crackling fire in a darkened room, snow illuminated by the flames, white and shiny against the windowpanes, drifting softly down from a blue-black sky. Peaceful. Romantic. I wore a new pink turtleneck sweater and white wool skirt, bought with money I earned chopping vegetables. Sam told me I looked beautiful. We cuddled on the O'Brien's couch in the den, waiting for 1964. The O'Briens were not at home. They had gone to a New Year's Eve party at Mr. O'Brien's lodge. Sam held my hand to his lips.

"We'll leave all our baggage behind us in 1963," he said, "and begin fresh and new in 1964."

Even the sound of his voice warmed me. He had on a loose navy long-sleeved wool polo shirt and soft smoke-gray pants made, I thought, of brushed velvet. Courtney later told me it was corduroy, a fabric I had never seen in Trinidad.

"I want to tell you about me," Sam said. "Then put it all behind us. Start a new page."

I could see sadness tighten the corners of his mouth.

"Later, Sam," I said.

"No, let's get it over with. Let it die with the old year."

He removed his arm from around my shoulders and shifted his body away from me toward the end of the couch. I felt the cold winter draft snake along the floor through the slit at the bottom of the door. It licked at my toes and opened the pores on the back of my neck.

Sam rested his head against the back of the couch and stared into the fire. He told me his story about a pregnant mother who bled to death because a white hospital turned her away. A father who was not dead, as Courtney had said, but might as well have been. He had abandoned Sam when he was only ten. Shame, his aunts had said. He couldn't face his son after the white man had reduced him to a child, his own son's age. A grown man who couldn't even get a doctor to treat his wife. And when she died, a grown man who didn't take his revenge, but he fled before his son saw how rage could burn itself down to impotence.

I listened but I barely understood. Bertha, blond and English, ran through my veins. White Americans had saved my family, though they had exacted their price. They had brought their Salk vaccine to my home and all my cousins, even the ones without Bertha's blood, black as night, were saved.

It was segregation, Sam told me. Jim Crow in America. I listened, and his words circled my heart and brought me almost to tears. His was a lonely childhood. He was passed from one relative to another in South Carolina until an aunt in Virginia took him in, where he finished high school and worked his way through Hampton Institute scrubbing floors in restaurants or anyplace else white people wanted him to clean. Hauling bags and boxes like a mule. When his aunt died, there was money in an insurance policy for law school.

He wanted to know about my childhood, but I could find nothing to say. How could I tell him how I suffered because one silly boy, in a moment of passion at the height of the Carnival season, had tried to make love to me and I had believed him? Would it make sense to him that my mother made me feel ugly because she was so beautiful? Could I explain how a look, a touch, a word unwisely said from either of my parents could make me crawl into myself and hide for days? What was my guilt for my mother's infertility compared to the heavy burden of guilt his father must have borne for his mother's death? How could I compare the cruel death of his mother to the nonexistence of my unborn siblings? How could my parents' transparent relief over my departure be compared to his father's abandonment? Could I say my father sent me to people he did not trust because he was afraid that Bertha still lived in me?

Now my background seemed privileged to me. I was spoilt. Selfish. I had a great uncle lynched in Georgia, a father reduced to silence for the price of a Salk vaccine, Trinidadians had lost Chaguaramus and Waller Field for ninety-nine years, but these injustices seemed insignificant next to the ones Sam had suffered, and I was ashamed to mention them. I had a beautiful mother, an intelligent father, two grandparents. Alive. Before Oshkosh, I had never washed dishes or cleaned a kitchen floor.

When the last chime rang out the old year, I made my New Year's resolution in the silence of my heart. I would love Sam forever. I would ask nothing for myself. I would make him happy. I would make him whole. I would stop my selfish preoccupation with myself.

The colorful balloons floated down from the top of the Times Square building in New York. I kissed Sam. He turned away from the television and touched my breasts.

CHAPTER 10

Sam and I had planned to be together again for my birthday at the end of January, but he did not come. He had final exams, he told me on the phone. He would see me at Easter. His letters came steadily, once a week. I wrote to him every other day. He called me, on Saturdays he said, so I wouldn't be lonely when the other girls went off on their dates. Now, even though the generosity that had seized them after Thanksgiving was beginning to wear away, I no longer cringed at their departure on Saturday nights. Sam filled my life. There was work, study, sleep and Sam's letters making it all bearable.

When Angela's curiosity finally got the better of her, she asked me about the letters. I told her about Sam. She had met someone too, she said. He was white.

"She'll soon find out what a mistake she's making," Courtney said when I told her.

I did not think Angela was making a mistake. I had known marriages between blacks and whites in Trinidad. They worked like any other.

But Courtney rolled her eyes. "Not here in these United

States of America." Angela said Courtney had a boyfriend, also.

"I saw a letter he sent," she said. "She had forgotten it between her books. I took it out and read it. The strangest letter. Not the kind you get from Sam. Well, how do I know what Sam writes to you? But I bet it's about love. This letter was all about buying a farm. He gave such details! How much the land costs, what they were going to plant, how he was going to train people to farm it. How she would teach the children in the village when she came back. Not the kind of letter a boy usually writes to a girl. And I wouldn't have thought it a boyfriend letter if I hadn't had to race to its end when Courtney entered the room. He had written, 'I'll always love you, Christopher.' Imagine!"

"She found you reading the letter?"

"She snatched it from my hand, of course, and tore it to shreds. Right in front of my face."

I took my chance to ask her that question again, the one I could tell from her eyes she had answered with a lie: "Is that why you two don't room together again?"

She put her hand on her hip and watched me closely. "I told you about the dolls."

She was lying again. Her voice had that same shrill quality as when she answered me the first time.

"Just because she had pincushions?"

"I told you they weren't pincushions."

I brushed her away with a wave of my hand.

"You don't believe me?" She came closer. "What if I told you I found blood on her rug? Chicken blood."

"Stop it, Angela."

"Yes, chicken blood. I'm positive. I know what they do. She hid the rug under her bed, but I found it. There were white feathers stuck to the blood. Chicken feathers."

Her eyes grew round and dark. "Voodoo," she said. "She was

doing voodoo here."

"You're crazy, Angela."

"Protect her if you want. Pretend it wasn't so."

"It could have been her period, for God's sake."

"And the feathers?"

"From her pillow."

"Wear blinders if you want, Sara."

But I had smelled burning roots in Courtney's room. I had seen smoke curling around four little coffins in the photograph on her bulletin board.

"Did you tell anyone?" I tried to hide my fear.

"How could I? They would have put both of us out of the college. They wouldn't believe I didn't do it, too."

"I think you were mistaken," I said.

"No. I know what I saw."

"Did you ever see it before?"

"No, but I know what they do."

"They?"

"The Negroes. In the bush. I heard about it in Guiana." Her lower lip curled. "Chicken sacrifice."

I became defensive of Courtney again, not for her sake but for mine. Once more Angela was driving that wedge between Courtney and me. *She's pure African, you know. No mixture like you. I could see you have white blood.* It was the African blood I wanted to defend.

"It's not chicken sacrifice, Angela. It's a religion. It's a way to pray to their gods. No more, no less than what your people do."

"My people?"

"I've seen them on Hosay morning, beating the half-moon dancers with whips."

"You're lying."

"Almost till they bled."

"That's a lie, Sara."

"I saw them with my own eyes."

"Years, donkey years ago. No more."

"Still," I said.

She narrowed her eyes. "That's the difference. We learned. We became educated. Courtney hangs on to her mumbo jumbo. Still."

Still.

In the Serpent's Mouth, off the coast of Icacos Point in the south of Trinidad, a boatload of Indians. My grandfather saw them. Years later he told my father, and my father told me. They had packed all their belongings, the things they came for when the English tricked them into believing that five years would pass before they could count them. After that, five acres of land. Or passage back to India. The English were certain they would not choose the Or, but some could not forget.

Two boatloads had left months before. This load was the last, so the ones who chose Or gathered up whatever the others had left behind. Their possessions as well: two hundred sacks of co-conut husks, five hundred pounds of copra, five hundred gallons of coconut oil, one hundred tons of brown sugar and as many tons of white, three hundred bags of rice—a lifetime of planting under a brutal sun collapsed into five, more than five years if you count a week to unpack bags, build huts in which to sleep, and a week to pack again, this time for India. Then there were the cows, bison, goats, the grass for so many cows, bison, goats. So many poles for Hindu flags, so many brass plates, so many brass bowls for Hindu prayers. A hundred and twenty men, women and children—the last of the ones who had chosen Or.

Out in the Bocas the Serpent yawned. He had not seen them when their pirogues left the beach at Icacos Point. Perhaps if he had, he would not have yawned; he would have let them pass. He had seen the old wreck anchored out at sea. They had bought it from the Englishman. Night after night after slaving on the cane field, they hammered nails and lifted planks of wood. Still it was too old, too decrepit, too small. Not fit for ten thousand pounds of human and animal cargo and much more. But they wanted to go home, even if the English were masters there too. They wanted to bathe in the Ganges; they wanted their ashes thrown in its muddy waters. So they packed up their belongings.

But the Serpent had been awakened from sleep. He was too angry for pity.

"Every last one of them drowned," my father told me.

The currents were strong in that passage between Icacos and Venezuela. The Bocas, we called it. The Serpent's Mouth.

Years later someone found them: a graveyard of skeletons of men, women and children, the remains of animals, brass planted with coral and seaweed.

When we went to the beach at Cedros, my mother warned me. "The Serpent will swallow you, too, if you swim too far out."

Still, Angela had said to me. But her people had died for still, for the past, for the donkey's years they kept to memory. And Courtney burned roots. For *still.*

Was there blood too?

Winter passed quietly. Sam brought me no more news of bombings and riots and beatings, and it seemed that all would be as he had predicted that Christmas: a new day, a new time of peace. Courtney, too, seemed to believe that things had changed. She still kept the photograph of the coffins pinned to her bulletin board, but she never spoke of it, and no matter how many times I visited her room that winter, I never again smelled the sweet odor of burning roots.

But winter brought new terrors of snow and ice I thought would never end. I never grew accustomed to the searing pain at the tips of my fingers and toes when I walked through the walls of snow from the kitchen to the dorm. The wind whipped across the grain fields and plummeted the temperature to levels in the thirties below freezing. Icicles formed on my eyelashes and on the tip of my nose. When the pain brought me to tears, these, too, froze on my cheeks and in the corners of my eyes.

Sometimes, while I waited for Sam, I thought I would die. By February I had fallen into a deep depression, smothered by the unrelenting dark, the total absence of leaves on trees, the disappearance of birds. I longed for sun—sun that warmed the earth, not the sun that could shine and still not cause grass to grow. I longed for green, for the smell of brown earth, for the warmth of rain.

"You act like a squirrel," the girls teased.

I was sleeping long hours, hoping to keep the days from happening.

"Humans don't hibernate, Sara."

But I did, or I wanted to until the land grew green again.

Then Easter came and the quiet ended. Three weeks before, Sam had called me bursting with excitement about a meeting that had taken place in Manhattan. Malcolm X, the man whose words about "chickens coming home to roost" so echoed Sam's own sentiments about the lesson America was beginning to learn from the assassination of President Kennedy, had announced that he was no longer a member of the Black Muslim party. He was going to form a new organization.

Sam had memorized Malcolm's X's words: "'A new organization dedicated to black nationalism as a political concept and form of social action against the oppressors.' That's what he said, Sara. 'Black nationalism.' And he called them *oppressors.* Right there in the heart of America's biggest and richest city. White men, police, all around him."

I wondered what had happened to the optimism that had

calmed his fury at Christmas. He seemed to guess my thoughts.

"Things had settled down around Christmas but it is back to business as usual in Alabama," he said. "Things are heating up in Mississippi."

"Will I see you at Easter?" I asked.

"Yes, of course. Why not?"

He called me again the following week. "I have to go to New York. There's to be another meeting," he said.

My heart dropped. "I won't see you then at Easter?"

"Yes. Yes, of course you will."

On March 12, Malcolm X announced his plans for the Organization of Afro-American Unity. We have dignity, he said. We will not be clubbed to death in Mississippi without defending ourselves. Each and every Negro will fight back in self-defense whenever and wherever he is being unjustly and unlawfully attacked.

Sam became enflamed with the trumpet call to recover, as he saw it, the Negro's manhood. Now. This was the hour.

I did not see Sam that Easter.

In April it snowed. In the sudden Wisconsin storm that ushered in the spring, George Wallace surprised his Southern supporters by wooing to his cause an unexpectedly large block of Northern votes in the Democratic presidential primary in Milwaukee. Sam said the snow was nature's tears for America. Things were getting worse, he said. Jim Crow was riding high again.

But the snow in April meant something else to me. It shattered memories I had stored in the imaginary world I had constructed through the books that made me safe. In the dingy reading room of the colonial library in Port-of-Spain, Trinidad, I had dreamt of Chaucer's Aprille, his shoures sote. All winter long I had comforted myself with the hope that when spring came there would be greenery sprouting from a soggy earth. There would be rain, warm and sweet. But no rain fell in Oshkosh in April that year, only snow drifting steadily down on fields hard and unyielding since winter. When the sun came out, the girls took off their coats. I still wore mine. April, and the air still chilled my bones.

Easter passed inconspicuously. Or almost. On Holy Thursday Angela went again to Molly's home and only Courtney and I remained in the dorm. We sat in the TV room and ate popcorn and pretended we were not lonely. On Good Friday I could not find her. I knocked on her door but she did not answer. I supposed she had gone with the nuns to the chapel, but later that night I saw white smoke curl out from under her door and I smelled again the sickly sweet scent of her burning roots. I saw her again briefly on Saturday. She came to my room early that morning to tell me she would not be going to the cafeteria that day. She would be fasting.

On Easter Sunday morning she was radiant. She told me that Easter was, for her, the most significant and auspicious moment in the liturgy of the Church. Christ crucified, sacrificed for man and then risen.

"It's all the same, everywhere. Our ancestors knew it too. There has to be sacrifice, Sara. You know what I mean. Before resurrection can occur, blood has to be shed. Now we eat His body and drink His blood."

We were on our way to church when she said this to me. Later when the priest put the host on my tongue, I remembered Angela's story of the blood and chicken feathers she had seen on Courtney's rug, and a shiver ran down my spine.

Not long after Easter, Sam invited me to spend a weekend in Milwaukee. "We'll have more privacy," he said. I remained so quiet on the other end of the phone that he had to call my name. "Sara? Sara?"

"But where would I stay?" I asked.

"With me," he said.

"Alone?"

He laughed. "You're a big girl, Sara."

"You think it's right?"

"I know you won't do anything you don't want to do."

I did not allow myself to think about what he might mean.

I told Sister Agnes that friends of the O'Briens had invited me to Milwaukee for the weekend. She had no reason to think the O'Briens would not be there. She wished me well and told me to take my mind off my books. I had earned a vacation.

Courtney, however, viewed my departure with suspicion. I ran into her on my way to the library and told her of my plans to meet Sam.

"American black men are not the same as West Indian men," she began, surprising me with her statement. It was the first time I had ever heard her make a distinction between people of African descent. "American black men think they know all about suffering and it's made them hard."

"Not Sam," I said, much too quickly. I felt the muscles in my throat constrict. "Sam's not hard."

"You don't know that. Don't think he's as sentimental as you. He won't forgive and forget so easily."

"What are you talking about?"

"Suffering. Slavery. Their brand of slavery."

"Slavery is slavery," I said carelessly, trying to brush her aside.

"True, but American slavery lasted longer. Then Jim Crow dug his claws into them. They think no one else is capable of understanding that kind of suffering."

"Yes, I am."

"Maybe," she said, raising her eyebrows, "but they don't think so. To them we're happy, free island natives dancing in the sun to steel band music and calypso."

"How do you know so much, Courtney?" I was being sarcastic, yet I could not shake my uneasiness.

"I just know," she said. "Because we didn't have signs on the bathrooms For Colored Only, and the conductor didn't tell us to go to the back of the bus, they think life was different back home. They don't know."

I looked away, resenting her for the shadow she seemed intent on casting over my happiness.

"Be careful," she warned.

"Careful of what?"

"What Sam thinks is the superiority of his suffering." She laughed bitterly. "Even suffering has its ranking order, you know. Sam can shut you out. Think you're too different from him."

"You don't know Sam," I said. I was almost shouting at her, needing to crush the doubts she was stirring in me. "I'm not Trinidad to Sam. I'm Sara."

"You don't have to raise your voice to me, Sara. I was just giving you some friendly advice. For your own protection."

But I needed her reassurance. "I thought you liked him."

"I do. But I don't love him and I'm not making the plans you seem to be making."

"I'm not making plans," I said defensively.

"Spending a weekend alone with a man is making plans."

"It's not going to be that kind of a weekend," I protested.

Courtney shrugged her shoulders and walked away.

Milwaukee shocked me with its blacks and its poverty. When the Greyhound bus I had taken from Oshkosh eased off the ramp from the highway, they were suddenly there. I saw them hanging out of windows in the tens of dozens from drab apartment buildings that leaned on each other, piles of broken bricks. I saw this all in slow motion, an illusion created, perhaps, when the bus suddenly slowed down and a deathly silence fell upon the passengers. The people on the street were brown like the people I had left in Trinidad, and yet they frightened me. When they turned to stare at the bus, I saw a guardedness and an anger in their eyes I had never seen before.

No one had prepared me. Sam had not told me there were black people in Milwaukee. Perhaps he had taken for granted that I would know, in spite of Oshkosh, that black people lived in all the cities in the north, pushed into tiny spaces in stacks of concrete. Had I so easily forgotten the clutter in New York, the pain in the eyes of the people huddled in corners on streets without trees? Oshkosh with its silence and trees and rosy-faced people made that all an ugly dream, a cruel fantasy. How could I have known that Wisconsin had its own blacks not far from where I lived?

I saw children thronging around steps of tenement buildings, dressed in clothes too big or too small, skipping rope next to mounds of garbage piled high against walls and on sidewalks. I saw young men, strong and beautiful as my Sam, slouched in dark corners and entranceways. Women in the streets called to women leaning over windowsills. I could hear no sounds, only see the movement of lips, mouths opened wide in laughter, and eyes that stung me. Dogs ran unleashed everywhere, their excrement dotting the pavement. I wanted to blot out the images, deny what I was seeing, but I could not turn away. I looked in silence with the others until at last the bus turned again and entered a wide avenue lined with trees and tulips in white boxes and houses so quiet that only the flutter of curtains behind closed windows signaled the presence of people within.

The sighs of relief from the passengers on the bus were almost audible. Sound and laughter returned. I remembered what Sam had told me during the snowstorm in Oshkosh that April. It was here in this city, Milwaukee, in the Democratic presidential primary just a few weeks ago, that George Wallace reminded the liberals that segregation was alive and well in all of America. Not only in the south.

Sam was happy to see me. Whatever specters of doubt Courtney had cast over me disappeared when he held me.

"I missed you." His kiss was long and deep. I believed him.

His apartment was not far from the bus station. Sam took my one small bag from me and said we could walk if I wanted to. It was a fairly warm day, though not what I would have called warm in Trinidad, but I agreed. I felt comfortable in the tan spring coat Courtney had lent me. Sam said it suited me. He liked the other clothes I wore, too—a white blouse with a lace collar under a yellow V-neck sweater and beige pants—two extravagances I had allowed myself with the money I made washing dishes. He held my hand, and when after three blocks we entered a park perfumed with cherry blossoms, the faces I had seen in the tenements receded from my memory. But Sam would shatter my forgetting.

"Did you notice," he asked when we were almost in the middle of the park, "that we are the only ones?"

"The only ones?"

"Don't you see? Except for those workers over there."

I followed his hand. He was pointing to three black men lifting garbage cans. Suddenly I noticed that the men digging flower beds were black, too.

Two men passed us. All I saw was the blue metal in their eyes. Hard-edged. Vicious. I flinched and let go of Sam's hand. He grabbed it back.

"Don't make them do that. Don't let them stop you from loving me. Ever."

In his own place Sam was relaxed and happy. He led me around his apartment oblivious to the pounding in my head, the tightness across my chest, apparent to me now that I was completely alone with him. What did he expect? What should I do? Where was I to sleep? Sam lingered in his bedroom. He wanted to show me his collection of books, he said. There were hundreds. Not just books about law, but history books, fiction, poetry. Rows of books on shelves he had built around his bed and on the wall near the window, stacked on raw wood planks held up by gray cement blocks. "Books about black people," he said. "And by black people." He handed me one: *The Invisible Man* by Ralph Ellison.

I would read it a year later but by then I would have already understood the meaning of its title.

In the kitchen Sam lifted my hair and kissed the nape of my neck right below the hairline. I felt the nipples on my breasts harden.

He insisted on cooking. Everything fresh: carrots, tomatoes, celery, cucumber, lettuce, sweet peppers, broccoli; fresh fish in butter sauce, lemon slices, baked potatoes, sour cream, chives. I had never seen a man cook before, only women: my aunts and my mother boasting; the men puffing out their chests like blow fish. *If you want to know the secret, Sara. The way to a man's heart.* It was strange seeing Sam at the stove, as if he had somehow usurped a right I held by having been born female. As if by insisting that he would cook he was insinuating that I was less than a woman. We almost had an argument when I fought for the stove. But he was adamant.

"Here." He handed me a glass of wine. "Relax."

And eventually my discomfort dissipated mostly because of the wine, and I watched, loving the way his arm muscles moved when he chopped the carrots in neat, even slices; the way he eased his broad shoulders past the open refrigerator door; the way his pants hugged his hips and brushed against his firm thighs.

We ate on a small round table in the space he had converted

into a dining room using an old blue couch to separate it from the living room. By the time we were finished, my tension was gone and my body felt fluid again.

We washed the dishes together, cramped in the space between the sink and the cupboards behind us. When our bodies touched, I felt as though an electric current had passed through me. Afterward we sat on the couch and Sam drew my head to his chest. I heard his heart beating steady and strong beneath my ear. He kissed the top of my head. I looked up at him and our mouths met.

I felt Sam's hand taking my blouse out of my pants long before slipping into my bra, but I did not stop him. I let his fingers cup my breasts and I stayed still when they moved down the back of my pants under the elastic of my panties, over my buttocks.

"Come. Come to bed." His whisper was urgent in my ear.

Later I wondered why my mother had made me so afraid of this moment. "Stay away from boys," she had warned, when my period came for the first time. "They can only cause you pain."

Pain. That was what I had associated with sexual intercourse. The kind of pain that gripped my womb in a viselike lock once a month and sent me doubling over for hours. Before coming to Oshkosh, I knew from my friend Zeta, basking in the glow of her clandestine affair with her married lover, that there was no pain. But images rarely leave us when they appear at those certain pivotal moments of our lives. Bent over with pain the day I became a woman, I accepted my mother's words as immutable fact. They sank into my subconscious to become solidified as myth. There was pain, but the sort of pain that intensifies pleasure because it is replaced so immediately, so completely by pure, distilled, unmitigated ecstasy. But the next time and the time after that, there was no pain at all. In the morning, nestled in the crook of Sam's arm, I was still glowing with remembrances of my utter happiness at those moments when the telephone rang and changed my reality.

Sam reached for the phone and my head slipped back onto the pillow.

"Hello? Hello? Oh, Harry!" He put his hand over the mouthpiece and whispered to me, "Long distance from New York. Harry Epstein." He removed his hand and spoke again into the phone. "Harry, what's up? What's going on?"

"No, really, I don't mind you calling me here."

"Man, forget about the time. Anything serious?"

"When?" Sam sat up in the bed. "Who's going?"

"You can count on me. I can be in New York on Monday."

"She's fine." He looked at me.

"I'll explain to her. She won't mind."

"No, man. Don't bother about the call. I told you to call me when it was a definite. I want to go. Thanks. See you Monday."

Sam hung up the phone, rubbed his hands briskly over his face, tugged at the sheets which were tangled around our bodies, and, finally freeing himself, he got out of bed. He didn't say a word as he walked to the bathroom. I heard water gush from the faucet and the swift swishing sounds of toothbrush against teeth. I waited, fearful of his return.

Sam was tense when he came out of the bathroom; he wound his arms in their sockets and flexed his fingers.

"What's the news?" I asked. I had gotten out of bed and put on my robe. I braced myself for the worst.

"That was Epstein on the phone," he said. "Harry Epstein. I met him when Malcolm X came to Columbia. He was sitting next to me when Malcolm said he was ready to send his people down to Mississippi and Florida with guns so they could protect the marchers." He rubbed his face fiercely with a towel.

I knew he did not see the anxiety in my eyes. His mind had already left the room.

"You know Malcolm has a lot of respect for Martin Luther King," he said, pulling on his pants. "But they don't see eye to eye on the solution to the problem of racism in this country. Anyhow, Malcolm was at Columbia, telling us that King's way is just not going to cut it. Black people are getting clubbed to death in the south and all we're doing is marching. Malcolm has these eyes. I don't know what it is exactly. You should see them, Sara. They're kind of like, transfixing. They just glue you to him as if he's speaking to you only. And he wears these thick glasses with dark frames. They make him look so intense. You *have* to listen to him. He's mesmerizing. There he is talking about the dignity of the black man. We're ready to give the Ku Klux Klan a taste of its own medicine, he says. Or something to that effect. Then, next to me, this white boy jumps up. Mr. Harry David Epstein himself. The guy on the phone. He jumps up and shouts, 'Right on, brother. Right on!'

"Malcolm looks at him and as cool as you can be, he says, 'We need you, brother, but we have to fight for ourselves. You get your brothers together. Then come back.' I tell you, Sara, it took a lot of guts for that guy to stand up and shout what he did because, I'm not kidding you, Malcolm could make white people cringe with all his militant talk. But that's Epstein for you. One self-confident, brave guy with convictions that could smoke you."

He took his sweater off the back of the chair and pulled it over his head. "He is something, that Epstein," he said. "I talked to him when the lecture was over. Asked him how he got so involved in colored people's business. He said the Holocaust ended less than twenty years ago and he was too young to do anything for his people, but he'd be damned to sit by and see it happen all over again. He's a weird guy. He's got some soul under that white skin of his."

"What did he want?" I managed to find my voice. I could

see Sam drifting farther away from me. I looked for my clothes and slowly began to dress.

"He wants me to go back to Mississippi with him."

"Why?" My voice was weak. I did not think Sam noticed.

"He's been there five months now. Working with CORE. Helping to organize the first community center for black people in Mississippi. Now he's with the voter registration drive." He spoke in clipped sentences, barely looking at me.

"What does that have to do with you?"

Suddenly he seemed to hear my voice. "Everything," he said quietly. "Everything."

The low tone of his voice scared me, but still I asked, "Why? What can you do? What are you going to do?"

"I don't know, Sara. I don't know."

"You have to tell me," I said. "I must know." My world was breaking up before my eyes. Sam was slipping quickly out of it. "Tell me." I had to struggle to keep my voice steady.

"Harry's white, Sara. If he can give up his job in New York, leave his family to help my people, you can't expect me to stand by."

"Stand by?"

"COFO has called a meeting on Monday. In New York."

"Are you going?" My voice was uneven.

"You're going back to Oshkosh tonight anyway."

"Yes, but I thought you'd be here. And next weekend—"

"Sara, this is larger than you and me. Can't you see that?"

"But last night?"

"Sara, I love you. Don't forget that." He tried to kiss my mouth. I turned and his lips brushed my cheek.

"How long will you be gone?"

"I don't know."

"Will you go to Mississippi?"

"If Epstein returns."

"Do you think he will?"

"He said he plans to."

"Then I won't see you again."

"Don't say *again* that way, Sara. This is not forever."

"When then?"

"Perhaps it'll be only for a month. I'll be back in July."

A wild thought flashed through my mind. "You knew! You had your plans made already! Is that why you did what you did last night?"

He steadied my shoulders.

"We did, Sara. Not I did it to you. And what we did was make love. It's what people do when they are in love."

"But you did it because you knew you were leaving." Tears welled in the corners of my eyes.

"I did it—we did it because we are in love."

Now I was crying, painful sobs that lifted my shoulders. Sam put his arms around me and held me to his chest. "Don't be afraid, Sara. I'll love you always. I won't leave you, ever."

"And suppose something happens to you in Mississippi?"

"It won't."

"Suppose—"

"Sara, what do you want me to do? Stay here with you while my people get killed and people like Epstein risk their lives?"

"You said it would be dangerous."

"Life is dangerous, Sara. You think you're all safe at the College of the Sacred Heart? All locked in tight, safe and sound? Negroes don't go to the College of the Sacred Heart, Sara. Haven't you noticed?"

"I go to the College of the Sacred Heart," I said.

"You, not us."

"What do you mean, not us? We're the same. We're black."

"Not us, Sara."

I had sung with Angela in the Hotel Dixon and wished I had put a hibiscus in my hair. "We're the same, Sam." My voice was hardly audible.

"To them you're different, Sara. You're a foreigner. You're going back to another country. They don't have to deal with you. But they won't give a scholarship to any of the black women you've seen in Milwaukee."

Nor to the son of a poor taxi driver. Ice-blue eyes in the rear-view mirror of the taxi. I wanted him to tell me why. Why me?

"Then why do you think they gave it to me?"

Sam shrugged his shoulders. "You're an intelligent girl. You figure it out. Figure out how you Catholics deal with a guilty conscience."

"What does Catholic have to do with it?"

"Religious people, then. Holy Rollers, rosary-saying, Our-Father-Christian people." Sam was shouting now. I saw the same eyes he had turned on Jim O'Brien—two tamarind seeds, hard and black. "Think about it, Sara. Think about what you and Courtney—even Angela—are doing for them. *Think!*"

He brought his face close to mine. His breath poured over me. I would only have to move an inch and our lips would meet, as they had last night. Now the muscles along his neck strained against his skin.

"So they won't have to have their own black girls in the college," I murmured.

"Yes." The muscles slackened. "Yes." The jaws loosened.

"Because with Courtney and me, they could say they have black girls."

"Yes." The acid left his eyes. Brown in an unruffled sea. Peace. I drummed out the terms.

"And all the time they're as racist as the next person."
"Yes."

"So Courtney, Angela and I are here to make them feel good."
"Yes."

The burning tool shed, my back blistering from the heat of the sun on the beach at Maracas Bay. The price, at last. The price.

"I couldn't know, Sam. I didn't—"

"Shh." Sam held me to him. "Shh. Just don't let them lie to you anymore."

Afterward, after I dried my tears, after I had convinced myself that I understood why Sam believed he had no choice but to go Mississippi, I still asked: "You'll be back?"

"Before the end of June."

I let that promise comfort me.

On the bus back to Oshkosh I decided I would return my scholarship to Sister Agnes. I would say to her, "I don't want it anymore. You give it to a black girl in Milwaukee. I won't let you lie through me. I won't let you use me to look good, to feel good." A hundred different versions. In each one I would tell her I was leaving. But when the bus pulled in at the station, other questions tormented me: What would I do? Where would I go? *What would I say to my mother?*

CHAPTER 11

Once, months before that Easter in Milwaukee when Sam had opened my eyes to my complicity in the betrayal of his people, I said to Courtney: "You know, really, we're lucky. We don't have to pay for tuition, books, board and lodging. Really, we're lucky."

We were walking back to the dorm from the hospital kitchen on a bitterly cold and dark winter evening and I was trying to find something cheerful to say to her. Icicles had formed from the tears the biting winds had forced down my cheeks. My ears ached. I could no longer feel my fingers, buried deep in my pockets under layers of wool. We walked through a trough of ice and snow. The week before a man had come with a machine and carved a path in the snow where the pavement was. The mounds of snow piled alongside the path reached almost five feet. I could barely see above them.

Courtney had sucked her teeth and then let out her breath, forming white clouds suspended in front of her. "We're doing the paying, you fool. We're the ones. You think this is easy."

I had thought she was talking about the cold.

Now, after Milwaukee, I knew better. I understood every-thing when I returned to Oshkosh.

I asked her the question I had asked Sam: Why us? This time she answered, "I have my own purpose. I know what I have to do."

"So what will you do?"

"Stay here till I graduate."

"How can you? Knowing what you do."

"Let the nuns worry about their own lies."

"But you are helping them, Courtney. They are using you."

"That's what you think."

"How could it be otherwise?"

"I have work to do when I return to St. Lucia. I will be able to serve my people better if I graduate."

And I remembered the letter her boyfriend had written. But still that was not a good enough reason for me.

"We can't simply turn our backs on all that's happening here," I said.

"There are other ways."

"Other ways to do what?"

"To do our part."

"Sam went to Mississippi," I said.

"That's his way."

"I'm going to give them back their scholarship."

"Don't be a fool."

"I don't want it anymore."

"And what will that prove? They'll just get another one of you from Trinidad."

"But it won't be me."

"Sam is going to need you," she said.

"I'm going to go to him in Mississippi."

"Not that way. He's not going to need you that way."

"I'm going," I said.

She looked at me. Hard. "Did he ask you to come?"

I tried to shift my eyes away from her but she held them.

"Did he?"

I didn't answer.

"No, he didn't," she said. "I told you he'd see you differently from him."

"It's not that," I said, irritated by the certainty in her voice. Her calm. Her self-assurance. "He didn't think I could come. That's all."

"Did he say that?"

"No, but he knew."

"Don't start lying to yourself now, Sara. If Sam wanted you to come he'd have asked. I'm not saying it has anything to do with how he feels about you. He probably loves you, all right, but he doesn't think you understand."

"I do."

"Maybe."

"I'm going to give back my scholarship."

"There you go. You don't understand, Sara. There are other ways to fight." She came close to me. The tight curls of her wooly hair glistened. Blue-black lights flashed in the soft mass of black upon black. "Obeah," she breathed. The word seemed so new. "Obeah."

Tall, thin men, their bodies hard and rugged like the trunks of coconut trees, their muscles taut from cheekbones to ankles, leopard skins draped across their shoulders, in their hands a long, knobbed pole. I blinked them away.

"Obeah," Courtney whispered again.

Gooseflesh rippled across my neck and down my arms.

"When the time comes, Sara, we'll help Sam."

I waited until the girls had left for summer, two weeks later. Cowardice? Then, I didn't think so. I told myself I wanted to face Sister Agnes alone. I wanted to wait until the girls had gone, taking their childish laughter with them. But it was Courtney who made me hesitate, her words ringing in my ears: *Another way to help Sam. Obeah.* I let the word flood my consciousness without moorings, without anchor. *Obeah.*

When I was a child, I used to try to pry apart the tendrils of vines that twisted and curled around each other in the lush fullness of the rainy season. But they always sprang back like the coils in my mattress and slipped into the curves they had made of one another. So it had been for me with obeah and Catholicism: they were intertwined. I questioned neither, though I taught myself to be ashamed of one. *When the time came,* Courtney had said. Perhaps.

Perhaps, too, it would mean nothing to the nuns if I told them: No, I don't want your scholarship. Perhaps they would find another salve for their consciences. And if these girls and their envelope-giving parents could carry their secrets and laugh, why not I? They had done their part for integration. They had helped their Negroes at the College of the Sacred Heart. Why should they care that not one black among them was American? Angela insisted on saris. I let the Knights of Columbus scare me into silence with their nightmares of burning and looting Negroes. Courtney kept her distance.

Angela had tried to look cheerful when the girls packed to go home that summer. I heard the promises between the laughter.

"I'll call you when I get home."

"Maybe you can spend some time with me this summer."

"I'll ask my parents."

I didn't have the heart to tell her that Molly's invitation to her home at Easter was the last she would get. That between the assassination of John F. Kennedy and the triumph of George Wallace in Milwaukee, ethnic distinctions had become irrelevant.

Now they saw her as they saw me—both of us black. We had served our purpose in Oshkosh. There was no need to take us home.

The day came finally that they were gone, and when the last car, heavy with luggage, bumped down the road over holes carved from the asphalt by the ice of that past winter, I went looking for Sister Agnes. Not even the newness of the freshly turned earth, the long stretches of dirt mounds and narrow canals smelling of the countryside in Trinidad before the planting of the cane fields; not even the flashes of tulips that suddenly had appeared in barrels at the end of the field where the college began, and which, since the spring, had made the walk to the college almost pleasurable, could shake my resolve, my determination to confront Sister Agnes with the lines I had memorized to say to her.

She was surprised to see me.

"Missing your friends so soon?"

I blurted out the words I had rehearsed before her sea green eyes, before the smile that had formed on her lips and her arms outstretched to embrace me could trick me into remembering her kindness to me, could cause me to have the slightest sliver of a doubt. I could not allow my thinking her incapable of deceit to fizzle all the promises I had made to myself, and the things I told Courtney I would do. I could not say nothing.

"I want you to take back your scholarship," I said. The words came out of my mouth clearly. Precisely. I did not raise my voice.

Nothing changed in her face. The smile remained. The eyes still sparkled. She embraced me. "Come. Come sit with me." She took my hand and led me to the leather couch that faced her desk.

"No." I looked away from her eyes. "I just came to tell you that."

"And what is that, Sara?" She sat down and placed her hand

on the cushion of the seat next to her. "Come here." She made tiny, gentle circles on the seat with her palm. I felt her pulling me to her, but I resisted.

I took a step backward. "I want to return my scholarship."

Her hand stopped still. "Have you thought this through?"

"When I was in Milwaukee," I said, "I saw hundreds of black people there. I think you should give one of them my scholarship."

"Just like that?" Sea green eyes forced me to meet them. "Just like that, Sara? I should go to Milwaukee and pick one of the Negro girls on the street and give her your scholarship?"

"That's not what I meant." I didn't know what to do with my hands standing there in front of her with nothing to lean on, nothing to latch onto. My knees felt weak. "May I sit on this chair?" I pointed to the armchair opposite the couch as far from where she sat as possible.

She did not stop me. Her hand remained on the cushion but she was no longer patting the leather, beckoning me to sit next to her. "What did you mean, Sara?" she asked.

"When I was in Milwaukee," I began again, "I realized for the first time how odd it was that Courtney, Angela and I were the only colored people in this college, and then I began to wonder."

"Wonder what?" She raised her eyebrows and challenged me to answer her. I looked away.

"I began to wonder why it is you had to go so far to find us. I mean, you had to go all across the United States, over the Atlantic, to find us. I mean, you had to go not only to St. Lucia, but to Trinidad and Guiana. I mean, there's Milwaukee, not even two hours away, but you had to go miles. I—"

She cut me off. "Are you finished?" Her voice, though soft, clashed against the escalation of my own with each "I mean" and forced me to look at her.

"Is there more, Sara?"

I struggled to find the rest, but when the words came out, they were not as harsh as I had planned them. "It seems to me, Sister Agnes, that you prefer to have us than them. I don't know why, but that's how it seems and I can't accept this."

"You think you're taking someone else's spot? Is that it?"

"Yes, but not that alone. I think that's how you want it to be."

She got up and walked to the window behind her desk. "You know, Sara, I had a lot of hopes for you." She had her back toward me but I could tell from the movements of her arms and shoulders that she was rolling her hands over and over each other. I knew I had touched a nerve. She turned around. "Is this what you want?"

"Yes, but I want you to know why. I want you to know that I don't want your scholarship because—" I stumbled. The words would not come. "Because," I tried again, "there are others who need it more."

Why couldn't I say what I really wanted to? Because you're living a lie through me. Because you're using me. Was it the sailboats that stopped me, the ones that drifted across her eyes? Was it because I didn't mean her alone, but all of them? Was it because the nuns in my school in Trinidad had already taught me that their goodness was not to be questioned? That the infallibility of the Pope was extended also to them?

"Where will you go?" Her question was cool. No guilt shaded her eyes.

"To Mississippi."

She was unprepared for my answer.

"Mississippi?" Now there was guilt. Her shoulders sagged. Her eyes turned misty and she reached for the top of the high-backed armchair at her desk. "Mississippi?" she repeated.

"I know what's going on here," I said.

"Oh. So that's it?"

"Yes," I said.

She sat down and regained her composure. "So you think you're more righteous than we are? Is that it? You've come to judge us." She spread her hands in front of her. "Let me tell you something, Sara, and listen well. The Church has been to a million Mississippis for longer than either you or I, or our grandmothers, great-grandmothers, great-great-grandmothers could remember. You talk about the Negro people in Milwaukee and I suppose you want to tell me about the Negroes in Mississippi, and then you'll tell me about the colored people in Trinidad, St. Lucia and Guiana. Well, Sara, to the Church it's all one family. All one people in need, and the Church ministers to those people and does not ask who or where they come from. Where they got their black skins. Where they were born. The Church goes to Trinidad, and yes, to St. Lucia and Guiana and Africa and India, and any other country where people are in need, and the Church does what it can. It's not just for you and Courtney and Angela. We educate Courtney, and she goes back to St. Lucia, and we educate Angela and the same happens. There's money here, Sara. The government here has money. It has money to educate the Negroes you saw in Milwaukee. We help where there is no money. No hope. Don't be so quick to judge us. We work where we are most needed."

Two lines popped into my head—"Love thy neighbor as you love thyself," and "Charity begins at home"—but I didn't say them to her. Years at a convent school in Trinidad had taught me to hold my tongue. Yet I came as close as I could.

"My grandmother always told us that we had to get our house in order before we could fix anyone else's."

For a moment she seemed shocked by my boldness. Her mouth opened and then closed again. She sat up straight. "Our house is in order, Sara," she said quietly. She touched the black crucifix at her breast and let out her breath. Her voice was strong again when she spoke. "The house of the Church is in order, Sara. What about you? Is your house in order? You will give up your scholarship and what will that do? I give you back your grandmother's advice. What do you think that will do to your parents? What about the other girls back home? Your cousins, your friends? What will they think? They'll only see your failure, Sara. Your failure, not your reasons. And what about the children in Trinidad that you could help if you become a teacher? What about your house, Sara?"

"I want to go to Mississippi."

"Why? Because you have a boyfriend there? You have no secrets, Sara. Mr. O'Brien told me."

No secrets? I was not surprised. The O'Briens had told her about the first time I visited them. It was only a matter of time before they would tell her about Sam, too.

"Sam's a friend," I said.

"A secret one."

I knew she was trying to bait me, but it was she who had secrets, burying them under the layers of half-truths she wove around me, the guilt she was trying to transfer to me.

"I didn't think you wanted to meet him," I said. "He's just a friend."

"And you'll go all the way to Mississippi to be with him? He means that much to you?"

"No. That's not it."

"Then what is? Do you know what's going on down there, Sara? Can you? Do you think you can understand?"

"Sam knows." She was breaking down my defenses.

"Yes, he knows. That's why he's there. But do you? He's not looking for some boyfriend-girlfriend tryst, you know. This is serious with him."

"That's not it." I barely heard my voice.

"That's why *you* want to go."

"No!"

"Then why?"

"I can't live with being here when that's there."

"Speak up, Sara. I can't hear you."

"I can't stay here telling your lies when I know you wouldn't have one of them in your college."

She opened the top drawer of her desk and took out a black leather book. She hooked her glasses carefully over her ears and adjusted them on her nose.

"Do you know who pays for your scholarship?" She opened the book. "Not us. Not the nuns here. The First Independence Bank on Main Street, Nickelstein's Diner, Marlow's Cinema, Ye Olde Record Shoppe." She ran her fingers lightly over the names. "The Knights of Columbus, Mr. and Mrs. Irving Salzer, Mr. and Mrs. Allan Upshaw, Mr. and Mrs. Bernard Kraus, Mr. and Mrs. Michael Held. Contributions, Sara, to a scholarship fund for you, Courtney and Angela." She looked over her glasses at me. "The fund would end, Sara, if you went to Mississippi. Not just for you, but for everyone else. Do you understand me? Do you want that?"

I felt the tears coming. I bit my lower lip and held it still.

"You have to think beyond yourself, Sara. Think how your actions might hurt other people. I know you're missing this Mr. Maxwell. This Sam."

"No. That's not it," I said again. The words trembled from my lips.

"These people don't see what your boyfriend sees in Mississippi. They think the Negroes are pushing too fast. Too quickly. They think they're forcing the hands of the white people in the South. I can't judge them and neither can you. I don't like what's happening in Mississippi. I don't like what the whites are doing, but I haven't lived in their shoes. 'There, but for the grace of God, go I.' Perhaps if I had slaves, and I had treated them well—

as some had done, Sara. Not all of them were cruel, you know. If I had freed them and given them land, I would find it hard to understand why they needed to sit down with me at my dinner table. And I wouldn't understand why they might want to burn down my shops. The people here in Oshkosh think the Negroes are moving too fast. People need time to adjust. Things fall into place but you can't push them."

"You think they are right?"

"Who? You mean the whites in the South? No, they're not right. But neither are the Negroes. When you put pressure on something it will give in, but it will only be a matter of time before it adjusts itself back out again. Like the seat you're sitting on, Sara. Get up. Look at it."

I did not move.

"The seat will cave in from the weight of your body, but in a few seconds it will balloon out again. Force, conflict, wars, they never set things right. That's how the people here see it. They think the courts should settle this matter. That's how change will last. When it's done that way, through the courts, change will endure. Nothing can be won with a war. And that's what this is. A second Civil War. People here don't think it's right. The South should know better how much there's to lose. People here won't take sides. They won't participate. If you go to Mississippi they'll think you're using their hard-earned money to support a fight they don't think is necessary. Or justified. And they won't take any more chances with any of you. That may mean Courtney, and Angela, too. Do you understand? I'm talking about their scholarships, also. Do you want that responsibility?"

There was no sea left in her eyes. Only green. Hard as emeralds and shining.

"Is Sam Maxwell worth all that, Sara?" She paused and studied her fingernails. "What was the name of the boy before Sam? Was it Eric? Yes, the boy who caused you not to finish high school. I'll have to tell the Immigration Department, Sara, if you leave here, you know. No scholarship, no college. No college, no student visa. You can't stay in America without a visa. You know that, Sara. What will you do?"

The tears spilled rapidly down my cheeks.

"Is that what you want? You'll return to Trinidad a failure. And because of the same problem. Eric then, Sam now."

She had boxed me in, closed in the sides and nailed the wood. With each word she spoke, I felt the walls of her room close in on me, squeezing out the air I breathed.

"Learn to control yourself, Sara. Learn."

Great-grandmother Bertha tied to a bed in St. Ann's.

I was still floundering, flapping like a fish struggling to disentangle myself from the net thrown over me when I found Courtney waiting for me outside Sister Agnes's door.

"Forget her. Forget them," she said. "Keep your eyes on your purpose." She put her arm around me.

Later, I told her what Sister Agnes had said.

"It's that horse crap they talk about universality," she said. "They use it when it serves them. All of us are brothers and sisters, they say. One big pool of black people. Yet they know what they're doing when they give to you and to me and not to their own black people. They know the statement they're making. You keep your mind on your purpose. Get your degree, then back to Trinidad."

I told her what hurt me most: that she said I wanted to go to Mississippi only because of Sam. That I didn't understand what was going on. Couldn't.

"Told you so," said Courtney. "That's how Sam sees it, too. And perhaps, you can't understand, but no, I don't think you want to go only for him." She smiled at me.

"How can I stay now?"

"You can," she said.

"How?"

"Your turn will come," she said. "Remember. Obeah."

The tall, thin men with skin like the bark of aged coconut trees. They stood there looking at me, waiting. I smelled the sweet scent of burning roots.

There was no summer school at the College of the Sacred Heart. For three whole months there would be no girls to confront in the dormitory. At first I took pleasure in that knowledge. Then, one week went by and the stillness scared me. The silence in the long, white corridors, the echo of three voices—Courtney's, Angela's, mine—bounced against the emptiness of rooms left gaping wide, beds stripped bare but for white mattress covers. No posters were left on the walls, no books on shelves. The girls had taken every shred of their presence, and left us with rows of empty bedrooms, stretches of bathroom stalls, cold, white tiles and polished chrome mocking: *Wasn't life better when we were here?*

Now in the quiet of the dormitory, Bertha began to trouble me, to fill me with doubts. What if my only reason was Sam? What if Sister Agnes was right?

I tried to avoid Sister Agnes. If I saw her on my way to the hospital kitchen, I hid and waited until she was gone, even if it meant being late for work. Her shadow taunted me. I was the willing reflection of her deceit. I was knowingly letting her use me to keep her conscience clear for Communion on Sundays. Every day I kept my scholarship, I was in complicity with her. I, too, was guilty. She had trapped me.

A blue-eyed black priest bearing gifts. My mother had not trusted those eyes. But now, unlike my father, I had no tool shed to set on fire. Silence was my only weapon against her.

I turned to Angela to rescue me with her cheerfulness, Angela, who had not given a single thought about the reason why she had been selected—except to sing praises to the generosity of the nuns.

"How did you manage last summer?" I asked her.

"Manage?" She made my question seem foolish. "Manage? I loved it. Courtney and I had the dorm to ourselves. We could do anything we wanted, anytime we wanted. It was fun."

"What did you do?"

"Lots of things. Not every day, of course, but we were busy. Lots of things."

I left her with the illusions she had created to make her own loneliness bearable. I didn't ask, Like what? Tell me one thing, Angela. One thing you did. But Angela had no ghosts, no Berthas, although she must have felt the silence, too—the emptiness, as I did.

CHAPTER 12

I was prepared for June to be the most difficult month. In the silence and loneliness of Oshkosh without Sam, without the chance to talk to him, to see him, I knew I would be haunted by the decision I had made to stay at the College of the Sacred Heart. That my guilt over my acceptance of and complicity in my betrayal would mushroom and mock me in that silence. But by the end of June those feelings would become much less significant, much less a source of torment than the frightening discovery that my weekend with Sam had not been without its consequences. That my mother had not been entirely wrong to have warned me of pain, to have tried to delay as long as she could the moment I would take a man inside me. She knew I was not ready.

But before that last week in June I thought only of July when my Sam would return. He wrote long letters filling me with such detail about Mississippi, I could have been there. He told me about the resistance he, Harry, and the others in their group were encountering daily as they tried to find ways for black people in the towns of Meridian and Philadelphia to register to vote in the coming presidential elections that fall. Philadelphia, Sam wrote, was a town seething with hatred, its name, "city of brotherly love," belying its reality. The Ku Klux Klan marched in broad daylight, bearing the messages of the white citizenry of Mississippi, spewing the hatred that the more genteel dared not voice.

"The best lack all conviction and the worst are full of passionate intensity," quoted Sam, and so it was in Philadelphia. Yeats's immortal words came to life on the streets of Mississippi, as the police stood smirking on the sidelines, dressed for war with guns slung high on their hips and clubs, freshly cleaned of the blood of innocents, beating an impatient rhythm on their palms. The responsible people of Philadelphia, the ones who later declared their shock over the events that occurred the third week of that June—the teachers, physicians, social workers, clergy— hid themselves behind closed doors and curtained windows, their silence giving the Klansmen authority. "Niggers!" the Klansmen screamed on their behalf, Sam wrote. "Niggers!" as if the word itself were a cancerous sore to be gutted from their bellies. *Niggers, go back to your stinking houses.*

I got a chance to see the news on TV now that the girls were gone for the summer, to see the senseless civil war between blacks and whites that offended the sensibilities of the people in Oshkosh, the war they found so unnecessary and unjustified that they wouldn't take sides. I saw blue veins straining against the contorted sinews of reddened necks. The children surprised me most. They held their mother's hands and mimicked their fathers: "Niggers! Niggers! Back to the fields, niggers!" So young. I thought of the games we played as children in Trinidad: Ring a ring of roses pocket full of posies/rise, Sally, rise, Sally/they all fall down. Those were not the games these children played: Get the nigger, Daddy/get the nigger, Daddy/get the nigger, Daddy, before the nigger gets me. I wondered what kind of adults they would make. What new world of their making was waiting to be born?

Sam said it was becoming more and more difficult for him to assume responsibility for persuading black people to leave the safety of their communities and risk bodily harm just for the right to vote. Fears die hard in Mississippi, even when the Department of Justice is on your side, he told me.

"And what if Johnson does not win the election?" Sam asked me one night on the phone. I longed to give him the right answer, but mostly to please him. The revolting images of man's inhumanity I saw on the television news, sandwiched between happy commercials, lingered now in my consciousness and I could no longer dismiss his tales as fiction. When the screen turned black, there was Sam to verify it all for me. Yet I was not affected as he was. What was happening in Mississippi was not as personal for me as it was for Sam.

"And what if Lyndon B. Johnson lost?"

Sam's voice was filled with terror. "Then Goldwater would win."

The words came out garbled as if he were strangling on them. I could feel his fear, but I did not understand.

Then, in Longdale, a small black community immediately north of Philadelphia, the Klan burned a black church to the ground. On the face of it nothing was special or significant about the burning. The Klan had already made a habit of burning the homes of black people, of destroying their property, but this fire touched a sensitive chord in Sam, the final disrespect he would endure.

"Even in war, a house of worship is sacrosanct," Sam said when he called, his voice straining with emotion. He and some of the guys in their group were going to Longdale the next morning to investigate. This was a crime that would not go unaccounted for.

That was the day everything changed, when I forced myself to look beyond the guilt that had been consuming me. I pushed it aside to make a space for Sam's suffering, for his feelings of pain, and in the sudden clearing, the slit that formed between feeling sorry for myself and feeling compassion for Sam, a reality I had been trying to ignore for days crystallized, and I came face to face with the likelihood that I was pregnant. I had felt tenderness around the edges of my breasts for some time now, but had fooled myself into believing my period was imminent.

Courtney had first caused me to worry when she had asked me casually, "You and Sam didn't get into anything in Milwaukee, did you?"

When I didn't answer, she pressed me. "You were smart enough to use something, weren't you?"

I looked away and she came close to me. "Then Sam used something, didn't he?"

I couldn't answer her. I couldn't tell her it never came up. That Sam didn't ask. Perhaps he assumed, but in all the times we made love that weekend in May, Sam never once broke the magic by asking.

But I didn't need to give Courtney an answer. She clicked her tongue and shifted her slanted almond eyes to the ceiling. "You better pray nothing happens."

Now, as Sam told me about Longdale, I felt the nausea mount in my throat, the same nausea I had suffered that morning and the morning before. As he gave me images of the desecrated church, its charred wooden frame reeking with the sour smell of rain-soaked debris fermenting in the sun, I fought against the heaving in my stomach, evidence of the possibility, the almost certainty now, of the child I bore in my womb. I saw the hollow anger of the people he described. I saw them wrapped in mournful circles around their ruined church and I felt the futility of their struggle.

"I don't think there's anything to be gained by your going to Longdale," I said to him, not realizing then how closely I echoed Sister Agnes.

Sam's vision was different from mine. "We want to know who did it," he said. His voice was tense with determination.

"But you already know. The Klan," I said.

"We want to prove it."

"And where will that get you?"

"We'll demand justice!" he shouted.

"Sam, for my sake, don't be a martyr."

I had meant those words in the idiomatic way I had used them many times before, but suddenly the word *martyr* reverberated in my ears, vibrating with the weight of hagiography—the stories the nuns had told me of the early Christians who were stoned to death for their causes, disemboweled by the vicious fangs of ravenous lions for the sake of their convictions. And I saw my Sam in a blinding flash of light, clearly, unmistakably, ablaze on a burning cross of the Klansmen. I became almost hysterical.

"Don't go, Sam. Don't go!"

When Sam hung up the phone, after telling me calmly that if his friend Epstein, whose battle this wasn't, was willing to go, then he, Sam, couldn't be less of a man, I felt the certainty of the fulfillment of my premonition.

Courtney called me to the phone on the night of June 21, the day Sam was supposed to go to Longdale. I thought the worst. My lips turned pale and trembled. Angela, worried for me, asked, "What is it, Sara? What's the matter?" Then Courtney told me Sam was on the line and the fear left my eyes. Sam was fine. He was alive. But he was crying. Three men, Schwerner, Goodman and Chaney, had gone to Longdale and had not returned.

❖

That night I knew I could not tell Sam I thought I might be pregnant. Not then. He was wreathed in guilt and grief over the disappearance of Chaney, Schwerner and Goodman, who, he told me, were on their way back to Meridian from Longdale when they were stopped by the police in Philadelphia for speeding. Chaney, a young black plasterer, was driving. He was arrested immediately and thrown in jail. The other two were also held. "For investigation," said Deputy Sheriff Cecil Ray Price, defending his actions. A "nigrah" driving two white boys was highly suspect. Price claimed he had to detain the white boys for their own protection. But he released them after only five hours had passed. And now, Chaney, Schwerner and Goodman had not returned to Meridian. Sam blamed himself.

"If only I had been there," he agonized. "If only—"

I told him it was too early for grief. His friends would be back. But he was inconsolable. He and Harry Epstein had been about to leave with their three friends when a woman came to their center, blood streaming down her face. Someone had hurled a stone at her from a passing car. Sam had no choice. He had to help her. Schwerner, Goodman and Chaney were already in the station wagon. Harry stayed back with Sam.

Sam had not listened to me, I thought. My entreaties had not moved him. Yet had he gone, he would not have been safe. Fate was working on my side. Later, Courtney would tell me the spirits had been listening to me, and I would remember that I carried a bag of herbs blessed by an obeahman and wore a St. Jude medal under my blouse.

Now Sam was saying: "I couldn't turn my back on her. She didn't want to come. I tried to persuade her. I promised her protection. I told her nothing would happen to her. You understand, Sara. You understand I couldn't just leave her and go with them."

He wanted me to ease his guilt, to help him find a way to live with the fact that he had escaped whatever misfortune had befallen his friends, but all I could think was that God had spared him for me. "No," I said. "You couldn't leave her." And I thanked God he was alive.

Soon Sam's agony, though I felt it acutely, became less important to me. When the waves of nausea left and I lay on my bed in the darkened room, I saw the horror of my situation spread out before me. My situation, not Sam's. Had I not told him simply because he had too much else on his mind? There were other times when he had called and I had thought my pregnancy possible. Why hadn't I said something then? Anything that might have led him to ask me more, to bring me to a full confession: *Sam, I don't feel well. Sam, I get sick in the mornings.* Was it because I had only myself to blame? I had been too much in love to be cautious. My excesses, those that had caused my father to so fear for my sanity that he would voice no opposition to my going to Oshkosh though he knew better, those feelings Sister Agnes had warned me to control, had once again entrapped me.

I looked at Angela on the bed across from me. I had called her girlish and yet even she knew that feelings left raw and naked could get you in trouble. She had mastered the disguise. She knew how to protect herself. I should not have made love to Sam. I knew when I went to Milwaukee it was possible. I should have controlled myself. And what could I do now? I stared into the darkness, terrified to confront the answer.

In the morning I rushed to the bathroom again, bile pushing against the edges of my mouth. Angela watched me silently as I returned to my bed. Some of her gaiety had left her when the girls had gone home for the summer, but still she said no word against them. If Molly had hurt her, she kept her pain to herself, but she also did not mention her friend's name again.

"Are you all right?" she asked.

My skin felt damp and clammy. I put my hand to my forehead. "I feel a little sick," I admitted.

"Do you think it's something you ate or drank?" She watched me more closely, a frown gathering in her brow.

"No."

"Should I tell Sister Agnes?"

I sat up abruptly, placed my hand over my mouth and shook my head vigorously.

"Are you sure?"

"Yes," I said. "Please, Angela. I'll be fine."

"Because if you aren't—"

I held her hand and forced myself to speak calmly. "I'm fine. Really I am."

She seemed uncertain at first and then a smile broke across her face. She patted the top of my hand. "I want you to know you can count on me if anything happens to you."

I felt her sincerity. There were only the three of us now. I felt she wanted to strengthen the bonds between us. "Nothing will," I said. Yet in spite of the friendship she offered, I didn't feel safe giving her the truth.

"Well, if . . . Courtney's not your only friend you know."

I let go of her hand.

Then for the first time, Angela asked me a personal question. "Are you going to see your other friend a lot this summer?" When I looked at her in surprise, she dropped her eyes. "You could have told me, you know." She brushed her hair off her shoulders and twisted it in a knot behind her head. "I hear you on the phone almost every night."

"I met him at the O'Brien's." I felt no remorse. She had told me nothing of her social life.

"Oh?"

"After Thanksgiving."

"So you'll be seeing him this summer?"

"I don't know. Maybe."

"Well, I'm not going to see mine at all."

I fought against the bile rising again in my throat.

"Why not?"

"He wants too much."

"Oh," I said weakly.

"You know what I mean. Girls like us don't do things like that back home."

I rushed to the bathroom.

Girlish Angela, bubbly Angela who struggled to keep her grades above C had proven she was smarter than I, more honorable than I. *Girls like us don't do things like that back home.* That was the shame that plagued me.

Courtney didn't have to ask me. She sensed immediately what was wrong. I now worked alongside her on the conveyor belt for the large dishwashing machine. This move was a sort of promotion from chopping vegetables. We were paid twenty-five cents more an hour. Together we scraped dirty dishes and placed them on the belt on which they would come out clean and dry from the machines. I hated the job. The half-eaten food strewn on the hospital white plates revolted me. On the first days I gagged uncontrollably, nauseated by thoughts of seeping wounds and bloody bandages. Courtney sometimes let me spend all my time on the clean end of the belt. She'd seen worse than this on the cocoa estates in St. Lucia, she said, when the insecticides the owners had brought from England polluted the water. Then pus oozed from open wounds on the bodies of the children.

For some time now I had wanted to ask her about her life in St. Lucia and about the boyfriend whose letter Angela had read, but I could not do that without betraying Angela. Now she had opened a way with her talk about cocoa.

"Do you know about growing things?" I asked her. Angela had told me that Courtney and her boyfriend had a farm together.

"No," she said. "Why would you ask?"

Her face revealed nothing. I searched for an answer that would not give away what I knew. "You mentioned cocoa and insecticides," I said.

"Yes. Well, yes. That was the English way. We were their guinea pigs. They tested the insecticides on us. You think they'd use it first in England? The children were already corpses before they died. The poisons had rotted away their insides. I've seen worse than this that makes you sick." She turned her back on me and drew the curtain down on her past.

Days later when I continued to gag in front of the dirty dishes, she watched me suspiciously. Sometimes, my hand across my mouth, I barely made the bathroom.

One day she questioned me directly.

"What are you going to do?"

I could not answer her.

"Have you told Sam?"

"No," I said.

"Good."

The tone of finality in her voice bothered me.

"I plan to tell him soon," I said.

"It's best you don't tell him. You'll have to deal with it by yourself, anyhow."

"Deal with it?"

"You have only two choices, Sara, and neither includes Sam. You know what they are. Tell me when you choose."

She had mentioned the unmentionable, not giving voice to it, of course, but I knew the alternatives. At night I worked out the one for which she'd given me no hope. When Schwerner, Goodman and Chaney came back, or when they were found, I'd tell Sam. We'd get married. I'd move to Milwaukee. I'd work.

Sam would go to school and work at night. When the baby came, I'd stay home for a while. Then I'd send the baby home to Trinidad. Didn't my mother want more children? But there my planning broke down, for I saw the shame and grief I would bring to my family. In only one year I would have crushed their dreams, their hopes that this daughter who had not become a swan could yet be redeemed.

Courtney was in the bathroom with me the next morning as I heaved into the sink.

"Did you choose?" she asked.

I shook my head.

"Did you tell Sam?"

"He has his troubles." I told her about Sam's work with the voter registration campaign and the three missing men. "When they're found, I'll tell him."

She shook her head. "The work he's doing down there is not going to end so soon. Don't expect him to come back for you."

"He will."

"Don't raise your hopes."

"Then what will I do?"

"That's for you to decide," she said. "Choose. Then let me know."

Three days passed and Sam didn't call. I telephoned him at the number he'd given me but no one answered. I fluctuated between hope and despair. Hope, that not hearing from Sam, not being able to get in touch with him meant he'd found his friends. He was too busy to call me, I reasoned. At best, the men had been found and they were hurt. Sam needed to be with them in the hospital. Despair, that they had not been found.

Angela now began to sense that something was really wrong with me. I tried to look cheerful for her, but I knew she heard the sounds I made in the bathroom. She thought I should see a doctor. She asked me again if I wanted her to tell Sister Agnes I was ill. I begged her to keep silent. She seemed to take pity on me.

"I'm here," she said, "if you need me."

Courtney said my nausea was psychosomatic. It wasn't normal for a woman to be so sick in the first few days. I had to free my mind, she said, or I would get quite sick and then they'd have to take me to the hospital.

My great-grandmother Bertha tied to a bed in a hospital in St. Ann's. Courtney frightened me into thinking of another alternative, perhaps one of the two she had in mind, but I pushed the thought away and invented another fantasy. I would leave college. I would return to Trinidad. I would live with my friend Zeta. My mother had written that Zeta was now living with a newspaper reporter. She had already shamed her family. I could do that. Zeta could help me raise the baby.

But I had none of Zeta's strength and self-confidence. One small rejection from a man had sent me cowering to my room for weeks. How would I endure the loss of Sam? And how would I survive my family's rejection? Trinidad was too small a place to find myself outside the circle of family and friends. I did not have Zeta's courage. I was no heroine.

The next time I gagged over the dirty dishes, I knew what choice I had to make.

"I've decided," I said to Courtney.

"Are you sure?"

I nodded. "Can you help me?"

"I know what to do."

I had smelled the incense she burned in her room under the photographs of four little coffins. Incense smelled like the roots the obeahwoman had burned the day the canal alongside my house ran red and I found my mother lying on her bed in a pool of blood.

"Have you done it before?" I asked her.

"It's you who have to be sure."

"But have you?"

She nodded. "Yes. Is that what you've decided?" She, too, did not name the unmentionable.

"Yes."

"You have to be absolutely sure."

"I am. Can you help me?"

"Yes, if it is right," she said.

She had one stipulation. "You must not tell Angela anything. Not that you are pregnant. Not what we are going to do. She will not understand."

Courtney chose a Sunday. Angela was going to sing at the Hotel Dixon. She would be away all afternoon. We had the day off from the kitchen. I asked her if it would hurt. She said perhaps I was having second thoughts. I said no. She said pain is relative. I asked her relative to what? Woman's pain, she said.

I knew she was talking about childbirth.

Every day of the five days until Sunday I prayed to St. Jude of the impossible cases for Sam to call me. I knew that something had gone terribly wrong with his friends. The newspapers in Oshkosh were cautious, but they reported that Schwerner, Goodman and Chaney were still missing. They gave no specific facts about the the Longdale Church burning or about Deputy Sheriff Cecil Ray Price's investigation: the irregularity of jailing three men and then releasing them suddenly after five hours. Soon I began to pray for them, too. Selfishly. If they turned up, Sam would call. I willed them to be released. I prayed that their captors' hearts would soften.

As Sunday approached, however, Schwerner, Goodman and Chaney became my enemies, standing between Sam and me, keeping my Sam from contacting me. Why did they have to go to Longdale? They had willfully walked into danger. Even I knew that there was something unnatural about people who would let their hatred fly in the face of God. People who would burn down His house of worship were people capable of anything, of committing the most atrocious crimes against humanity. Did the voter registration workers think they were immune from the wrath of such vicious men? Were they so anxious for martyrdom? I would not have gone to Longdale without protection. I would have left the investigating to the investigators. I would have sought help. Surely among the police in Mississippi there were those who were not corrupt. Surely there were those who could be moved to righteous anger over the senseless cruelty inflicted on people who had done nothing wrong, who had only asked to be permitted to exercise their right to vote.

In my desperate need for Sam, in the chaos of emotions that ran through me, I blamed Schwerner, Goodman and Chaney for the decision I now had to make. If they had not gone to Mississippi, if Sam were not consumed with grief, I would not be alone. He would have called. He would have come. He would have worked out this problem with me.

Sunday was not as I had hoped, dark and dreary. There were days like that in the early summer in Oshkosh when it seemed that the sun would never rise. Sheets of rain poured down from a blackened sky. Sometimes between their glistening streaks, the drops hid small, hard pebbles of ice that struck with vicious force the delicate flower buds of plants still trembling with newness from the just-thawed earth. It was such a day that I wanted. A day that would lash out at me, berate me for the abominable thing I was about to do. But Sunday was a sunny day, a warm and beautiful day. A picture postcard day. The sky was blue, the clouds white and cottony and all around me the greenery shimmered. Nothing foreshadowed the terrible thing I was about to do.

Angela expressed reluctance to work on such a day and filled me with guilt.

"I could stay out in the sunshine all day and look at the wind dance through the trees," she said. I had never before heard such poetry from her. My plans for the afternoon were made even more sordid.

"Couldn't you, Sara? It's days such as these when Oshkosh feels like home. Do you hear the sounds of the trees? Remember, Sara?"

I remembered.

Once, in the early spring, the O'Briens took us to their summer house north of Oshkosh. When we saw the lake shimmering blue, we rushed into it, so desperate were we for the sea. But the blue was not the sea blue we knew but an ice blue, and it took two woolen blankets and a fire to stop our bodies from shivering.

So, too, one day in the winter, when the sun burst through the clouds and lit up the sky, I remembered Trinidad. I ran outside to the sun that day, believing it would warm me.

"Today is not a day for staying indoors," Angela sang. "I think I'll call Mrs. O'Brien. Maybe they won't mind if I don't go to the hotel. What are you going to do, Sara? Maybe I'll do what you are doing."

She didn't wait for my answer.

"Maybe I'll just go, anyway. It'll be good to sing on a day like this. What are your plans, Sara?" She came to my desk where I was sitting, staring at a book, pretending to read, wishing the sun would not feel so warm and familiar on my skin.

"You're not going to stay in and read all day." She was playing with her hair, tossing it from side to side.

I wanted to cry. Innocent, girlish, self-controlled Angela. She could stop seeing her boyfriend because she didn't do things that good girls weren't supposed to do.

"Why don't you come with me? You haven't for a long time. Not since Christmas. Why don't you? Sometimes they wonder when they see I'm East Indian. You make it authentic. We could sing "Yellow Bird" together. If you want, you could just hum. Here, let me show you."

I must have had tears in my eyes when I turned to face her. I saw the reflection of my unhappiness in her face. She wrinkled her nose as if some unpleasant odor had wafted across the room and then forced a thin smile.

"It was only a suggestion," she said. "I didn't mean you had to go. Really, you don't have to. Why don't you go for a walk with Courtney? It'll do you good. Look, I'll see you when I come back."

That was the way it was with Angela.

Courtney came for me as soon as Angela left. "We'll do it in my room," she said. She seemed so detached. I wondered if she really knew what we were about to do. We had not named it yet—not even discussed it. Courtney had a way of making me feel that there was no need to question what she said. She knew everything. In her hands there was no reason for doubts.

"Did you tell Angela you won't be home tonight?" she asked me as we walked toward her room.

"No," I said.

"That was foolish. She'll be looking for you."

"Do I need to spend the whole night in your room?"

"That's what I told you three days ago. Have you changed your mind?" She stopped and watched me carefully. Her eyes were expressionless.

"No," I said quickly. "Why do you think that?"

She turned her face away and continued to walk toward her room. "I'll tell Angela for you. I'll find something believable to say." She opened her door.

The first thing I noticed was that the bulletin board had been covered with a black felt cloth. Then I saw that all the cosmetics had been removed from her dresser, which was now draped with a white cotton sheet. A wide-mouthed, speckled blue enamel basin sat on top of the dresser, long green leaves floating within, in a shallow pool of water, leaves unlike any I had seen in Oshkosh. The books, too, had been removed from her desk, which was covered with a white sheet as well. The dolls Angela feared were laid against the back of the desk, one in the middle, the others at either end. In front of the middle doll was a thin, long, pointed silver rod, no more than one-sixteenth of an inch thick and about six inches long. Next to the rod was a clear bottle containing a dark brown liquid. Little solid black flecks, slightly thicker than grains of sand, were suspended in the fluid, defying all earthly laws of gravity. Next to the bottle was a large, speckled blue enamel cup that matched the basin on the dresser.

The floors of the room were bare. Courtney had removed the two white shaggy rugs that were usually in front of the two beds. The nuns had never taken out the extra unneeded bed when there were no other girls to share Courtney's room with her. Courtney had predicted that she would not have a room-mate even before we were told that the girl had decided at the last minute to go to the University of Wisconsin.

Courtney's bed was, as usual, neatly covered with the thin, pale pink corded coverlet that we all used. It was pushed next to the other bed, which had been stripped except for brown rubber sheeting that lay in the middle of the mattress. At the foot of that bed, which I assumed was for me, another enamel basin, a white one, was filled with clear water. Alongside was a stack of white rags.

The curtains in the room were drawn, shutting out the sunlight, but a strange light trembled against the walls. I looked across the room to the other desk and saw six thick candles flickering on top of the bookcase. I drew in my breath. Courtney held my hand and whispered softly, "Don't be afraid."

"Is this obeah?"

She pressed my hand. "Don't be afraid," she repeated.

"Do we need the candles?" I asked.

When I was a girl, we put candles on the graves of our dead relatives on All Souls Day. Dressed like a bride in my First Communion clothes, I clutched my bouquet of white candles and trailed behind my mother and aunts along the tiny, paved paths that divided the cemetery into street blocks. Once, kneeling beside Bertha's grave, a sudden breeze stirred the flames on the candles I had planted in a cross in the earth that covered Bertha. I felt the heat first, rising from Bertha. Then I saw yellow flames licking the frills on my white organza dress. A man with hair like black lamb's wool rushed toward me and wrapped me in the folds of his thick, black cape. The women dropped to their knees.

"A miracle!"

"A vision!"

My mother screamed.

Now the fear of being consumed by fire returned to me.

"Didn't you use candles in your church?" Courtney asked.

"When we prayed to the saints."

"Same thing," she said, and tightened her grip on my hand. "Come. Come close."

I fingered the St. Jude medal that dangled from the chain around my neck.

"There's nothing to be frightened of," she said. And I followed her because there was no place else to go, because I had already committed myself to a course of action, and because her voice was soothing and comforting to me.

"What we are going to do now is very simple," she said. "Don't be afraid. I will take care of you."

I let her calm my fears.

"I want you first to be sure, because when we do this, there is no turning back for either of us."

I wondered why not for her, and I asked.

"Because I am with you in this all the way," she said. "Do

you want to change your mind?"

I asked her about the white sheets on the dresser and desk, and about the enamel basins. I avoided the silver rod and the black-speckled brown liquid.

"Decorations," she said. "To make it feel like home."

I guessed she meant St. Lucia. I gathered my courage and asked about the dolls.

"They have nothing to do with you," she said, and frowned at me. Then, as quickly, her mood changed and the frown disappeared. "More decorations," she said. She waved her hand across her face as if she were swatting away a fly. "Like home."

"And what about that?" I pointed to the bottle, the needle and the cup.

"You'll find out soon enough."

"Will it hurt?"

"Do you want to do it?" she asked.

"I have no choice," I said.

"Everyone has a choice. Even you, now. Are you sure this is the right one?"

"This is the only thing I can do."

She seemed to accept my answer as final—unchangeable. She walked to the desk and poured the liquid into the cup.

"This will make you drowsy," she said. "It'll help you forget."

I took the enamel cup from her and put it to my lips. The second the liquid touched the nerves in my mouth I spat it out onto the floor, revolted by its bitter, burning taste.

Courtney clapped her hand tightly over my mouth. "No," she said sternly. "Don't do that again. If you know what you have to do, do it and take the bitterness."

She removed her hand from my mouth. "There," she said. "Go ahead. Drink."

I swallowed hard in gulps, quickly. Once the liquid passed my lips it did not taste as bitter or as burning, or at least with each gulp I took, less so. At first the small, solid, black flecks scratched the roof of my mouth, but even that sensation died away as I drank. Then I heard Courtney's voice in the distance: "Drink. Don't be a baby . . . baby . . . baby," and I slipped downward, legs first, into a pool of warm, salty water.

I knew when the rod entered my womb between my legs. I felt the blistering heat of a blow torch sear my flesh. I tried to scream, but something firm and hard clamped down on my mouth and my cries exploded in my head. Frantically, I snapped my legs upward to pull my body out of the water, but my ankles were held in a vise-like lock and I was yanked farther downward.

That was when I saw the mermaids, their smiling dark eyes lighting up their brown faces, their outstretched hands beckoning me. I grasped on to one of them when a sudden warm current rushed down my legs and tremors of pain rolled across my womb. She brushed her long, thick curls against my forehead and along my cheeks and soothed me. I recognized her. She was the mermaid who had seduced my cousin to the ocean floor. Desperate to forget that dreary, chilly island with her lies about motherhood, he had followed her to his death.

And I would have done the same had the sea cow not come to save me. For I was filled with such nostalgia for home, swimming with the mermaids among the dazzling pink coral flowers and the swaying locks of tall, luminescent, green sea grass, that I would have gone with them to the bottom of the sea. But at the very moment when a million tiny bubbles like beads of pearl rushed out of my mouth, the sea cow rescued me. She rode through the water a dark, giant shadow, pushing the sea, glazed like glass, in a V behind her. In a fizz of white water, the mermaids scattered. The sea cow wrapped her dwarfed arms around me and held me close, and then, in one swift movement, she lifted me upward to the surface of the sea. When we broke through the water, air rushed through my lungs. I gasped and coughed with the newness of it.

My first conscious sensation was of the smell of burning roots.

Courtney was bending over me, wiping my forehead with a damp towel. "Did it hurt you?"

"I had a dream," I said.

"A dream?"

"I dreamt I was swimming with the mermaids in Maracas Bay."

I drifted to sleep. When I woke up Courtney's room was the way it had always been: deodorant, lotion, face powder on her dresser; books on her bookshelves and on her desk neat piles of paper, a stapler, a pair of scissors, Scotch tape in a holder. There were no candles on her dresser, no smell of burning roots. The curtains were pulled back. I could see a bright moon outside.

"Were you scared?" Courtney asked.

"No," I said. "I never felt afraid but the sea cow took me away."

"What?"

My head swirled.

"What?" she asked again.

The image of the dark shadow that had snatched me from the mermaids shimmered before me.

"You said the sea cow took you away," Courtney was saying.

"No. I was with the mermaids," I said. I pushed the image away.

"Don't feel bad," she said.

I knew what she meant.

"We couldn't have done it if it wasn't meant to happen. It happened for a purpose. You'll see. Spirits don't die, not even the spirits of unborn children. She'll be with you again."

"Oh, Courtney," I said. "What a nice thing to say." And sleep overcame me again.

CHAPTER 13

I slept until noon the next day. Courtney woke me up and told me it was time to go to my room. I did not remember getting into my bed. I slept again until morning. When I opened my eyes, Angela was in the room, sitting on the chair at her desk, her body twisted around so that she faced me. I remembered thinking that she did not seem worried. She had on a pale yellow nightgown; the skirt fell in the hollow of her thighs and flapped against her legs.

"So you're finally awake," she said. She was chewing vacantly on her thumbnail.

I rubbed my eyes and tried to focus on her face. "I must have slept for hours," I said.

"Almost eighteen."

"What time is it?"

"Six."

"I slept so long?"

"Eighteen hours," she repeated.

"And you got up this early?"

"I couldn't sleep."

237

I didn't want to ask her why. Memory was returning to me. The mermaid, the sea, the dark shadow of the sea cow were drifting in and out of my consciousness.

"You stayed so long in Courtney's room," she said.

I felt a heavy cloud descend upon me. I wrapped myself in its darkness.

"Courtney said you stayed up all night and all morning," Angela said.

"Yes." I said. I fought to keep my eyes open but a sea cow was riding me to the surface of the sea.

"What could you possibly have to talk about that kept you up so long?" Angela was insisting.

I touched my mouth to keep my lips from trembling. "Things," I said. A profound sadness spread through me.

"What things?" asked Angela.

I held back my tears. "We talked about home," I said. "She told me about St. Lucia." How easily the lies came!

"It didn't seem to have made you happy," she said. She was watching me closely.

"It made me homesick."

"Hmm," she said and turned away.

I thought she was finished with me and I shut my eyes, but she had another question. "Did you see her dolls?"

"Yes," I said quickly, a little too quickly.

"Did they frighten you?" She had turned back around and was looking at me. A quizzical frown had gathered above her eyebrows.

"No," I said

She kept looking at me as if she expected me to say more but when it was obvious that I was not, she smoothed the furrows on her brow with the palm of her hand and got up.

"Well, are you going to stay in bed all day or are you getting up?"

I hoisted my body to a sitting position and swung my legs slowly to the side of the bed.

"Do you need help?"

"No," I said. "Why?"

"I just thought you would," she said.

I walked toward the door.

"Oh, Sara," I heard her voice singing out sweetly to me. "Your period's come?"

I reached for the back of my nightgown. It was stained with blood.

The next day was the fourth of July, Independence Day in America. Angela and Courtney went to the O'Briens'. Courtney said she would explain that I was too ill to join them. At first I was glad they had left me alone, but less than ten minutes later the darkness engulfed me and I panicked. When the mermaids crowded around me, I rushed outside to the sun.

But everything in that pristine town mocked me. The smells of hickory smoke and barbecued meat hung in the stillness of the air and mixed with the sweetness of the red rose bushes that climbed up trellises on the sides of blue and white houses. Near the end of the street, two lovers kissed. When they broke apart the woman laughed, a gay, sunny laugh that floated to my ears on the warm July breeze. The man kissed her again and she rose on the balls of her feet and twisted her heels in the air like a dancer. I felt old. I felt my presence tar their Edenic world.

Courtney came to see me that night. "You have to be at work tomorrow," she said. "Don't forget."

I did not look at her. She lowered her voice and whispered, "It's over, Sara. Try to forget."

"I feel terrible."

"Pain?"

"No."

"The bad feeling will go away. It's only natural."

Natural when I had laughed in the face of Nature? I clasped my hands over my mouth to strangle the cry that rose in my throat.

"It will go away," she repeated.

"What I did was so unnatural."

"You think you have that kind of power? You can't cross Nature," she said.

"I stopped it from happening." I still could not, would not give it a name. Say, I stopped a baby, a child, from happening. Tell her my mother almost gave her life for what I so easily discarded. Three operations in England before I was four and an obeahwoman burning roots to make one more miracle.

"You had nothing to do with it, Sara." She seemed to pity me now. Her voice was kinder. More gentle. "Do you remember what I told you about the spirit? We couldn't have made it happen if it wasn't supposed to happen. It has a purpose, you'll find out. You couldn't do it alone, believe me."

Yes. Yes. The obeahwoman with all her roots couldn't save the child in my mother's womb. Yet I had done more.

"Tell me more about the dream you had swimming with mermaids in Maracas Bay."

"I should have died then," I said. "Like my cousin." I had told her the story about my cousin's drowning.

"If you had stayed with them you would have died."

I shut my eyes and squeezed them together. Still the tears broke through.

She held my shoulders firmly and shook them. "Sara, get a hold of yourself."

"I should have died."

She didn't answer me.

"What am I going to do now?" I was a child in her hands.

"Join the living."

"I want to see Sam."

"Call him."

"I know he won't be there. He's never there. I know I won't hear from him until those men come back."

"Pray, then," she said.

"Pray?"

"Yes. You now have a spirit to pray to. Ask her to help you." She left me.

I became more and more morose, haunted by the memory of swimming with the mermaids between the coral and the dancing sea grass. I went to work the next day and the next and did things that made me acceptable, normal, in the eyes of others. I talked—even smiled—and scraped mottled food into the churning electric grinder: half-chewed meat, bright orange and green carrots and peas, potatoes heavy with gravy. I stacked the clean dishes: cups, saucers, plates in separate piles; knives, spoons and forks in little blue plastic barrels with tiny holes. Later, around the kitchen table I ate in the circle of people who wore white nets on their heads like me and didn't talk much. I was in bed at night before ten. But I did these things in a trancelike state, a billowing fog that drew me ever closer to its dark center. And in this darkness I walked each afternoon from the dorm back to the hospital kitchen, across the lawn in front of the college, past the rows of high windows, staring. Row upon row. Three of them. Sixty windows, looking. And sometimes the brightness of the white—veil, cape, long skirts flattened against the clear glass panels near the front door—jolted me, but it never stopped me. Then one afternoon the brightness stood right before me, blinding me. Sea green lost in white.

"Sara, Sara."

I broke through the fog.

"Something's troubling you, Sara. Can I help? I want to help."

I tried to force the mermaids to leave me.

"Sara, Sara. Talk to me, Sara."

But I did not answer her.

"It's not so bad, Sara. We can reconsider some of your concerns if you want. If they are troubling you, you don't have to take the scholarship. We can make arrangements. Work-study. You could pay for your tuition."

"I . . . I . . . ." The mermaids lingered.

"What's troubling you, Sara? The circles under your eyes are so dark. Are you well? Do you feel sick?"

The splash of a tail fin. They were gone.

"No. No. I'm fine. I'm late for work."

"You should rest."

"I'm fine."

"Will you come by later? We'll talk."

"Yes. Yes."

"Remember, Sara. We're here to help."

My father had let me go to them because they were a nursing order. Were they nurses for the mind or nurses for the body?

I turned in time to escape her arms, the white of her sleeves stretched out like wings to enclose me. I ran into the darkness. Sister Agnes shouted after me, "Tomorrow. Come by tomorrow. After work."

The next day Courtney came to help me. "Pray to her," she said.

I had not gone to work that day. I had been sitting in my room for hours staring blankly through the window, my eyes seeing shapes and colors that my brain did not acknowledge. Seven days had passed since the sea cow had saved me from the mermaids. July 9, 1964. Sam still had not called. I needed him, I needed to speak to him to make me whole.

"Pray to her," Courtney said again.

Perhaps I was going insane. Perhaps I was already insane. Perhaps the inevitable was happening to me: the legacy of Great-Grandmother Bertha fulfilled, my father's unspoken prophecy, Sister Agnes's warnings. It was this painless explanation of the source of my depression that freed me to take the step into the world that Courtney wanted me to enter. If my memory of the mermaids and the sea cow was simply the manifestation of my growing insanity, then in a perverse twist of logic it would be reasonable, as it is reasonable for the insane to do the unreasonable, that I would act upon the advice Courtney now gave me, no matter how illogical.

"I told you the time would come for you to help Sam. Obeah, the way of your ancestors. Pray to your spirit."

Tall, thin men like the trunks of ancient coconut trees, their muscles glistening from cheekbones to ankles. They beckoned me.

"Pray to her."

The Intermediaries, the beloved of God. I had learned to pray to the saints in grammar school. Human prayers said directly to Him, that could not find their way to Him, were carried to Him by these beloved. I shut my eyes.

A thousand eyes shone from the leopard skins that fell across the shoulders of these men, tall and thin like the trunks of ancient trees. They guided the spirit of my unborn child, my saint, up. Up. Up.

I was still facing the window, my eyes shut, when Angela called my name. "How many times do I have to call you?" She was standing right next to me. "It's your friend. He's on the phone."

Two bodies had been found in the Mississippi River, their wrists and ankles bound by chicken wire. They were tied to each other with a thick brown rope around their necks, chests, thighs and legs.

"Like the kind of rope you used to skip with when you were a child," Sam said. The bodies had not been identified but the police believed they were those of two of the three men missing since June 21.

Sam didn't begin his conversation with those words. First, he told me he loved me and that he was sorry he hadn't called. I felt the dense clouds rise from my brain. I began to cry.

"What is the matter, Sara? Are you okay? Are you all right?"

But I didn't tell Sam what had happened to me. I couldn't burden him with more troubles when he was searching desperately for his friends. I told him I missed him. I told him I loved him. I had faith in him.

"It's all over, Sara. It's done. I don't think I can stay here anymore."

I asked him what was done.

"We found them."

Sam said he would wait until the bodies were positively identified. He expected the third body to show up in the next few hours. He would return when it was over. Mississippi had killed the joy in him and he needed to see me, to believe in life again.

He needed me to believe in life again. What irony. I could not tell him now about my lost pregnancy, not when he needed me.

Madness was not attractive to me after Sam called.

How quickly I grew up that summer. *Summer.* Just to say the word felt strange and new and grown-up. No summer existed on the island I had left. There were August holidays, the dry season, the wet season, but no summer. Summer as opposed to what? The sun was always present in the morning to heat up the earth, grass was always green, the sky, forever blue. To know summer, to say summer, meant you had been where there was winter, that you had traveled out of the tropical zone. To do that you had to be grown-up, making your own money. Or rich. And when I was a child, rich did not come to black skin on my island.

I knew some people, though, were neither grown-up nor

rich, who had traveled. They had followed parents gone to England to collect on England's promise of motherhood: a factory job, schooling for their children, decent health care in exchange for two million barrels of oil, one hundred tons of asphalt, six hundred acres of sugar cane estates. By the time they learned to use word *summer* they knew they had been duped. Rage strangled the words in their throats, words they would have used to explain they were owed much more, that they had paid too dearly for an exhausting factory job, inferior schooling and inadequate health care.

But it was too late for them to return to a home that took the sun for granted. Summer had taught them grown-up realities like working till daybreak, saving up pennies, patching peeling plaster walls. Summer was an endless trap of preparing for a winter cold that penetrated to the marrow, paying debts owed from the winter before when no jobs were available for island people in London's wet slums, when the roof leaked and the children went hungry. Summer made a man or woman out of a child, and so it did me that summer in Oshkosh.

I felt as if I were forty, if forty was the age when you took a good look at yourself, assessed your worth, for better or for worse, accepted it and moved on. I carried Bertha's genes, but that did not mean I had to end up like Bertha. I was not crazy, nor would be, no matter what I saw in my father's eyes, or Sister Agnes's book learning told her. But I had changed; I had grown up. I would not be the same again. I had accepted the illogic of the insane and it had matured me. Why couldn't I ask Courtney what she had done? Why did I feel I had to defend her dolls from Angela's prying? Why did my dreams of mermaids and a sea cow disturb me so deeply? Courtney made it seem all so sensible. The spirit of my unborn child could help me. And I believed her. Not believed her in a conscious sense, but my soul—was it my spirit?—responded to her. And wasn't she right?

Had Sam not called me at the very moment when I prayed to my little saint? Wouldn't he be coming back to me? Hadn't my little saint found the bodies of his dead friends and made it possible for him to leave Mississippi?

What Sam said should have moved me to tears. I cried but not because of the horror he described. I cried because I loved him, because he said he loved me, because he said he would be coming back to me. I should have cried when he told me about his two friends.

"You know, Sara, I still hoped that, somehow, they were alive. If James were alone, or if he were with two other black people like himself, then I would have known there was no hope. I mean, it was possible that they would have killed him, but when they let them out, I felt they had a chance. They let James out because of Andrew and Michael. I figured they just wanted to shake up Andrew and Michael. You know, to warn them to stay out of 'nigger business,' to frighten them out of their wits. Let them be a lesson to other white people. I never figured they would kill their own. But those two were Jews. I should have known. Racism in Mississippi is as deep as the river."

"How soon do you think the funeral will be?" I asked, my mind fixed on Sam's returning.

"I couldn't go down to the river tonight. I didn't want to see. Hearing about it was enough. God knows what they did before they tied them up. Jesus!"

"At least it's all over," I said.

"Shit." Sam began to sob again. "Shit. Shit. Crackers are so evil. You'll never know, Sara. Never."

"I feel what you feel," I said.

"You can't, Sara. You don't know."

"I know what it is to lose a friend." I was thinking of Nancy— her burning forehead, her frozen legs, the silence into which I withdrew myself because nobody seemed to know that a part

of me died when she died of polio. The unfairness of her death—
my guilt—haunted me for months. Why pick her from the many
in our school? If her father had known a Captain McNeil, she
would not have died. It was unjust.

Sam seemed to pull his words from my mind and then he
distorted them, and I was ashamed I had thought of Nancy.

"There is no justice," he said. "Not for black people in
America. If all I lost was a friend—friends—it would be fair. I
could grieve like a normal person. I could mourn. But this is
much greater than losing a friend. They didn't even have the
chance of bad luck. I know the two bodies they found were
Michael and Andrew. The racist bastards. Even if they had to kill
their own people, they would give back the bodies. But they
wouldn't bother to give back the body of a black man. God,
what they did to James! This is bigger than losing friends. This is
the whole black race chopped up into little pieces and thrown
in the Mississippi River. That's what they did to James. It's about
what they want to do to you and me, Sara."

I fished for the right words to comfort Sam, to tell him again
that I shared his grief, that I understood how he felt. *The whole
race, they want to chop up the whole race in little bits.* The violence of
that image silenced me.

"They tied them up with rope and wire," Sam was saying.

This was a kind of racism I did not understand. The racism I
knew, the kind my parents whispered about, might lead you to
suicide, but it didn't tie you up with rope and wire and drop
you to the bottom of a river. The English colonists were less
crude than that. More devious. My father's friend took his own
life. No Englishman put the bullet to his head.

"Simply because one stupid clerk laughed in his face when
he fired him." My mother struggled to understand.

The British had made my father's friend a manager on their
sugar estate. Thinking they meant for him to manage and not

able to accept his role as their token, their contribution to native participation in management, he demanded that the clerk
obey his orders. But the clerk was English and he complained
to the English boss and the English boss told the Trinidadian
manager: "Everybody else, but you don't order around an Englishman, even if he is a clerk."

"That incident broke him," my father said. "They had been
undermining him for a long time."

Now Sam was telling me about chicken wire.

"They used chicken wire to hold their wrists and ankles
together. Then they must have put them on top of each other
and tied them together with rope. They say the two had turned
so blue they looked black in the night. You know the rope they
used, Sara? The kind you used to skip with when you were a
child."

A grown-up summer. Men using the playthings of children
to do their bloody work. I, carrying the guilt of a convent of
nuns and using my silence as a stone. I, stopping a child from
growing and letting Courtney persuade me that I had set a
spirit free. "Oh, Sam," was all I could say.

"I'll come back after the funeral."

"Oh, Sam."

A funeral was held in Meridian, but not for Chaney,
Schwerner and Goodman. "They had turned so blue they
looked black in the night," Sam had said. Only they were black-
blue not blue-black. Black that sank to the bottom of the Mississippi River. Black that rolled in the red clay silt of the Mississippi, jammed between stones in narrow crevices she carved
just for occasions such as this, because the river remembered
how she had allowed steamboats to roll over her when she well
knew, had seen the Africans all right, when they were forced to

drag their chains on deck, that those boats carried—and safely, too, thanks to her—fully grown men and women forged into chattel, their hatred smoldering embers in their eyes. The Mississippi clutched the two blacks she found and hid them till their black turned blue, and she allowed fish to bite the men in the eyes, ears, mouth so they would not be recognized. When she released them in the dark of night, not even the Mississippi police could tell if they were black turned blue or blue turned black.

Sam must have known his mistake the same moment that I did. The information was reported on the ten o'clock news, between stories about Mickey Mantle's home run and Lady Bird Johnson's rose gardens: "Two Negro bodies, found in the Mississippi River, were identified as those of Henry Dee, a sawmill worker, and Charles E. Moore, a college student. Their bodies were tied with wire and rope. Authorities say there appears to be no connection between these deaths and the disappearance of three civil rights workers on June 21."

Two Negro bodies. Would the announcer have said two white bodies? Sometimes only three words are necessary to start a person thinking. *Two Negro bodies.* Had he said two Negroes, two Negro men, the bodies of two Negroes, I would have felt only grief and disappointment that they weren't Chaney, Schwerner and Goodman; that there would be no funeral; that Sam would not be coming home to me; that I could not lay on his heart the burden I carried of the spirit I had set free. But the announcer said *Negro bodies*, as if to imply that saying *the bodies of two Negro men* would place too much weight on their humanity and make their deaths a shame, embarrass people after dinner. It was enough that the network had allowed the announcer to squeeze the brutal murder of two men between a ball game and the sprucing up of America's sidewalks.

A piece of Mississippi slipped through a crack in my heart

and touched me directly. What if they were talking about *my* Negro body? Would they have said, *the body of a Negro woman*, or merely *a Negro body*? Would they have tried to diminish my humanity, also?

Sam caught the fear in my voice when he called to tell me of his mistake.

"Those two dead men meant nothing to those white people. What if it were you?"

"Are you all right, Sara?"

"It's just . . . "

"Why are you so upset?"

I told him about the news report.

"That happens every day. I get numb sometimes," Sam said.

"Were they beaten?"

"God knows."

"Didn't you find out?"

"Beaten, tortured, then killed. That's the way it goes here."

"How can you stand it?"

"I've been telling you. Haven't you been listening to me? It's getting me down. I need to see you."

"When will you come?"

"Are you okay, Sara? You sound different. Is everything all right?"

"I'm fine. Really, I am. When will you be here?" I asked him again.

"After the funeral."

"Will you stay?"

He was silent for a few seconds. Then he said, "I can't. Not till we find Michael, James and Andrew, but I'll stay awhile. I should be in Oshkosh in two weeks. Definitely in two weeks. To the day."

"Fourteen days?"

"Fourteen days," he promised.

CHAPTER 14

Oshkosh is hundreds of miles away from Mississippi, light years different in temperament. In July 1964 Oshkosh basked self-righteously in that distinction. For one, the town had no Negroes, so it had no Negro problem. Secondly, if Oshkosh did have Negroes, it would not have resorted to name calling, stone throwing, dog fighting. Oshkosh had style. The good news, that of important people, was put on the front page; the scandals were set in fine print and stuck in columns after the weather and the obituaries.

Oshkosh had Saturday parades with blond baton twirlers in white uniforms with brass buttons, the red, white and blue of the American flag, bratwurst and sauerkraut, creamy American cheese and hand-pumped milk. Oshkosh had *The Music Man*, Robert Preston dancing down wholesome, clean streets. A big brass band, seventy-six trombones. The barbershop quartet. Marian, Madam Librarian, freckled-faced children, obedient teenagers, buxom women and good-natured fathers. But no Negroes. Definitely no Negroes.

Negroes in the neighboring towns, perhaps, but not out front.

Negroes behind cooking pots in kitchens, Negroes in back corners of factories, Negroes come and gone at harvest time, Negroes, with mules, digging ditches from dawn to dusk on farmlands that seemed to stretch beyond the horizon. But Oshkosh had no Negroes disturbing Saturday morning parades with colors that clashed against the pale pinks, whites and beiges of the way Oshkosh thought America should be. When New York City got ugly that July, and all because of Mississippi, Oshkosh clucked its tongue in disbelief and disapproval. Over Negroes in Mississippi? Oshkosh would never allow things to get so out of hand. Oshkosh had class.

Then, one afternoon, while I was walking with Angela from the cafeteria to the dorm, a group of boys and their girlfriends called us niggers.

We had seen them standing at the corner ahead of us— teenage boys in blue jeans making awkward advances to giggling, red-faced girls. A common sight on Saturday afternoons in Oshkosh: miniskirted girls with newly developed breasts and rounded hips throwing pimpled-faced boys into confusion. I had noticed one of the boys nudging another, and they all turned and looked at us. This was something new. Different. They had never paid attention to us before, so consumed were they with their adolescent forages into sexual terrain still strange to them.

"Niggers!" they shouted as we passed them.

Later in our room, Angela told me that this was the way her boyfriend's parents saw her, too.

"I lied," she said, "when I told you I wasn't going to see him because he wants too much. He broke up with me. I didn't break up with him. He said his parents had threatened to stop paying his college tuition if he kept on seeing me. They said they didn't want him going out with a nigger."

"But you aren't a Negro."

"He said we are all the same to them."

Angela with her sari, me with my accent, wishing I had worn a hibiscus in my hair and we were all the same to them. We were niggers in that good-news town. They did not care that Angela's grandparents had come from India of their own volition to work on the land as indentured laborers, or that mine were forced onto plantations with whips and chains, or that Bertha's blood ran in my veins, English and white. Our skin was not white. We were black. We were niggers.

We grew closer that day, Angela and I, our public humiliation forging a bond between us that had not been there before. Perhaps Courtney noticed that our friendship had deepened—nothing escaped her eyes. Perhaps this was the reason she left me alone. Or perhaps I was the one who avoided her. Whatever the reason, I was glad she was not there to whisper to me about spirits, relieved I could pretend that the mermaids and sea cow were part of a bad dream that had no truth in my reality.

Twice I had nightmares but they were about two black-blue bodies floating down the Mississippi: Henry Dee's and Charles E. Moore's. The second time I dreamed of them, two mermaids with sea grass hair were doing cartwheels in the water around them. But in the morning there was the sun, and Angela not letting *nigger* stop her from laughing, and no Courtney to remind me otherwise. Most of all there was the knowledge that there was one less day before I would see Sam again.

Ten days after I had spoken to Sam, four days before he had promised he would return to Wisconsin, I had my second conversation with Sister Agnes since that day she called me foolish for wanting to give up my scholarship. She was waiting for me outside the hospital kitchen. The dark circles under my eyes had disappeared. I was sleeping again, counting the days until Sam. The fog had retreated. I could smile at her when she smiled at me. With my eyes. She seemed satisfied. She gave me some literature on a work-study program the college was considering. I told her I was interested. I knew she was scrutinizing me closely. I was careful.

"Can I work with a student visa?" I asked. "Will Immigration permit it? Is it legal?"

"This would have to remain our little secret." She winked at me.

The next evening, Courtney appeared suddenly at the doorway of the TV den where Angela and I were watching David Janssen make his weekly escape in *The Fugitive*.

"You seem to be in good spirits."

I struggled against the power of her choice of words, her mahogany face, her African mask eyes. The fog that had smothered me was threatening to return.

"Where have you been?" I asked.

"Here. If you had wanted to see me."

"I haven't seen you at work."

"They changed my shift," she said.

"You didn't tell me."

"You didn't ask."

"I couldn't find you," I said.

Angela made a shooshing sound through her teeth and put her finger on her lips.

"We're disturbing her," said Courtney. "Do you want to come to my room?"

My heart somersaulted in my breast. I was angry for that betrayal for I had almost fooled myself into believing that her sudden appearance was not affecting me.

"Anything special?" I asked.

Angela hushed us again.

"If you don't want to come—" Courtney began.

"No, of course not." I got up.

"Just want to know how you are doing," she said.

"I'm fine." I was next to her now in the hallway.

"You don't have to come to my room if you don't want to," she said. Her eyes pierced mine.

"Why wouldn't I?"

Courtney shrugged.

"What's your new job?" I asked.

"Delivering food to the patients," she replied. "I like it better. I waved to you the other day but you didn't seem to see me."

I saw her. Pretended I hadn't, and that night the mermaids got muddled in my dreams of Henry Dee and Charles Moore.

"When is Sam coming?" she asked.

"In four days."

"Are you going to Milwaukee?"

"I'm not sure."

"Hmm," she said, and frowned. When her face settled back again it was a blank slate, revealing nothing.

Inside her room my eyes were instinctively drawn to the dolls on her dresser, the ones I had so lightly dismissed with Angela, once calling them pincushions. Now I remembered how they sat there next to the speckled blue enamel basin filled with long leaves floating in water, like locks of mermaids' hair.

"So she made it happen for you?"

I knew which "she" Courtney meant. She, the spirit of the unborn child. How did she know the child was female? I dared not ask, dared not acknowledge that moment again.

"Sam called soon after you spoke to me."

"I know."

"But he didn't find his friends," I said.

"She knew they were the wrong bodies," she said, "but she wanted them to be found. She wanted them to know they were killing Negroes every day and nobody noticed. Sam's friends were three in a hundred and nobody would have noticed if two of them hadn't been white."

I squeezed my eyes shut and broke the lock the dolls had

placed on me. When I opened my eyes again, I found my peripheral vision. On the bulletin board, the photograph of the four little coffins was lost in a maze of newspaper clippings pinned to the board with thin, long needles like the ones she kept in the dolls.

Courtney's eyes followed mine. "Did you hear about New York City?"

I shook my head.

"They're scared in Milwaukee now," she said. "And Oshkosh is so close to Milwaukee, you know the people here must be afraid, too."

"Afraid of what?" I asked.

"That it's spreading," she said. "That the Mississippi is going to flow backward into the north. Can't you hear how quiet it is here?"

I could feel her pulling me again into her world: rivers defying nature and the laws of gravity, silences that spoke, spirits deciding when they would be born. I wanted to leave her room but she reached in front of me and pulled out one of the needles that had been stuck in the center of a newspaper photograph, one that, at that very moment for some inexplicable reason, my eyes were being drawn to as if it were a magnet. The picture showed an adolescent black boy sprawled on his back on a road, his T-shirt lifted up to his rib cage, his dark cut-off pants pushed down below his hips, exposing a belly like a baby's, with a dark, thick liquid curling from it and forming a shallow pool beneath him. A few seconds passed before, blinded by the innocence of that belly, its hairless smoothness, I noticed the other liquid that had streamed from his temples.

"His name was James Powell," said Courtney. "He was only fifteen. In New York City they kill children."

"What happened?" I could barely find my voice.

"They blamed him for starting the riot in Harlem. He taunted a white man, took out his knife and threatened to make him pay for Mississippi. But the white man was a policeman, and he shot the boy."

There was no caption under or near the picture. But I knew how Courtney knew the details. She had read the papers I had been avoiding because I did not want to hear any bad news between two dead Negroes floating down a river and Sam's arrival.

"The people in Harlem rioted," she said. "The riot's going on now."

"I didn't know you still kept up with the news."

"So Sister Agnes was right, then?" Her tone was bitter. Unforgiving.

I squirmed under her question, guilt constricting the muscles in my throat. Her eyes pinned me to her like the newspaper clippings on her bulletin board.

"It was only Sam after all. Wasn't it, Sara? Only Sam."

"No," I said. "I hate it all, also. But it's too much. Too much."

"Too much?"

"I thought it would be simple. I would force Sister Agnes to give a scholarship to a black girl in Milwaukee. That would be enough. A start. But this is too big. It's too much. It won't ever end. I didn't think it would be so bad."

"What did you think?"

"Sam will be back soon," I said.

"He won't stay."

"He loves me."

"You better start letting go."

"I'm doing that, Courtney. All of it, except Sam. All that stuff about spirits. I feel better now. I was depressed. I know I was. Just leave me. I don't want to hear your talk again."

She came in. "You're in it now. Sam needs you."

I stepped away.

"I told you our time would come. It's your spirit."

"No, Courtney. No. No more. I'm finished with this."

"You're not. This is only the beginning."

"Courtney, don't you know what we did? Doesn't it bother you? It was wrong, Courtney. Wrong. Stop this now."

"Sam needs your spirit."

"Stop it, Courtney. It was an abortion! An abortion!" I was shouting at her, my hands over my ears to shut out her voice, cool like ice, washing over my back.

"That's what you European Negroes call it. Well, sometimes it's that. Not always." She pulled my hands from my ears. "Listen. You listen to me, Sara. When they brought us to the plantations in this country, and in yours and mine, we called it life. Go ahead, feel sorry for yourself, feel guilty, look for answers their way. Mississippi, St. Lucia, Dominica, Trinidad, it was the same for women like us. We bred for them. We made more slaves for their plantations. We made children to be killed their way, with whips and chains, to be treated like animals. To wake up with the sun, in pens meant for animals. To grovel under the whip, to mate under the whip, to sleep under the whip. Some of us said no. We gave back our unborn children to the ancestors. You call that abortion? We call it life. Think how your spirit has helped us already. She will help us again. Think how, if you did have a child, it would stop Sam from doing what he has to do. Think, Sara. You can't run away. The spirits connect you and me and Sam and Mississippi and all black people in America. Remember that."

The fire in her eyes burned me. She let go of my hands and I ran to Angela.

PART THREE

CHAPTER 15

The women in my hometown in Trinidad did not think my grandmother was mannish simply because she seemed to them to be more than they could be, to be able to do more than they could do; because she appeared to scoff at the code of manners and behavior that safeguarded their femininity. Their word for her, mannish, actually masked a greater fear: that my grandmother possessed powers an obeahman had given her.

There were stories. I had not paid much attention to them until now in Oshkosh. Before Oshkosh I thought the women said what they said because they envied my grandmother. She had given birth to six sons, more than that, six sons who survived infancy, a miracle in her day when it was not unusual for a woman to lose half of her babies, even her life. She never stayed in bed long either, after they were born. By the third day they would see her with my grandfather, pulling the cows from the open pasture into her fenced-in backyard. Soon they were saying an obeahman in Sans Souci had made her mannish, had given her the same power he had used to lure Bertha to him.

I knew that obeahman. We passed him on our dizzying trips along the winding curves to Sans Souci. His polished tin hut glittered in the sun, almost blinding us as we skirted past dangerous precipices plunging to the rocks that stood sentinel at the edge of the sea below. No one in my family acknowledged he was one of us, not even my father who told me about Bertha. Yet now, in Oshkosh, I was to suspect that the bag of herbs my mother put in my bath water between her Hail Marys when I was sick had probably been blessed by him, so, too, the one I now hid at the bottom of my drawer in my room in America.

They said that right before my grandmother became mannish, children clung to her like flies. She could cure any illness. The first time she proved her powers, she was in the ninth month of pregnancy, only three days before the birth of her first son. A terrible storm raged that night, but my grandmother ran through the howling wind to take her herbs to her neighbor's three-year-old son who was shaking like a baby's rattle with the malaria a mosquito had injected into his leg. The next morning the boy's fever broke and his shaking stopped. He was running to her with kisses by the time her first son was born. And so it went, the people in her town said: More cures, more kisses. The children loved her and followed her everywhere while she kept breeding son after son till she had six. The women were envious. Then someone found out about the obeahman in Sans Souci.

He was the one, they said, who had burned his black magic into the heart of blond Bertha, my grandmother's mother. Why else would a white woman go mad with desire for a man with skin the color of ebony and hair tight as the wool on the back of a fat black lamb? He had passed his magic through Bertha to my grandmother. They could see it no other way, the people in the village, when their children ran to my grandmother with their kisses. She had put a spell on them, they said. *Watch out for the children.*

My grandmother was in the ninth month of her seventh pregnancy when these rumors cut a vicious swath through her village. Her seventh son was born with the umbilical cord wrapped around his neck like a noose. He died within minutes.

My mother had her own superstitions: "Watch out for the soucouyant that lives in the silk fig tree."

I laughed at her.

"If you had black-and-blue marks on your legs and arms, you wouldn't laugh so easily."

Everywhere in Diego Martin, Toco, Blanchiseusse, Sans Souci trees groaned under the weight of overripe fruit. Black-and-blue bites marked the legs of the children.

"It's the vampire bat," I said.

"You'll find out one day, little miss with the big mouth who reads too much. You'll find out."

Suddenly, one starless night, a ball of fire fell out of a black sky into a clump of silk fig trees and peeled back the soft, yellow bark of the tree trunks like the succulent segments of a ripe grapefruit. The fire sizzled, gained ground and flared up again, burning nothing but itself. Then the fire went out as suddenly as it appeared, leaving its scars behind: the imprint of its roundness pressed into the pulp of the split tree, faint traces of charred bark, a metallic odor that overpowered the sweet smell of crushed figs.

"A meteorite," I said to my mother.

"A soucouyant," she countered. "It was changing its skin under a silk fig tree."

"Always a silk fig tree?"

"Always."

"Don't you know bats love figs?" I asked in my youthful arrogance, books my only guide. "Can't you see that people make up stories because they don't know how to keep the bats from eating their figs? Or how to explain stars that fall from the sky?"

"Hhrump," she said, "Hhrump. You better watch your mouth. There's more to things than meets the eye."

Was there more to things than met the eye? In the laughter of mermaids and the appearance of the sea cow, perhaps. In the coincidence of Sam's phone call and my prayers to a spirit, perhaps. In the surfacing of two black-blue Negroes thought to be blue-black, perhaps.

Maybe my grandmother had magical powers. Maybe Courtney did, too. Maybe a soucouyant did live in the hollow of a silk fig tree, and burned with desire on hot, starless nights. Maybe the man who walked on Bertha's grave on All Soul's Day was the obeahman I saw in Sans Souci, his skin the color of ebony, his hair thick and curled like the wool on the back of a fat black lamb. Maybe it was he who saved me that day when he wrapped me in the folds of his long black cape and smothered the fire that licked the hem of my white organza dress.

The women dropped to their knees and shouted: "A miracle! A vision!"

I would discover that Angela, too, believed in miracles. One day I asked her if she did. I was fighting the memories Courtney had caused me to recall with her talk of spirits. I hoped Angela, who loved the light, would dispel the darkness that rolled toward me like a fog out at sea.

"Of course, silly, I believe in miracles. I'm Catholic."

"Yes," I said, "but you weren't *always* a Catholic."

"My father and his father."

"I'm sure your grandfather was a Hindu or a Muslim. In India everybody is a Hindu or a Muslim. Your grandfather came from India, didn't he?"

Angela wrinkled her brow and narrowed her eyes. At first I

thought she was going to chastise me for prying into her personal life, but in the characteristic way she had of ending a conversation that was unpleasant to her, she looked past me in silence. I was about to say something about the weather—anything that would send her the message that I had no intentions of challenging her in the cruel way I once did when I told her I saw the half moon dancers being whipped until blood ran down their shoulders—when she looked directly at me again.

"Yes, when he was in India, my grandfather was a Hindu."

We were having lunch, alone in a little room outside the nuns' dining room. The nuns had closed the cafeteria, of course, once the girls had left for the summer. Naturally we were not allowed to eat with the nuns, but we had to have our meals at the same time. When I was not working, I ate with Angela; when I was, she ate alone or with Courtney. We never complained about this arrangement. We were scholarship girls.

"Did your grandfather convert?" I asked her.

"Yes, but not willingly."

"Was he forced to convert?"

"Oh, it was nothing like that. Not like force. He wanted a civil service job and in those days people thought that all Indians were good for was cutting cane or planting tomatoes. Circumstances have changed, but in my grandfather's time only brown-skinned Negroes worked in the civil service. They used to say Indians were too small to be firemen or policemen. I suppose they also thought the dirt from the land remained permanently under our fingernails and that's why they kept us out of city offices. My grandfather liked math. He wanted to be an accountant so he converted to prove to them he was a Western-style modern man."

This was the most Angela had ever said to me about her family. I wanted to know more.

"Was he successful?"

"Very. He made good money before he lost it drinking. His relatives ostracized him when he converted. That was too much for him. He drank himself to death. When my father married my mother, she had to convert, also. They couldn't have got married in the Catholic Church if she hadn't converted. I never really thought they cared because by that time a lot of Indians had converted and our relatives were more or less on good terms with us. But one day—one of the holiest of the Hindu religious days—I caught my parents burning incense to Krishna. That was the day my mother taught me that you must keep your thoughts and feelings to yourself and never let people see into your heart."

I knew what she meant. She had told me once: *Don't let them see into your heart, Sara.*

"My grandfather became Catholic, you know, and not Anglican, because he liked the saints in the Catholic Church. My mother said praying to the saints was like praying to the different gods in the Hindu religion. And," she said, smiling mysteriously at me, "I like the fact that saints can make miracles."

CHAPTER 16

S am came as he said he would, fourteen days after he called to tell me about the mistake he had made by not going to the river that night to make certain that the two black-blue men they had fished from the Mississippi, tied together with chicken wire and skipping rope, were not, as he had thought, his two co-workers, Schwerner and Goodman. He telephoned from Milwaukee, saying he would come the next day and stay a week with the O'Briens so he could be with me. After that he had to return to Mississippi. *Had to*, he said. I heard the resolve in his voice. I realized the impossibility of persuading him otherwise. We agreed to meet in the park. We wanted to be alone the first time we saw each other, and I couldn't be sure that Angela and Courtney would not be at the dormitory.

I saw Sam through the tangle of bushes that partially surrounded the park bench I had chosen. Nervousness perhaps, an overpowering feeling that it would be better for me to see him before he saw me, led me to pick that bench. I could not shake off my fear that Mississippi had carved its misery so deeply into him that he might no longer be mine; that suffering might have wrung him so dry that when he saw me, he would speak hollow words and I would know that nothing was left for me, no space remained in his heart. I did not want to find myself in the open, the sun on my face, my humiliation visible, for all to witness.

I thought I would know how he felt by the way he walked. If quickly, he was anxious to see me. If slowly, he had left me already. I would also be able to tell by the expression on his face. From where I sat, I could detect if he seemed distant, preoccupied by a reality or a place where he wasn't at that moment, or if he was eager to see me, and was searching me out through the maze of green benches and leafy bushes that twisted and curled around the edges of the paved walkways. But when I saw him, his clothes were what caused me to shiver in the heat of the summer sun. Gone were the tailored slacks and the soft knit jerseys he usually wore. Sam, his face bright with the eagerness I wanted, his step quick and anxious as I had hoped, was wearing an indigo print dashiki embroidered in white at its collarless neck, blue denim jeans flared slightly at the bottom, brown sandals and no socks.

He was in front of me before I knew it. He had rounded the bend of the bushes while Oshkosh's pink faces turned pale at his sight. A Negro in African garb walking boldly in daylight in the middle of their downtown park? A Negro in No Negroes Oshkosh? Sam wrapped his arms around me and held me until the earthy, sweet smell of his body eased back the glare of their stares and the memories returned, warm and familiar, the man in the strange clothes the same Sam who had loved me in June.

"You've changed," he said, unknowingly echoing my earlier fears about him.

Had he changed? Yes, but not in the way I feared. When he kissed me, pressing his lips against mine with such passion his body shook, I knew I had not lost him.

"Me?" I asked when finally my trembling eased and the sweetness remained.

"Yes, you. You've changed. What has happened to you?"

"I thought you've changed." I waved my arms in circles in front of his chest, hardly able to get the words out of my mouth.

He laughed. "Oh, this." He tugged his dashiki. "I saw them looking at me." He tossed his head sideways toward the few people who were still staring at us. "Do you like it?"

"You never wore it before."

"So what do you think?"

"It's different for you."

"No, it's right for me. It's who I am now."

I did not speak.

"It scares them, I know. Or makes them angry. In this dashiki I'm not just a black man they named Negro, but a black man who has a homeland, a whole continent of ancestors, a culture, traditions that go back centuries."

One man was still glaring at us. Sam stared back, engaging in a contest of will and indignant righteousness. The man lost. He shifted his eyes and turned away.

"Things are going to be different now," Sam said.

I felt icicles encircle my heart.

"So what about you? You seem changed."

"A lot has happened," I said.

"In Oshkosh?" He opened his eyes wide in mock disbelief.

"No, with me."

I had not intended to expose myself then. Not there in the wide open spaces where Oshkosh's brass band marched down rows of tree-lined streets in the Sunday sun. I had chosen a park bench for the camouflage of trees I had hoped would hide me, but the sunlight streamed through the leaves and made fanciful shadows on the ground that resembled the delicate, intricate patterns of old lace, with spaces where the sun shone through, and ribbons of darkness that glowed at the edges. If I had planned the moment to tell Sam what had happened to me, if he had not caught me off-guard with his sudden discovery that I had changed when I, at that moment, was transfixed and frightened by the change in him, I would have found a darkened corner, a sheltered space inside a house in which to make my confession. I would not have blurted out the words so starkly. I would have found ways to soften their hard edges. I would have found explanations to ease the harshness of the truth they conveyed.

"I had an abortion," I said. No elaboration. No explanation.

The leaves on the bushes behind us flipped over in the sudden breeze and bared their delicate undersides to the sun's harsh rays. The shadows dipped and shimmered on Sam's face.

"I thought so," he said.

"Thought so?" I stared at him.

"Every time I called you sounded so sad, but when I asked you, you always said you were okay. Yes, I thought it was possible. I knew we didn't do anything. To protect you, I mean. I had hoped it wouldn't happen."

"That's all?" I could hardly believe his words.

"It's not like that," he said. "These are different times. We do different things." He removed his arm from across my shoulder

What different things? I thought. "Doesn't it bother you?" I asked aloud.

"When it occurred to me that that could be the reason you always sounded so sad, I thought, if she is pregnant, we'll get married." He examined his fingernails. "Then, in Mississippi," he said, not raising his head, "I thought, if she's pregnant, she wouldn't tell me."

His words fell like a shroud around his shoulders and darkened his face. He had impersonalized me: if *she* is pregnant, he had said. *She.* I saw my pregnancy as he must have, an inconvenient barrier between him and Mississippi.

I heard no shame in his voice, shame that I wanted and hoped for, that would let me know he loved me. Only guilt. His conscience was affected rather than his heart, which should have been, for being careless with the love he had sworn.

Suffering makes a man hard, Courtney had told me. Had the suffering Sam had witnessed in Mississippi hardened him too?

"Why?" I asked. "Why wouldn't I tell you?" My mouth felt dry.

"You'd know having a baby wasn't possible. Not at a time like this."

I wanted to close the spaces between the leaves, to stitch together the holes in our lace cover. I wanted to drape us in darkness. I was the one besotted by love, following the mermaids to the bottom of the sea. Sam was swimming free to the surface, his head above water.

"But I worried for you, though," he said. "I guess I fooled myself into believing you were all right. I mean, that you weren't pregnant."

"But you didn't ask?"

"I suppose I didn't want to know. There were other things—"

" . . . to keep your mind off me." I finished his sentence.

Sam's arms closed me tight to his chest. "I'm sorry, Sara. I'm sorry. Forgive me."

Shame at last. I held on to him. The park closed in on us. The trees became solid walls and sheltered us.

"I knew what had to be done if you were pregnant. I should not have left you to do it alone. There is no excuse."

At another time I would wonder why he knew so easily what had to be done. I would think of all the possibilities I had discarded, all the alternatives I eventually realized I did not have. I went to Courtney because there was nothing else left for me to do. And then all that kept my legs from folding under me was thinking about doing it for him. What filled my mind when I followed Courtney to her room was that I wanted to keep more trouble away from him when he was troubled. But for Sam only one choice existed and his guilt had to do with not facing that choice with me. Yet, then, at the park, that was enough for me. His shame, the tenderness in his voice, the intimacy of his touch were sufficient to comfort me.

"How did you do it?" he asked at last.

"Courtney did it for me in her room."

"Did it hurt?"

I shook my head, no. Then, remembering the one single moment of pain, the sharp point of the needle before the mermaids came, I said, "Just a little."

"Are you okay?"

"Yes," I answered.

"It'll never happen again."

I closed my eyes and made myself warm and safe with his words. "Yes," I said. "Never again."

"Do you feel bad? Guilty, I mean?"

I told him about the mermaids. I told him what I was able to tell him about the mermaids, what made sense to me. I told him that Courtney had put me to sleep and I had dreamt of mermaids. He smiled. I told him not to. He asked me why not.

"When my cousin drowned," I said, "I thought mermaids had seduced him to the bottom of the sea."

"Well, they didn't seduce you."

I told him that I could not understand my dream. It seemed real and made me feel strange. He asked me how so.

"I think," I said, for the first time giving voice to my fears, "that Courtney used obeah to do the abortion on me."

I half expected him to laugh, to grab me by the shoulders and shake me, to tell me to put a rein on my imagination, but instead he stayed silent for a long moment and then said carefully, as if having given much thought to choosing his words: "I thought she would. Courtney has never broken her link to our African ancestors."

We did not leave the park right away. Sam wanted to tell me more about Mississippi. He couldn't leave Mississippi, he said, until Schwerner, Goodman and Chaney were found. He was resigned to the fact that they were dead. He should have been there with them. He should have died, also. His eyes grew damp as he said this.

I hugged him and let him empty himself into me. I forgot my pain, the abortion, my fear that Courtney had used obeah. Only Sam's grief mattered. He told me about the dogs let loose on innocent people, and the fire hoses that pitched bodies writhing to the ground. The more I listened, the more I felt a chasm open wide between us. His words whipped me with their implications: *Never. You could never have known that kind of suffering on your banana bush island.* I became frightened by the difference that he seemed to be suggesting lay between us, and, desperate to bind him to me, I told him again that I loved him. He said he loved me, too.

"With your whole soul?"

"With my whole soul."

Nothing, I said, was more important to me than our being together.

The moment I said that I knew I had made a mistake. The muscles in his face stiffened and two hard lines appeared around his mouth. He looked so strange that I wondered if I knew him at all, if I had not dreamt him up. If I had not made him into the man I hoped I would find after Eric disappointed me.

"We are important, Sara," he said quietly, "but there are other things more important than us, other things more important than our being together."

I raced to change the subject, afraid he'd say more,

remembering Courtney's warning about the suffering of black American men. I told him about my days now at the College of the Sacred Heart. How lonely I was. How it was becoming more difficult to face the nuns now that I knew the truth about their reason for giving me a scholarship. How I was glad that most of them had gone to their retreat house on Lake Erie. They needed the prayers, I said. Still, it was hard to be civil to the ones who were left, especially Sister Agnes. I searched for anything to make him think I had my share of suffering, too. But he looked away and said, "Those nuns should be doing something more important than sunning themselves on Lake Erie. Too much is going on."

I asked him about me. Should I be doing something more than spending my days in Oshkosh?

"Where else can you go?"

"I could go to Mississippi with you."

He smiled, a half smile. "It's not the same for you as it is for them. It's their country."

"But don't you want me to come with you?"

"It's not about that."

He's not looking for some boyfriend-girlfriend tryst, Sister Agnes had said.

I felt ashamed.

He touched my chin. "Hey, I'll be back."

Courtney was waiting for us on the O'Brien's porch. The Knights of Columbus had asked for Angela again, so Courtney had come alone. I saw her head bobbing against the vivid magenta and pale pink of the fuchsia hanging from white baskets below the cornflower blue frames on the windows of the O'Briens' pretty white house. She spotted us a block away and bounded down the steps toward us.

"Did you tell him?" she asked breathlessly when she reached us.

I nodded.

She hugged Sam. "We were praying for your friends when you called," she said. "Did Sara tell you?" She looked at me.

"No," I said.

"Did she tell you about the spirit?" she asked Sam directly. He shook his head.

"We prayed to her. It was she who helped them find Henry Dee and Charles Moore."

Sam turned away from her.

"No. It's true. Ask Sara. Tell him, Sara. Tell him." She grabbed my arm. Her eyes disappeared. An African mask. Only the hollows were left where the eyes should have been. "Tell him, Sara."

The sea cow rose and raised her stumped arms to embrace me.

"Let's go inside." I felt Sam's arm around me.

"Wait. There's more," said Courtney. "She did more."

"Who?" Sam faced her now.

"The spirit. Sara knows."

"She means the abortion," I said.

The sea cow removed her arms. Tears welled up in her eyes.

"I know," said Sam. "She told me."

"That's not all it was."

Sam took his arm away from me and reached for Courtney's hand. "Come, let's go inside."

I followed them up the steps and saw Mrs. O'Brien take Sam in her arms and press his head into her bosom. Courtney looked back at me, her eyes now filling the sockets of the African mask, glaring at me. I felt a strange emptiness in the pit of my stomach, as if there were a hollow space where my womb should have been. My skin felt as if it were pulled against my hip bones, and some mysterious force seemed to be holding my legs and feet to the ground.

Inside, Mr. O'Brien embraced Sam, too. "Good work you're doing there, Sam. Good work. It won't be wasted. Everything will turn out fine in the end."

Sam shook his head. "Those guys didn't have a chance," he said.

"I'm sorry," said Mr. O'Brien. "I know what this means to you."

"We think we can help you find them."

It was Mrs. O'Brien who spoke but for a second I thought it was Courtney. The two of them were standing together, their arms linked around each other's waists, watching Sam and Mr. O'Brien. I saw Courtney's lips move, but it was Mrs. O'Brien's voice I had heard. Soft. Maternal.

Jim O'Brien shot her a dark look. "No, not that again, Martha."

She moved closer to Courtney. Or was it Courtney who moved closer to her?

"I think we should tell him, Jim."

"Tell me what?" Sam frowned.

"About the letter."

"It's nothing," said Mr. O'Brien. "I don't want to get your hopes up."

"What letter?"

"Something a friend of Martha's sent her. I wouldn't pay attention to it if I were you."

"My friend Madge Sinclair. Her grandfather and mine were friends."

"Did you know Martha's grandfather was an abolitionist?" Mr. O'Brien spoke directly to Sam.

"You told me that the first day I met you," Sam said dryly.

"When Martha lived in Boston—"

Mrs. O'Brien interrupted him. "Madge told me a man came to her office and gave her a letter for Dick Gregory. She works for the NAACP in Washington."

"Dick Gregory?" Sam's eyes grew dark.

"It's about that twenty-five thousand dollar reward he announced he would give to anyone who had information about Schwerner, Chaney and Goodman."

"I told you, that letter is a hoax," said Jim O'Brien. "Martha, don't do this."

"I don't think it's a hoax, Mr. O'Brien."

Now the eyes disappeared again. Mr. O'Brien must have seen it, also. He blinked his eyes and Courtney was still there. The mystery silenced him. He turned pale and stumbled backward.

"Are you ill, Jim?"

The eyes returned.

"No. No."

"Do you want some water?"

But before Mrs. O'Brien could move, Courtney had slipped away. In a few seconds she was back again, handing Mr. O'Brien a glass of water.

"Here." Courtney had to force him to take the glass from her. She held his hand and wrapped his fingers around the glass.

"What's the matter with you, Jim?" Mrs. O'Brien touched his shoulders.

"Nothing. Nothing. I'll be back in a minute."

But he had seen Courtney's eyes disappear. Angela had, too. I remembered how she had backed away from Courtney that first day I met them. Beads of perspiration were forming on Jim O'Brien's forehead when he left the room.

"Tell me more," said Sam.

Mrs. O'Brien turned her head in the direction of the door where her husband had gone, but Courtney pulled her back. "Tell him about the letter, Mrs. O'Brien," she urged.

Mrs. O'Brien pushed her hair off her forehead. Her hair was grayer than I remembered. Her eyes darted anxiously from the door to Courtney and back.

"Tell him how you got the letter," said Courtney. She moved between Mrs. O'Brien and the door, breaking the older woman's line of vision.

"What's all this about a letter?" Sam asked.

"My friend Madge sent it," Mrs. O'Brien began slowly.

"Yes. Yes. The one who works for the NAACP." Sam was growing impatient.

"Madge said that they get piles of mail every day from all sorts of kooks telling them they know the whereabouts of Schwerner, Chaney and Goodman. But this man was different. She said he looked like a gentleman. Someone who wouldn't pull a prank or anything. He just walked directly to her and handed her an envelope addressed to Dick Gregory. Here." She reached inside the top of her blouse and pulled out a white envelope from her bosom. "It's a copy." She handed it to Sam. "He gave this to Madge. He told her that if Dick Gregory didn't do anything about the letter, she had to. It was her responsibility, too. She now had the truth. Madge was scared, of course. She didn't know what to do, but the man made it sound so personal to her. As if it were *her* responsibility. Hers, personally. He left before she could get his name or address, but she knew he'd be back if she didn't do something soon. She couldn't sleep. I knew you were coming, and that you'd be returning to Mississippi. I told her I would give the letter to you. Perhaps you could do something."

Sam was reading as she spoke. His lips moved rapidly.

"I do feel as though it's also my responsibility." Mrs. O'Brien nervously fingered the collar of her dress. "But Jim says it's none of our business."

"It gives the exact location," Sam said, looking up from the letter. His voice was a step away from tears. "Almost to the last detail. Between two hundred and four hundred feet off the road. Five to eight miles off the right, heading south from Philadelphia. Exact! Exact details!" The words strained between his teeth. "He knows. Killed by a gang. Buried in a field. He knows. They're dead. Andrew, Michael, James. Buried. This man knows."

"I told Jim that." Mrs. O'Brien murmured.

"I'm sorry," said Courtney. She embraced Sam. He bent into her arms.

"I think he also knows who killed them," said Mrs. O'Brien quietly. "He doesn't say so in the letter, but I believe he does."

"Why didn't you give this to the FBI?" Sam raised his head.

"We thought you should."

"Me?"

"Maybe you could give it to Dick Gregory. Jim didn't want us mixed up, involved. He thought it would be better coming from him. He thought—"

"I know what he thought," Sam said gruffly.

"It's not like that. He thought Dick Gregory would have more influence. We knew you were going back to Mississippi."

"Yes," said Sam. His eyes were expressionless.

"Well, maybe now you can find the murderers. If you take the letter to the FBI they'll find the man who wrote it. He'll tell them everything."

"They wouldn't believe him," said Courtney.

"She's right," said Sam.

"Then what will you do?"

"I'll try to speak to Dick Gregory. Maybe there's another way."

"We'll pray for you," said Courtney. She looked steadily at me as if daring me to contradict her.

"I will, too," said Mrs. O'Brien. But she could not know what Courtney meant.

The knob turned on the door that had closed behind Jim O'Brien. The door opened and closed again. Mrs. O'Brien jumped.

"I'm sorry, Sam," she said, looking nervously at the door. "Really I am. I thought there was some hope. Something we could do . . ."

"It's fine. Fine," Sam murmured.

"I better see how Jim's doing. Take care of Sam, Sara." She squeezed my hand. But Sam did not seem to hear her. When she left, he turned to Courtney.

"Do you think this letter is real?" he asked her.

"I'm sure it is."

"I don't know if Dick Gregory can do anything. If he can get this letter to the right people in the FBI, perhaps."

"He'll do that. We'll help. Ask Sara."

"Sara?"

"Remember I told you her spirit found Henry Dee and Charles Moore for us?"

"Courtney, this is too big for that."

"Tell him, Sara."

The sea cow broke through the water, turned and then dove down deep into the sea. She vanished. Not a trace of her was left. Not even bubbles.

"Courtney said my abortion released a spirit. The day I prayed to her, you called and told me they had found two bodies in the river."

"She'll make it happen again," Courtney said quickly. "She'll help you."

"I need some air," said Sam.

Courtney pressed his arm. "Obeah," she whispered.

He looked at her. "How, Courtney? Here in Wisconsin?"

"Do you want us to pray?"

"I'll be back," he said.

"Do you?"

"Yes."

"We'll wait."

But Sam did not return.

That night Courtney knocked on my bedroom door. The moment she entered my room I smelled roses, the sweet odor of crushed leaves and decaying petals. I was grateful Angela had not returned. Pink rouge was smeared across Courtney's mahogany cheeks, her mouth was painted an ugly red. At her throat, tied around her neck by a piece of straw-colored string, was a tiny pouch, like my bag of herbs an obeahman had blessed that I hid beneath my clothes at the bottom of my drawer. My eyes jumped directly to it and she noticed. She touched the pouch and her lips drew back. A smile of recognition. Instinctively I got out of my bed.

"No. Don't be afraid," she said quietly. "I come for your help."

My legs moved me backward.

"It's about Sam's friends," she said. "Don't be afraid."

My heart bounced in my chest. Her eyes, gentle and serene, should have calmed me. Her hand upon my arm, when she reached me, was soothing.

"You've seen me like this before," she said.

I found my voice. "No. Never."

"Yes. When you swam with your mermaids."

I shut my eyes and forced the sea cow to retreat.

"We have to pray again, Sara. You must help me. I can't do it alone. Sam will take the letter to Dick Gregory but it must be placed in the right hands. We need you to pray to your spirit. We don't know the enemy. If you ask her, your spirit will show us whom to trust in the FBI. Then Dick Gregory will be able to take the letter to the right man."

The smell of roses sickened me. I clamped my hand over my mouth to hold back the nausea. I asked her to leave.

"Sam needs us," she said again.

I told her I would call the nuns.

She narrowed her eyes. "You're not like Angela," she said. "Don't forget that."

I said I would scream. She smiled, caught my hand and pressed her fingers deep into my flesh. "Sam needs your spirit," she said. She forced me to face her. "Don't turn away. We need you."

I struggled to get away.

"Sara, Sara." Her voice brushed over me like the feathery ends of the soft, wide ferns that grew in back of my grandmother's kitchen. I was a child, no more than six. I was running in a forest of ferns; my naked legs made swooshing sounds against the leaves.

"Sara, Sara. Don't be afraid. It's only me."

It was Carnival time in Trinidad. My cousin was disguised as a medicine man. "Look, look," he said, " I'll take off the mask." But I crouched down deep in the fern, shaking with fright.

"Come on, Sara. Don't be silly. Come out of there. You'll get scratched."

I thrust my head deeper between my knees. I was certain that when he removed the mask there would be nothing there.

"Snake will bite you."

My deepest fear. Still I stayed low in the fern, trembling. He shook his rattle of beads strung on animal skin and growled behind his mask. Long, dry grass hair dangled from his head, white cowry shells circled the dark holes where his eyes should have been, white paint was streaked across his cheeks. I knew he was not my cousin. When I screamed, he laughed.

My father plucked me out of the fern. My uncle chastised him. "That's what comes from letting her see Tarzan movies. The child is afraid of her own people. You tell her only one half of the story. You tell her about the English blood, the French blood, the Carib blood, the Spanish blood, but you don't tell her about the African blood."

I remembered he was the one who had told my father our new name. "Afro-Caribbean," he had said. "Or African West Indian. Black. Any of these. Not colored West Indian." He had been to America and to Africa.

"Don't be afraid of me, Sara," Courtney was saying. "Know yourself, Sara. Love yourself. Open yourself to your spirit, Sara. To our ancestors."

She left me, trailing dead roses behind her. I remained there, feeling no sensation in my legs or in any other part of my body. Later I wondered how I got into bed, for I was stunned to stillness by the sudden tenderness in her eyes, the seductive soft-ness of her voice. Her words filled my ears: *Love yourself. Open yourself to your spirit. Know yourself.* Now I felt an urgency to remember, to know, to understand, to love a past that had terri-fied the child in me. I pulled the blankets over my head and let the sea cow, the crying manatee of my dreams, return. I surren-dered myself to her. She had circled me all evening. Now I opened my spirit to her.

The darkness surrounded me, penetrated my senses and en-tered my every pore.

I must face the truth, I must unravel the mystery Courtney wanted me to confront: Had I released a spirit to the ancestors? Had the sea cow saved me for a purpose?

I would have drowned if I had stayed with the mermaids. They would have taken every bubble of breath from my lungs and stopped up my mouth with their sea grass hair. And yet I would have followed them willingly and happily to the ocean floor.

But the sea cow came.

In the darkness I forced myself to face her. Was she good or evil? Had she saved me or damned me? I remembered the stories my father had told of the old Amerindian god, the Orehu, the manatee of the Guianas. The Waraos loved her but they feared her as well. They knew that in a storm she could ride them on her back to safety. And yet there were times she had dragged them down to the bottom of the sea. It was the sea cow that had lured my cousin to his death, that had caused him to drown.

> We have lingered in the chambers of the sea
> By sea-girls wreathed with seaweed red and brown
> Till human voices wake us, and we drown.

I must live with this paradox. I must accept this contradiction. To have lingered in the chambers of the mermaids was to have died. To have been saved by the sea cow was to drown in the conflicting voices of conscience and history.

I must see, like Courtney, that my abortion, so antithetical to life, was necessary to release a spirit that would help us. Had the African women not made the same choice? They would not give birth to slaves for the white man's plantation. Was it so easy for them to live with blood on their hands?

I must think the way they thought. Courtney had warned me about searching for answers the European way. There was no blood on the hands of my African foremothers. Blood was everywhere, but it sprayed from the whips in the hands of white men. Blood was everywhere, but it was not on me. Blood was on the hands of the murderers of Chaney, Goodman and Schwerner. My spirit would expose them all. I squeezed my eyes shut. I let the darkness lead me to light, the silence, to sound.

Bertha lingered on the edges of my consciousness, but I did not fear her. I saw the ebony man with hair like lamb's wool. I saw him sending his signals to the sun, but I did not fear him. I lay on my bed and let the silence and darkness envelope me, take me to that fat triangle where the sea cow lived, the delta at the mouth of the Orinoco. I let the silence and darkness take me where the river muddied the waters near my island home, off the coast of Venezuela with her history of violence and brutality: the genocide of the Amerindian people, their vast Amerindian empires crushed by the savagery of white men who could not understand why brown-skinned people welcomed them to their lands, offered them water with berries, and then were surprised to anger because the whites took everything— all the gold and emeralds, all the jewels, everything, even the women. Later, two million barrels of oil, one hundred tons of asphalt, six hundred acres of sugar cane. Everything. Not even the tumbling waters of the Orinoco River could wash away that horror.

I rode on the back of the sea cow across the Atlantic, her ocean floor littered with the bones of the dead: Africans who jumped ship; others thrown overboard when the cargo weighed too much. I rode on the back of the sea cow over cotton fields in Georgia, the winds whispering bloody tales of torture in my ears. Across Alabama, down the Mississippi the sea cow took me, down to that other delta where the water ran red.

On the banks of the delta I saw the letter writer. I would have thought as Madge Sinclair had thought when the man had handed her that letter addressed to Dick Gregory: this was a gentle man, a kind man. This was a man who would not lie, who would tell the truth about the horror in Mississippi.

He recognized me immediately.

"Sara." He called me by name.

The Mississippi grumbled past us. I looked into the clay red water and knew his name—Jesse Chrisman.

"No more hanging from trees like ripe fruit."

"What, Jesse, what?"

He twisted his tie to the side of his neck and pulled one end above his head as my grandmother had done with her kitchen towel the day I told her I was leaving for Wisconsin.

"Strange fruit," he said.

I needed no explanation. I knew what he meant.

"Tell Sam everything is true. Tell him I know where his friends are."

The darkness rose around him.

"Tell him."

The darkness circled his chest and spread to his neck.

"Tell him to follow what I said. He'll find them there."

"Jesse." I could not see him. "Jesse."

There was nothing before me: no sound, no light, nothing— only the dark.

CHAPTER 17

S am was waiting for me next morning on the bench on the lawn in front of the college. He had called to tell me to meet him there. He looked tired. Dark rings circled his eyes. His eyebrows seemed thicker than they were the day before and they bunched beneath his furrowed brows. He had changed his clothes and was now wearing a brown dashiki and brown slacks. His duffel bag was on the ground next to his feet. My heart sank. I knew he had come to say good-bye.

"You look as if you didn't get any sleep last night."

"A little." He kissed me on my cheek. "I didn't mean to leave so suddenly last night."

"I waited for you."

"I came back to say good night but you had left already," he said.

I clasped my hands around my knees. "It was getting late," I said. "We had to get back to the dorm."

"I should not have left." His voice trailed. A silence grew between us and deepened. He seemed barely aware of my presence. I had put on the white skirt and blouse he once told me

287

he liked and wrapped my waist with the richly woven Ghana-
ian kinte cloth he had given me for Christmas, but he did not
seem to notice.

A squirrel rushed by us, stopped suddenly, stood on its hind
legs, sniffed the air and then scrambled back in our direction.
An oak nut lay on the ground close to Sam's bag. The squirrel
stared at the nut, made two attempts to move toward it, and on
the third, snatched it quickly between his front teeth and scur-
ried up a tree. Both Sam and I heard the soft thud of the nut
hitting the ground, so absolute had the silence grown between
us. We turned in unison to see the squirrel scamper back down
the tree and then pause as if to ask our permission, his two
round black eyes darting left and right.

Sam laughed. "Go on, take it." The squirrel raced toward us,
clamped his teeth down on the nut, and sped away.

"They never cease to amaze me," I said. "In the height of
summer they never forget there's going to be a winter. They
don't let all the food that's there for them now distract them. He
could spend his time eating but instead, he is storing for the
future. None of the animals in Trinidad have that instinct. It's
eat now and they're sure to find more later. Easy living." I felt
Sam's eyes on me, but I babbled on unable to stop, conscious
that I was trapping myself, that with each word I was feeding
him the very images I wanted to rectify—Caribbean people
were all happy-go-lucky natives singing calypsos in the sun under
coconut trees on the beach. I felt as if I were stuck in quicksand.
The more I twisted and turned my body in the sand, the deeper
I sunk in the ground.

"They always remind me of cane fields," I said, pointing to
the wheat fields. "Then I think, isn't it funny that on the same
stretch of land that gets so hot and grows wheat that looks like
sugar cane, snow falls and freezes it solid? Isn't it funny, the sun
and the snow . . . "

Tears brimmed my eyes. Sam reached for my hand and squeezed it. I put my other hand to my mouth to stop the flow of words. He moved it away.

"We're different, Sara," he said. "We come from two different places. Yours with blue sea and bright sunshine, green grass and happy people; mine with cement and bricks and cold winter months."

My knees shook and I rested my hands on them to hold them still. I wished I could take my words back. I knew what he was trying to say to me. I had opened the way for him with my silly talk of squirrels and wheat fields. I wanted to tell him that there was no difference between us. I knew better now. I had dreamed of Jesse. I understood him.

"We have thunderstorms, also," I said. "And we are not always happy."

"You know what I'm saying." He looked directly in my eyes.

"That you're leaving."

"It's my people's fight, Sara. I have to stay until it's over."

Once he had said it was my people's fight, too, but that was when the hurt was still raw in him and he needed me. Now he had grown hard and tough with the pain. He had encased the tender part of himself in a shell. The battle was his and his alone. He saw only the suffering of *his* people, *his* black American people.

"And when do you think it will it be over?" I looked away from him.

"When we have our civil rights. When we can vote, eat where we want to, sleep where we want, live where we want. Get the best education. You don't have that fight in Trinidad."

On New Year's Eve, when he told me the story of his family, I thought he was right. Then, I thought my own misfortunes were insignificant next to his. But now, since I had ridden on the back of the sea cow to the delta out of the Orinoco, there were hundreds to exonerate: my grandmother who burned kerosene lamps until dawn for her sons, all in vain. Only one in two hundred thousand would get the chance to go to university in England. None of her sons would, though one was a genius in physics and had a photographic memory. Later, that number rose to five in two hundred thousand, and some went crazy trying while the sons and daughters of the colonists partied in the night. The future in Trinidad belonged to the children of the colonists. Or so they thought.

No, our pain mattered, too. I had witnessed my father's humiliation, just for a vial of vaccine. Fishermen by the hundreds were banned from Chaguaramus and Teteron Bays. There would be no Sunday picnics on those beaches for natives. Hundreds of farmers were forced off cocoa lands in Waller Field Park: *Why farm anyway? We'll sell you what you need to eat. Tomatoes and avocados are bigger in Florida.* For ninety-nine years! Not once did the British ask the people in Grenada, St. Vincent, St. Lucia, St. Kitts, Jamaica, Barbados or Antigua if they wanted the Americans to build military bases on their land. Ninety-nine years were exchanged like copper pennies for fifty destroyers that already had seen battle.

I wanted Sam to know my father's anger. I wanted him to know about two million barrels of oil, one hundred tons of asphalt, six hundred acres of sugar cane, and cocoa, also. All for England. Worst of all, there was the destruction of hundreds for whom the unwritten laws of discrimination under colonization were so deeply embedded in their souls, they no longer knew who they were. They had surrendered a past, a tradition, confused by the motherhood England offered. If England was mother, what was Africa? I was afraid I was losing Sam, but I had to explain those hundreds.

"You have no monopoly on suffering or struggling," I said. "Did you think black people were always in Trinidad? We came in chains just like you. Slavery was the same. There weren't two kinds."

Not too long ago I had said of Americans—black and white— what Sam had so lightly said about Caribbean people. I believed they lived in a fairy tale world without troubles, a world of big cars, huge mansions, loads of money, all the heart could desire. How ignorant I had been of the extent of the slave trade, the suffering of black Americans. We tend to be so insular, watching only the doors to our own homes.

"Colonialism is no different from what you have here," I said.

Sam smiled grimly. "You didn't have Jim Crow. If you knew what goes on in the South, if you went there, if you were American . . . black . . . "

His tongue lingered on the words, *American, black.* I shut my eyes against the bitterness in his voice.

"If you were born here, you wouldn't say that. You'd know how much worse Jim Crow is."

I was frightened now. Would it matter if I told him about the hundreds and he understood, and yet I lost him in the end?

"How can you compare colonialism to the kind of racial segregation we have here? How can you, Sara? They are two different experiences, totally different."

"They may be different ways of making people believe they are nobody, but they both hurt the same way," I said, but I was sinking deeper into the quicksand I had created for myself. "You think there is only one way to suffer and one way to fight. You think going to Mississippi is the only way for you to fight, but there are better ways if you want to win."

"Tell me," he said. He was challenging me.

"Go back to New York. Become a lawyer so you can help from a vantage point. From a position of strength. I think doing that makes more sense than just giving your life away in

Mississippi.You think you'll have better luck than your friends? Mickey's dead. So are Andy and James.That's what they got for their way of fighting." Tears rolled down my cheeks. "What good would you be to your people dead? Don't you think they will kill you just the same way? Take the letter to Dick Gregory. Do what you can to persuade him to give the letter to the FBI. Bury your friends and come back."

He put his arms around me and pressed my head into his shoulders. "Sara," he said, "I'd feel like a vulture if I did that. I can't simply walk away to my ivory tower and come down only when everything is over. There wouldn't be enough water in the world to wash away the blood from my body if I did that."

I lifted my head from his shoulders and backed away from him. "You wouldn't be a vulture," I said. "You'd be doing what you can do best. Not everyone has the capacity to be a lawyer." I was desperate. I needed to find the right argument to convince him, so I twisted the callous injustice that caused his mother's death to serve my own ends. "Wasn't that what your mother would have wanted for you? Don't you think you have the responsibility to change the laws that took her life?"

He dropped his arms, reached into the pocket of his shirt and pulled out a pack of cigarettes.

"When I was in Mississippi," he said, lighting a cigarette, "I met a doctor. A brilliant man. He was born in Alabama but moved up north to New York with his family when he was about fifteen. He went to college in New York and to medical school at Cornell. He had a big practice in Queens. Made loads. He told me that the day after those four girls were killed in the bomb explosion in that church in Birmingham, he closed his office and moved back south. I asked him why. He said too much blood. I didn't understand him at first and then he explained."

Sam took a long drag on his cigarette and blew out slowly. I watched the smoke curl up gray in the sunlit air.

"He said he returned to Mississippi because he was drowning in blood." His voice was softer now, sadder. "Some nights he would wake up and blood would be everywhere—on his hands, his chest, his legs, all over the bed. He would smell the blood on him when he went to work the next morning. No amount of cologne would smother it, not in his new car, nor in his big house, nor in the fabric of his fancy clothes. Then he realized what he was smelling was the blood of the hundreds of people who made it possible for him to have the life he now had, people he never met, like Sojourner Truth, Harriet Tubman, Frederick Douglass and the unnamed ones who died for every breath of freedom he took, every luxury he enjoyed. He said the only way he could wash away the blood was to go back to Mississippi and finish the work they had begun. If not for them, he would not have been a doctor. He had to do his part. I understood. I cannot do less. *That*, Sara, was what my mother would have wanted."

He was drifting further away from me. Afraid of losing him completely, I made another foolish statement, and regretted it. "That man is useful in Mississippi because he's a doctor. If he hadn't taken the time to get his education he would not have had as much to offer. You, also, will have a lot to give back when you become a lawyer, but you can't be there and go to law school at the same time."

Sam dropped his cigarette on the ground and crushed it slowly beneath his feet into the cement that surrounded the bench. The furrow on his brow grew closer together, his eyes dull and sad.

"You've just proven, Sara," he said, picking up the burnt butt of the cigarette, "how different we are. My friends' lives are not worth less than mine. And they, too, would have liked to have been able to stay in school. Andy and James were students like me. Don't you think they had dreams too? I couldn't have them die for nothing."

"That's not what I meant."

How logical Courtney had made it seem when she told me to keep my eyes on my purpose. Get my degree, she said. That was what she was doing.

"Perhaps not." He shrugged his shoulders.

"This was the advice Courtney gave me. It makes sense."

"For her. For you. This is not your country. Why can't you understand that, Sara? It's not the same. You can leave this behind. I can't. And even if you stay here, you always have some-place else to call home. When life gets too ugly here, you can dream of home. Well, America is my home. Here. I survive or die here. There's nothing else."

"Then you're going to stay in Mississippi?" I tried to quiet the fear pressing against my heart. "Does that mean it's over between us?"

"I didn't say so," he said.

I grabbed onto the hope he offered. "Then you'll come back when it's over?"

"A long time may pass before it's over."

How rational men are, I thought, how sure and decisive. I envied him. My emotions were taking control of me, breaking me down, but his voice was steady, his face calm. Hours before he had said he loved me, but now he did not seem bothered that weeks, maybe months, might pass before we would be together again. And all for a cause. My abortion, the child we had lost, was insignificant in the light of that cause. He had put reason over feeling, the good of the group over his personal desires.

The obeahman from Sans Souci burned his magic into the heart of my great-grandmother Bertha. It was her love for him that drove her to madness. *Hold on to a man too tight and he drowns you.* When I invented the story about how my cousin drowned, I had mixed up the sexes. The woman was the one who would hold on to the rope too long. The woman would plunge with her lover to the bottom of the sea until she lost all consciousness.

I wrapped my arms across my chest and breathed in deeply, fighting to keep my head clear. "I thought you loved me."

"I do," he said.

"I don't think you'll come back."

"I will."

"I mean, to me."

"Of course I will."

"I could help you."

"How?"

"Courtney plans to pray for you. She said my spirit—"

Sam cut me short. "Yes," he said tersely. "Everything helps."

"Don't you believe what Courtney says? I thought in the park you said—"

"Yes, I said Courtney hasn't forgotten Africa, but these times call for more than that."

"More?"

Sam's eyes burned acid, like tamarinds. "More than obeah. We need guns, weapons. There is a war going on."

"Courtney says—"

The sizzling heat did not leave his eyes. "Good. Let her pray. You pray. Let her use obeah."

I was losing ground again. I wanted to tell him I understood *his* suffering. I shared *his* vision. "I had a dream last night," I said. "I dreamt about the man who wrote that letter."

He looked at me and waited. I could see his irritation deepening the folds in his forehead, but I went on. I had to show him.

"He said everything he wrote in that letter is true. You'll find your friends buried where he said they would be."

"I'm going to speak to Dick Gregory."

"My grandmother made the same sign when I told her I was coming to America."

"What sign?"

"In my dream, Jesse—"

"How do you know his name?"

"As soon as I saw him I knew his name: Jesse Chrisman."

Sam was listening to me intently now.

"He made a noose with his tie."

"A lynching. But how did you know his name was Jesse?"

"I just knew."

"Jesse Chrisman is the name of the man who wrote the letter to Dick Gregory. You must have seen the letter at the O'Briens."

"I didn't."

His face grew dark.

"I dreamt it," I repeated. But Sam didn't believe me. He sat in silence for a moment, then stretched his legs and turned to me.

"Tell me about the sign your grandmother made."

"My great-uncle was lynched in Georgia."

He kissed me. "You don't have to say that for me, Sara."

"It's true. My grandmother said it's true."

"You never told me about this."

"It didn't come up." I told him how it happened; that Mrs. Clancy told me that my great-uncle thought that because he was a dentist, white people would see him differently.

"Yes," he said, "the educated ones are the easiest to fool." He smiled. "Like your nuns in the College of the Sacred Heart."

His smile cut through my heart. I knew what he meant. Like you, he was saying, people like you who could be used so that people like the nuns at the College of the Sacred Heart could say with impunity that they were not racists.

"They have too much to lose," he said. "They want to be fooled."

My guilt deepened. I lowered my head but Sam continued to talk, unaware of the impact of his words on me.

"I would rather go to Mississippi now before my head is so full of my own self-importance that I think my life is too much to risk."

"And my life?" I mumbled. "The love between us? The life we could have together?"

"We won't have a life worth living together until I do this," he said.

"And you'll come back to me?"

"I'll come back to you."

It was not much of a promise but he had not excluded the possibility of an "us" together. However different he saw himself from me, however guilty I may have appeared in his eyes, he still wanted a life with me. I held on to that hope and offered him a gift—the only one I thought would seal the bargain between us, make it impregnable, make it impossible for him not to return to me.

"Courtney and I will pray for you," I said again. "I think her prayers brought that letter to us." *How I wish I could believe that, really believe the way Courtney believed.* "I know Dick Gregory will convince the FBI to pay attention to the letter. I know you'll find your friends."

Sam kissed me again. I wrapped my arms around his neck, closed my eyes and lost myself in his embrace, making an eternity of the moment.

Long after Sam's bus left, when the smiling faces of a blond man and woman blowing smoke rings in a sea of golden marigolds became a blur on the sky blue cardboard plastered on the back of the bus, I still felt the pressure of Sam's lips. But now the sensation of his lips on mine was as alien to me as the land I stood on, land that for months could seem like the land I knew in Trinidad, with its green grass and wheat fields as familiar to me as the sugar cane fields I knew, and yet so different when the bitter winter wind stripped leaves off trees, turned grass ashen and froze the earth to stone. I had accepted my alienation from the girls in the dormitory. Their history, their tradition, their culture had taught them that they were different from me, superior to me, but that I should feel this same alienation from Sam, Sam whose skin was as dark as mine, whose hair curled as mine, was too painful to accept.

I put my fingers to my lips to touch the spot where Sam had kissed me. I forced myself to remember the times when we had made love, when he had held me, when he had said he loved me. I tried to regain that reality. The other was an illusion he had created because Mississippi had unleashed her cruelty on his spirit and blinded him to all that connected us: our love, our common history of the enslavement of our African great-great-grandparents. Frightened by this new feeling—how strange Sam seemed to me when he was no longer in my presence—I swore to myself I would do what Courtney said had to be done. I would reach out to the spirit of my unborn child if she would connect me to Sam again, if she would keep Sam safe in Mississippi and return him to me. I would reach out to her for Sam, for the hundreds in Mississippi fighting for the rights of blacks to vote. I would reach out to ease my guilt.

Sam called me from Washington two days later. He had taken the letter to Dick Gregory. He told me that Mr. Gregory acted as if he were expecting him. The man had sent him the letter, too, he said, and he thought they were onto something big but he didn't think the FBI would go for it. Mr. Gregory had told Sam he believed the FBI did not want to find Schwerner,

Goodman and Chaney. They didn't want the facts smeared all over America, the truth hung out on the clothesline for everybody to see. They had years of experience with dirty laundry. No one knew how to hide it better than they. They didn't want the world to see white Americans as dirty, murderous racists. They didn't mind if the world *knew* this, but *seeing* was different. Seeing opened the possibility that the world would feel sorry for the nigrahs, and then where would that leave white people?

The same had been true when the newspapers showed the photos of half-dead Jews coming out of concentration camps in tattered black-and-white striped pajamas. The Jews were walking skeletons with sockets for eyes. Their bones seemed to be popping out of their skins. People felt sorry. Red-blooded white Americans felt sorry and guilty, even when they didn't want to do anything, as when they hadn't wanted to do anything for that boatload of Jews. They just turned them back, you know. A whole boatload turned back once they hit the Louisiana shore. Now every schoolchild in America is reading *The Diary of Anne Frank*. That's the guilt trip these people are afraid of. What if guilt pushed them into making Killens's *Youngblood* compulsory reading? See? Dangerous stuff. So they don't want to find those boys. They don't want people to see what happened. Imagine if the three had been tortured? White America will have to see the fruits of its racism.

Sam said he had a hard time convincing Dick Gregory that the FBI might believe the letter told the truth, and that they couldn't risk not trying. He did not tell Mr. Gregory about the spirit Courtney said I'd freed, but he came as close as he could. Sam knew Mr. Gregory was a spiritual man so he told him he had people praying over the letter. The ancestors could make things happen that we could not, he told Mr. Gregory.

Dick Gregory looked interested when Sam mentioned the ancestors, and asked what he meant by "they could make things happen." Sam said that by some stroke of luck Kenya popped into his mind. He told Mr. Gregory that when the Kikuyus wanted to return to their ancestral home in the highlands, the English told them it was too late, that they had lost their home forever. And so it seemed: the English had guns. A small squadron lined up on the crest of the hill was all the English needed, or so they thought, and thousands of Kikuyus would fall before the bullets in spite of nights of war dances to the ancestors and war chants that had once led them to victories over the wide plains of Kenya, in spite of spears chiseled to deadly accurate points, and mojos that had proven their power in past confrontations. But the English had not counted on the spirits. Not even ten thousand guns were strong enough against such a powerful force.

Dick Gregory was impressed. Yes, he knew about Jomo Kenyatta and the Mau Maus. "Was that how they did it?" he asked.

Sam told Mr. Gregory the spirits of the ancestors gave the Mau Maus their courage. They weren't afraid to look into the face of death. When a hundred fell, a hundred came back.

"That's what we need here," said Gregory. "An underground army. I don't mean the Sojourner Truth-type underground army. That was good in its day. But now in 1964, with Schwerner, Goodman and Chaney gone, vanished from the face of the earth because those racist bastards willed it, we need something stronger. Bigger, more ferocious."

Sam said at that point Gregory's eyes grew wild, darting from one end of the room to the other. He snarled, reared up his head and bared his teeth.

"A panther," he growled. The words rumbled in his throat. "A black panther."

Sam said he had no trouble after that convincing Dick Gregory to give the letter to the FBI.

"We'll let them know we know," Gregory said. "We'll put them on notice."

A week later the morning paper carried the headlines: 'Tipoff' Message Held Valueless—Letter to Gregory is Called No Aid to FBI in Search. Phrases and sentences in the column below leaped out at me, lashing my eyes to water. *The letter writer. Jesse Chrisman. Mentally ill. A former psychiatric patient. A nuisance. He sent letters weekly to the FBI. Claimed he had the solution for every unsolved murder. His "specialty": black victims of racial violence.* Despair washed over me. I knew a long time would go by before my Sam returned to me.

CHAPTER 18

I was ready this time when Courtney came with her painted face. I had waited for her all morning in my room. Angela watched me closely. Was I homesick? she asked me. Was I missing the girls? My boyfriend?

I saw her only in shadows crossing the room, coming by my bed, sitting next to me. I heard my voice in echoes: No, I wasn't homesick. No, I wasn't missing the girls. Yes, but Sam was coming back soon.

Angela invited me out to dinner. She was to meet one of the girls, Elise Ziebert, in Milwaukee. She was taking the bus there. Elise's mother had promised to drive her back to the college.

I shouted my answer. "No, I cannot go with you."

The harshness of my voice must have startled her. Her face crumpled almost to tears.

"Did I do something to you, Sara? Have I hurt you?"

Her eyes looked so innocent. I wanted her to leave. I needed to be alone with my brooding, my despair. Part of my consciousness took in the significance of her invitation: this was the first time since the girls had left for the summer, promising to call, that one had asked her out. How worried I must have made her that she was willing to take the chance of Mrs. Ziebert having to endure the embarrassment of taking two black girls to dinner.

"Do you want me to stay?" she asked. "I'll stay with you."

I softened under the mist that gathered in her eyes. "You don't have to, Angela. I really want to be alone."

I read and re-read the news article about Jesse's letter when she left. I asked myself repeatedly whether he was a dream or a vision, the kind of vision the Roman Catholic nuns at my school in Trinidad wanted me to believe occurred with regularity, in-explicable appearances, physical forms of the dead floating out of thin air: Our Lady of Fatima, Our Lady of Lourdes. And yet brilliant men and women, including the Jesuits whom I thought the most learned men in the world, believed this possible. The Pope hid the secrets of the three girls from Fatima in his vault in the Vatican, eking out bits and pieces to his flock of millions who waited with impatience when first he said five years, then ten, and who did not question him either when he said perhaps never. Were the secrets too frightening, too powerful, too tragic to reveal? Yet no one doubted their presence. No one doubted that the Lady had appeared.

And my Jesse, was he a vision too? The newspaper reported he was a crazy man fixated on racial violence. Only a crazy man would search trees for fruit hanging from ropes, drop nets in the Mississippi for fish without fins, dig up freshly covered earth as if he knew, as if he expected, there'd be treasures there more precious than diamonds.

There was madness in my family, also. Its source was the same as that confusion of identity that caused Jesse Chrisman to plummet irredeemably into the darkness of irrationality. Like my great-grandmother Bertha, he was foolish enough to be-lieve that all human beings were essentially the same, that color and culture were accidental differences, the result of place, time and one's fortune or misfortune in the world.

My great-grandmother died tied to a bed in a mental hospital in St. Ann's. Was loving a black man evidence of her insanity? Her family set her afloat among the seaweed in the turgid waters of the Sargasso Sea. Abandoned by those she loved, those she once thought loved her; spurned by those who believed she was a victim of the ebony man's dark magic, Bertha drifted in the darkness until human voices woke her and she drowned.

I, too, would embrace the dark and enter the unknown. Had the darkness not led me to Jesse? I rode on the back of the sea cow to the delta in the Orinoco, back to that other delta in the Mississippi River, and I was not afraid. I would not be afraid now.

To which side could I attach myself? To black America? Sam had told me that even if I tried, I could never understand the suffering of black Americans. To white America? White teenagers called me nigger. To Trinidad? I could not bring such shame on my parents. My cousin hauled coal in Newcastle, preferring to coat his lungs with black soot, that slow death, over having to say: "I've failed. I want to come home." And when he did return, the sea cow took him down.

Or did I belong to Europe, to the countries of some of my ancestors, to the Europe that educated me, taught me to spurn the soucouyant, the diablesse, the duene, and then, when I had rid myself of superstitions, when I had been willing to say that the mystical beliefs of Africa were primitive, the Roman Catholic Church asked me to believe that the Virgin Mary had visited three girls in France, and that, in a wooden cylinder in Turin, Italy, lay the shroud of Jesus Christ, His blood etched into that ancient linen, the imprint of the places where the nails had entered His hands and feet still clearly visible.

No, I would enter the dark. If I closed my eyes, if I suspended all I knew by reason alone, my past existence before I came on earth would be known to me, and I would reach a reality that none of my books, or any learning I could have achieved in my lifetime on earth, would ever have made accessible to me.

I had known this before. Why else had silence sometimes scared me? At times I heard at the center of the silence an implosion of sound that pressed against my ears like air against the inside of an inflated balloon. Why else had darkness frightened me? I saw shadows and shapes and light when my reason told me there were none.

I would welcome the dark and the silence. The spirits of my past would no more harm me than would the living beings around me. I would open myself to them without fear, without rejection. I would live my whole reality. I would use the bag of herbs my mother had so secretly given to me. I would take the bag of herbs out from the shadows of its hiding place.

When the sun came down, Courtney knocked on my door. I had prepared for her.

In the bathroom at the College of the Sacred Heart I had made an ocean of a bathtub, filled with water as warm as the water that rolled across the burning sands along the coasts of Trinidad. I poured in spoonfuls of salt and swirled the water with my fingers until it tasted of the sea and sent tiny currents rippling to the hard edges of the tub. I sprinkled the herbs an obeahman blessed in his hut in Sans Souci. They floated to the top of the water like flecks of green seaweed crushed against the cupped ridges of pink coral flowers.

I placed my naked body in the ocean I had made and the salt entered my pores, the herbs encircled my limbs. I opened my

palms and spread my fingers wide. I let my arms lie limp at my
sides. I let my head fall, weightless, onto the back of my neck. I
drifted in my ocean and it purified me. The water curled around
my parted legs: the warm waters of the Atlantic lapping against
the shores of Africa, connecting me, attaching me—Trinidad to
Africa, to the past, to the beginning.

Bertha came for me. The stream of frigid water she trailed
brushed against my neck and caressed the sides of my face. Her
long blond hair like the locks of mermaids swirled around my
arms. She pulled me upward to her cold northern chamber in
the Atlantic. I did not resist.

We would have been trapped by icebergs if Calypso had not
saved us. We heard ping, pang, pinkety, pang of her steel band
pans and swam toward her.

> *And*
> *Ban*
> *Ban*
> *Cal-*
> *iban*
> *like to play*
> *pan*
> *at the Car-*
> *nival;*
> *pran-*
> *cing up to the lim-*
> *bo silence*
> *down*
> *down*
> *down*
> *so the god won't drown*
> *him*
> *down*

down
to the is-
land town

Bertha made a path in the icy waters for us with her warm breath, and led us through a narrow channel to the center, to the stillness of the wide Sargasso.

out of the dark
and the dumb gods are raising me
up
up
up
and the music is saving me

Calypso stayed with us and we floated on a bed of seaweed, Africa and Europe to the east, the Caribbean beneath us.

I felt safe drifting with my great-grandmother Bertha on the green-grass seaweed, the ping, pang, pinkety, pang of Calypso's music intoxicating me, mesmerizing me, taking me upward, then down, to a limbo silence far away from the currents that stalked us—the prongs of ice from the north, the steam rising from Africa.

I would have stayed there, so enchanting was Calypso's music, but the darkness I knew I needed lay beyond this limbo. It was past silence to new sound, past the dark to new light. This was the darkness I had tried to reject when I hid my bag of herbs an obeahman had blessed. Now I struggled to free myself of the entangling embrace of Bertha's long, blond tresses. Calypso's music, they said, was what drove Bertha to madness. My legs beat the water to froth and I tore at the seaweed entwined in my hair. Unfettered, I plugged my ears shut with my fingers. Calypso retreated.

Like the sea cow of my dreams, I dove down deep past the silence, past the pull of the currents from the frigid zones of Bertha's home in the north, past the sounds of Calypso's pans, luring me to her coral caves in the south. Deeper and then straight ahead to Africa. I surfaced above water. The tips of my fingers and toes were crinkled like the ridges on a washboard. Dead skin on the balls of my feet and the knobs of my elbows sloughed away like the scales on a lizard, and new skin appeared, smooth and blood-tinged as a newborn baby's.

I stepped out of the tub, the ocean I had made. I dried my body. I put no lotion or oil on my skin, nothing that would remove the ocean from me—my connection to my past, the reality I would enter with Courtney. I left my skin ashen white with salt.

I wrapped the bedsheet around me like a sarong and used my pillowcase as a headdress. I tied its four ends into two knots that stood like the spikes of a crown on my head. I applied lipstick over the edges of my lips and past the corners of my mouth, and rouge the color of rose mangoes on my cheeks. I blackened my eyebrows with pencil. How instinctively I knew that this face I made protected my real face. In the mirror the reflection I saw was no longer mine.

I opened the door for Courtney. She took me by her hand, her face, like mine, a mask. I followed her.

The flames from the candles on her dresser and around her bed threw flickering shadows on the white square piece of cloth spread out at the foot of the bed. I was not afraid. On All Souls' Day, when the tongues of fire on Great-Grandmother Bertha's grave licked the hem of my organza dress and threatened to consume me, the ebony man with hair like lamb's wool wrapped me in his wide cape and saved me.

Courtney bade me to sit on the center of the cloth. I obeyed her. The candles surrounded me. A flaming necklace. I was not afraid. No fears, either, when Courtney lifted a little white hen from her dresser drawer. I saw the small, feathered body lying still in her hands. Only its tiny black eyes blinked: shiny balls drowning in the white that engulfed them.

Courtney put my hands on the wings of the hen. She did not speak. I did not need her to speak. I knew what she wanted me to do. I had done it a hundred times before in my dreams of a thousand years ago. I clasped the hen between my legs and brushed the soft feathers on its back. I stroked the top of its head and felt it tremble slightly, then grow calm against my thighs. I felt the strong, steady beat of its heart where its feathered breast touched my skin.

Courtney sat opposite me on the floor outside the cloth. Her beauty astonished me. I saw lakes and rivers and deserts and plains and mountains in her eyes. A thousand gazelles and antelopes, deer, impalas and wildebeests. Zebras, giraffes and camels. Elephants, hippopotami, rhinoceri. Chimpanzees, monkeys and gorillas. A thousand flamingos. Falcons, hawks and cormorants. Ten thousand weaverbirds. Pelicans, parrots, macaws and eagles. And tens of thousands more. Across her cheekbones, the sand dunes of the Sahara, the silt of the Nile, the ridges of the mountains of Zimbabwe. On her lips, the crushed purple of cocoa pods, rubies from Namibia, still encrusted with the surface of the earth.

She called me by a name I did not recognize.

"Nguni!"

And another.

"Fulani!"

Still another.

"Bambara!"

I felt the chords in my throat vibrate. Blood pulsated at my neck.

She called me by other names.

"Azandi!"

"Zulu!"

"Dagomba!"

"Mende!"

"Masai!"

"Idoma!"

My tongue felt heavy. I wanted to speak, but no words came. She said another name.

"Yoruba!"

A blast of wind slammed into the center of my back and pitched me forward over the hen. My head crashed to the floor. The room spun around me: a million circles swallowed into a vortex at its center, faster and faster until nothing was left, no movement, no sound, no color, no light.

I felt her then, my little Yoruba. I felt her when she entered my soul through my heart. My blood poured hot through every vein in my body when she came into me. My breath stayed still.

"Yoruba," Courtney called to me again. My head rose from the floor under a power not my own.

"Yoruba," Courtney called.

The strings of my vocal chords vibrated, and my voice, like the voice of a child, rose sweet and high.

"I'm here."

"Yoruba," Courtney called again. "What shall we do?"

"The man with six hundred children shall be sacrificed," I said.

"How?" Courtney asked.

"The man with six hundred children shall sprout from a tree."

"When?"

"Before the rain falls."

"Yoruba, what shall we do?"

"The rain will make rivers, but no water will fall on them."

"On who, Yoruba?"

"The ones they have buried in the basin. The rain will make rivers but no water will fall on them. But the man with six hundred children will hang from the tree like fruit."

"Why Yoruba? Why will he hang from the tree like fruit?"

"Because he knows."

My voice rose higher: the sounds of a baby who had not yet learned to speak, longing for its mother.

"He has told them where they are. The ones they have buried in the basin."

"And what shall we do, Yoruba?"

"Make sacrifice."

The voice of a baby; the newness of the words scratched my throat.

"But the man with six hundred children now hangs from the tree like fruit and the rains will make rivers, but no water will fall on them."

Courtney placed her hands on mine. "Let go, Sara."

I resisted her.

"Let go."

I did not want to go back. I did not want to return to my body.

She pried my fingers off the wings of the hen. The pain when her nails dug into my flesh cooled my blood. I let go and felt Yoruba leave me. She passed through the tips of my fingers. Out. Air rushed through my nostrils and filled my lungs. I breathed on my own again.

"Now! Now!" shouted Courtney. She moved my hand to the neck of the hen.

I had grown cold. Tremors rippled down the sides of my face into my shoulders and along my arms.

"Now!" Courtney shouted again.

The hen lay quiet, waiting, its neck outstretched. Its eyes

stared into mine. They were expressionless.

"Little Yoruba," I murmured.

No flicker of light in its eyes. No sign of recognition.

"Now!" Courtney shouted.

My fingers twitched and curled around the neck of the hen. "Now!"

I tightened my grasp. I pressed my fingers against its feathers. *My little Yoruba.*

"Twist it!"

I stretched the hen's neck. I held the bottom of its neck with my left hand, and with my right I twisted until I felt the tiny bones crack and fall apart. And yet the hen uttered no sound. *My little Yoruba.*

Courtney placed a knife in my hand. "Take it."

I knew what I had to do. I had done it hundreds of times before in my dreams of a thousand years ago. I put the knife to Yoruba's throat and slit her neck. The blood poured down my fingers and sprayed my arms and splashed on my dress.

Again I saw Jesse Chrisman. He was a school principal, the father of six hundred children. I saw him sprouting from a tree like a fruit. And I saw my great-uncle Thomas. He was swinging like a sack of coals from a branch of a tree in Georgia.

"Oh, my grandmother. Oh, my grandmother, how right you were."

Courtney raised her fingers to her lips and motioned me to be quiet.

Nothing could hold back the grief I now felt. I saw a forest of trees sprouting black men; fish without fins anchored to a rock in the Mississippi; human cargo folded like chairs stacked on trays in the bottom of ships, heads bent almost to knees, lips upon backs, whispering. Suddenly, the splash of three who jumped: a woman and two children, preferring to drown when they reached the turquoise waters of the Caribbean, preferring the black to the blue, hating the white sand, the pristine beaches, the playful surf. And how correct they were in their hatred. Years later, when laws were made declaring them human, not chattel, sandy beaches and turquoise waters would still not be theirs. They would be given to Americans for ninety-nine years. But humans, the laws had stipulated, not white. My grief rose higher. Courtney whispered in my ear to be quiet. "Shh. Shh. Be still. You must stop now."

A ship with trays of folding chairs, black bodies, cargo shipped out from those way stations on the islands in the Caribbean to plantations in Virginia, Louisiana, Alabama. Cargo floating up the Mississippi. Thousands bent under the blistering sun in cotton fields, backs split open. Blood everywhere.

"Shh." Courtney clapped her hand over my mouth. My tears drained through her fingers. "Shh. She will hear you."

But the beat of the drums was what I heard. Boom! Boom! Boom, boom, boom! Boom! Boom! Boom, boom, boom! The sounds echoed down crystal-clear rivers, cascaded over rushing waterfalls, crashed against the smooth sides of black boulders, rose through the bush of fat-trunked trees. Green leaves shivered in the sudden winds. The drumbeat swirled through their spaces. Boom! Boom! Boom, boom, boom! The drums rose higher. A flock of pink-feathered ibis floated up into the air. Boom! The water buffalo stampeded. Boom! Boom! The drumbeat came closer. Courtney took me by the shoulders and shook me.

I wailed as if I were one of the women in the village mourning their dead.

A slap across my face. I put my hand to my right cheek. The drums were in Courtney's room now. Tall, thin men, their bodies like the trunks of coconut trees, their muscles glistening from cheekbones to ankles, pointed their long canes bidding me witness: See. See all this.

I wailed as if I were one of the women in the village mourning their dead.

Courtney shouted my name. "Sara!"

I did not recognize it.

"Sara!" she repeated.

I knew I was Yoruba.

"Sara! Sara!"

A slap to my left cheek. I put both my hands on my cheeks, but now new hands were on my shoulders shaking me.

Boom! Boom! The drumbeat retreated. The pink-feathered ibis faded into the sky. The trees shrunk to waxen sticks, tongues of fire licking at their tops.

"Sara, it's Angela at the door. Quick, Sara. We have to clean this up. Quick, Sara."

Courtney whispering, moving back and forth, her arms full, dripping blood. Through her whispers I heard Angela's voice, and knocking on the door.

"Open the door, Sara. Is anything wrong? If you don't open the door now, I'll get Sister Agnes. Now, Sara! Open the door! Courtney, what are you doing to her? Courtney! I'll tell! Open the door now!"

In a distance I saw Courtney blowing out the candles. Everything went dark until she turned on the light, and then I saw blood everywhere, and a dead chicken.

"*Yoruba!*"

"Here, put this on." Courtney pulled off the sheet I had wrapped around my body and took the pillowcase from my head. "Here, put your arms in." I felt her nightie slide over my breasts. "Come, come help me." She tugged my arm.

Angela was pleading now. "Don't make me do this, Courtney. I don't want to get you in trouble. Just open the door and let me in. Sara!"

"Hurry up, Sara."

I struggled with the nightie Courtney had thrown over me.

Outside the room: "Sara, open the door."

Inside the room: "You must help me, Sara."

Courtney spread a thick quilt on the floor.

The blood. My little Yoruba.

The light brought clarity: a dead chicken, candles, many of them. I scrambled to my feet and gathered them up from the dresser and from around the bed.

"Put them in here," Courtney pointed to the center of the quilt. "Here, help me with this." She held the two corners of the cloth upon which the dead chicken lay.

I heard Angela's footsteps racing, then fading down the corridor. I grabbed the other corners of the sheet. Angela would know what had happened. She had told me about the white chicken feather and dried blood she had seen on Courtney's rug.

"Quick!" Courtney commanded. "Quick!"

We wrapped the chicken in the quilt, mopped the floor with the towels and hid everything under the bed.

Footsteps returned. More this time. The drumbeat was on the door now. I heard the key click. Mounds of white next to Angela rose to the ceiling and hovered over me, veils billowing like wings behind them. I cupped my hands and they formed a funnel above me: tiny flakes of snow. They melted to water as they fell on the warmth of my hands.

I spent two weeks in the psychiatric ward of the hospital. Sister Agnes said I had a nervous breakdown. Temporary insanity. It was easy for her to define it so. She had been looking for traces of insanity in me from the moment I had arrived in Oshkosh. But I knew I had not gone mad. I knew I was saner than ever before.

They made Courtney leave the college. She came to see me. She told me not to cry for her. She was glad to be going home to St. Lucia. She left me her dolls, the ones that stood on her dresser with the pins in them. I keep them with me now.

Sam wrote me one letter and then I never heard from him again. He told me what I already knew, that Jesse Chrisman was lynched by a mob of white men. They came to his house at night, the day Dick Gregory took his letter to the FBI. It was the same night Courtney and I prayed to the spirit to help Sam find the bodies. I was glad Sam stayed in Mississippi. He had his work to do.

EPILOGUE

On August 4, 1964, an obeahman stood on a hill in Sans Souci making signals with the sun. Bertha stood beside him, an Englishwoman, his wife, her hair trailing behind her, loosened strands of bleached rope. The ebony man with hair like black lamb's wool grimaced in the sun. Too much light. It was not right. There were the dead to unearth. He placed his body in front of his hut, but the shadow he cast was still not enough. The sun glittered and gleamed off the tin walls he had polished. Tears filled his eyes.

The ebony man with hair like black lamb's wool pulled his Bertha to him. Round and round he spun her till the rope that was her hair caught the nails on his hut and twirled like twine around the tin he had shone, blocking out the light. When the darkness he caused draped over the earth, he stood on the edge of the ridge over the frothing waves and summoned the winds. The winds whirled around him and sent the sun spinning into the sea. He lurched for the eye of the hurricane, caught it in the palm of his hand, and then, facing northward where the Big Lands were, he let loose the vulture.

The carnivorous beast curled back its talons, its sharp nails pointed with cruel intent toward the dark, swollen sea, its ancient scales glittering under the eerie sheen of the electric light blazing across the sky. The bird dove low, swooped across the water and cut deep welts in the silver-edged froth, raising mountains of metallic gray waves in its wake.

The beast rose again, this time ripping its sharp beak across the charcoal clouds, gnashing open deep chasms of light, ice-blue and jagged—a ferocious beauty painted in the sky.

Circling the edges of northern Trinidad, past Toco and Balandra, the vulture chiseled razor-thin streaks of destruction a mile inland with the iron tips of its wings. The tops of coconut palm trees whizzed through the pounding rain. Galvanized roofs, planks of wood, whole houses flew light as feathers in the raging wind. The vulture would have done more—flattened villages, taken lives—but something made it pause. Pity, perhaps. The beast turned its beady-black, red-rimmed eyes on the people below and remembered where it was: Sans Souci. A land that had known no pity, no compassion, no succor. Who had so aptly named it that the French colonizers would concede the translation? Sans Souci. Without care. Perhaps the old Amerindian warriors, their bitterness turned rancid when even the land could not protect them from the brutal guns of white men. Or perhaps the Africans, pronouncing their fatalistic acceptance of the dominance of a Mother Earth whose motives they did not always understand. Why had not the land here on the other side of their ocean saved them from slavery, from the white man's cruelty?

The vulture pondered this, too. It folded in its wings, its heart aching with the memory of a bloody past. It would not participate. The bird sat on the outstretched limb of a giant immortelle, its roots clutching desperately to the edge of a cliff that had already lost trees more majestic than this one under the furor of the sea. Sans Souci. The vulture waited. When the people reached safety, the vulture rose. It spread its wings like plates of armor and beat the air, lifting mountains of winds behind. Then, with thunderous speed the vulture headed north-westward, its beak pointed to where the black dead lay restless, sprawled across the torrid south of North America—Mississippi, Alabama, Tennessee, awaiting its vengeance.

People who would know said that there had never before been storms such the ones in Philadelphia, Mississippi, that August 1964. Three miles south of Burrage Farm, where Mr. Olsen Burrage had built his dam at the bottom of the valley to collect rainwater for his cattle, Mississippians shook their heads in despair over the torrents of rain that would surely cancel their annual Neshoba County Fair. That year, more than any other, they needed to meet on their old stomping ground: there were agitating nigrahs to stop, nigrahs threatening to turn back the clock on years of white Mississippian progress.

They had stopped Medgar Evers. Gunned him down cold in the hazy stillness of an early dawn. In front of the doorway of his own home, they widowed his wife before her eyes, snatched innocence from his children in that split second. Yet nothing seemed to stop the rising roar of feet marching closer, thousands of feet pounding the asphalt on city streets. How to silence Martin Luther King whose voice was more powerful than any war weapon they had known? How to put out the flames Malcolm X was stoking with his fiery breath? How to stop them all?

The white Mississippians needed to meet at the Neshoba County Fair that year. But it rained. It stormed. The rushing water scratched away State Highway 21 and then curled into the gravel pits dug out by the floods. Mud caked the road to Burrage Farm, known to white Mississippians as Old Jolly Farm. But the vulture would permit no celebration that year. No jolly heaving of bellies swollen with alcohol and faces turned blood red with laughter over plans to stop marching feet. Trees leaned against each other, limp with water. The temperature rose. One hundred degrees. The earth released hot steam.

On August 4, 1964, two cars loaded with men, FBI agents sent by J. Edgar Hoover, turned off Highway 21. They knew where to go.

Sweat pouring down the sides of his face, Agent Henry Coleman, Jr. led his men straight to the dam. He held a stick over his shoulders which he would need to measure the ground. His feet sank into the soft red clay on Olen Burrage's farm. The ooze curled around the edges of his brightly polished black shoes. He hadn't walked far when a blob of mud squished into the narrow space between his right shoe and his ankle. He spat on the ground in disgust and bent over to fish the mud out. At that very moment, something buoyed by a sudden wind—perhaps the excrement of a vulture circling the dead—grazed his forehead. He swiped the mess away with his hand and too late realized that his fingers were muddy. He looked up helplessly at his men. They grinned back sheepishly at him.

"It's hard to keep the dirt off you in these places, sir," one of them said.

Agent Coleman shook his head sadly and wiped his fingers, in resignation, on his pants. By the time he reached the edge of the dam, the Mississippi clay from Olen Burrage's farm was on his face, hands, pants, socks and shoes. Yet the ground here was dry. There was no water at the bottom of the dam.

Agent Coleman questioned his men.

"Mystery to me," one of them answered. "You'd think with all that rain."

Rain will make rivers, but no water.

Agent Coleman shrugged his shoulders and began counting his steps. Twenty paces. Three hundred and ninety-eight feet from the east end of the dam. He stopped walking, turned full circle and surveyed the ground. His men watched him from the sides of the dam. Suddenly, he broke into a smile. His eyes sparkled with confidence. He was a man sure of himself now, certain of his knowledge. He lowered his stick, marked the earth and then walked quickly around to the other side. Ninety-seven-and-a-half feet from the west end he put another mark on the earth. He walked back to the east end. He counted ten more paces from his mark, thirty footsteps, four hundred feet. He made another mark. He walked back to the west end. One hundred feet. He waved his stick triumphantly in the air and then jabbed it viciously into the earth.

"Here," he shouted to his men. "Dig here. This is where they are."

Most people concluded that Agent Coleman had been tipped off, so certain was he of the exact spot where Schwerner, Goodman and Chaney were buried. Those who understood the South said that tipping off wasn't necessary. The *New York Times* reported that the FBI would not disclose its sources.

But we know, Courtney, we know. We know what Jesse did. Was that you, too, Yoruba, letting me know you exist?

ABOUT THE AUTHOR

Elizabeth Nunez was born in Trinidad and immigrated to the United States after secondary school. She is a CUNY Distinguished Professor of English at Medgar Evers College of the City University of New York. She received her Ph.D. and M.A. degrees in English from New York University, and her B.A. degree in English from Marian College in Wisconsin. She is the author of four novels: *Discretion*, published this year; *Bruised Hibiscus*, which won an American Book Award in 2001; *Beyond the Limbo Silence*, which won a 1999 IPPY Award—Independent Publishers Book Award in the multicultural fiction category; and *When Rocks Dance*. Nunez is coeditor of the collection of essays *Defining Ourselves: Black Writers in the 90s*. Her essays and short stories have appeared in anthologies and magazines. The director of the National Black Writers Conference sponsored by the National Endowment for the Humanities since 1986, Nunez chairs the PEN American Open Book committee, which focuses on providing access for people of color to various aspects of the publishing industry, and has served as an evaluator for national and local programs in the arts and education. She is the recipient of numerous awards and honors, including fellowships at the Yaddo and MacDowell colonies and the Paden Institute; the YWCA Woman of Distinction Award; the Sojourner Truth Award from the National Association of Black Business and Professional Women's Clubs; and the Carter G. Woodson Outstanding Teacher of the Year Award. Nunez was awarded an honorary doctorate in Humane Letters from her alma mater, Marian College, Fond du Lac, Wisconsin, for her contributions to the arts and education.

Look for Elizabeth Nunez's powerful novel
exploring an intricate lovers' triangle—
and the myriad ways desire can betray
those who have fallen under its spell.

For twenty years, Oufoula has carried a secret in his heart, a secret of his
love for a woman named Marguerite—a woman who is not his wife.
Though they have been separated for two decades by Marguerite's call
for propriety, Oufoula refuses to let his desire wane. When the lovers are
at last reunited, the rekindling of their passion forces Oufoula to come to
terms with his true feelings: Is he willing to sacrifice his marriage, his
career, and the very foundations of the life he has struggled to create, all
for the love of one woman?

**"I recommend this novel ten-times over. I was due for a smart,
well-written novel with depth of breadth and scope,
and I got it in *Discretion*."**
—TERRY McMILLAN, author of *Waiting to Exhale*

Published by One World/Ballantine Books.
Available wherever books are sold.